CAUGHT BY A MADMAN

Kimberly stepped into the alley. "Do you need some help?"

The man looked over at her. He was cute, with glasses and a crooked smile. "You're a lifesaver," he said, readjusting the swaddled baby in his arms.

"You look like you could use an extra hand," Kimberly said, grinning.

"Thanks a million." He held out the tote bag. "If you could just open the car door, then put this on the floor back there, I can do the rest."

"No sweat," she said, taking the tote bag from him. It was a bit heavy. She turned and opened the back door. "So how old is he?" she asked over the baby's cries.

"Two months," the man replied.

Kimberly bent over and set the bag on the floor. Then she noticed something strange. There was no infant seat in the back. And she didn't see anything to hold a baby in the front passenger seat either.

"Can you take him?" she heard the young dad ask.

Still half-inside the SUV, Kimberly started to turn toward him. She reached out for the baby, but hesitated.

There was nothing in the blanket but a lump of clothes and a small tape recorder.

Suddenly, she felt the man grab her arm and twist it.

Kimberly struggled.

She opened her mouth to scream as the man pulled back his hand, clenched in a fist. It felt like a hammer-blow to the side of her face.

Then she didn't see anything, just blackness . . .

Books by Kevin O'Brien

ONLY SON

THE NEXT TO DIE

MAKE THEM CRY

WATCH THEM DIE

LEFT FOR DEAD

THE LAST VICTIM

KILLING SPREE

Published by Kensington Publishing Corporation

KEVIN O'BRIEN

LEFT FOR DEAD

PINNACLE BOOKS
Kensington Publishing Corp.
http://www.kensingtonbooks.com

PINNACLE BOOKS are published by

Kensington Publishing Corp.
850 Third Avenue
New York, NY 10022

All Kensington titles, imprints, and distributed lines are
available at special quantity discounts for bulk purchases for
sales promotions, premiums, fund-raising, and educational or
institutional use. Special book excerpts or customized print-
ings can also be created to fit specific needs. For details, write
or phone the office of the Kensington special sales manager:
Kensington Publishing Corp., 850 Third Avenue, New York,
NY 10022, attn: Special Sales Department; phone: 1-800-221-
2647.

Pinnacle and the P logo are Reg. U.S. Pat. & TM Off.

First Pinnacle Books Printing: July 2004
First Printing (with preview of *Killing Spree*): December 2006

10 9 8 7 6 5

ISBN 0-7860-1847-X

Printed in the United States of America

This book is for my sister-in-law, Judy O'Donnell O'Brien.
Jude, you're a treasure . . .

ACKNOWLEDGMENTS

For his friendship and support, I'm grateful to my editor, John Scognamiglio. Thanks also to everyone at Kensington Books, especially the terrific Doug Mendini.

Another great big thank you goes to Kara Cesare, Meg Ruley and my friends at the Jane Rotrosen Agency.

This book couldn't have gotten off the ground without my Writers Group pals, David Massengill, Garth Stein, and Soyon Im. I'm also grateful to my good friends, Cate Goethals and Dan Monda, who weathered through early drafts of this book and came back with suggestions for improvement.

Thanks also to my neighbors at the Bellemoral, especially Brian Johnson and David Renner; the gang at Broadway Video, especially Paul Dwoskin; and the folks at Bailey/Coy Books.

For their friendship, encouragement and help, I'm grateful to my friends, Lloyd Adalist, Dan Annear, Marlys Bourm, Terry and Judine Brooks, Anna Cottle and Mary Alice Kier, Ed and Susan Kelly, John Saul and Michael Sack, Dan and Doug Stutesman, and George and Sheila Stydahar. And a huge thank you to my pal, Tommy Dreiling.

Thanks also to my family for all their love and support.

Chapter 1

She made up her mind. She would tell her husband all about it when she got back home. A full confession. She felt a tight knot in her stomach. She dreaded this talk. Still, better Frank hear the truth from her than from somebody else.

She was five blocks from the house, walking their Jack Russell terrier, Cosmo. It was eleven-thirty, and a chilly, autumn wind crept through the night air. She and Frank had just returned from an awful party. They'd flipped a coin over who got dog-duty. Connie had called heads, and it had come up tails. So she'd put her coat back on, grabbed the leash and a couple of pooper-scooper bags, then let Cosmo lead the way out the front door.

Connie Shafer was thirty years old, with green eyes and shoulder-length, wavy, auburn hair. She'd dressed to the nines tonight, a simple, sleeveless black dress that showed off her thin figure, and on a delicate chain, the gold heart-shaped locket Frank had given her last Valentine's Day. Connie's two-hundred-dollar Amalfis made a curious click-click sound on the sidewalk.

They lived in a town house in Redmond, not far from one of the main shopping areas. Their neighborhood had sprouted up in the mideighties, a maze of little roads with new split-level and rambler-style houses dwarfed by tall, old trees. There wasn't anyone else out at this hour, so Connie had plenty of time to think—sometimes out loud.

"I'm sure half the people at the party know," she muttered, pausing for a moment while Cosmo sniffed at a tree trunk. "That Hannah has such a big mouth . . ."

Cosmo pulled her farther down the sidewalk, beneath a sputtering streetlight and past a gnarly old oak. Someone had left their recycling bins on the sidewalk. Connie stepped around them.

The party had been at the home of a former coworker from their Microsoft days. Connie and Frank had met while working there. Half the people at tonight's soiree had been at their wedding four years ago. Both Frank and Connie had since moved on to other jobs. But before leaving, Connie had become involved with a coworker, Gary Levinson.

It lasted only a week, after months of flirting. Talk about a long build up to nothing. At the time, she'd been pretty miserable at home—with Frank ignoring her while he focused on his new job. And there was Gary, a bit older (thirty-two at the time), divorced, nice eyes, and saying all the right things. It didn't matter he was balding and about twenty pounds overweight. Gary made her feel special.

Connie ended it. She couldn't stand the sneaking about. Besides, after a few times with Gary, he didn't seem so charming anymore. In fact, she realized he was a jerk. Whenever they'd gone out to eat together, he'd treated the waitpeople like crap—always a bad sign. Moreover, she heard from several coworkers that he was a backstabbing sleazeball.

Connie had heard he'd quit Microsoft and moved to California, so she hadn't expected to see him at tonight's gathering. But there he was—even fatter and more bald—with yet another Microsoft refugee, Hannah Van Buren, hanging on his arm. Big Mouth Hannah.

"Oh, Gary's living in Bellevue now," Hannah had told her, nibbling on a cheese puff. "We've been going together since July. He's awesome. But then I don't have to tell you,

Connie. You had a little thing with him a while back, didn't you?"

"Not really," she replied, with a half-smile, half-grimace.

"That's not what he told me," Hannah retorted in a singsong voice.

Connie noticed a couple of party guests turn to stare at them. Maybe she was paranoid, but she felt people staring all night. Nervously fidgeting with her gold heart-shaped locket, she clung to Frank most of the time. She managed to avoid Gary—until Frank went to the bathroom. Then Gary slithered up to her and kissed her on the cheek. "That's for old times," he whispered. "I'm with Hannah now. Going on four months . . ."

"That's swell," Connie said. They deserved each other.

Frank came back from the bathroom, and suddenly Connie was standing with the two of them. She just wanted a hole to open in the floor and swallow her up. "Honey, you remember Gary Levinson," she heard herself say.

The two men shook hands. Frank was very cordial—as usual. He was good at small talk, chatting amiably with Gary.

Then out of the blue, Gary said to him: "I hope you're taking good care of this gal of yours, and treating her right." With that, he excused himself to cozy up with Hannah by the hors d'oeuvres table on the other side of the room.

Frowning, Frank turned to her. " 'Treat this gal of yours right.' What the hell does he mean by that? Who does he think he is?"

Connie merely shrugged.

Twenty excruciating minutes later, they'd left the party and driven home, hardly saying a word to each other in the car.

"He knows," Connie murmured, pulling out a Baggie to scoop up after Cosmo. How appropriate, cleaning up a mess. It was what she had to do when she got home. Damage control. She loved her husband. The thing with Gary was merely a momentary lapse, an embarrassment—like a hiccup or a fart. It was just something disgusting she'd let happen. And she was sorry. Would he understand? Would he please forgive her?

Connie stepped into an alcove by the condominium at the end of the block. She deposited the loaded poop-bag in a Dumpster, then quietly closed the lid.

Giving the leash a little tug, Connie started out of the alcove. But she stopped abruptly. She may have even gasped. She wasn't certain. She wasn't certain of anything—except the man standing on the corner across the street. He seemed to be staring at her.

Had he heard her talking to herself? Had she been talking out loud a moment ago, or just thinking?

Cosmo tried to go back toward the Dumpster. Connie had to tug at the leash until he obeyed and followed her. She headed back home.

She glanced over her shoulder at the man. She couldn't see his face, swallowed up by the shadows. But he was tall and gaunt. He wore a windbreaker and baggy pants. He hadn't moved from his spot on the corner. She had no idea what he was doing there. He didn't have a dog with him. It wasn't a bus stop. Was he some homeless guy? In Redmond? This was the suburbs, for God's sake.

Connie moved on. She told herself not to look back. She didn't want him to know she was afraid. Maybe if she just kept walking, he'd stay where he was and leave her alone.

Cosmo wanted to stop and sniff at another tree, but she jerked at the leash. Despite her resolve, Connie peeked over her shoulder again. She let out a little sigh. The man wasn't on the corner at the end of the block any more. He must have moved on.

Then Connie saw something out of the corner of her eye. A shadowy figure darted into the little alcove where she'd been just a minute before. It was him.

Her heart seemed to stop for a moment.

She could see his silhouette, half-hidden behind a fence.

He was lurking in that dark niche, watching her. She couldn't see his eyes, but she felt them on her.

She couldn't move or breathe. Then Cosmo pulled on the leash, and made her turn away. *Only four blocks from home,* she told herself, *you're going to be all right.*

Connie picked up the pace a bit. She didn't dare run, because he'd probably chase after her. She pulled Cosmo into the center of the street. She'd read somewhere that one way to discourage a possible attacker while walking alone at night was to go down the middle of a road—no shadows or trees for anyone to hide behind, no nearby bushes to camouflage a crime.

The night was so still. She heard the click-click of her high heels on the pavement and Cosmo panting. She even detected the sound of some cars in the distance. But she didn't hear anyone behind her. Connie nervously fidgeted with her gold locket. She dared to look back once more.

No one. Or was he hiding again?

Three blocks back, a Mercedes turned up the street, followed by a silver SUV.

Connie returned to the sidewalk. She felt a bit better. No one was about to attack her while a couple of cars were driving by. She glanced over her shoulder and squinted at the headlights, illuminating the roadway. No sign of her phantom stalker. The cars must have scared him away.

Connie began to breathe easier. She continued toward home, and the cars passed by, first the Mercedes, then the SUV. Maybe she should tell Frank about her little scare. She could squeeze some sympathy from him, before she told him about Gary. Would he ever forgive her?

She was less than two blocks from the town house. Cosmo wanted to stop and sniff another tree. Connie studied the darkened street. The creepy man must have run off or he'd gone Dumpster-diving in that alcove. She and Cosmo were alone—and very close to home. Still, she felt unhinged. The dread in the pit of her stomach hadn't quite gone away, because she had to have her talk with Frank.

Cosmo moved on, pulling her along. Two blocks ahead, Connie saw a car turn and come up the street toward her. The headlights blinded her for a moment, then she noticed the vehicle was the silver SUV that had driven by just a minute ago. As the SUV came closer, it slowed down, then crawled to a stop.

Connie kept walking, but hesitated as she saw the driver's window roll down.

"Excuse me," the man called gently. *"I'm sorry, I'm holy cross . . ."*

Connie stopped and stared at the man inside the car. She couldn't quite see his face. And she was pretty certain she hadn't heard him right. "I beg your pardon?" she asked, taking a step toward the SUV.

Cosmo seemed to resist. He was straining the leash.

"I'm totally lost," the man said, more clearly. "I wonder if you could help me. I'm *working for sessions treat . . ."*

"What?" Connie asked.

"I'm looking for *chessions* street . . ." he repeated, but it was still a little muddled.

"Oh, *street,"* Connie said. He was talking as if he had a mouthful of marbles. She still couldn't quite see his face either. "What street were you looking for?"

"Zeelshions Street."

"I'm sorry, I still can't hear you . . ."

Connie took another step toward the car.

Frank Shafer glanced at his wristwatch again: 12:20. He'd already changed into a flannel shirt and sweatpants, watched part of Leno, and knocked off a beer.

Connie had been gone nearly an hour. Usually Cosmo did his business within ten minutes. Something was wrong.

Frank had stepped outside twice already, looking up and down the block. No sign of them.

Damn it, if she'd planned on taking this long, she should have brought along the cell phone. Frank couldn't figure out what was going on. Connie had seemed pretty tense most of the night—ever since they'd arrived at the party. Had he said or done something to upset her?

Frank paced around the living room. He kept looking out the front window for her. He'd turned the TV volume to mute a few minutes ago. He wanted to hear if anyone was outside.

He did hear something: a scratching on the front door, then an abbreviated bark. *Cosmo.* He always strained at the leash and clawed at the door to get back in, because it was their routine to give him a dog biscuit after a walk.

Frank hurried to the door. He was so happy for Connie and Cosmo's return that he wouldn't be mad at her—at least, not for a minute or two. Right now, all he wanted to do was hug her. He flung open the door.

Cosmo looked up at him. The dog was whimpering. His leash trailed behind him, dragging on the ground.

Frank noticed something tied around the handle end of the leash. It looked like a black handkerchief. He squatted down, and Cosmo nuzzled up beside him. The dog was trembling.

"Jesus, what's going on?" Frank murmured.

He gazed at the black silky material tried around the leash handle. He'd seen it before, earlier tonight, while Connie was getting dressed for the party.

He was staring at his wife's panties.

Megan and Jamie had known each other seven weeks, and they were totally in love. They were so wrapped up in each other, and so heady with bliss that it was a bit disgusting. As they played on the swings together in the kiddie playground, several people smiled warmly at them. Jamie noticed one woman roll her eyes and sneer, but he decided to ignore her. He and Megan were a cute couple, and they both knew it. Damn cute.

With a disposable camera, Jamie chronicled their cuteness, their love, and all the fun they were having that Sunday afternoon. It was a crisp, overcast day, and the leaves on the trees had turned to vibrant hues of orange, red, and yellow. Megan looked gorgeous—her cheeks rosy and her black hair all wind-swept. Jamie had taken some terrific photos of her hanging from the monkey bars. He wanted to save some on the roll for later—so he could shoot a few photos of her in bed.

"Next, let's play hide and seek," Megan suggested, calling to him from the top of the slide. "Okay? "

"Let's go back to your place and play it," Jamie replied, grinning.

Megan just laughed, then pushed off and sailed down the slide.

As Jamie pulled her up, she gave him a kiss. "Close your eyes and count to fifty. Gotta find me before I'll let you take me home."

Jamie plopped down on a bench, closed his eyes, and started counting.

"No cheating!" he heard Megan call.

"Stay in this section of the park!" he called back. Then he went back to counting. He kept his end of the bargain— going all the way up to fifty.

Once Jamie opened his eyes, he suddenly felt very much alone. He shrugged it off and started scoping out the kiddie park area.

Megan was wearing a yellow pullover. She should have been easy to spot. But he didn't see her.

Jamie peeked around a few trees—and even peered up at the branches. He and Megan had climbed a couple of trees earlier, and she was good at it. But he didn't see her hiding up in any of the limbs.

He circled the restroom facility—a plain, small brick unit with the men's room on one side, and the women's on the other. Megan wasn't in the bushes behind the building.

As he passed the women's doorway, Jamie almost bumped

into a girl coming out of the lavatory. Lugging a backpack, she had a pierced nostril and a green streak in her hair.

"Excuse me," Jamie said. "You didn't see anyone else in there, did you? My girlfriend and I are playing hide and seek."

"Nobody's in there," she muttered, with a wary sidelong glance at him. She moved on, then adjusted her backpack. "You can check it out if you want . . . freak."

Jamie looked around to see if the coast was clear. He'd never stepped into a women's bathroom in his life. If anyone saw him, they'd probably think he was a major pervert. He poked his head past the door: just as dirty and smelly as any public men's room—only no urinal. "Meg? You in here?" he called, his voice echoing. Both stall doors were open. The place was empty.

He tried the men's room—on the off-chance she'd been gutsy enough to stow away in no-woman's-land. But the bathroom was empty.

When Jamie stepped back outside, a chilly wind stirred up, and he shuddered. He noticed two big piles of leaves at the edge of the park. Had Megan buried herself in one of them?

"Come out, come out, wherever you are!" he called, swiping at the mound of leaves. He walked into them—until he was up to his knees in dead leaves. "Shit," he muttered, kicking at the pile. He glanced around the empty park. "Meg?" he called out. "Megan? Babe? Okay, you win!"

Jamie's eyes locked on the row of cars parked along the roadway that snaked through the park. When he'd told her to stay in this section, he'd considered this road a boundary line. Nevertheless, Jamie hurried toward the line of cars. Some of them appeared to have been abandoned. Megan wasn't hiding behind any of the vehicles. Jamie even peeked underneath the cars. No sign of her. Something was wrong. Where the hell was she?

"Okay, Meg, you win!" he announced loudly, lumbering

away from the last automobile at the edge of the park area. "I give up, babe! Game's over, okay? Meg? C'mon, I'm getting tired of this . . ."

Across the roadway, he'd caught the attention of a couple, who had stopped to stare at him. They must have taken him for a crazy man, yelling at nobody. If Meg was in the vicinity, certainly, she could hear him too.

"Megan? Baby?" Jamie couldn't help it, but his voice was cracking. "The game's over. Goddamn it, I'm serious! I'm going home, okay?"

Jamie glanced around. It didn't make sense. If someone had grabbed her, she would have screamed. He lumbered back toward the park bench. Maybe if he just sat and waited for her, she'd come out of her hiding place.

As he passed under a tree, he heard twigs snapping. Leaves drifted down past him. Jamie looked up.

"I can't believe you gave up so soon!" Megan teased him. She was sitting on one of the lower branches.

He managed to laugh. "You scared the shit out of me, goddamn it. I thought someone had abducted you." Shaking his head, Jamie watched her climb down. "I looked up there, for God's sakes, and I didn't see you."

"That's because I was in that other tree," Megan said, nodding at a tall oak by the roadway. She jumped to the ground, then gave him a quick peck on the cheek. She was a bit out of breath. "After you looked up this tree, I came down from the other one and hid up here. Pretty smart, huh?"

"You're a friggin' genius," Jamie muttered. "C'mon."

They crossed the road—into another part of the park, where a path wound around the beautiful Dahlia Gardens. Megan put her arm around him, but Jamie pulled away. "Oh, don't be a sore loser," she said, giggling. "Huh, you should have seen yourself ducking into the ladies' toilet. It was pretty funny."

"Yeah, hysterical," he replied, cracking a smile, despite himself. He couldn't stay mad at her.

Megan kissed him, then ran toward a big pile of leaves

between the gardens. Jamie chased after her. Megan jumped into the leaves, then let out a scream.

Jamie laughed—until she screamed again.

"Oh, my God, my God!" she yelled, recoiling and scrambling out of the leafy pile. Megan had tears in her eyes. She ran into his arms. "Something's in there," she gasped, trembling. She started to choke on her words. "A dead animal—some *thing*—"

Jamie stepped toward the hill of leaves, now scattered and blowing in the chilly wind. He hesitated, then brushed some leaves off the top of the stack.

"Please, Jamie, don't," Megan cried, turning away.

He felt a cold and hard object against his fingertips. He dug past the top layer of dried-up leaves and lawn waste. Something smelled like rotten fruit. It was wrapped in a clear plastic bag. Jamie swiped a few more leaves away. He could see a woman's face and a pair of heavily made-up eyes staring back at him through the plastic. Her mouth was painted dark red, and she had a beauty mark on her cheek.

"Oh, Jesus," he whispered.

Jamie told himself that it might just be a mannequin. But he brushed away a few more leaves, and he saw the plastic bag was tied around the woman's throat.

Her blue-white hand—frozen with rigor mortis—clutched at a something near her neck.

It was a gold heart-shaped locket.

Chapter 2

She'd checked into the Westhill Towers Hotel in downtown Seattle under the name Mrs. George Mowery.

The *real* Mrs. Mowery was home in Salem, Oregon, where she lived with George and their two kids. Selma Mowery always stayed home whenever George went to Seattle on business.

Yet for the last two years, Westhill Towers's records showed Mrs. Mowery had joined her husband on eighteen out of twenty-three of his overnight stays there. Selma had no way of knowing. The credit card bills with the hotel payments went to George's work address. And Selma never phoned the hotel. She always rang his pager or cell phone. She had no idea her husband was seeing someone else.

The "other" *Mrs. Mowery* was also married. And her husband had no idea she was seeing someone else either. They lived outside Seattle. Whenever George planned a trip, he'd e-mail her, and she'd think of some excuse to spend a couple of nights in the city. She had a friend backing up her cover story this time. They were supposed to be on a shopping spree for a couple of days. She stole George's idea, and got herself a cell phone. No reason for her husband to call the hotel if he could reach her on the cell. No reason for him to suspect anything.

She liked being Mrs. George Mowery whenever George came into town. But she had no intention of taking the name on a full-time basis. She didn't want to break up his marriage—anymore than she wanted to ruin her own. They loved their spouses, yet needed the diversion. What she had with George was love with boundaries.

At the moment, she wasn't too happy with her surrogate husband. George had left her alone tonight while he'd gone off to wine and dine a client. She wasn't supposed to wait up. He'd apologized profusely, and promised they'd be together the entire day tomorrow. But that didn't make tonight any easier.

She stared at the Seattle skyline, the twinkling lights of a Saturday night. She saw it all—past her own reflection—through the floor-to-ceiling windows of the small gymnasium on the thirty-seventh floor of the Westhill Towers. She was on the treadmill, clocking in at twenty-one minutes, with 244 calories burned so far. Perspiration dripped from her forehead, and her T-shirt was soaked. It clung to her shoulders and back. She'd been pacing herself to the oldies music piped over a speaker system. Right now, the Beach Boys' "Wouldn't It Be Nice?" kept her moving in place.

She'd come up to the gym so she could blow off some steam. It beat sitting alone in their room all night. For a while, an overweight man and his two skinny adolescent kids—a boy and girl—had been in the gym, too, going from one weight and cardio machine to another. The boy kept staring at her. So she had a little fun with him.

She'd gotten her two front teeth knocked out when she was a kid—thanks to a girlfriend fooling around with a tennis racket during a slumber party. Every few years, she was fitted for new permanents, and had to wear a temporary retainer with fake front teeth. She could take it out with the flick of her tongue. This was one of those temporary interims. So—when that obnoxious teenage boy gawked at her for the umpteenth time, she smiled, then took out her teeth with her tongue. The kid actually shrieked. He was horrified. It was the one good laugh she had tonight.

The dad and two kids had left shortly after that, about ten minutes ago. Now she was alone.

A section from the newspaper was rolled up in the cup-holder on the Treadmaster's handlebars. The newspaper was four days old, and folded over to page three. But the headline grabbed her attention:

"REMBRANDT" KILLER CLAIMS FOURTH VICTIM

A female corpse discovered in Seattle's Volunteer Park on Sunday afternoon is now considered the latest victim of an elusive serial killer the police have dubbed, "Rembrandt."

The victim, a Redmond resident, Constance Shafer, 30, had been missing for 72 hours before the discovery of her body, buried in a pile of leaves near the park's Dahlia Garden. Shafer had been shot in the chest. In a pattern consistent with Rembrandt's previous three victims, Shafer's face was made up with lipstick, false eyelashes, and rouge. A plastic bag had been tied over her head.

Shafer was last seen by her husband, Frank, at 11:30 Thursday evening when she stepped out to walk the family dog. She never returned.

King County medical examiners estimate that Shafer had been dead less than 12 hours prior to the discovery of her body. "The killer or killers appear to have held the victim in captivity at least 48 hours before she was shot," said Seattle Police Chief, Norm Christoff. "This repeats a pattern established with the others victims."

Police would not confirm if any of the women had been sexually abused.

The last victim, Jan Kirkabee, 20, a student at Seattle Pacific University, had been reported missing on September 3. A jogger discovered her body by the Fred Gilman trail in Renton two days later. Kirkabee's throat

*had been cut. Medical examiners estimated that she
had been dead no more than 8 hours.*

*According to Dr. Arlene Landis, a criminal psychi-
atrist following the Rembrandt case for* The Seattle
Post-Intelligencer, *"This killer believes he's an artist.
He's probably very pleased with the nickname, Rembrandt, which is unfortunate. It's quite likely he places
the plastic bags over his victims' heads in order to preserve the painstaking cosmetic make-over he has given
them. In many cases, he has even cut and styled the
victim's hair. Considering the populated areas he has
left the bodies, we can conclude that he wants his victims discovered before the bodies decompose and while
their makeup is still fresh. He wants people to see his
handiwork."*

*Medical examiners could not determine if the vic-
tims were "made-up" before or after their deaths. None
died from suffocation, despite the plastic bags placed
over their heads.*

*The first victim, Nancy Hart, 23, a newlywed from
Wenatchee, was found on November 19, last year. She
had been shot in the chest.*

*Nearly six months later, on May 17, the body of a
Boeing employee, Barbara Tuttle, 34, was discovered
in a junkyard not far from her home in Woodinville.
Her neck had been broken.*

"Oh, God, enough of this," she muttered, rolling up the
newspaper section and stuffing it back into the treadmill's
cup-holder.

She'd heard about this Rembrandt killer. It was all they
talked about on the local news lately. Apparently, the police
weren't any closer to catching him. She didn't want to read
about him. She'd have nightmares tonight.

For the next few minutes she let her mind go blank. She
watched a ferry glide across Puget Sound's calm, moonlit
water. Suddenly, she felt so forlorn. People were going places,

and here she was, running and running, and going nowhere. She should have stayed at home. Saturday night alone in the city was utter misery.

"Oh, screw this," she muttered, switching off the treadmill. She felt her pulse, and wandered over to the window. Gazing outside, she caught her breath. "Quit feeling so sorry for yourself already," she sighed. "You'll be with him later tonight and all day tomorrow."

The music stopped. She glanced up at the clock on the wall. It was almost eleven. The gym would be closing soon. She imagined them automatically locking the door and turning off the lights from some switch down at the front desk. Just her luck, she'd be locked in here until six in the morning. George would think she'd ditched him.

Well, then he'd know how it feels to be ditched, she thought, heading toward the women's changing room. She'd come to the gym, wearing a sweater over her T-shirt, with her room card in the pocket. She'd left the sweater in a locker in the changing room.

She walked past a row of lockers. Her footsteps echoed on the tiled floor, and there was a steady drip sound from a faucet in the bathroom. Finding a stack of towels, she wiped the cold sweat from her forehead. She felt a chill. She needed to take a shower, but not here. Without the oldies music playing, the place was kind of spooky. Too damn quiet.

All at once, a locker door slammed.

She jumped at the noise. Her heart rate had just started to return to normal after the treadmill, but now it was leaping off the chart. For a moment, she couldn't move. She just listened. Nothing.

She'd thought she was alone in here. How could anyone have gotten past her without her seeing? Maybe the noise was from the men's room next door.

The security in this place wasn't so terrific. Her plastic card room key was supposed to open the door to the workout room, but the door wasn't locked. Anyone from the street could have walked into the hotel, taken an elevator up to the thirty-seventh floor, and let themselves into the gym. And there was no lock on the women's changing room door either.

Someone could be hiding in the very next row of lockers, or in one of the shower stalls, or maybe in the sauna.

She shuddered. "Oh, quit creeping yourself out," she grumbled. She wished she hadn't read that stupid newspaper article.

She hurried to her locker. Her hand was trembling as she worked the combination. It was one of those new changeable combination locks. She'd set it for her birthday June third: 6–0–3.

She was dialing the three when she heard another noise. It was a sudden, mechanical hum. Maybe the heater in the sauna, or a vent activating automatically. Whatever it was, *it wasn't a person,* she told herself.

She got the locker open, then pulled out her sweater. "Honey, sorry I'm taking so long!" she nervously called out. "I'll be right there!"

She felt stupid, talking to no one—just in case she wasn't alone in this changing room. Who was she trying to kid?

She closed the locker door and started toward the center aisle. Then she stopped dead.

A shadow swept across the tiled floor.

She glanced up at the ceiling. It was polished metal, almost like a mirror. She could see her own reflection. And she saw a man, standing on the other side of her locker, in the next row.

She gasped.

He looked up at the ceiling, too. His face was a bit blurred. But she could tell he was smiling at her.

* * *

On the thirty-seventh floor, a hotel security man switched off the lights in the small gymnasium and the two locker rooms. The place was empty. It looked clean. He failed to notice a pair of white panties dangling from the treadmill's handlebars.

* * *

"There's another one," he said. "Christ, that damn thing is huge! It's bigger than a squirrel. That makes eight so far. I told you, ten's my limit. If I see two more rats, I'm out of here."

"Oh, don't be such a pansy," Phillip Banach told his brother. He was wearing coveralls, construction boots, work gloves, and over his nose and mouth, a mask which he'd dabbed with peppermint extract. It helped camouflage the pungent smell of the junkyard. The place was about half the size of a football field, with trails winding through hills of debris. Phillip turned toward his brother. "Y'hear what I'm telling you, *pansy?*"

"Hey, you're the homo here, bro," Alan Banach retorted. He'd put on an old pair of galoshes and wrapped duct tape around the cuffs of his jeans, but he still hated stomping through all this foul garbage. "Flies and rats and stench, oh my," he said, tugging a small oriental rug out from under a loaded garbage bag. Half of the rug had been scorched in a fire or something. He tossed it back amid the rubble. "I can't believe you and Damien do this every week," Alan continued. "What kind of gay men are you anyway, sloshing through garbage? You should be dealing with fabrics and colors."

Actually, Phillip and his partner, Damien, did deal with fabrics and colors. They ran the Banach-Tate Antique Gallery in Bellingham, Washington. Phillip's brother, Alan, was their accountant, and they did a good business in their posh little store. Most of their stock was acquired in estate sales, but once every week or so, unbeknownst to their snooty, rich clients, the two men searched for antique treasures in this dumping grounds off Interstate 5, a few miles south of the city.

Damien was visiting his ailing father in Everett that Sunday. So Phillip had tapped Alan to come along on this afternoon's scavenging expedition. It was a two-man job. Some of the pieces they uncovered here could be pretty heavy.

"You know, we're totally wasting our time. We'll never find anything here," Alan announced, sifting through the garbage. He glanced up at his brother—in his coveralls, picking through another mound of debris. "All we'll come up with is more rats. I'm telling you, if I see two more, we're out of here."

"Has it ever occurred to you that maybe you've seen the same rat eight times?" Phillip retorted. "Stop your belly-aching. We're not wasting our time. For your information, Damien and I once found a headboard here that we repaired and refinished, and ended up selling to a woman from Portland for a thousand dollars."

"Oh, for chrissakes, you've told me that stupid headboard story about a hundred times. It happened in—what, like—nineteen ninety-seven? Get yourself some new material, bro." Alan picked up an empty jar and waved it at his brother. "Hey, I have an old Noxema jar here! Whaddaya think we can get for this? A couple of hundred bucks?"

His brother didn't respond. He was staring down at something.

"I'm telling you, Phil," he called. "No one throws away anything any more. They sell their junk on eBay. Phil?"

Alan squinted at his brother, who was still studying some object amid another heap of debris. Phillip Banach fell to his knees and started digging through the trash. Alan figured his brother must have struck gold.

But then he stepped closer.

Philip swept aside a Burger King bag and some other garbage, uncovering what looked like a woman's nude corpse.

"Holy Jesus," Alan murmured. "Is that—"

He didn't get the next words out. He saw the dried blood between her bare breasts. A plastic bag was tied over her head, and someone had made her up with dark red lipstick, false eyelashes, a heavy application of rouge, and a beauty mark by her mouth.

Phillip started to untie the cord from around her neck.

"You shouldn't touch her," Alan warned. "You—"

Once again, Alan was struck dumb. His brother didn't seem to care about disturbing police evidence. Phillip tore away at the plastic bag. Alan suddenly realized his brother's intention: he was trying to help the woman breathe.

She was still alive.

Chapter 3

"Can you talk, honey?"

Her eyelids fluttering, she tried to focus on the plump, black nurse at her bedside. She didn't want to talk. She didn't want to move. All she wanted to do was go back to sleep until the pain in her chest went away. Her head hurt too, worse than any hangover.

The nurse reached for the telephone on the night table. She punched a couple of numbers. "Our girl's up again," she said.

The patient saw the intravenous tube in her arm and some kind of monitor near the nightstand. "What—what happened?" she managed to ask.

"Up—and *talking,*" the nurse said, then she hung up the phone. She pulled a pen-light from her breast pocket, then leaned over the bed. She shined the light in her eyes for a moment, then gave her a warm, reassuring smile.

The nurse had a pretty face, a pale cocoa complexion, green eyes, and a short pageboy hairstyle with auburn streaks. "I'm Sherita," she said. "What's your name, honey?"

The woman just stared back at her. "What happened to me?" she whispered in a raspy voice. Her throat hurt too.

Sherita seemed to read her mind. At the night table, she poured some water from a plastic tumbler into a glass with a bendable flexi-straw. "Take it easy now," she purred, bringing the straw to her lips. "You've had a rough time of it, honey. But you're going to be okay. You're a fighter. You practically came back from the dead. Your name ought to be Lazarus, but they've got you down as 'Jane Doe.' You're in a hospital in Bellingham. We've been taking good care of you."

Sherita set the water glass aside. Some commotion out in the hallway distracted her for a moment. But she kept talking in a calm, soothing voice. "A lot of people have been rooting for you, hon. You're lucky to be alive. If not for a couple of little holes in a plastic bag, it might be a different story. You were six hours in surgery. The last three days, you've been drifting in and out, mostly out. But you're up and talking. And that's a good thing. Can you tell me your name?"

Now that she'd had some water, her throat didn't hurt quite as much any more. It would be easier for her to speak now—if she could answer Sherita. She gazed up at the nice nurse, and slowly shook her head.

She had no idea what her name was.

" 'Albinia?' " Sherita said, glancing up from a paperback called, *Names For Baby*. She sat at Jane Doe's bedside, a Tootsie Pop in her free hand. " 'Alcina?' " she continued, " 'Alda . . . Aldora . . . Aleria . . .' "

Frowning, Jane Doe shook her head. They thought she'd recognize her name if she heard it, and someone suggested going through a Name-Your-Baby book. She forgot which doctor had this brainstorm. So many of them had been in and out of her room for the last twenty-four hours, she couldn't keep track. She felt so weak and frail, everything seemed muddled.

Two police detectives had questioned her last night, but it was pointless. She couldn't remember who she was—or how she'd ended up in the hospital with a hole in her chest and a bad bump on her head. Nor did she recollect someone shooting her five days ago. The more questions the detectives asked, the more upset and frustrated she became.

She hadn't been out of bed yet, but apparently, a policeman was guarding her door, and they'd beefed up security on this particular wing of the hospital.

Sherita and a couple of the doctors said the extra precautions were to keep all the reporters out. Maybe. But what they weren't telling her was obvious. Whoever had tried to kill her probably wanted to finish the job.

Did this killer know that she didn't remember him at all?

This morning, one of the doctors had tried to explain how her amnesia had been caused by the trauma, shock, and injury. She'd just nodded and pretended to understand as he explained about the workings of the frontal, temporal, and parietal lobes. He said amnesia was a temporary condition, lasting from a few seconds to a few hours. Only in the most severe cases did the memory loss continue for weeks or months. Hers was a form of retrograde amnesia. "But you're one for the record books," the doctor had admitted. "Completely forgetting one's own identity, that's not retrograde amnesia. That's *As The World Turns* Amnesia. It only happens in movies and soap operas."

She'd had no idea what he meant by *As the World Turns*. At the time, she wondered if the doctor thought she was faking. It was almost as upsetting as her interview with those two police detectives. She felt so stupid and useless, a total disappointment to all these detective and doctors who wanted her memory to work for them.

" *'Alethea?'* " Sherita said, slouching a bit in the chair. " *'Alexandra? Alexis?'* " She gave the Tootsie Pop a quick lick, then peered up from the book. "Tell me it's not *Alexis*. Remember that show, *Dynasty?* That Alexis, she was a real bitch."

Jane Doe just shook her head.

"Girl, you don't remember *Dynasty?* Joan Collins? She was *Alexis*. Let me tell you, she was mean. I loved that show. Me and my girlfriend, we used to call it, 'Do-Nasty.' "

Shrugging, Jane Doe glanced down at the bedsheets. "Sorry. I don't know it."

With a sigh, Sherita went back to the baby-naming book. " 'Alfonsine?' " She laughed. "Hell, who would name their kid, Alfonsine?"

Jane Doe cracked a tiny smile. "Maybe someone named Sherita isn't in a position to criticize."

"Well, aren't you the smart ass?" Sherita chuckled. "It's a family name. Sherita is my favorite aunt."

"Sorry," she murmured, gazing at the bedsheets again.

"Did you have a favorite aunt when you were a kid?" Sherita asked.

"Dig, dig, dig." Jane Doe gave her a shrewd look. "You don't give up, do you?"

"Nope." Sherita nursed the Tootsie Pop for a moment.

"Well, thanks for not giving up on me," she whispered.

Sherita glanced down at the book again. " 'Alfreda . . . Alice . . . Alina . . . Alison?' "

Jane Doe kept shaking her head. She didn't think this would work.

Last night, she'd dreamt she was playing on the beach with a handsome, sporty-looking man and an eleven-year-old boy. They both had wavy golden-colored hair and the same guileless smile. She was with her husband and son. The three of them were laughing and playing tag with the waves along the shore. But then she remembered she had to have her portrait painted by some artist, and he wanted her there on time. He was very strict about that. She watched her husband and son stroll along the water's edge without her. They didn't seem to realize she'd stayed behind. She tried to call to them, but couldn't remember their names. She felt a pain in her chest—as if something had speared her heart.

She'd told the doctors that she had a husband—and a son, who was about eleven years old. But even as she'd described the man and boy in her dream, she'd had a feeling they were lost to her. Where were they? Why hadn't they come for her? Didn't they miss her? She felt so alone.

She'd also told the doctors about the artist in her dream.

She didn't remember his face. She hadn't really seen him. But in the dream, she knew he was waiting for her.

" '*Alma . . . Aloha . . . Althea . . .*' " Sherita continued, her eyes on the book.

"I have a name you might help me with," Jane Doe interrupted. "It's *Rembrandt.* Who is he?"

Glancing up from the book, Sherita worked on her Tootsie Pop for a moment. "He's an artist, Dutch, I think," she answered steadily. "It's also a brand of toothpaste."

"And it's what they call this man who tried to kill me," Jane Doe said.

Earlier, she'd heard a couple of doctors talking outside her door when they'd thought she was asleep. One of them wanted to show her a newspaper. He figured if she read about what had happened to her, it would trigger her memory. His colleague argued that it was a terrible idea, and reading about "Rembrandt" might only traumatize her further. She kept hearing that name, whispered about.

"Do they think he'll come after me?" she asked.

"You don't have to worry about that," Sherita assured her. "You have a couple cops on babysitting duty, just outside the door, honey. Nobody's getting past them."

Jane Doe sighed, and tugged at the bedsheets a little. "I bet they're hoping Rembrandt tries to pay me a visit," she muttered. "That way, they'll catch him. Am I right?"

Frowning, Sherita pitched her Tootsie Pop in the wastebasket. She picked up the book again. "I don't know what the cops are thinking, honey."

"I hope they don't kill him," Jane Doe said.

"Even after everything he did to you?" Sherita asked.

"Oh, I'm not being nice," she replied. She shrugged helplessly, and her voice cracked as she spoke. "What if he dies without telling anyone? Don't you see? Right now, he's the only person in the world who knows me."

"This clown offered me three hundred bucks."

"Three hundred—just for taking her picture?"

Sherita nodded. She picked the lettuce off her prewrapped turkey and Swiss on rye. "Those reporters are all dying to get a look at her. Might as well be Madonna in that private room." She ripped open a small bag of barbecue potato chips.

Sherita never ate anything that was actually cooked in the hospital cafeteria. She bought only prepackaged stuff that came from an outside vendor. Serving her patients their dinner, Sherita often wanted to warn them that the food was so fatty and low grade, they were guaranteed to come back with heart problems—or a parasite.

Her friend, Naomi, had no qualms over the cafeteria fare. She didn't work at the hospital, but was meeting Sherita there for lunch. Naomi eagerly dug into the fried chicken— even though it was dripping in grease. Like her friend, she was a big girl. But Naomi was white, with a corkscrew-curly blond perm and a pierced nose. At twenty-six, she was a couple of years younger than Sherita. They'd first met at a Weight Watchers orientation five years ago. They'd both decided life was too short to live without real cheese or ice cream, and walked out during the break. Naomi and Sherita had been friends ever since.

They met for lunch or dinner every week or so—usually some place nicer than the hospital's cafeteria. At this hour, it was crowded, and all the good tables—the ones by the windows looking down at the parking lot—were taken. Sherita and Naomi had to settle for a two-top by the bus station.

"So—are you going to take the three hundred bucks or what?" Naomi asked, working on her fried chicken. "That's like—half your rent for the month."

"I don't care," Sherita said, scowling. She munched on some chips. "I'm not doing that to her. I told you, she's a nice lady. She doesn't want her picture in the paper. Hell, she's been through enough."

"My friend at work, Cindy, she's been following the newspaper stories," Naomi said. "And she thinks this Jane Doe is faking. Cindy says she's holding out for the publicity or a book deal—and *then* she'll start talking."

Sherita rolled her eyes. "How can you hear what your friend Cindy says when she's talking with her head up her ass? I'm Jane Doe's nurse. I've been looking after her for six days now. I'd know if she was faking. She doesn't remember a damn thing. Poor girl's all alone, and she's scared."

With a sigh, Sherita picked up her sandwich again. "I only hope this guy coming in today . . ." She trailed off, then took a bite from her sandwich.

"Who's coming in today?" Naomi asked. "What are you talking about?"

"Nothing," Sherita shrugged, her mouth full.

"Oh, c'mon, you started to say something. Now, give. Is somebody coming in to identify her today? Some guy?"

Sherita dabbed her mouth with a napkin. "This is on the hush-hush, okay? The newspapers and TV people don't know about this. Swear you won't tell anyone?"

Naomi leaned forward. "Swear to God and kiss my elbow. What is it?"

"Well, you're right," Sherita admitted, her voice dropping to a whisper. "They're bringing in someone this afternoon—up from Tacoma. He says he's her husband. He gave the cops a couple of photos that—I guess—looked enough like her. And he described her fairly accurately, even mentioned a birthmark on her elbow. They think this guy's on the level. I hope so—for her sake."

Sherita turned to a man sitting alone at the next table. "Excuse me, hon, could I borrow your salt?"

He handed her the white plastic salt shaker. Sherita salted her sandwich, then handed the shaker back to him. "Thanks, honey." She turned to her friend again.

"I think he's interested in one of us," Naomi whispered. "I saw him looking over at us earlier. He's cute."

Sherita glanced at the man, whose nose was in a newspaper.

"Did I tell you?" Naomi continued. "I joined an Internet dating service. It's really fun, and cheaper than you'd think . . ."

Naomi was whispering. But the man at the next table

could still hear her. He'd been listening to every word they'd said to each other.

The nurse's friend was right: he was interested in one of them. For the last four days, he'd been following Sherita Williams, trying to find out all he could about her.

She lived alone in a rented house. Contrary to the decals on the door and front windows, the place didn't have an alarm system. He knew when her boyfriend came by, and when she was alone. He knew her hours at work, and where she parked her car in the hospital lot. He knew the patient with whom she spent the most time, a woman they called Jane Doe.

He had placed Jane Doe into a Dumpster in North Seattle a week ago. He'd expected her corpse to be discovered in that Dumpster—or possibly in a nearby garbage dump. He hadn't counted on her ending up—alive—in a junkyard nearly ninety miles away in Bellingham.

Sherita Williams said her amnesia wasn't an act. But that was just a temporary condition. If this man coming in today was truly her husband, he might help her recollect certain things.

He had to act quickly.

At the next table, Sherita was listening to Naomi talk about the three candidates who had answered her ad on the Internet dating service. She turned to borrow the salt from the man at the next table again. She did a double take.

His lunch tray was there, but he was gone. He hardly touched his food.

Sherita got up and swiped the salt off his table, and sat back down. "That's funny, I didn't see that guy take off," she muttered. "Did you?"

Naomi frowned. "No. But I'm telling you, he was interested in one of us. I saw him looking over here a lot."

"Well, I'm off the market," Sherita said, salting her sandwich.

"Huh," Naomi replied. "So—you're probably the one he's interested in. Typical. I'll bet he shows up again and goes after you. I'll just bet."

Chapter 4

"Does this freak you out or anything?" Sherita asked, applying some mascara to Jane Doe's eyelashes.

"You mean, am I having flashbacks to the last time someone put makeup on me?" Sitting in the hospital bed, Jane Doe kept still while Sherita worked on her eyes. She sighed. "No, I'm not 'freaking out.' But I vaguely recall a woman doing this to me while someone else was watching."

"Where? In a department store?"

"I'm not sure. I just remember thinking she was using way too much makeup, and I'd end up looking hideous."

"Hmmm, you want a tip?" Sherita said, reaching for the face powder brush. "Never get a make-over in a store that also sells corndogs."

"I'll take that under advisement," she chuckled. "Thanks."

"You're welcome, *Tammy,*" Sherita said.

They had found out her name: Tammy Phelps. Her husband was Lon, a night watchman at the University of Washington branch campus in Tacoma. They lived there—along with their twelve-year-old son, Dwight. Lon had told the police Tammy had been missing for eight days.

The only one of those names remotely familiar to her was

Tammy. Could it be her name? Was Lon the sporty, handsome man in her dream?

She hoped so. She desperately wanted to see her husband and son. The names Lon and Dwight would soon become familiar to her again. She would recognize them. The search for her family—and her true identity—would soon be over. Lon was scheduled to meet with her in an hour.

She'd been nervous about this reunion ever since this morning, when they'd told her about Lon. With a little help from Sherita, she'd finally crawled out of bed and walked a few steps—to and from the bathroom. Sherita gave her a sponge bath, and brushed baby powder though her dark brown hair to absorb some of the oiliness.

She also had a chance to study herself in a mirror for a while. In addition to the flat, lifeless, shoulder-length hair, she was pale and gaunt, with dark circles under her green eyes. "My God, I look awful," she told Sherita.

"Well, what the hell do you expect, girl?" she replied. "You're recovering from major surgery, and you've been in bed, eating bad hospital food for nearly a week. Relax, you're a knockout. I'd kill for your cheekbones and waistline."

Nevertheless, Sherita borrowed some makeup from one of the nurses—along with a lavender silk robe that a patient had left behind. Jane Doe didn't dare ask if the robe's former owner had departed from the hospital on her own or in a box. She didn't want to know.

"My stomach feels funny, butterflies," she said, checking Sherita's work in a hand-mirror. Sherita had laid the rouge on a bit heavily, but she didn't look too bad. "Is this what it feels like, going on a date?"

"Huh, I can't remember that far back, honey," Sherita replied. "Just keep in mind, he might not be your husband. I saw the photos he brought in, and they're a little out of focus. In one, you're standing at a distance, and in the other, you're squinting in the sun. And the birthmark he said was on your elbow, it's much farther down on your arm."

Jane Doe shook her head. "Please, don't. I need for this to be my husband. I saw the photos too. They look like me, they do. I—I almost remember them being taken."

Sherita smiled tightly. "I know you want this to be the Real McCoy, but I don't want to see you get your hopes shot down, honey. There are a lot of people—reporters and curiosity-freaks—who would say or do just about anything to get a look at you. This Lon Phelps could be one of them."

At three-fifteen, a couple of doctors came into her room. Apparently, they wanted to observe how Tammy Phelps reacted when seeing her husband again.

"I hope he's your dream man, honey," Sherita whispered. Then she stepped over toward the window—out of the doctors' way. She glanced toward the door.

Two police detectives, sporting suitcoats and ties, ushered in a man. He had glasses, a goatee, and slick, long brown hair. He saw her and broke into a grin. He was skinny, and dressed in jeans, an old, soiled sportshirt and a jean jacket. "Tammy? Baby?" he whispered.

Wide-eyed, she stared back at him.

"Don't you know me, sweetheart?"

She didn't know him at all. She didn't feel any kind of connection to this man. She glanced at Sherita for help.

"Tammy, it's me, Lon," he said, the smile running away from his face. "What's going on? You gotta remember me, baby. I'm your husband. I've been real worried about you, doll."

Gazing at him, she felt herself shrinking back. She slowly shook her head. He wasn't the man of her dreams. As much as she tried, she couldn't conceal her disappointment. She felt stupid, having spent the last two hours trying to look pretty for this stranger who didn't even bother putting on a clean shirt for her.

"C'mon, baby. How about a kiss?" He took a step toward her.

"No, get away," she said steadily. Jane Doe shook her head. "You're not my husband. I might not remember much, but I'm sure you're not my husband. I've never even met you."

Lon Phelps glared at her. "Hey, now cut the bullshit—"

One of the cops took hold of his arm.

"You're not Charlie," she whispered.

"Listen, bitch," Lon Phelps growled. "You can't do this—"

The detective pulled at his arm. "All right, Mr. Phelps," he said. "That's enough—"

"You left me once, and you're not doing it again!" he hissed. "Dwight is my kid too. Where is he? Goddamn it, Tammy, I want to see my son!"

Breaking free, he pushed aside one of the doctors and charged toward her. Recoiling, Jane Doe screamed.

The detectives swept down on Lon Phelps again, then tore him away from her bedside. "Get him out of here!" one of the doctors yelled.

Lon Phelps lunged toward the bed once more, but the two detectives restrained him. Jane Doe clutched the bedsheets to her throat, and turned her head away. He kept calling her a whore and a bitch. As they dragged Lon Phelps toward the doorway, he kicked the night table and sent a water pitcher crashing to the tiled floor. Both doctors were doused.

Eyes closed, Jane Doe curled up and pressed her face to the pillow. She could still hear Lon Phelps lashing out obscenities at the detectives as they led him down the corridor.

"Good God, they sure did a bang-up job of screening him," she heard one of the doctors mutter. "What were they thinking?"

The other doctor was asking if she was all right. She felt Sherita hovering over her.

"Yes, yes, I'm all right," she answered, eyes still closed. She was shaking inside. She just wanted everyone to leave—except maybe Sherita.

As if reading her mind, Sherita announced she would clean up the mess Lon Phelps had made. "It's okay, you go on," she told the doctors. "You better dry off. I'll look after our girl."

After the doctors shuffled out the door, Jane Doe opened her eyes. She took a couple of deep breaths. She was still trembling.

Sherita came from the bathroom, then wiped the water off the floor with a towel. Retrieving the tumbler, she set it on the night table and stepped up to Jane Doe's bedside. She stroked her hair. "Well, hon, if that was your husband, I've got news for you. He's as crazy as a road lizard."

Jane Doe managed to smile up at her. "I guess that was kind of a bust, huh?"

"Not totally," Sherita said. "Who's Charlie? In the middle of that fiasco, you said to psycho-man: *'You're not Charlie.'* "

"I did?" she asked.

"Is Charlie the guy in your dream?"

She stared up at Sherita, then let out a little laugh and nodded. Tears stung her eyes. "Charlie's my husband," she heard herself say. "Charlie Ferguson. I met him my freshman year at the University of Oregon in Eugene. Charlie Ferguson. And—and our son's name is Brian." Suddenly she had a hard time getting her breath. The flood of memories and facts were coming at her. She remembered her mother and father. She married Charlie in Las Vegas. They were both still in college at the time. Her mother was furious.

"We live in Seattle," she said, sitting up in the bed. "On Cascadia Avenue. It's not far from Lake Washington. That's where we were in my dream. We were walking along the water's edge."

"Are you still Tammy?" Sherita asked. "You said the name was familiar."

She laughed and shook her head. "No, no. Tammy— Tammy was my best friend in junior high school. Tammy Lampley. We both had a crush on Brad Reece, the cutest guy in our class. We were in Ms. Hockins' homeroom. I remember it all." She was smiling and crying at the same time. The recently applied mascara ran down her cheeks. "God, Sherita, I remember everything. I know who I am. My name is Claire . . . Claire Ferguson."

Sherita grinned, then took her hand and squeezed it. "Nice to finally meet you, Claire Ferguson."

"God, you're such a goodie-two-shoes. I can't believe you won't even tell me her first name."

Sherita pressed the button for the elevator again. She wore her tan raincoat, and had a big purse hanging from her shoulder. She shook her head at her coworker, Angie, a stout Korean nurse in her early forties. "Sorry, hon, I'm sworn to secrecy," she said, glancing up at the numbers over the elevator door. "A handful of doctors, the cops, and me—we're the only ones who know about it. To everyone else, she'll stay Jane Doe."

"At least tell me what the husband's like." Angie nudged her. "Weren't you there when they brought him in today?"

"Yeah, but it wasn't her husband," Sherita said. "It was some whacko."

The elevator finally arrived, and the doors opened. Sherita and Angie stepped inside. No one else was in the elevator, so Sherita felt free to talk. "I knew something was wrong with those photos he gave the cops. From what one of them told me, I guess this guy's wife took a hike with their kid five years ago, and . . . well, someone on the force will have his ass in a sling for letting that looney-tune in to see her."

"So—do they know who her real husband is?" Angie asked.

The elevator stopped on the first floor, and two people stepped on.

Sherita just smiled and shook her head at her friend. The last she heard, the police couldn't find a Charles or Claire Ferguson on Cascadia Avenue in Seattle. Before clocking out tonight, she'd stopped by Jane Doe's room. They'd given Jane Doe a sedative. She'd been groggy and a little out of it. "Why hasn't Charlie been in to see me?" she'd whispered, grabbing Sherita's hand. "Why don't they get a hold of him?"

"It's just taking them a while to track him down," Sherita had replied. "You'll see your man tomorrow, I'm sure."

But Sherita wasn't really sure at all.

Angie and the other two passengers stepped off at garage level B. Sherita said good-bye to her friend, and continued alone to level C.

She'd done a lot of running back and forth today, and her feet hurt. Strolling toward her car, Sherita looked forward to a long, hot shower and trying some peppermint-scented foot lotion she'd just bought.

Space 29, level C of the underground garage had been Sherita's parking spot for over a year now. The florescent lighting, low ceiling, gray walls, and the cold concrete were so familiar to her that she rarely felt squeamish walking to and from her car—no matter what the hour. Right now, she didn't see anyone else around. She heard cars moving on the level above, a faint rumbling and tires screeching in the distance.

She dug the keys from her purse and started toward her red Honda.

"Sherita?"

She stopped in her tracks. The voice wasn't familiar. A mystified, half-smile frozen on her face, she glanced around. "Who's there?" she called.

Sherita heard footsteps, but no response. She still didn't see anyone. The smile faded from her face. "What's going on?" she said loudly.

Out of the corner of her eye, Sherita saw a figure silhouetted in the doorway to a maintenance area. Then she blinked and he was gone. But the door was closing on its own—very slowly.

Sherita started past a row of cars—toward the entryway. She didn't see anyone in the maintenance area beyond that door. A shaft of light from the other side was narrowing as the door almost closed. But Sherita grabbed the handle, and pushed it open again.

"Is anyone there?" she called.

To her left she noticed the open door to a boiler room with some machinery churning out a loud, continual humming noise. Straight ahead, another open door—to what looked like a broom closet. A bare lightbulb hung from a cord in that little room, and it swayed back and forth as if someone had just brushed against it. Shadows swept across the walls full of shelves, cluttered with cleaning supplies.

Sherita paused in the doorway and stared across the hall to that closet. She listened to the loud, mechanical drone from the room next door. For a moment, she couldn't move. She'd been lured here hoping to see the man who had called her name. Now, she didn't want to see him. She just wanted to get the hell out of there.

Sherita shook her head. "Fuck this," she announced.

Backing out of the doorway, she half-expected someone to come at her from behind. She anxiously pulled shut the door, which must have been on some sort of slow-spring hinge. For a moment, it felt as if someone was pulling at the handle from the other side. Giving up, Sherita swiveled around and ran to her car. Her heart was racing, and she could hardly breathe. Fumbling with the keys, she glanced back over her shoulder.

The door was wide open again.

"Sweet Jesus," she murmured.

With her hands shaking, she could barely insert the key into the car door. She kept looking around for this stranger, praying at the same time that she wouldn't see him. She finally got the car door open, then ducked into the vehicle. Within seconds, she shut and locked the door, and started the ignition.

Sherita peeled out of the parking space. Then it suddenly dawned on her that she should have checked the backseat. She slammed on the brakes. The screech echoed throughout parking level C. Sherita froze for a moment, then peered into the rearview mirror. She reached back and patted the empty seat. No one.

Catching her breath, Sherita drove the three levels to the

garage exit. The cashier on duty sat in his booth. Sherita was glad to see a familiar face. She thought about telling him what had happened down at level C, maybe even suggesting the police search the area.

But what could she have told him? All that happened was someone had called out her name. A door had mysteriously opened and shut by itself a couple of times. And she'd gotten scared.

With a sigh, Sherita showed the guard her employee parking pass. Except for "thank you," she didn't say anything to him.

On her way home, Sherita thought that perhaps she'd imagined hearing someone call her name. Maybe the door to the maintenance area opened and shut on its own. Perhaps the person who called to her was one of the many custodians she knew. It might have been a reporter. The hospital lobby was full of them. It could have been anyone.

But the one "anyone" she couldn't stop thinking about was Rembrandt.

Chapter 5

"Claire, what's the last thing you remember before you woke up here in the hospital?"

Wearing the lavender robe she'd inherited yesterday from Sherita's other patient, Claire sat in a wheelchair, facing Dr. Emily Beal. The psychiatrist leaned forward in the beige leather chair. Behind Dr. Beal was a wall full of diplomas, a mauve sofa—and on it, a plainclothes detective with a tape recorder in his hand. Claire tried to avoid eye-contact with him.

"I know it's hard, Claire," Dr. Beal said. "Take your time answering."

Emily Beal was about forty—and pretty, with short-cropped, carefully styled brown hair. She wore the hospital's white topcoat over her Donna Karan dress. Claire had already had a few sessions with her, and always felt a bit frumpy around the chic doctor.

It didn't help that Dr. Beal usually talked to her with this condescendingly sympathetic smile—a well-meaning, I-Really-Understand-And-Feel-Sorry-For-You simper that was supposed to reassure Claire, but had the opposite effect. Dr. Beal was giving her that look right now.

"I'm sorry," Claire muttered. "I can't remember. I really don't know how I ended up here."

She was drawing a total blank. The doctor might as well have asked her to solve a problem in advanced physics.

"It's all right, Claire," Dr. Beal said in a soothing tone. "Let me ask you another question. Do you remember driving into Seattle with your friend to go shopping? You were planning to stay the night at a hotel and see a show. Do you recall that, Claire?"

"I'm sorry," she answered again, shrugging.

Apparently, within the last hour or so, someone must have come forward with this story about her disappearing during a shopping expedition with a girlfriend in downtown Seattle.

"I don't remember any shopping trip into the city," Claire admitted.

"It's okay, Claire," the psychiatrist said patiently. "We're making excellent progress. We're on the road to recovery, Claire."

She tried to smile. She wished Dr. Beal would stop calling her "Claire" every ten seconds. Since remembering her name yesterday, Claire noticed most of her doctors overusing it. They seemed to try too hard for a sense of familiarity and closeness that just wasn't there.

The only people who really knew her were her husband and son. So where were they? She'd told the doctors yesterday. She was still a little muddled with figures, and didn't remember the phone number or exact address. But they could find her husband and son at home: Charles, Claire, and Brian Ferguson on Cascadia Avenue in Seattle. Charlie taught twentieth-century literature at the University of Washington. Maybe they could track him down there.

"You know, my husband might be able to tell you where I was last," Claire offered, drumming her fingers on the arm of her wheelchair. "Maybe then I'll remember this shopping trip downtown. Charlie could fill in the blanks for us, Dr. Beal. You know, help clear away the cobwebs?"

Emily Beal's mouth twisted into a frown, and she shifted a bit in the chair. "Claire, can you remember the last time you saw Charlie?" she asked. "What were the two of you doing?"

Claire stared back at her. Again, she drew a blank. It was an easy question: When did she last see her husband? Was it a kiss good-bye at breakfast as he went off to teach classes at the university? Or was she waving at him and driving off with her "friend" to spend the night in a hotel downtown? Why would she do that—when they lived only about fifteen minutes away from downtown Seattle?

Dr. Beal sighed. "Can you remember where you and Charlie last went out to eat, Claire? Or a present he gave you on your last birthday?"

"A pearl necklace," Claire answered. "He gave me a single-string pearl necklace."

It was very simple and elegant, something Dr. Beal would wear. Claire remembered thinking Charlie must have spent at least a couple of hundred dollars, and they couldn't afford it.

No, that wasn't her last birthday. It was their anniversary, and because money was so tight, they'd agreed ahead of time not to exchange presents.

Claire remembered how she'd become an expert at coupon clipping, and hunting down bargains at secondhand shops. She knew when they marked down the beef, pork, and chicken at the supermarket. She bought in bulk and froze it.

Charlie was in graduate school, working as a teacher's assistant. They lived in a rented two-bedroom rambler she fixed up with nails, glue, paint, and window treatments. She had an art studio in the basement, but could steal away only a few hours a week to paint. Her work was slightly derivative of Edward Hopper, but good for an occasional two or three hundred bucks a month when a piece sold at some café or street fair.

Most of Claire's time was spent with their two-year-old, Brian. Sometimes she also babysat a neighbor's son the same age as Brian. It brought in some extra money.

"This is what happens when you get married and have a baby while still in college," Claire's mother declared during a weekend visit around that time.

"Actually, we're very happy, Mother," Claire told her.

But on that anniversary, when Charlie went against their pact and bought her a gift, Claire wasn't happy. It didn't help that Brian had pitched a fit when a neighbor-friend picked him up for the night. And Claire's attempt to cook Charlie's favorite meal (beef brisket, twice-baked potatoes, and green bean casserole with the Durkee's Onion rings on top) was a disaster. The brisket was one of those reduced cuts of beef she always bought on sale. An old shoe, marinated and cooked at 350 for an hour, would have been more tender and flavorful.

She was still crying over the dinner when Charlie gave her the fancy-wrapped, small gift box—which just had to be from a jewelry store. They were sitting at the folding card table in the kitchen, and she'd replaced the ever-present, washable plastic tablecloth with a checkered polyester one. Cosco wine goblets took the place of jelly glasses. There was a candle glowing on the table—along with their plates and the half-eaten dinner.

"But we had an agreement," she said, unwrapping the gift. "We weren't supposed to exchange presents . . ."

Then she opened the box and saw the pearl necklace. "Oh, my God, Charlie! What were you thinking? We can't afford this."

"Do you like it?" he asked, smiling hopefully.

"That's not the point!" she snapped. "I don't know how we'll pay this month's phone bill and you're making out like Donald Trump! Where am I going to wear this anyway?"

Then she saw the hurt look on his handsome face. Claire apologized, and kissed him.

That night, she came to bed wearing the pearl necklace— and nothing else.

She loved telling her girlfriends that story. Maybe that was why she remembered it so well. She still had the pearl necklace, of course, and always wore it on special occasions. She remembered wearing it to a funeral. But she couldn't remember whose funeral it was.

Her memory was coming back in fragments. There were big pieces still missing. She could remember Tammy Lampley from high school, and her girlfriends from college. So—how come she didn't know this woman who accompanied her shopping in downtown Seattle? What was she blocking out?

"Charlie gave me that necklace years ago," Claire murmured. "We were living in Oregon at the time. It was before we even moved to Seattle."

She glanced over at the detective on the sofa. He quickly looked away. This time, he was the one who seemed to be avoiding eye-contact. Claire turned to Dr. Beal, who intently stared back at her.

"I'm not remembering something," Claire said. "And I don't mean when I was attacked. It's something else. I've blanked out on a big chunk of my past. And you know what it is, don't you?"

Dr. Beal's mouth twisted to one side. She glanced down at her notes.

Claire leaned forward in the wheelchair. "What's the missing piece? Why can't you tell me?"

The psychiatrist sighed. "I think it would be better, Claire, if you remembered these 'missing pieces' yourself."

"Obviously I don't want to remember." Claire sat back. "It's something painful, isn't it? Why do you want me to work so hard—only to relive something painful?"

"Because we'll need you to do just that, Claire," she replied. "How else are we going to know how Rembrandt got to you?"

The police guard sat in a folding chair outside room 311. Lanky and handsome, the twenty-nine-year-old black cop kept his hair cut so short he was nearly bald. The name tag on his uniform read: Taj Harnell. The door beside him was open. Taj had his nose in a copy of *Sports Illustrated*, but then he saw someone out of the corner of his eye, and glanced up from the magazine. "Hey, doc."

"Oh, hi, Taj," the doctor said, very soft-spoken. He stood by the door opposite 311.

Taj didn't remember meeting him before, but so many doctors came and went in there. For a moment, he thought the doctor was trying to peek past him inside the room.

"She isn't in, doc," he said. "Is there anything I can help you with?"

The doctor nodded at the empty bed inside room 311. "That's Jane Doe's room, right?"

"Yes, but she's not a 'Jane Doe' anymore."

"Oh, so they've identified her. Good." He craned his neck to look inside her empty room again. "I'm one of the surgeons who operated on her when they first brought her in. I was just checking up on her. So—they must have tracked down her family then."

Getting to his feet, Taj pulled a pen from the top of the clipboard. "Can I tell her you stopped by, doctor—?"

The doctor smiled and shook his head. "Oh, no, that's all right. I was just popping by—like I said. In fact, I stopped in about an hour ago, and no one was here, not even you."

"The patient has been gone most of the morning," Taj said. "But she should be back from Dr. Beal's office within the hour. Sure you don't want to leave a message?"

The doctor shook his head again. "No, but thanks anyway." He gave a cocky, little salute and started to back away. "I'll come by later."

Taj watched the doctor walk down the hallway until he disappeared around a corner.

The detective on Dr. Beal's sofa was beginning to look very uncomfortable. Claire figured he also knew about the "missing pieces" of her past. She shifted in the wheelchair, then turned to Dr. Beal. The psychiatrist had that same sad, sympathetic smile.

"Earlier you mentioned that you live on Cascadia Avenue in Seattle," she said. "What can you tell me about that house, Claire?"

"We bought it, because of the third bedroom," Claire said.

She remembered that they'd planned to turn the extra room into a nursery. She'd been pregnant when Charlie had taken an offer from the University of Washington. At last, they had some money, which promptly went into the new home. It was one of the happiest times in Claire's life. She painted the nursery walls: a cartoon jungle with friendly tigers, giraffes, Curious George–inspired monkeys, and smiling elephants.

When Julia Maye Ferguson was born, three different sororities from the university sent flowers. Mrs. Donovan flew in and stayed for a week, helping with Julia. She'd been a considerate—though slightly distant—grandmother to Brian, but she simply adored the new baby. Claire's mother had always been rather critical of her. But with Julie it seemed Claire had at last done something right as far as her mother was concerned.

Charlie, who had been working practically around the clock when Brian was a baby, made up for lost time with his new daughter. At night, Claire often found him waltzing around the nursery with Julia in his arms. The cartoon jungle creatures on the walls seemed to smile at them, while Charlie softly sang "The Lion Sleeps Tonight."

Like any only child who suddenly has to share the spotlight, six-year-old Brian was slightly jealous, but very much in awe of his little sister. Claire and Charlie did their best to make sure he didn't feel neglected. Brian worked toward the same goal. He found all sorts of ways to demand their attention. If he wasn't suddenly throwing his arms around his mother or father—and not letting go—he was getting into trouble.

One afternoon, Claire was lulling Julia to sleep. It took several choruses of "The Lion Sleeps Tonight," and one too many *"a-whimbo-whack-a-whimbo-whacks"* before the baby finally succumbed. Brian was back from kindergarten, snacking in front of the small TV in their breakfast nook. Claire hoped to grab a short nap on the sofa. She was just nodding off when she heard a shriek from the kitchen. She could tell, it wasn't the TV.

She sprang from the couch and raced toward the kitchen. Reaching the doorway, Claire stopped dead and let out a scream.

Brian lay sprawled on the tiled floor. His golden hair was matted down, soaked with blood from his forehead. His eyes were open, and he stared back at her. For a moment, Claire thought he was dead. "Oh, My God!" she cried.

Then Brian started to giggle.

She realized the "blood" was ketchup. The half-empty bottle was still on the counter. Brian began laughing so hard that he curled up on the floor.

"Oh, real funny!" she hissed, a hand still over her heart. "You almost scared me to death! I'm not amused, no sir . . ."

But Claire cracked a smile. Brian brushed at the ketchup on his forehead and licked his fingertips. "I want french fries with this!" he loudly declared, rolling on the floor.

Past Brian's dizzy laughter—which, by now, was a bit forced—Claire thought she heard Julia crying up in the nursery.

"Hey, hey," Claire whispered. "All this screaming, if you woke up your little sister, you'll wish you really were dead. I mean it now, simmer down. Clean yourself up and put what's left of the ketchup back in the fridge."

Claire wondered if it was too much to wish for a measly twenty-minute nap. She went to the foot of the stairs and listened for a moment. She didn't hear a peep, but went upstairs to check anyway.

She crept toward the nursery door. Still, not a sound—except the TV downstairs, and Brian running the water in the kitchen sink. Claire tiptoed to the crib and gazed down at her daughter. She felt a sickly pang in her stomach. *She's not breathing.*

For a moment, Claire told herself she was being silly. How many times in the last three weeks did she go through this panic, this same false alarm? There was nothing wrong, there couldn't be.

She reached down and touched Julia's tiny hand. It was slightly cold, lifeless. *No, no, no, this isn't happening. Please, God . . .*

"Julia!" she screamed. Claire scooped the infant into her arms. Her baby girl didn't squirm or cry—as she had only a few minutes ago. It was as if someone had severed all the joints inside her little body, she was so limp.

Clutching the baby to her chest, Claire raced down the hall to Charlie's and her bedroom. She grabbed the phone and dialed 9-1-1. She told the operator that her baby had stopped breathing. She didn't want to say that her baby was dead. But Claire knew she was.

It didn't keep her from trying mouth-to-mouth resuscitation on Julia. She finally stopped when she heard the ambulance siren in the distance. Pulling her mouth away from Julia's, she glanced toward the bedroom door.

Dazed, Brian stared back at her. She would never forget the horrified expression on Brian's face: his big green eyes gaping at her with utter dread, the lower lip quivering.

Everything after that was a blur. She didn't remember calling Charlie's office at the University of Washington. Her neighbor, Nancy, must have come over at about the same time the ambulance arrived.

While one of the paramedics attended to her daughter, Claire asked Nancy to take Brian. They labored over the infant for ten minutes. Claire knew they were all hoping for a miracle. She knew her baby daughter was dead. Yet when one of the paramedics covered Julia with a blanket, Claire screamed and tore off the coverlet. "No, no, no, don't cover her up," she cried. "Don't take her away, please . . ."

They let her hold the baby until Charlie got there.

She wore the pearl necklace to Julia's memorial service. A social worker from the hospital had given Claire and Charlie the literature and the talk on Sudden Infant Death Syndrome. She'd warned Charlie and Claire that they might blame themselves—or each other. And try as they might to find a reason for their child's death, they couldn't. Claire played over in her head those last few minutes when she was holding Julia, trying to lull her to sleep, wishing more than anything that she would stop crying and be still. She couldn't help wondering what might have happened if she hadn't put Julia down for that nap. Would her baby have been spared? Or maybe she would have died later that night. Claire knew it was useless to wonder, but she couldn't help it.

Brian, as the surviving sibling, was a classic textbook case. For a while, he was afraid to step inside the nursery. And he didn't want to go to sleep—for fear he'd never wake up. Charlie or Claire had to stay in the bedroom with him until he nodded off. He demanded their constant attention, and seemed worried about their mortality too.

Claire knew exactly how he felt, because she kept thinking another horrible catastrophe would soon happen to them. She and Charlie read the literature. They tried to make Brian feel safe and loved—without smothering him. They told him as much as they thought he'd understand about SIDS, stressing that it only happened to infants—not to older children or grown-ups. They reassured him that he'd been a good big brother to Julia.

Every time she reassured Brian, Claire used the same argument on herself. She couldn't avoid the nursery forever. She couldn't blame anyone. She had to quit worrying that some other horrible thing would happen. She needed to sleep.

The literature had a section for mothers who had been breast-feeding their SIDS babies. Claire read up on what to do about the painful swelling and discomfort. But there were no instructions in the book to remedy the soreness in her arms. No one seemed to understand that her arms actually ached from not holding her baby.

She tried not to cry in front of people. Charlie was the only one with whom she let down her guard. He didn't talk about Julia much. But he listened. Somehow, Charlie made her feel they would survive this. In his arms, she felt safe.

Sitting there in Dr. Beal's office, Claire longed to see her husband again. If only she could bury herself in his arms for a few minutes, everything might become clear again. She wouldn't have to block out certain memories, because Charlie would protect her.

"Claire, remember the other day, when you told me about your dream?" Dr. Beal asked. "Remember, Claire, you said you were with a man and a boy on the beach?"

Nodding, Claire gave her a wary sidelong look. She gripped the sides of the wheelchair.

"You said the man in your dream was Charlie, and the boy was Brian. The boy was eleven years old." Dr. Beal sighed. "But Brian was only six when you lost Julia. So—that was a long time ago, wasn't it?"

Claire nodded again. "I guess so." She sighed, and rubbed her forehead. "Listen, can't you just call my husband? Why can't I see him? I'm sure if you brought Charlie in here, I'd start remembering things right away. Are they even *trying* to locate him?"

Dr. Beal shifted in the beige leather chair, then cleared her throat. "Claire, you haven't lived at the Cascadia address in Seattle for almost five years."

Numbly, she stared at the psychiatrist.

Claire remembered moving day. She remembered standing alone in the empty nursery. Charlie had long ago turned it into an art studio for her. It had taken several coats of paint to cover up the cartoon jungle she'd created on the nursery walls.

She didn't notice until moving day—when the room was empty and the sun poured through the windows—that despite all those layers of paint, the smiling elephants, tigers and monkeys were still slightly visible on the walls. They were like ghosts, and she was alone with them.

Charlie wasn't around.

Her premonition after Julia's death must have come true. Something else had happened, something horrible.

Tears stung Claire's eyes. She glanced at the detective on the sofa, who still wouldn't look at her. Claire turned to Dr. Beal. "My husband, Charlie," she whispered. "He's dead, isn't he?"

Dr. Beal didn't say anything. She just smiled—that same pitying smile.

Chapter 6

The young East Indian orderly pushing Claire in her wheelchair was named Yuvraj, at least, his nametag said as much. Claire had asked Sherita how to pronounce his name, and she'd replied: *"Damned if I know. He's been here two years, and I've always called him 'honey.' Nice guy though."*

Yuvraj seemed to read Claire's mood, and said nothing as he steered her down the hospital corridor. In every room they passed, Claire noticed patients with family members—some with entire clans gathered around their beds; others with just one person at their side. Claire saw their rooms full of flowers, beds with Get Well helium balloons tied to the side rails, framed photos of loved ones and Get Well cards on nightstands.

Meanwhile, Yuvraj was pushing her toward her stark, empty room: not a single flower, card, or side-table photo. Not a soul.

She had a guard outside her room, and dozens of reporters who were dying for a chance to talk with her. But they only knew her as Jane Doe, the lone survivor of Rembrandt's killing spree.

Word had spread around the hospital about her, and these excursions from her room always made Claire a bit nervous. Sometimes, while Yuvraj or one of the other orderlies was wheeling her down the hallways, she'd notice doctors, nurses, and other patients staring at her. Did they know who she was? Every once in a while, she'd catch a stranger looking at her, and she'd wonder, *Is that Rembrandt? Would she recognize him if she saw him again?*

Dr. Beal had given her a copy of a photograph, which someone had passed along to the police. It was a snapshot from the family album of Mr. and Mrs. Harlan Shaw. While Yuvraj navigated down the corridor, Claire studied the picture.

The woman in the photo was pretty—with a creamy complexion and wavy, dark hair. She was an improvement over the rather sickly, pale woman she'd seen in the mirror for the last few days. Claire looked happy in the photograph, which had been taken in a beautiful garden. The lean, silver-haired man with Claire in the picture stood nearly a foot taller than her. Though handsome, his smile seemed forced, a bit stiff. That was her husband, Harlan Shaw, a little bit stiff, a little too serious.

She remembered him now. He was a good man. But he wasn't Charlie. He wasn't the husband she'd desperately wanted to see again. With Harlan due to see her in a couple of hours, she felt as if the wrong guy was coming by to take her out on a date. But at least she had a little time to prepare herself, work up some enthusiasm and act happy to see him.

Brian wasn't coming along. Dr. Beal had braced her for that. According to Harlan, Brian was fine, but couldn't come to the hospital tonight. The eleven-year-old boy Claire had remembered in her dream was actually seventeen now. His father had been dead for five years.

Claire now knew what had happened in those intervening years. But she didn't want to think about Charlie's death, and how awful it had been to be poor again—without him. She didn't want to recall the struggles, the loneliness, and all the trouble Brian had given her.

Meeting and marrying Harlan Shaw had been like a godsend—at least, for a while. They'd been together eighteen months now.

And he was coming for her.

Claire said hello to the guard at her door. Yuvraj helped her from the wheelchair into her bed. Someone had just changed the sheets, starchy with tight hospital corners. Claire set the photo on her nightstand, then sank back on the pillow. She thanked Yuvraj as he dimmed the light. He quietly closed the door behind him.

Claire turned on her side, and slid one hand under the fresh pillow. Something sharp stung her fingertip. Snatching her hand away, she noticed the blood on her finger. Claire flipped over her pillow to find a slightly crushed, long-stemmed red rose—complete with thorns.

Bewildered, she stared at the rose for a moment, then finally picked it up. She wondered who could have left it. The person who had made her bed? Someone on the hospital staff who felt sorry for her? Sherita?

Claire set the rose in her water glass on the nightstand. Laying back on her pillow, she sucked at the blood on her pricked fingertip, then stared at the single, long-stemmed rose—beside the photo of Harlan and herself.

She'd gotten her wish for flowers and a photo on her nightstand—and a husband coming to visit. Only none of it seemed quite right.

The husband was nearly a stranger to her. As for the rose, she had to consider the possibility it was from someone who didn't wish her well.

"Well, I didn't give it to you, honey," Sherita admitted. She was changing the dressing and bandage on Claire's chest wound.

Claire tried not to look down at the sutures and the swollen, shiny patch of torn flesh between her breasts. She kept staring at the rose on her bedside. "Who do you think it's from?" she asked.

Finishing with the bandage, Sherita shrugged. "I don't know. One of the orderlies probably who has a crush on you.

Listen, you've got about forty-five minutes to start looking pretty for your husband. And from his photo, I'd say he ain't hard on the eyes."

Claire sighed. "This Rembrandt killer, he might have left the rose—to show how close he is to me."

"He couldn't have gotten past the guard—"

"Well, maybe he did," Claire argued. "Maybe this is his way of letting me know how vulnerable I am."

"Oh, for God's sakes," Sherita said, helping Claire readjust her nightgown. "You think he'd sneak past the guard and leave you a flower—as some kind of threat? He'd have to be crazy."

"That's just the point, Sherita. He is crazy."

"I'm telling you, the flower is probably from an orderly who's warm for your form."

Claire rolled her eyes. "Just the same," she murmured. "Could you throw it out for me, please?"

Gathering up the old bandages, Sherita nodded. "Sure thing, honey." She snatched the rose out of Claire's water glass, then stuffed it in a plastic bag with the used bandages. "I'll be back in a bit to help you get ready for your hubby." She smiled. "Nervous?

Nodding, Claire sucked at her fingertip, which still stung a bit from the thorn prick. "Scared," she replied.

"Well, I sold a couple of the single roses today," Janice from the gift shop, said. Twenty-five years old, she was pretty—with trendy, black-rimmed glasses, short-cropped flaxen hair, and a clingy sweater that showed off her aerobicized body. She busily replenished the Altoid tins in the counter display.

Sherita stood on the other side of the register from her. "Do you remember who you sold them to? It's important."

Pausing, Janice glanced over the rims of her glasses at Sherita. "Hmmmm, a little kid and an old lady."

"You didn't sell one to a man? A long-stem red rose?"

Janice shook her head and went back to the Altoid display. "Not today."

Sherita glanced at the refrigerated locker with the glass door. All the cut flowers were on display in there—along with their prices. The single roses were ridiculously overpriced.

"So—did this kid come in here and break his piggy bank for you?" she asked.

Janice squinted at her. "What are you talking about?"

"I'm talking about nine bucks for one lousy rose," Sherita replied. "That's a lot of greenbacks for a little kid to be throwing away."

Janice sighed. "He was buying it for his father. His mother was in a car crash yesterday, and she's in a coma. They don't think she'll make it. So his dad sent him in here to get the mother a rose."

Drumming her fingers on the counter top, Sherita frowned. "And junior told you all this? He volunteered the information?"

Janice nodded. "Yeah. Why? What are you getting at?"

"Did it sound like he'd been coached?"

"I don't understand what you mean," Janice said.

"Never mind," Sherita said, heading out of the gift shop. "Thanks, Janice."

"I need to find out if we have any current adult female comas. This one was in a car accident and admitted yesterday—or the day before."

The thin, gangly young man glanced up from his computer. "I can't help you, Sherita," he said. He was sitting at one of four desks in the empty office. The other employees in the billing department had left just a few minutes before—at five o'clock. But Sherita had caught Glen Lehman still at his desk, buying concert tickets online.

"You have to be in hospital administration for us to give you information like that," Glen explained. "And you're not in administration, Sherita. So I can't access it for you."

Sherita nudged him. "Not even if I buy you a six pack? Your choice of the brew."

"That's all? Just a six pack of beer?"

She sat on the edge of his desk. "That, and I promise not to kick the hell out of your skinny, white ass."

Chuckling, Glen started typing on his computer keyboard. "Coma patients," he murmured. "Current, female . . ."

He stopped clicking on the keys, then stared at the computer screen for a moment. "Closest thing we have to what you want is a twenty-year-old female, now comatose, admitted two nights ago. But she wasn't in a traffic accident. She OD'ed."

Sherita frowned. "Can you get a listing of females recently admitted with injuries sustained in traffic accidents?"

Sighing, Glen started typing again. "I should charge you another six pack, but since I'm such a prince . . ."

Gazing at the screen once more, he shook his head. "Nothing. Closest I have for you is a female DOA from a traffic accident three days ago. All the other current traffic accident patients were patched up in the ER."

Cocking his head, he glanced up at Sherita. "You sure this female coma patient is here? Or did somebody just make her up?"

"Thanks, honey." Sherita patted his shoulder, then headed for the door. "You're right. Somebody made her up."

"It's true," Sherita said, touching up Claire's cheeks with a powder brush. "I checked with Janice, who runs the gift shop. An orderly came in and bought a long-stem red rose from her this morning. She didn't remember who, which is no big surprise. Janice has always been a space case." Sherita handed Claire a mirror to check on the makeup job.

Claire eyed her skeptically, then glanced at her reflection.

"So we threw that rose away for nothing," Sherita continued. "But let's not sweat it. Your hubby will be here any minute, the genuine article this time."

Claire handed the mirror back to her. She thought about what a lousy liar Sherita was. Obviously, Sherita had done a little snooping around, and found out something about the red rose. Was the truth really so awful that she didn't want to tell her?

There was a knock on the door, then Dr. Dwoskin poked his head in. "Are you ready for some company?" he asked.

Claire nodded nervously.

Dr. Dwoskin stepped in, followed by a man in a business suit who must have been a plainclothes cop. Then Harlan came in. Tall and handsome, he wore a pressed dark blue shirt and a tie she'd bought for him last Christmas. He carried a bouquet of mixed flowers and a large manila envelope. He had tears in his eyes as he smiled at her.

"Hi, honey," she said.

"Hi, sweetheart," he replied, barely getting the words out. He took a step toward the bed, then hesitated and glanced at Sherita, Dr. Dwoskin, and the cop. He didn't camouflage his annoyance. "Think I could have a couple of minutes in private with my wife?" he asked.

Dr. Dwoskin nodded, and the cop appeared disappointed. They filed out of the room. Sherita tailed after them, pausing at the door to give Claire a thumbs-up sign.

Once the door shut, Harlan set the flowers and the envelope on the nightstand, then he turned to Claire. "If I don't kiss you soon, I'm gonna die," he whispered. "Is it okay? Are you in pain, sweetheart?"

She nodded. "It's all right. I won't break. Just be careful around my chest." She laughed skittishly. "Huh, that sounds funny, doesn't it?"

Harlan rushed to the bed and wrapped his arms around her. He kissed Claire on the lips, then pressed his face against hers. His smell was familiar, Cool Water. But something very unlike Harlan Shaw was happening as he held her. He began to cry.

She'd never seen her stoic husband shed a tear, not until now. Claire stroked his salt-and-pepper hair. "It's okay, honey," she whispered. "Everything's all right. I'm safe now. You found me. We're going to be fine. . . ."

Claire figured if she kept saying it, she might actually believe it.

Sherita had guessed quite accurately that the plainclothes policeman was one of the head honchos. Lt. Roger Elmore was tall, with a crew cut and a sun-creased face. Sherita led him down the corridor—out of earshot from Taj, who sat erect in his folding chair—no reading material in sight. She told the lieutenant about the red rose and someone stalking her in the garage.

"I don't mean to get anyone in trouble," she explained— shooting a glance over Lt. Elmore's shoulder at the guard. "But obviously, this maniac was in her room. And he's in this hospital. 'Rembrandt' or whatever you call him, he knows where she is. He knows the weak links in your security—"

"Now, wait a minute," the lieutenant interrupted. "What makes you so sure it's Rembrandt? One of those guys from the press could have been following you around last night. And one of them could have left that rose for her too."

"A reporter would go to all the trouble of having a kid buy the rose for him? And he'd coach the kid with some stupid story about his mother in a coma—"

"Some of those reporters will do anything to goose up a story," Elmore said. "We aren't telling them much. I wouldn't be surprised if one of them decided to get creative."

"Well, in addition to getting creative, someone also got past your security. Whether it was a reporter or Rembrandt or Santa Claus, I thought you ought to know." Sherita paused. "And I thought you'd give a shit."

Harlan emerged from her bathroom with the flowers in a large tumbler. "Did the doctors say how soon you can come home?" he asked, setting the arrangement on her nightstand.

Claire self-consciously touched her hair. "Not yet. I'm

still a little wobbly. Plus I think they're waiting for me to remember things. My memory's kind of fuzzy."

She felt awkward around him. They were both trying hard to ignore the tension. She'd come back from the dead, and even the familiar felt strange. She desperately wanted things to be normal again.

Harlan pulled a chair close to her bedside, then sat down.

"How's Brian?" she asked. "Why couldn't he come?"

Harlan cleared his throat. "You don't remember?"

Claire shook her head. "What? Did something happen to him? They told me Brian was all right—"

"He is—as far as I know," Harlan replied. He leaned forward in the chair. "Sweetheart, Brian ran away the night before you disappeared."

Numbly, she stared at him. "Wh—why did he run away?"

Harlan sighed. "Beats me. Why did he take off the other two times?"

Claire rubbed her forehead. She recalled an argument between Brian and Harlan one evening, months ago. Brian had grabbed some of his things and stormed out of the house. But he'd come back the very next afternoon. A few weeks later, there had been another quarrel, and he'd run away again. He'd phoned her after the first day—to tell her he was fine. That hadn't stopped Claire from worrying herself sick—until Brian slunk home two days later.

"Do you know where he might be?" she asked.

"I think he's staying with one of his buddies," Harlan muttered, slouching a bit in the chair. "Must be someone we don't know. The high school called, and he hasn't shown up for classes. Then again, I'm not surprised."

"It's been over a week," Claire said. "What's being done about it? Did you call the police?"

"Of course, I did. I called them about you too sweetheart. This has been—like the longest week of my life. But I found you, Claire. And don't worry about Brian. He's a big boy. Heck, you know how independent he is. He can take care of himself. I keep getting hang-ups whenever I answer the phone—or the machine answers. I'm sure it's Brian, wanting to talk to you. He'll be back—once he connects with you. He came back the other two times. Right?"

Claire couldn't answer him. She had this awful feeling in the pit of her stomach. Something had happened to Brian, something she was blocking out.

"He'll be home soon enough," Harlan continued. "Now that I've finally found you, I'll pour all my energy into finding Brian. You'll see, things will be back to normal. We can put this all behind us."

He reached for the envelope on the nightstand. "Tiffany sends her love, by the way." He handed her the envelope. "She made this for you."

"Oh, how—how is she?" Claire asked. She started opening the envelope. She couldn't look Harlan in the eye. She should have asked about her six-year-old stepdaughter. Tiffany was Harlan's only child from his first marriage. Claire hadn't adopted her, but they were planning on it.

Tiffany had made her a "Get Well" card with watercolor flowers. She'd printed in crayon: *"To Mom—I Miss you. Love, Tiffany."*

"Oh, how sweet . . ." Claire started to say.

A knock on the door interrupted her.

"Am I butting in?" the woman asked, peeking past the doorway into the room. "Are you two making out?"

Claire recognized her friend, Linda Castle, whose frosted, light-brown hair was cut in a Dorothy Hammill style that had been popular in the late seventies. At forty, Linda was a couple of years older than Claire. She'd been best friends with Harlan's first wife, and she was Tiffany's godmother.

"The natives are getting restless out there," she announced, breezing into the room and closing the door behind her. "I think they want 'in.' "

She wore a pink pullover and khaki pants. A ribbon was tied around her wrist, holding a foil helium balloon of Garfield saying, *You're Sick!* on one side, and *Get Well Soon!* on the other.

She turned to Claire, and put a hand over her heart. "Oh, Claire, you're a sight for these sore ones. I can't believe we finally found you—and up here in Bellingham! You should see all the "Missing" fliers we posted all over Seattle. That's where we thought you were. Huh, only ninety miles off!"

She hurried to Claire's bedside and planted a kiss on her cheek. "I'm so glad you're sitting up, and—and, well I thought you'd have the IV tube in your arm and another tube up your nose. Y'know, half in a coma and drooling. Ha, ye gods, listen to me!" Linda squeezed her hand. "Anyway, I pictured you looking a lot worse, sweetie."

"Well, thanks, Linda," Claire said, working up a chuckle. "You should have seen me before my nurse-friend outside helped me get made-up. She also found this robe for me."

Linda laughed. "Huh, she should stick to taking temperatures and changing bedpans."

"I think she looks wonderful," Harlan piped up.

Linda tied the balloon ribbon to the railing at the foot of the bed. She gave Claire a wink. "I'll come by tomorrow with some of your things. So—how soon will they spring you from this joint? You must take this husband of yours off my hands. He's been an absolute baby this whole week."

"We're still not sure when she can come home," Harlan explained.

Claire managed to smile at them both. She imagined Linda bringing over dinners for Harlan and Tiffany. She was a terrible cook too, suffering from the delusion that her runny, fatty casseroles were just about the living end. Her husband, Ron, didn't seem to mind though. He was a heavy-set man with a boyish face and a thick dark brown toupee that combed over to the side. Claire always thought he looked like Bob of Bob's Big Boy. They didn't have any children.

"Harlan, my head is splitting," Linda said. "Could you be a doll and run down to the gift shop? I need aspirin, one of those pocket-size ones ought to do."

"I'm sure the nurse could give you something—"

"I'm trying to get rid of you, knucklehead," Linda said,

rolling her eyes. "Claire and I need to get in a little girl-talk before that flatfoot, the doc and the nurse traipse in here. Do you mind? All we need is a couple of minutes alone."

With a sigh, Harlan got to his feet. "You still want the aspirin?"

"No. Just keep them out for a minute or two, and I'll be your slave for life." Linda pulled Harlan's chair even closer to Claire's bed. "And don't worry, Claire and I aren't going to talk about you."

Harlan gave Linda a wry smile, then he gently kissed Claire on the forehead and stepped outside,

Linda sat down. She took hold of Claire's hand. "I wanted to talk before they come in and it all starts getting official with the questions and statements," she whispered. "Really, how are you doing, kid?"

Claire nodded. "I'm okay, but I'm worried about Brian. I don't remember him running away."

Linda stared at her. "And you really can't remember anything else that happened?"

"Well, it's all kind of muddled."

"You don't remember the—plans to go into Seattle with me? You know, our *shopping* holiday?"

Claire shrugged. "I've been told that's where I disappeared, but I don't remember any of it."

"Really?" Linda's eyes narrowed at her. "You aren't holding anything back, are you, Claire?"

She slowly shook her head. "No. Is there something you know that I ought to remember?"

"No, nothing," Linda said, with a tight smile.

"Are you sure?" Claire asked. Her friend acted as if they shared some secret.

"Really, there's nothing," Linda repeated.

Claire wondered if, once again, a well-meaning friend felt she was better off not knowing some terrible truth.

Chapter 7

"Anything going on?"

"Nothing, nada, bupkis. She's asleep."

"Did they find out anything? Did Little Girl Lost get some of her memory back?"

"Naw. Cops were in there most of the night. Her friend and her husband did all the talking. Here, you want the paper? There's a good article about the Seahawks."

"Thanks . . ."

Claire heard a newspaper rustling, then one guard said good-bye to the other. They changed shifts outside her door at eleven o'clock. She'd been wondering how long she'd been lying here in the dark, and now she knew. Just an hour. But it seemed longer.

So the guard called her *Little Girl Lost,* and he said it with a heavy dose of sarcasm. Were the police and hospital staff fed up with her?

Dr. Dwoskin and Lieutenant Elmore had spent nearly three hours tonight in this room, talking with her, Harlan, and Linda. A few other doctors and plainclothes policemen came and went during the exhausting interview. They fortified themselves with stale coffee in Styrofoam cups. At one point, Yuvraj brought in her dinner. Claire barely touched her ham, which had a rainbow gleam to it. She just picked at her mashed potatoes and carrots. She let Harlan have her Jell-O cup.

Meanwhile, Harlan and Linda gave their accounts of what had happened in the forty-eight hours prior to Claire's disappearance. The police and the doctors kept hoping some detail in their stories might spark her memory.

"When I came back from the meeting with my civic group on Friday night, Claire was—acting a little crazy," Harlan told them, hunched over in his chair. "Brian had run away again. He'd packed up and slipped out that afternoon, I guess. He didn't leave a note or anything, just took off. Claire figured out he was gone, and she wouldn't stop crying. She kept screaming at me that I must have done something to make him leave. I hadn't, but there was no reasoning with her. She was hysterical, poor thing. I didn't know what to do, so I called Linda and Ron, and they came over."

Claire didn't remember any of it.

According to Linda, Claire was *"practically bonkers"* when they arrived. "She was crying nonstop, and trying to pick a fight with Harlan. I knew she was worried sick. She'd been through this with Brian a couple of times before, and I don't know how she kept bouncing back. I mean, Brian is a sweet kid, but well, don't get me started on some of the pranks he's pulled. Anyway, I could see what Claire needed was a couple of stiff drinks and a change of scenery. If she'd stayed home, all she would have done was climb the walls and keep snapping at Harlan. So—I helped her pack some overnight things, and took her back to Ron and my casa. After a couple of brandies, she slept like a baby in our guest room . . ."

Claire had been in Ron and Linda's guest room, but didn't recall ever sleeping in there. She could picture the room: Linda's framed, ugly yarn-and-glue flower pictures that hung over the twin beds; a fake spinning wheel planter in the corner, holding a yarn-wire-and-pipe-cleaner flower arrangement; a bookcase with their collection of plastic snow globes from forty-eight states (*"All we need is Delaware and North*

Carolina, and we'll have all fifty," Linda bragged). Some of those airport trinkets were so old, the snow had turned brown. Claire wondered how she could remember the brownish snow in those cheesy little globes, and not recall ever having slept in that guest room.

"I got up early the next morning, made hotel reservations in Seattle and bought tickets for a play." Linda continued. "I figured a day of shopping in the city might take her mind off things. And by the time Claire got home on Sunday, Brian might come back . . ."

The overnight stay in a Seattle hotel made sense to Claire now. She didn't live twenty minutes away on Cascadia Avenue any more. Harlan's house was on one of the San Juan Islands, a ferry ride, then another seventy miles south to Seattle by car.

Ron and Linda Castle had their own boat, and kept an SUV parked in the mainland harbor. Linda and Ron had grown up on the island, and both were expert sailors. The last time Claire remembered being on Ron and Linda's boat had been three months ago—in the middle of summer. She and Harlan had gone sailing with the Castles and spent the day in Victoria.

In a daze, she listened to Linda recount their trip across the bay to Anacortes nine days ago. Linda described the weather and sailing conditions. In the car, she and Claire had talked about what they would buy and the show they were going to see. "I know she was thinking about Brian, but I thought it best to steer clear of the subject," Linda said with a pout.

"We arrived too early to check into the hotel, so I parked the car in a pay lot a couple of blocks from Nordstrom and Pacific Place." She turned to Claire. "Remember? We used my coat to cover up the suitcases in the back?"

Claire just shrugged and shook her head.

"Well, anyway, we hit Nordstrom first. After a while, we decided to split up and meet again in an hour. I wanted to storm the shoe department, and I told Claire, 'Meet you in scarves at one-fifteen.' Claire nodded—and waved. And that was the last I saw of her—until today."

At this point in her story, Linda became teary. She talked about how she waited and waited in the scarves department—until nearly two o'clock. She had Claire paged in the store three times—to no avail.

"I figured maybe she got tired and went to the hotel," Linda said. "But she wasn't there. So when I checked in, I told the desk clerk to be on the lookout for her. I didn't know what else to do. I called Harlan from the room, and asked—very casually—if he'd heard from Claire. I didn't want to worry him. Anyway, we had theater tickets, and when Claire didn't show up by seven-thirty, I knew we were in trouble. I phoned Harlan again, and he called the police."

Linda turned to Claire again. "I guess you never even made it to the hotel, did you?"

Claire didn't know how to answer her. It was as if Linda expected her to say yes—not because she actually remembered, but more to back up what Linda was saying. Earlier, when they were alone, Linda had acted as if they shared some kind of secret. Claire had a feeling her friend was fabricating this whole *shopping* trip tale to protect that secret. Were they keeping something from Harlan? Or was he in on it?

She wondered about Brian too. It was true, he'd gotten into trouble in the past. Had he done something really awful this time, something she'd blocked out? Maybe that was why he'd disappeared. She wanted to ask them: *"Did Brian really run away? What aren't you telling me about my son?"*

But Claire couldn't raise that question in front of the police. Still, it frustrated her. No one seemed to care about Brian's disappearance, just her own.

"Claire, you never got to the hotel, did you?" the lieutenant asked. "Did someone approach you in the department store?"

"I really don't recall any of this," Claire admitted. "I'm sorry . . ."

They kept trying to spark her memory for another half hour. They finally called it quits at nine-thirty. Looking disappointed and depleted, Lieutenant Elmore, Dr. Dwoskin, and the two detectives who had been there for the last hour, all wandered out of her room.

Linda lingered on. Claire grabbed her hand. "Is there something you're not telling them I should know?" she whispered, her eyes pleading.

Linda shot a look at Harlan, then glanced back at her. She let out a little laugh. "Ye gods, no. I don't think I left out a damn thing about the entire weekend—except when I took my potty breaks." She kissed Claire on the cheek. "See you tomorrow, Claire. Okay? Now, I'll scram, give you and the ball and chain a little privacy."

Once they were alone, Harlan wrapped his arms around Claire. She tried to return the hug, but it was awkward. He embraced her as if she were a frail old lady. He must have been scared of hurting her.

"Thank Tiffany for the card," she remembered to say, patting Harlan on the back.

He started to pull away, but Claire grabbed his hand. "Harlan, were you telling the truth about Brian? Did he really run away? Or is he in some kind of trouble?"

He sighed and shook his head. "Sweetheart, it's like I said earlier. He left without any explanation. We have the police on the island looking for him. Now the Bellingham and Seattle cops are working on it too. If Brian has gotten himself into trouble, we'll fix it. He'll be okay. You just think about getting well."

Then he'd said good-bye, giving her a long, yet chaste kiss on the lips.

That had been at least two hours ago.

Now she was alone, wide awake in the hospital bed. Or had she dozed off for a bit? Images drifted in and out of her head. She could see Linda, slouching to one side in the hardback chair with her legs crossed, talking to the police and Dr. Dwoskin. Then she saw Linda at the wheel of Ron's Jeep. Claire occupied the passenger side. It was night. Someone stood outside the vehicle—at the driver's window. Claire couldn't see his face. But he had a gun. Her eyes closed,

Linda was muttering something under her breath. It took Claire a moment to realize her friend was praying.

"We can't just sit here!" Claire remembered saying. *"We have to do something!"*

Linda opened her eyes and turned to her. "Pray, Claire," she whispered.

Claire screamed.

Suddenly, she was awake again. Had she screamed out loud, or just in her dream?

Claire started to reach for the lamp on her nightstand, but a pain shot through her chest. She'd stretched the surgical stitches. She lay back and caught her breath.

Then she heard it. A chair scraped against the tiled floor— as if someone had accidentally bumped into it. She could tell, the sound didn't come from outside. It wasn't the guard in his folding chair by her door. The sound came from within her room.

The hairs stood on the back of her neck. Clutching the bed sheets to her chest, Claire stayed very still. She wondered how anyone could have snuck past the guard. It didn't make sense. Yet she could feel this person, watching her in the dark. Was it him? Was it Rembrandt?

Claire wanted to scream, but she couldn't even get a breath. Was she dreaming again?

She blinked and tried to adjust her eyes to the darkness. Then she heard him clear his throat. *My God, this is real. Someone's in the room with me.* She couldn't move. Her heart was pounding. She saw a figure standing in the shadows.

"Who's there?" she finally whispered. She barely got the words out. "Guard? Are you the guard?"

"He went to buy himself a chocolate bar," the man whispered in a too-friendly, almost singsong voice.

Claire felt herself trembling. "I'll scream," she said.

"I won't hurt you," he cooed. "Just turn on the light. C'mon, don't be afraid . . ."

She hesitated, then reached for the lamp on her nightstand. Her hand fanned at the air until she found the light switch. She turned on the lamp.

A brilliant flash blinded her, and she shrieked.

"Just one more," she heard the man say. "C'mon, doll. I need a good shot of you."

The camera flash went off again.

Claire covered her face. "Stop it!" she cried. "Get out! Get out of here!"

It was like another horrible nightmare. But Claire was wide, wide awake.

"We've confiscated the film," Lieutenant Elmore said, sitting behind his desk. He popped a Tums in his mouth. "He and his crummy tabloid won't be running any photos of your wife, Mr. Shaw. I assure you, we're doing everything we can to keep her name and her face from the TV and newspaper people. They still know her as Jane Doe."

Harlan Shaw stood in front of Elmore's desk, having refused to sit when the lieutenant had offered him a chair. Elmore's office had a case full of trophies and citations, and a glass wall that looked out to a bigger workspace. One woman and several men—all in plain clothes—were busy at their desks, talking on their phones, or working at computers. A couple of the younger detectives were goofing around in the corner of the big office, tossing a Nerf basketball through a hoop that hung on the wall.

"You still haven't answered my question," Harlan said, glaring at the lieutenant. "I want to know how a reporter got into my wife's room in the middle of the night. I understand yesterday afternoon someone left a rose under her pillow. What kind of security do you have in that hospital? Who's in charge of my wife's safety? I'd like to talk to this guy, because he's not doing his job."

"Believe me, Mr. Shaw, it won't happen again," Lieutenant Elmore said.

"Well, are you the one who screwed up?" Harlan pressed.

Elmore sighed, then he nodded toward the window—at the room full of detectives behind Harlan. "Detective

Timothy Sullivan is in charge of security at the hospital. And I've already had a talk with him—"

"Is he out there?" Harlan turned to look at the people in the work area.

Elmore got up from his desk. "I've handled it, Mr. Shaw—"

Harlan threw open the door and stepped out of Elmore's office. "Detective Timothy Sullivan?" he called.

Everyone stopped to stare at him. Then a couple of the plainclothes officers turned to glance back at the two younger detectives, who had been playing Nerf basketball a moment before. Harlan marched toward the two younger cops.

One of them was a short, black man. His friend was white, about thirty, and good-looking with brown hair and a little dimple in his chin. "I'm Tim Sullivan," he said, setting the Nerf ball on his desk. "Can I help you?"

All at once, Harlan grabbed him by the shirt collar. "Yeah, you can help by doing your goddamn job!" he growled. "My wife has been through hell—"

"Whoa . . . wait a minute," Tim Sullivan said, holding his hands up. "Listen—"

"No, you listen, you cocky son of a bitch." Harlan pushed him against the wall. "You're in charge of security at that hospital, and I swear to God, if somebody else slips by one of your so-called-guards and bothers my wife, you'll wish you were dead!"

"What are you talking about?" the cop asked, wide-eyed. He shook his head. "Who are you?"

Lieutenant Elmore and another detective pulled Harlan away. "C'mon now, Mr. Shaw," the lieutenant said. "We have this under control . . ."

Harlan gave Tim Sullivan a final shove, tearing at his shirt. "Worthless piece of shit," he muttered. "Call yourself a cop? You're supposed to protect people . . ."

Dazed, Tim Sullivan stared at them. Elmore and the other detective led Harlan back to his office.

The black cop turned to Tim. "Since when have you been in charge of security at the hospital?"

"Since I don't know," Tim Sullivan replied. "That guy's half-out of his mind." Straightening his tie, he watched Lieutenant Elmore step back into his office with the man who had just attacked him. "Who the hell was that anyway?"

"I think he's Harlan Shaw."

"Who?" Tim asked, still catching his breath.

"Harlan Shaw. His wife's the amnesia case in the hospital. You know, the one Rembrandt left for dead."

Tim glanced back toward Lieutenant Elmore's office again. "Huh," he murmured. "No wonder the poor son of a bitch is half-out of his mind."

"You won't hear a peep about it from Harlan, but I guess he really gave that moron-detective a piece of his mind this morning," Linda said.

She was pushing the empty wheelchair, and walking beside Claire in the corridor. Claire kept a hand on the support rail along the wall. She'd been in the hospital nine days now, and still felt a bit wobbly on her feet.

Linda had brought her a couple of nightgowns, Claire's favorite robe, her slippers, and some other things from home. Claire was wearing the robe right now, a near floor-length blue terry-cloth number with white piping.

"Ron was in the hallway at police quarters, and caught the whole thing," Linda continued. They passed a couple of rooms with the doors open. "Ye gods, what a depressing place," Linda whispered. She fanned her hand in front of her face. "And the smell. PU. How do you stand it? Anyway, Claire, I don't think you have to worry about any more visitors in the night. They're screening everyone who tries to come on this floor. You know, I've noticed some people gawking at us. Do you suppose they have any idea who you are?"

Shuffling along, Claire tried to keep her balance. "A handful of doctors and nurses know me by name," she explained. "To everyone else, I'm still Jane Doe." She sighed. "Whew, and right now Jane Doe would like sit down."

Linda helped her into the wheelchair. "Let me push myself, okay?" Claire asked. "It's the only kind of cardio I get here."

Claire maneuvered the wheels while her friend walked beside her. "Could you do me a favor, Linda?" she asked. "Next time you come by, could you bring my address book? It's on the kitchen counter, near the phone. And underneath it is a stack of papers. The car pool list is there with the numbers for Brian's high school friends. It's on yellow paper. Could you bring that too?"

"Claire, honey," Linda groaned. "Really, I'm sure the police have already contacted Brian's chums. If you start calling up his entire class, you'll just be wasting your time—"

"Well, I have plenty of time on my hands here," Claire replied, an edge in her voice. "So let me go ahead and waste it. Will you bring me those things, Linda?"

She cleared her throat, and gave Claire a pinched smile. "Certainly, Claire. Whatever you want."

"Thanks." She glanced up at her friend, who looked so uncomfortable for a moment. Claire stopped moving the wheelchair.

"I remembered something last night," she said.

Linda frowned. "What are you talking about?"

"I don't know when it happened," Claire explained. "But you and I were in Ron's Jeep. It was nighttime, Linda. I remember being very scared. Someone stood just outside the car—by the window on the driver's side. From where I was sitting, I couldn't see his face, but he had a gun. And you—you told me to pray. Do you remember anything like this happening? Does it sound familiar?"

Linda squinted at her, then let out a little laugh. "Ye gods, no." She moved behind Claire and started pushing the wheelchair. "A man with a gun coming at us—in the Jeep? Sounds like you had a nightmare to me. I'd just forget about it if I were you."

Claire stared straight ahead. "But I'm trying to remember, Linda," she said. "Isn't that what all this is about?"

Chapter 8

"Well, I thought you might have heard something, Dottie," Claire said. She'd taken the nightstand phone near the window, where she sat in the easy chair. The cord was stretched across the tiled floor. She was talking to the mother of Brian's best friend. "Brian has been missing for over ten days now. Derek must have some idea where he is. Could you have Derek call me?"

"He's not home, Claire."

"Well, when Derek comes home—"

"He's in Europe," Mrs. Herrmann interrupted. "And there's no way we can get in touch with him, Claire. He's backpacking all over the continent. Derek won't be back until Christmas."

"I had no idea," Claire murmured. Brian never mentioned his friend was planning a trip. "When did this happen?"

"He left a week ago Saturday morning. It's something he's always wanted to do."

"Saturday morning?" Claire echoed. That was the same day she'd disappeared—and the morning after Brian had supposedly run away. "You took him out of school?"

"Yes, that's right."

"Um, does Derek have a cell phone number where I could reach him?" Claire asked. "It's really important—"

"I'm afraid not." Dottie Herrmann paused. "How are you, Claire? I understand you were in some kind of accident. A mugging or something?"

"That's right," Claire lied. "But I'm doing much better now." She stared out the window at the hospital parking lot and the woods beyond. It was a gray, overcast afternoon.

The story they'd given the people on the island was that Claire had wandered out of the department store, then someone stole her purse and knocked her unconscious. Everyone knew that she'd been missing, and that the search for her had been focused in the Seattle area. If they hoped to protect Claire from Rembrandt and a vulturous press, only a handful of people could know she was "Jane Doe." *We're saying you've been in a Seattle hospital for the last week,"* Harlan had told her. *"I don't think anyone will press you for more details. Folks around here are too polite for that."* The only people on the island who knew the truth were Harlan, and Ron and Linda Castle. Everyone else got the cover story.

"I'm sorry I haven't had a chance to visit you in the hospital," Dottie Herrmann said on the other end of the line. "I wanted to send flowers, but Linda Castle told me not to bother. She said you were coming home soon."

"Yes, that's right," Claire replied. "Listen, Dottie. I'm surprised about Derek's sudden trip to Europe. You let him go by himself?"

"He's old enough."

"Do you suppose Brian might have snuck off to Europe with him?"

"No, I don't think so," she answered, an edge in her voice. "One reason we agreed to let Derek go on this trip was to put some distance between him and your son. I don't mean to be unkind, but we feel Brian has been a bad influence on our Derek."

"I beg your pardon?"

"Derek never got into bit of trouble until he met up with your son," Dottie Herrmann explained. "There, I've said what I needed to say. Let's not discuss it further. I sincerely hope you'll be out of the hospital very soon, Claire. I'll pray for you—and Brian too. Good-bye."

Claire heard a click on the other end of the line. "What the hell?" she muttered to no one.

She wanted to call Dottie Herrmann back and tell her she was delusional. Talk about denial. During Claire's first conference at Brian's high school, his homeroom teacher warned her that Brian's new friend, Derek Herrmann, was a troubled kid. According to Brian, Mr. Herrmann often beat Derek.

The first time he slept over at their house, Derek stole three checks from Claire's checkbook. She noticed them missing the next morning while at the Safeway. That afternoon, Claire sat Derek down and talked with him. He denied all culpability at first, but after a half-hour, Claire had made him feel so guilty, he was confessing, apologizing, and crying. He said it would never happen again. Just the same, Claire hid her checkbook and purse whenever Derek Herrmann came by. He still stayed over at their house occasionally. The poor kid had to have some refuge from his father's beatings.

Still, Claire often wished Brian would find himself another best friend, someone who wasn't a potential candidate for *America's Most Wanted*. Then again, she couldn't entirely blame Derek Herrmann for getting her son into trouble all the time. Brian was no angel.

It was no excuse, but Brian hadn't exactly had a cushy childhood. Despite everything they'd told him to the contrary, Charlie and she had figured Brian somehow blamed himself for his baby sister's death. That went on for a couple of years. Then when he was twelve, Brian's father got sick.

Claire had discovered the mole a few inches above Charlie's left butt cheek—below his tan line. Charlie thought it was a wart, or a little patch of eczema. Claire thought it was gross, and wanted him to get rid of it. He tried Claire's Oil of Olay, Ambesol, and even some of Brian's Clearasil for a while. Nothing worked. Then the mole started to bleed, and Claire demanded that he have it checked.

When the doctor called back about the biopsy results, he

asked Charlie to come into the office. That was all he had to say. They knew it was cancer. The dermatologist simply gave the cancer a name: a Stage III melanoma, vertical growth.

Charlie started chemotherapy. Brian had to watch his father become sicker and sicker. Brian's thirty-four-year-old dad showed up to his class's science fair with a cane. And later, at a sit-down lunch in the cafeteria, Charlie had a seizure. "Well, Brian will have to change schools now," he later said. "He'll never want to show his kisser in that place again."

They went into debt trying herbal, holistic, and acupuncture remedies their insurance wouldn't cover. Charlie began spending more time in the hospital than out. And Claire was usually by his side or in a waiting room. Brian came home from school to an empty house—and an empty refrigerator. He learned how to do the shopping, laundry, and the cooking. For several months, he lived on frozen pizzas and microwave dinners. He was very independent, and insisted he was fine by himself. In fact, at times, Brian wouldn't even speak to her. He'd refuse to visit his father, or talk to him on the phone. Charlie wasn't hurt by this. He told Claire that their son was protecting himself from the impending loss.

There were other times when "Mr. Independence"—as Claire sometimes referred to him when talking with Charlie—would have dinner ready for her when she came home at night from the hospital. Brian would fix her a hot dog, or Sloppy Joe's, or a grilled cheese sandwich and tomato soup. Comfort food. Brian was very often there for her when she didn't expect it.

After Charlie died, Claire and Brian moved into a small, two-bedroom apartment. She'd survived near-poverty as a newlywed, but being poor again—without Charlie—was utter misery. She hated borrowing money from her mother, who was ailing. Claire's paintings weren't making enough to support them. So she got herself a clerical job through a temp service. And Brian got himself into trouble a lot.

The first time Claire was summoned to a meeting with

Brian's high school principal, she had to leave work. Her boss caught her off guard, and asked if Brian had gotten hurt. Claire didn't have time to think up a lie. The truth was so humiliating. "No, Brian's all right," she heard herself say. "He—he's in trouble. He skipped class and stole a six pack of beer from a grocery store near the school."

According to the principal, Brian's teachers liked him—despite some of his mediocre grades and outbursts in their classes. He was also quite popular with his fellow freshmen—as well as many upperclassmen. "I think Brian's running around with a group who are a little too mature for him," the principal told her. "In fact, they're a little too mature for themselves. Anyway, Brian won't say who coaxed him into stealing the beer, but it seems to be a case of peer pressure. I understand Mr. Ferguson died last year. I wonder if you've considered having Brian talk with someone, a therapist or psychiatrist . . ."

They couldn't afford it, but Claire didn't tell him that. She merely thanked the principal for his advice, and agreed that two days' suspension seemed fair.

The school secretary asked Claire to fill out some paperwork, and they stepped into her office. Through a narrow window by the door, she could see the waiting room, and Brian slouched in a hard-back chair. He caught her eye, then glanced away, visibly ashamed. He reminded her of Charlie, the same wavy, golden hair. Claire had to take a couple of deep breaths to keep from bursting into tears. She started to fill out the suspension forms.

"My daughter, Kim, is in Brian's homeroom class," the secretary said. She smiled at Claire. She was a slim, pretty Asian woman. The name plate on her desk read: *Ms. Soyon Wright.* "He's a handsome young man, Mrs. Ferguson," she continued. "And very popular. You know, they have that dance class for the freshmen on Thursday nights. Kim tells me Brian is one of the best dancers there. All the girls want to dance with him."

"Really? I had no idea." Claire stopped writing, and

stared at Ms. Wright. She wondered what the school's secretary was getting at.

"You know, kids can be awfully cruel. There are a couple of girls in particular, who are frequently the butt of jokes, and they're picked on. One of the girls, Sally, she has a weight problem. And there's another freshman, Jessica, she just doesn't fit in. Well, high school kids can be pretty vicious." She sighed. "Mrs. Ferguson, I think you should know something about your son. At dance class, the boys still choose the girls for most of the dances. Like I said, all the girls want to dance with Brian. But every class session, your son always picks Sally for at least one dance and Jessica for another. My daughter overheard some boy ask him why in the world he did that—when he could have his pick of any of the girls. Do you know what your son's answer was?"

Claire shook her head.

Ms. Wright smiled. " *'I just feel like it,'* he told him." She set another form in front of Claire. "I only need your signature on the bottom of this one. Anyway, don't be too hard on him. He has a good heart."

Claire kept telling herself that. She tried to remember Ms. Wright's story two months later when a call from the police woke her up. Brian and two friends—upperclassmen—had been arrested for trespassing, being drunk and disorderly, and indecent exposure. With two six packs of beer, they'd jumped the fence at a private country club, then went skinny-dipping in the club's pool. A night watchman had seen them, and telephoned the police.

Five weeks later, Claire received a call at work. Brian had skipped summer school, and was one of four passengers in a stolen car, stopped by a patrolman down in Tacoma. The kids in the vehicle were on their way to the beach. Two bottles of liquor, a two ounce bag of marijuana, and various drug paraphernalia were also found in the stolen vehicle.

"What exactly do you want me to do with you?" she asked Brian later. "Would you tell me? Because I don't know how to handle you any more. You're out of control. You were in a stolen car! And there were drugs! Who are these *jerks* you're hanging around with?"

"I won't see them any more," Brian muttered, tears in his eyes. "I promise. And I didn't have anything to drink—or smoke. I swear. I'm sorry, Mom. I just wanted to go to the beach."

"I'm terrified," she admitted. "Brian, I keep thinking the next call from the police is going to be the capper, and you'll end up in some correctional facility for minors. Is that what you want? Because that's where you're headed . . ."

Two months later, Claire got another call—in the middle of the night. It was from the nurse looking after her mother.

After the funeral costs and medical bills, there wasn't much left from her mother's estate. But Claire paid off a chunk of their debt, and set a little aside for Brian's college. Her mom would have wanted that.

One of the last conversations she'd had with her mother had been about Brian. She hadn't told her mom about Brian's brushes with the law and his trouble at school. An ailing old woman shouldn't have to hear such troublesome news about her only grandchild. But on the phone the last time they'd spoken, Claire's mother had seemed to know. "You're worried about Brian, aren't you?" she'd asked. "He'll be okay, Claire. Brian's a good boy. He'll be all right."

Claire thought about that last conversation some time later—after eight months, two more visits to the school principal, and one more trip down to the police precinct to escort Brian home. She was standing in line at the Burger King near work, waiting to order her lunch. Over the Muzac system came "The Lion Sleeps Tonight." Suddenly she could see Charlie waltzing around the darkened nursery with little Julia in his arms, singing that tune. She thought of her mother—and Brian. Would he really be all right, as her mom had said?

All at once, Claire felt this awful, aching sadness rising within her. Tears welled in her eyes. She let out a rasp, and knew she couldn't control it. She didn't want to start sobbing in the middle of the stupid Burger King.

She ran out to the parking lot, almost getting mowed down by someone peeling away from the drive-thru. The car horn blared. "Stupid, fucking bitch!" someone yelled from the window. "Watch where you're going!"

Claire reached the sidewalk on the other side of the drive-thru. She didn't want anyone seeing her. Tears streaming down her eyes, she ducked through a gap in the trimmed hedges bordering the Burger King, and found a row of empty benches by a deserted car wash. Claire plopped down on a bench and cried.

After a couple of minutes, she dried her eyes and blew her nose. Then she realized someone was standing at the end of the bench. Claire glanced up at a tall, handsome man with salt and pepper hair. He held a Burger King bag. "I wasn't sure what you were going to order," he said. "So I just got you a cheeseburger, fries, and a Diet Coke. Is that okay?"

He sat down on the bench and set the bag between them. "I know I'm imposing, but you looked like you could use a friend—and some lunch. My name is Harlan Shaw."

Later, over dinner at home, she told Brian all about him: "He's a widower. His wife died—along with her best friend— in a car accident fifteen months ago. He has a four-year-old daughter. They live on Deception Island, up in the San Juans. I mean, it's like a vacation spot for a lot of people, and he lives there year round. He's manager at a chemical plant on the island. He's really very nice. I think you'll like him. And isn't it sweet how we met?"

"Yeah, Mom," Brian grunted, rolling his eyes. "It's a *Whopper* of a good story."

"You know, this will be my first date in seventeen years," she said, exasperated. "I like him, and I'm a bit nervous about the whole thing. Would it kill you to be a little supportive?"

Brian was supportive, and even cordial to Harlan, whom he thought was *"okay, for someone who acts like he has a stick up his butt."*

To Claire, Harlan was godsend. He was rescuing her from loneliness, debt, and a life she hated.

He took her and Brian out of the city for a weekend, and they stayed at his house on the island. It was a beautiful home. She imagined the guest room becoming Brian's bedroom, and her son starting fresh at a new high school. She could take him away from his seedy friends. Harlan helped coach a summer softball team for high school boys. She told herself that he'd be good for Brian.

Harlan's daughter, Tiffany, developed an immediate crush on Brian. He in turn was charming toward her. They went sailing with the Castles and Harlan's best friend, Walter Binns, on Walter's boat. And there was a barbecue. Despite some initial misgivings about their minivacation on the island, Brian seemed to have fun. In fact, he fell in love with sailing.

After Harlan proposed, Claire checked with Brian. "Is it all right with you?" she asked him, on the ferry coming back from their third trip to Deception Island. "Be honest. Speak now, or forever put a lid on it, kid."

"Well, he's Joe Serious, kind of a tight-ass, y'know? I mean, I'd like to see him get drunk and silly. Maybe then, he'd lighten up a bit."

"Sorry, but that's not going to happen. Harlan told me he used to have a drinking problem—after his wife died. But he conquered it. Now, he allows himself just one beer a day—before dinner, that's it. I think that's commendable. I'd rather have Joe Serious than a guy who gets drunk every night. So—aside from his general lack of silliness, do you have any other objections to Harlan?"

Brian shrugged. "Well, it doesn't matter what I think. I'll only be around a couple of years before I head off to college, You're the one who has to live with him, Mom. Do you love this guy?"

"Not the same way I loved your father," she admitted. "But I like him. He's a good man. I can see myself living with him and being very content. I can see *us* living with him—if you can behave yourself and stay out of trouble. Do you think you can do that, honey?"

Brian nodded. "I'll try, Mom," he said. "I really will."

So the first friend he made on Deception Island was Derek Herrmann, the check-stealer. They were off to a bang-up start.

But Claire had thought she could keep her son from sliding back to his old ways. She'd hoped Harlan would be a good influence on him.

The phone still in her lap, Claire stared out the window of her hospital room. She remembered Brian running away on those two previous occasions. Both times, he'd come back, promising he'd try harder to stay out of trouble and get along with Harlan. What had happened this last time? Why hadn't he returned yet?

It seemed too much of a coincidence that Brian had run away, she'd disappeared, and Brian's best friend, Derek Herrmann, had suddenly taken off for parts unknown in Europe—all within a twenty-four-hour period.

Brian had other friends. Claire consulted the car pool list. She'd call every mother on that list. One of them had to know something of Brian's whereabouts.

Claire pulled herself out of the chair, and took the phone over to the windowsill. She dialed Becka Goodwyn's number. While counting the ring tones, she noticed it drizzling outside. She watched the rain drops hit against the glass.

Then she saw him. He was just a blur, moving through a bald patch in the forest—just beyond the parking lot. He wore a black windbreaker and a hunter's cap with the ear flaps. He held something in his hands. Claire couldn't tell what it was. He peered up toward her window for a fleeting moment, then he ducked behind a tree. She didn't get a good look at his face. The brim of his hunter's cap obscured it.

"Hi, you've reached the Goodwyns," she heard a recording on the other end of the line. Claire hung up.

Biting her lip, she stared out the rain-beaded window. The man was peeking around the tree. He held something up to his face, binoculars or a telescope of some kind. He was watching her.

"Oh, my God," she murmured. She put down the car pool list. All the while, he was staring up at her with those binoculars. Or was it a camera? Claire stepped back from the window, and almost tripped over the phone cord. She made her way to the door and opened it.

The guard sprung up from his chair. "Are you okay, ma'am?"

She pointed toward the window. "I think someone's spying on me. He's down by the parking lot with binoculars or something . . ."

The guard grabbed his cellular from a clip on his belt, then he hurried to the window. "This is room three-eleven," he was saying into the phone. "I'm with the victim. She spotted someone spying on her from the wooded area by the north parking lot . . ."

"I didn't see his face," Claire interjected. "But he was a white man, tall, medium build. He wore a black rain-slicker, and this strange hunter's cap."

Claire listened to the guard repeat the description to his associate. She was still unsteady on her feet. Moving to the window, she had to grab onto the nightstand, the edge of the bed, and then a chair.

"No, I can't see anyone from here," the guard was saying. Hunched over the sill, he peered out the window. Rain continued to slash against the glass. "Advise you patrol the area . . ."

Claire came up to his side. She braced a hand against the wall. She gazed down at the thick, wooded area. She expected to see him hiding behind a tree or some bushes.

But the man in the hunter's cap had disappeared.

Chapter 9

"Oh my God, are those Pepperidge Farm cookies on sale?" Sherita Williams asked her friend.

She was pushing a shopping cart down aisle nine at the Quality Food Center not far from where she lived. It was Sherita's day off. She'd met her friend, a thin, black woman named Monica, for coffee and a trip to the store.

"If I get the cookies, I really ought to put back the Klondike bars," Sherita told her friend. "I really shouldn't have both. Otherwise, next time I come here I won't fit through the aisle."

She fished two boxes of ice cream bars from her cart. "I'm putting these back." She retreated to the freezer section.

He didn't follow her. He stayed in the cookie aisle—a few feet behind her friend. Neither one of them had noticed him so far. He knew when not to stick too close.

He'd gotten close enough to Sherita already; the other night in the hospital's underground garage, he'd stood just a few feet away, watching her from the janitor's closet. He'd planned to abduct her that night, and keep her for a few hours—until she told him what he needed to know about Jane Doe. Then he would have gotten rid of her. No makeup, no plastic bag, no shallow grave. It would have been a burial at sea—or in the most remote part of a forest. He wouldn't have wanted this one found.

Sherita Williams would have been dead that night—had she not suddenly turned and run away. And she moved fast for a big girl.

There were other occasions he'd been close enough to touch her. He'd sat near her at lunch three times in the hospital cafeteria. One night, through her bedroom window, he'd watched her undress and go to sleep. This was his second time shopping with her.

She passed by him to rejoin her friend. She put a box of Klondike bars back in her cart, then loaded three bags of Pepperidge Farm cookies in there after it. "I'm keeping one of the Klondikes—and a bag of cookies for myself," she announced. "I'll give the other two bags of cookies to a couple of my patients. Jane Doe could use some cheering up, and she doesn't have to worry about her weight, damn her."

"Who's the other patient?" he heard Monica ask. He followed them further down the aisle.

Pushing her cart, Sherita let out a sigh. "Oh, her name is Tess Campbell. She's just down the hall from Jane Doe . . ."

There was an announcement for a cleanup on one of the aisles. For a moment, he couldn't hear what Sherita was saying.

". . . complications, and she lost the baby," Sherita went on. "Hydrocephalus. Talk about sad. Oh, and she's all alone. No husband, no family. Huh, I should get her and Jane Doe together. Jane Doe lost a baby too, a SIDS case. The two of them might help each other out."

"Does she have any other kids?" Monica asked. They headed toward the check-out line.

"Who, Tess?"

"No, Jane Doe."

From the next checkout line, he could see the hesitation on Sherita's face. "I can't say, hon," she finally replied. "I shouldn't really give out any details about her."

The line moved, and Sherita pushed her cart forward. Her friend started flipping through one of the tabloids near the checkout stand.

Frustrating as it was, he had to admire Sherita's self-control when it came to disclosing information about Jane Doe. In all the times he'd eavesdropped on her conversations, Sherita hadn't given away anything he could really use—at least, not yet.

He'd never overheard Sherita say when the husband and friend were visiting. Subsequently, he always missed them. From either one, he could have learned Jane Doe's true identity. And then he could track her down once she was out of the hospital.

Funny the way things worked out. She'd been a last minute substitute for a blonde he'd been trailing at the Westhill Towers. She'd been there for a convention, and unwittingly kept eluding him and joining up with friends. The blonde never knew how close she'd been to becoming his fifth victim. She and a girlfriend had just left the hotel gym when this attractive brunette walked in. And she had been alone.

She didn't have a purse or wallet with her. In the hours that he held her captive, he never asked for her name. And she never told him. She'd just kept begging him not to hurt her.

So he would have to find out her full name from her nurse. He would get close to Sherita Williams again. He'd catch her alone, and she would tell him everything he wanted to know about her patient.

In the meantime, the clerk was ringing up his groceries. Sherita's line wasn't moving. Her friend found something in a tabloid called *The National Tattler*. "Is this really Jane Doe?" she asked.

Sherita's mouth dropped as she glanced at the newspaper. "Oh, my God," he heard her whisper. "Oh, no . . ."

* * *

"Feast your weary eyes on page two," Linda Castle said, tossing the tabloid on Claire's lap. "You're practically *The National Tattler*'s cover girl."

Claire was sitting in the easy chair by the window in her hospital room. Linda plopped down on the edge of the unmade bed. "I'm sure when Harlan sees that, some heads will roll on the hospital's security staff."

Hesitating, Claire opened the tabloid magazine. She stared at the blurry photo on page two—beneath a splashy banner: *"Tattler Exclusive! The First Look at 'Jane Doe,' the Amnesiac Mystery Woman 'Made Over' and Left for Dead by the 'Rembrandt' Serial Killer!"*

Claire recognized herself in the murky picture. It had been taken from outside—with a telephoto lens. She was staring out the same hospital window now, and wearing the same robe she had on in the photo. Fortunately, the image was so grainy, she doubted even her closest friends could identify her in it. But that was little solace for having her privacy violated.

Claire read the caption below her photo:

"From her window in a Bellingham, WA., hospital, the patient known only as Jane Doe, is the sole survivor of the 'Rembrandt' serial killer, terrorizing women in Washington state."

"Wouldn't you know?" Linda said. "The one time they put your picture in the newspaper, you're in your bathrobe and your hair's a mess. The shutterbug must be that hunter-guy you said you saw in those woods the day before yesterday. Huh, I bet they stopped the presses for you, Claire."

At the bottom of the page Claire read a teaser: *"For The Full, Horrifying Story on the Rembrandt Murders, Turn to Page 17!"*

Linda's cell phone rang. She dug it out of her purse. "Hello? Oh, hi, hon . . . Yeah, I'm with Claire now. What's going on with you? Well, I was going to make a stew, and bring some of it over to Harlan and Tiffany."

Claire glanced up from the newspaper, and cleared her

throat. "Linda?" she whispered. "I hate to be a killjoy, but they don't like you using cell phones in here."

Linda distractedly nodded at her, but kept on talking into the cellular: "I have plenty of ground beef in the freezer, and that would stretch it out . . ."

She kept discussing dinner plans until a nurse poked her head in the doorway. "Excuse me, ma'am?" she called, an edge in her tone. "Use of cellular phones isn't allowed in this hospital."

Linda waved her away, and kept talking.

"Ma'am, did you hear me?" the nurse asked pointedly.

"Hon, I have to call you back," Linda said into the phone. "I'm getting it in stereo now. Apparently, I'm committing this huge crime and they'll shoot me at sunrise for talking on a cell phone here. Isn't that the stupidest thing you've ever heard?"

Once Linda clicked off the phone, the nurse nodded at her, smiled curtly, then moved on. Turning toward Claire, Linda rolled her eyes and frowned. "Ye Gods, only a few days ago, you couldn't remember a thing, and now you're Miss Know It All, quoting hospital rules to me, no less."

Speechless, Claire just shook her head.

"I'm kidding, silly!" Linda laughed. She climbed off the bed. "I'll step outside so I can talk to my husband without getting yelled at. Ha! Be right back."

Linda breezed out the doorway. Claire stared after her for a moment, then glanced down at the tabloid in her lap: *"For The Full, Horrifying Story on the Rembrandt Murders, Turn to Page 17!"*

Until now, she hadn't seen a single news article or TV report on the Rembrandt murders. Everyone had been protecting her: screening newspapers and magazines that came into the room, and otherwise occupying her during local TV news broadcasts. Before her own encounter with Rembrandt, she hadn't been following the case. Living on Deception Island, she'd felt removed from so many things happening on the mainland. She'd had no interest in the Rembrandt murders.

Now, she was interested. Claire turned to page 17. She winced at all the headlines and photos crammed into the two-page spread.

"PRETTY MAIDS ALL IN A ROW," was emblazoned across the top of page 17. Portraits of Rembrandt's five victims stretched beneath the bold headline. The first woman was a blonde with a pretty smile. She looked like someone with whom Claire might have been friends. *"Victim 1,"* said the caption. *"Nancy Hart, 23, had married her high school sweetheart only four months before her disappearance last November. She was shot in the chest."*

All the captions were like that with a bit of personal information to humanize these *"pretty maids."* Barbara Tuttle, whose neck was broken, loved plants and had a greenhouse in her backyard. Karen Ferrigno, stabbed eleven times, was a cat-fancier, and volunteered at an animal shelter. Connie Shafer, shot in the chest, did numerology and astrology charts for her friends. All of the dead women had been attractive and reasonably young. The last portrait was just a silhouette, and carried the caption: *"Jane Doe, midthirties, shot in the chest, and found in a garbage dump in Bellingham, WA. She's the only victim to have survived Rembrandt's murder rampage. What can she tell us?"*

Claire numbly stared at page 18. Under the headline, *TRAIL OF TERROR,* the tabloid featured a small map of Western Washington, with a circle marking the area where each victim lived, and an "X" where each one was found—after Rembrandt had finished with her. An arrow pointed to the location of the Bellingham dump where she had been discovered. *"Jane Doe found here,"* read the explanation in a little box beside the map. *"Like the second victim, Barbara Tuttle, she was also found in a garbage dump. But Jane Doe survived. Investigators are protecting her identity."*

Another column on the same page showed sketches of where Rembrandt might have hid his victims before killing them. *"REMBRANDT'S DUNGEON OF DEATH,"* said the headline.

He holds each victim several hours or several days before he kills them. He even feeds them. Autopsies on victims, Barbara Tuttle and Connie Shafer, revealed the presence of K-rations in their digestive systems. Where does Rembrandt keep his captives?

The sketches employed a "woman" symbol most airport rest rooms use, showing how a victim may have been held in various confined quarters. That doll-like figure in a dress was shown lying on its side in an underground bunker; standing at the bottom of a well; and tilted against the wall of an attic crawl space.

The tabloid carried photos of other serial killers: Ted Bundy, David Berkowitz, and Albert deSalvo.

Claire got chills as she stared at the composite sketch of "Rembrandt," based on the description of _"a dark-haired caucasian man in his midthirties"_ seen with the third victim, Karen Ferrigno, in the parking lot of Sea-Tac Mall, where she disappeared. It was an eerie half-photo, half-rendering of a man in a dark jacket, T-shirt, and black pants. In one hand he held a gun, in the other, a knife. The mouth, a plain line, was obviously drawn-in, as was his hair. But the eyes appeared real and menacing. They seemed to gaze at her from the page. Claire wondered if this was an accurate facsimile of the last human being those poor women had seen before they'd died. He seemed so creepy and unreal.

She didn't recall meeting anyone who looked like that.

The telephone rang, and Claire jumped a bit. She closed the tabloid. She didn't want to look at that half-real, half-cartoon face any more. Moving over to the nightstand, she grabbed the phone. "Hello?"

"Claire, it's Sherita. How the hell are you?"

"I'm the hell fine," she replied, sitting down in the bed. "How are you? Isn't it your day off?"

"Sure is, thank God. I'm calling because I need a huge favor from you. I want you to drop in on a patient just down the hall in room 304. Her name's Tess Campbell. She lost her baby a couple of days ago. Hydrocephalus. Very sad. And there were complications in the birth, so she's laid up for a while. Anyway, Claire, she's all alone. No husband, no family."

"Well, what do you expect me to do?" Claire asked.

"Be a friend to her. You lost a baby too. Go talk to her."

"About what? Our babies' dying? I don't think either one of us want to talk about that, and it's the only thing we have in common."

"Oh, for God's sakes, I'm not asking you to donate a kidney here, hon," Sherita said on the other end of the line. "I told Tess you might drop by. All I'm asking is that you get off your ass, walk down the hall, and introduce yourself to her. Would it kill you?"

Claire hesitated before answering.

"Might even help you out, girl," Sherita continued. "Take your mind off your own worries."

Claire became aware of someone standing in the doorway. She glanced over her shoulder. Linda stared back at her, then cleared her throat.

"Okay, I'll go talk to her," Claire said into the phone. "I guess we have something else in common after all. We both have a nutcase for a nurse. Her name's Tess?"

"That's right, Tess in three-oh-four. She's expecting you."

"Swell," Claire muttered. "Listen, I need to scoot. I have company. Was that all you were calling me about?"

"That's it, hon."

"Well, thanks for thinking of me on your day off, Sherita," Claire whispered.

Linda closed the door. She swiped the tabloid off the chair, then sat down. "Guess who beeped in while I was talking to Ron," she said.

Claire hung up the phone. "Who?"

"Ellen Roberts. She says you called her yesterday, and grilled her for fifteen minutes about Brian. And then you got her son, Michael, on the line and interrogated him for ten more minutes."

Claire frowned. "I simply asked them a few questions. You make it sound like I strapped them each to a chair and used the brass knuckles."

"Well, you can't go calling everyone up and asking them about Brian."

Claire said nothing. She'd already called all the mothers on the car pool list—and talked with over a dozen of Brian's friends. No one had a clue as to her son's whereabouts. She'd even asked about Derek Herrmann's trip to Europe, and the possibility that Brian had gone with him. A few of the mothers expressed surprise over Derek's sudden departure; others didn't know a thing about it.

"Harlan already phoned several of Brian's friends and their families when he ran away two weeks ago," Linda went on. "It's beyond pointless that you're calling and hounding them again. In fact, Claire, I hate to say this, but it's downright embarrassing. I mean, it's a family matter. The whole island doesn't need to know that Brian ran away from home."

Claire frowned at her. "What's it your business anyway, Linda?"

She straightened in the chair. "Well, it becomes my business when Ellen Roberts phones me and asks what's wrong with you. Plus, she star-six-nined your call. She wanted to know why she got this hospital here in Bellingham when we've been telling everyone you're in Seattle. I had to make up this elaborate story about how the Seattle number is routed through Bellingham. That's another reason you shouldn't be calling all these people. You'll blow our cover story."

Claire rubbed her forehead. "Do we really need a 'cover story,' Linda? Is it necessary to lie to people about a mugging and my recuperating in some Seattle hospital? Why not simply tell everyone the truth?"

"Well, now, you're just not making any sense, Claire," Linda sighed. "It's common knowledge that Jane Doe is in a Bellingham hospital. That's why we're saying you're in Seattle, dear. The fewer people who are clued into the fact that you're Jane Doe, the better." She motioned toward the tabloid on the foot of the bed. "I mean, do you want everyone knowing that's you? You were missing for a week, and practically the whole island is aware of that. Do you want them to make the connection? So you were mugged, and you're in a hospital in Seattle. That cover story is for your protection, your privacy."

Claire looked her in the eyes. "You know, Linda, I have a feeling that you and Harlan are giving *me* a cover story. There's something you're not telling me, something you're keeping from me—and from the police."

Linda glanced toward the closed door, then squinted at her. "What, are you nuts?"

"Did we really go shopping together in Seattle? Because I don't remember it at all. And I know I've never spent the night in your guest room. You made that up, didn't you?"

"Why would I make it up?"

"That's exactly what I'm asking you, Linda. Something happened, and you're covering it up. Does it have to do with Brian? Is that why you don't want me calling people and asking—"

Linda shook her head. "Claire, you're talking nonsense—"

"Do you expect me to believe that within a twenty-four-hour period, Brian ran away, his best friend took off for parts unknown in Europe, and I disappeared? Isn't that a pretty strange coincidence?"

"It's not so strange, considering Brian has run away twice before. And if I were Dottie Herrmann, I'd have sent that kid to Europe too. Hell, with all the trouble Derek was into—along with Brian, I might add—I'd have given him a one-way ticket to Timbuktu ages ago."

Linda got to her feet. "Now, I'm sorry you don't remember Brian running away. But you're the one who broke that news to us the night he took off. And I'm sorry you don't remember how Ron and I tried to be good friends, and put you up for the night. It's exactly as I told the police, Claire. The next day, I took you to Anacortes on the boat, and drove you down to Seattle. I'm not lying, or keeping anything from you. Quite frankly, I resent your accusations."

With a sigh, she glanced down at Claire on the bed. "I should be hurt, Claire, but I'll just chalk up your suspicions to the stress and strain you've been under."

Claire stared up at her. "No, Linda," she whispered. "Chalk up my suspicions to the fact that you're a bad liar."

Linda shook her head and clicked her tongue against her teeth. "Well, I see there's no reasoning with you while you're in this mood. I'll come by tomorrow. Call if you need anything—or if you want to apologize."

She shot Claire one last wounded look, then headed out the door.

Linda Castle climbed into her sports utility vehicle in the hospital visitors' parking lot. She pulled the cell phone out of her purse and pressed the speed dial. She gazed at the hospital through the windshield while listening to the ring tones. Someone answered on the third ring.

"Hi, hon," Linda said. "Listen, I tried to discourage her from calling half the island about that son of hers, and she got all uppity with me. Honestly, I wanted to smack her. We really have to move her out of this hospital before she starts to remember things. I mean it. The sooner the better . . ."

"Do you want me to close this door, ma'am?" asked the guard outside her room.

Still sitting on the bed, Claire glanced over her shoulder at him. "Yes, thanks very much." Once he closed the door, Claire curled up on the bed.

She didn't give a damn if calling Brian's friends and their parents had made certain people uncomfortable. She needed to find her son. She didn't want to think that Brian could have run away and decided to *stay* away this time.

Claire closed her eyes for a moment. She felt herself

drifting off. Then an image flashed in her mind. She saw the hospital door open. In the doorway stood that half-photograph, half-cartoon of a man from the tabloid. He stared at her, unmoving, unblinking. He held a gun in one hand and a knife in the other.

She quickly sat up, and glanced back at the closed door. She felt her heart racing near the fresh scar on her chest.

"Shit," she muttered, getting to her feet.

Claire brushed her hair, put on some lipstick, then buttoned up her robe. She nodded and smiled at the guard as she stepped outside, then she headed down the hallway toward room 304. She figured Sherita was probably right. Maybe she needed to take her mind off her own worries for a while.

The door to 304 was open, and Claire peeked inside the room. A thin woman sat on top of the bed with a remote control device in her hand. She wore a beautiful, long, red kimono and black embroidered slippers. Claire figured she must have prepacked the outfit in her maternity overnight bag.

The patient's big blue eyes were glued to the TV—on a bracket high on the wall. She was pretty, despite a slightly weak chin and a long neck that made her look a bit like a bird. Her wispy, delicate blond hair was pinned back behind her head.

"Tess?" Claire asked, working up a smile. She paused in the doorway.

The patient turned to frown at her. "Wouldn't you know? My one opportunity for unlimited amounts of bad afternoon–TV, and people keep interrupting me. What do you want?"

Momentarily speechless, Claire glanced at the TV. A couple were screaming at each other while a TV-therapist sat between them, caught in the crossfire.

"Well?" Tess prompted. Then she sighed and rolled her eyes. "Oh, Jesus-Mary-Joseph. You're the woman from down the hall that Sherita told me about. I was praying you wouldn't come."

Claire let out a stunned laugh. "Huh, you sure know how to make a girl feel welcome."

Tess shot a final look at the TV, and switched it off with the remote. Then she turned toward Claire again. "C'mon in," she said, with mock enthusiasm and a forced smile. "Pull up a chair, and let's swap dead baby stories. That's what you're here for, right? Sherita said you lost a baby daughter in a crib death about ten years ago. Gee, that's tough. I lost a baby son, hydrocephalus. You want to hear the corker? According to a couple of the nurses, he was just about the most beautiful baby they've seen around these parts in a long time. But I wouldn't see him, because I knew he was going to die. I knew during the delivery. See, they didn't catch it on the ultrasound. Can you believe that? Talk about a screw up. I've had four different lawyers come in here unsolicited, saying I have 'a terrific case,' bless their greedy little hearts. It's like I lost a baby and won the lottery. How about that? Aren't I the lucky stiff?"

Claire walked around to the foot of her bed. The fake, almost manic smile was still plastered across Tess Campbell's face. Yet tears were locked in her eyes. Claire noticed she had a large strawberry mark on the left side of her face. It went from her cheekbone to halfway down her neck. Irregular in shape, it resembled an outline of Africa.

"Whew! I feel better now," Tess went on. "I'm glad we had this little talk. Thanks for stopping by. You can go now."

Claire studied her. "Does this caustic routine work with everybody?" she asked.

Eyes downcast, Tess wouldn't look at her. "It seems to scare off the lawyers and social workers," she muttered. "I don't need anyone trying to cheer me up. I don't need anyone feeling sorry for me either. And if one more person tells me that I'll get over this, I'm going to punch their lights out."

"I lost my baby eleven years ago," Claire said. "I'm still not over it."

A tear ran down Tess's cheek, and she quickly wiped it

away. She still wouldn't look at Claire. "I'm sorry, I really am."

"Her father died five years ago," Claire heard herself say. "Cancer. I'm still not over that either—even though I've remarried."

"Jared, that's my baby's father, he's dead too. A skiing accident." She let out a sad laugh. "Having his baby was going to be my way of getting over Jared's death. He was going to keep living through this baby. I guess the joke was on me." She pulled a Kleenex from the pocket of her kimono and wiped her eyes. "Huh, Sherita was right. We do have a lot in common. It's almost scary. Now, all you need is a high-rolling, Bible-thumbing, fundamentalist insane bitch for a mother, and I'd say you and I were the exact same person."

Claire sat near the foot of the bed. "Well, my mom and I butted heads a lot, but we had a pretty good relationship in the years before she died."

"You're lucky," Tess grunted. "When I called my mother and told her that Collin died—that's my son, Collin. When I told her that he'd died, she said it was my punishment for having a baby out of wedlock. She said I was going to hell, and the baby's soul was also damned to hell. So—I told her, 'Fine, that means I get to spend eternity with my baby.' And I said, 'I'd tell *you* to go to hell, old woman, but my baby and I don't want to see your sorry-ass self down there, so just piss off.' I think she's praying for me right now, as we speak."

"Was she always that way?" Claire asked.

"Pretty much borderline. But she really hopped on the crazy bus around the time I went to college. I remember her telling me when I was nineteen that this thing here . . ." Tess pointed to the strawberry blemish on her face. "She said it was the mark of the devil. I always thought it looked like South America, myself."

"Really? Because I was thinking Africa."

Tess laughed. "Well, anyway, I've had it all my life, and suddenly she tells me it's Satan's imprint or something like that. Anyway, she's a piece of work. She didn't even ask why I was still in the hospital four days after I had the baby."

"She didn't?"

"Nope," Tess frowned. "Anyway, F-Y-I, there were some 'complications.' But I shouldn't have to stay here too much longer. How about you? Why are you here?"

"Didn't Sherita tell you?" Claire asked.

Tess shook her head. "She just said your name was Claire, and that you'd lost a baby to SIDS about ten years ago, and you might stop by. So what are you in here for?"

Claire hesitated. "Um, I was mugged outside a department store in Seattle, and I—" She trailed off, then shook her head. "No, that's not true. Two weeks ago, I was left in a garbage dump with a bullet in my chest, a cosmetic makeover, and a plastic bag over my head."

Tess stared at her. "Oh, my God," she murmured. "You're Jane Doe. And here you are, trying to cheer *me* up."

Claire shrugged. "Mostly I'm here for selfish reasons," she admitted. "I'm trying to take my mind off my own worries. See, I have a seventeen-year-old son, who ran away the day before I was attacked, and I don't remember it." Her voice cracked. "I don't know where he is . . ."

She couldn't help it. She started to cry.

"Oh, here." Tess plucked a couple of Kleenex from the dispenser on her nightstand, then handed them to Claire. Then she opened the nightstand drawer and pulled out a box of chocolates. "And take a couple of these. My girlfriend, Mary Lou from Seattle brought them up. They're Godiva."

Tess smiled at her. There was nothing fake or forced about the smile this time. It was genuine.

With Tess, Claire felt as if she'd made her first real friend in years. Nearly all of her acquaintances on the island had been chummy with Harlan's first wife, Angela; and she couldn't help feeling she'd merely *inherited* their friendship. She wasn't particularly close to any of them, including Linda.

Her new friend lived in Bellingham, only a ferry ride and a thirty-minute drive from Deception Island. Tess had recently moved from Seattle, figuring the recently dubbed, "All American City" was a better place to raise a child. A real estate agent, she relocated to her company's Bellingham office, where business was on a steady rise. She hated leaving her friends. But she had no real family, and her baby's father had been dead for three months when she'd made the move.

"Jared was sweet," Tess explained to Claire, the morning after their initial meeting.

Wearing their robes over some scrubs Sherita had pilfered for them, Claire and Tess had snuck away to the physical therapy room on the second floor. The two of them were still a bit weak, so they'd limited themselves to some very, very light stretching on the mats together.

"He was thirty, but just a kid at heart," Tess continued, wincing a bit as she turned her shoulders one way, then the other. "I had no hopes of marrying him. From the time I was a kid, I'd pretty much figured I'd be alone. Maybe it's my birthmark. You learn to drop the happily-ever-after pipedream when you grow up with something like this on your face and a crazy mother always telling you that you're ugly. Anyway, Jared made me feel pretty—and loved."

"You *are* pretty," Claire said.

"I never thought so. Even without the birthmark, I'd say I was only so-so. But I think I would have been a terrific mom." She paused for a moment, then went back to her stretching. "Anyway, about Jared, he wasn't exactly Mr. Responsibility. He was always off skiing, sky-diving, bungee jumping, or something like that. He wasn't mature enough for marriage—no less fatherhood. But when I got pregnant, I figured, 'I'm thirty-five. It could be my last shot.' Then Jared died, and I knew I had to have this baby."

Tess stopped stretching, and caught her breath. "So what about your baby?" she asked Claire pointedly. "I lost mine. What are you going to do to get Brian back?"

"Well, I had this idea last night," Claire said, sitting up with her legs stretched in front of her. She pointed her toes. "I'm thinking of going public. You know, let the reporters in, and make a statement: *'I'm Jane Doe. My real name is Claire Ferguson Shaw. If anyone knows the whereabouts of my son, Brian Ferguson . . .'* "

Frowning, Tess shook her head. "You don't want to do that. If you blow your cover, the police might not be able to protect you from the press and God knows who else. And you'll probably get a ton of false alarms, fake Brians falling over themselves for a chance to meet you . . ."

Claire said nothing. She knew about false alarms. Every time the hospital front desk called to say she had a visitor, her heart leapt. She couldn't help thinking it could be—just might be—Brian. Then of course, it would be Harlan, or Linda. And she'd feel so disappointed.

"Brian might not want to be in the spotlight," Tess continued. "If he truly did run away, he might be in some kind trouble. You mentioned he'd been in some jams with the police before. You don't want to make trouble for him, do you?"

"No, I don't want to do that," Claire muttered.

"Why not hire a private detective? I know they probably don't have any on Gilligan's Island—"

"Deception," Claire interjected, grinning tiredly. "Deception Island."

"But I'm sure we could find someone in Bellingham," Tess continued. "We'll both be out of here within a few days. I think you need to go shopping with a girlfriend in the city again. Only this time, I get to be the girlfriend. The city will be Bellingham, and we'll shop for a private detective together. And I promise, Claire, I won't let you out of my sight."

"You know, Tess is the best post-op medicine you've prescribed for me so far. She's giving me hope."

Claire sat on top of the bed while Sherita changed the dressing on her chest wound. "I'm really excited about this private detective idea. But I'm not saying anything to Harlan or Linda. This is something I need to do independently of them. Thank God for Tess—and for you, Sherita. Honestly, if not for you two, I'd don't think I could stand it here. You two have been my salvation."

"Oh, cut it out," Sherita said, smiling. "You making me feel underpaid." She started to replace the bandage on Claire's chest. "You're healing pretty well here, honey."

"But not healed completely," Claire said, her eyes avoiding the scar. "Not yet."

"I mean it, you and Claire are the only real friends I've made in this place." Tess shrugged, then took another bite of the Nestle's Crunch bar. "Not that I expected to make any friends here. I thought I'd be leaving this hospital with a baby."

She sighed. "Anyway, Claire made me stop feeling sorry for myself. And so have you."

Tess glanced around the visitor's lounge on the third floor. There was an older couple, having a quiet conversation on the sofa across from them. Three other visitors sat separately in the orange bucket seats lined against the wall. No one paid attention to the game show on the muted TV set, bracketed to the other wall.

No one seemed to be watching them either.

"You've been wonderful," Tess continued. "And I don't just mean your kindness to me the last couple of days. I'm really amazed at the way you've held up during your own ordeal. How long has it been now—I mean, since the traffic accident? How long has your wife been in a coma?"

"Five days," he replied in a low voice. "And I'm not so amazing. I take just one day at a time. Tell me more about your friend, Claire."

"I can't," Tess replied, nibbling at her candy bar. "It's kind of the same way you don't want me telling anyone about our talks. She's—well, she needs her privacy."

Her eyes narrowed, Tess smiled at him. "You suddenly seem uncomfortable."

He quickly shook his head. "Not at all. But I need to get back to the ICU, and see my wife. Then I think I'll catch a couple of winks down in this lounge I discovered in the basement. They have a couple of sofas in there, and I can stretch out. No one seems to know about this place, but it's very nice."

"Your own private little retreat," Tess said.

He nodded. "Why don't you come down and meet me there at six? You can be my wake-up call."

Tess shrugged. "Sure."

"And if I wake up early, I'll run down the street and get some Chinese for us. I'll bet you're sick of hospital food. You wouldn't object to dinner with a married man, would you, Tess?"

She laughed. "I think I'll be safe. Where is this little hide-away lounge?"

Tess took elevator D down to the basement. He'd told her to turn right after the elevator. She walked alone down the yellow-painted cinderblock corridor.

Tess was wearing her red kimono and the embroidered slippers. She'd washed her hair, and put on some lipstick and a touch of mascara. She kept reminding herself that this wasn't a date. He was married. Still, she had a little, harmless crush on him. They had a connection—not that anything would ever happen. She just liked being with him.

He'd said to take another right at the entrance to the South Annex, where the cinderblock walls were painted an ugly blue. But before turning that corner, she spotted someone at the end of the main hallway. It looked like a custodian. She thought he was wearing a uniform, but he moved across the hallway so quickly, she couldn't tell. He was there for only a second.

Biting her lip, Tess hesitated. She kept staring down that hall, waiting for him to reappear. After a few moments, she moved on, turning down the annex with its ugly, narrow blue walls. He'd said she would come to a door with a little window in it. The door was unlocked.

As Tess opened the door, she was greeted with a mechanical, churning sound. It sounded like a big washing machine.

He didn't tell her there would be some hospital equipment in the hallway after she went beyond that door. She was surprised to see a couple of gurneys and a stainless steel table on wheels blocking her path. She wondered if she'd taken a wrong turn. How could such an out-of-the-way place be open to the public? She hadn't told Claire or Sherita about this little rendezvous. They might not understand her wanting to spend time with a married man. Still, Tess would have felt better if someone knew where she was right now. Hell, she didn't even know where she was herself. And she hadn't seen another soul down there—except for that janitor.

A fire extinguisher was the landmark for the next hallway. She was supposed to take a right, but stopped in her tracks. *"Just go down to the double doors at the end of that short hallway,"* he'd told her.

He didn't mention that the fluorescent overhead in that corridor was malfunctioning. It sputtered on and off. She noticed two big laundry bins against the wall, and finally, the double doors. She didn't see any light coming through the crack between them.

"I might have the lights off in there if I'm still napping. But go ahead and wake me," he said.

Tess took a few steps into that corridor. All the while, she kept thinking, *Something's wrong here.* She paused and glanced down at the laundry bins. Both hampers were half-full of sheets and bedding. The fluorescent light above kept flickering.

Past all that mechanical churning sound, she heard some-one in back of her clearing his throat.

Tess swiveled around.

"Excuse me, ma'am," the janitor said. He was a middle-aged black man with gray at his temples and dark little skin-tabs sprinkled on his face. He leaned on the long handle to a dry floor-mop. "Can I help you?"

Tess caught her breath. "Um, no thank you," she said. With her thumb she indicated the room behind her. "I'm just—headed into the lounge to meet a friend."

"That's not a lounge, ma'am. This whole area is mainte-nance."

"Are you sure?" she asked. "A friend told me to meet him in the basement lounge."

"Well, there's a lounge down here for the maintenance crew, but that's in another wing." He nodded at the double doors. "That there's a storage area." He set the mop against the wall, then walked past her to the doors. He swung them open. "See?"

Tess gazed into the darkened room. Amid the shadows, she saw stacks of boxes against the walls, a few broken-down gurneys, and some more steel tables—gleaming in the dim light. "I must have gotten the directions mixed up," she heard herself say.

The janitor reached for the light switch, and flicked it on. But the lights didn't work. "Um, looks like a short in the electricity."

Tess felt a shudder pass through her. She ducked out of the cold, gloomy storage room and almost bumped into one of the laundry bins.

The janitor stepped out of the storage room after her. The double doors were still swinging behind him.

"Um, sir, could you do me a favor?" Tess asked him. "I need to get back up to my room on the third floor, the North Wing. Could you walk me to the elevator?"

He nodded. "Of course, ma'am."

"Thank you," she said. "I'm just a little worried. I don't want lose my way again."

With the janitor at her side, Tess retreated past the laundry bins. The light overhead was still flickering in the narrow corridor. She glanced back toward the end of the hallway—at the darkened storage room. With a slow, dying flutter, the double doors continued to swing back and forth.

Leaving the cold, dark storage room, he stuffed a handkerchief and the small bottle of chloroform into his jacket. He traced the steps Tess and the janitor had made only three minutes before. Moving down the hallway with the flickering overhead, he passed the laundry bin, where he would have stashed Tess Campbell's body. Under the top layer of dirty sheets, he'd hidden a pair of custodian's coveralls. From that corridor, it was only two short passageways to level A of the underground garage, where his SUV was parked. No one would have noticed a custodian wheeling a laundry bin.

Tess Campbell wouldn't have been like the others. From her, he'd have found out a lot more about "Claire." And he would have rewarded Tess for the information. He'd have covered up that strawberry mark of hers. Tess would have looked very pretty when they found her. He hated seeing his careful plans go to waste.

He rang for the elevator.

The gift shop was on the first floor. It closed at seven, not quite an hour from now. The blonde, Janice, was on duty this evening. He noticed she always wore clothes that accentuated her figure. Tonight, she had on a clingy, black cowlneck pullover and tight jeans.

He bought a pack of gum and a single yellow rose. He said it was for his wife in the ICU.

"Oh, I think yellow roses are so pretty," she said, while wrapping tissue around the flower. "Everyone gives red roses. You're different, that's cool."

She counted out his change for him.

"You know, you found the right job for yourself, Janice," he said, glancing at her nametag. "You make people feel good—when they really need it. You have a beautiful smile too."

Her face lit up. She seemed dazzled by him. He'd gotten that same smitten look from a couple of the others before her. He wished he could have kept that expression on their faces after he'd made them up.

"Well, thank you," Janice said.

A car alarm went off. It happened at least once every night. But usually, the sirens, beeps, and buzzes died after a few moments.

This car alarm had started up at least a minute ago, and it was still going strong.

"Damn it to hell," the parking attendant grumbled. He grabbed his walkie-talkie, stepped out of the cashier's booth, and locked up after himself.

He trotted down the ramp. It sounded as if the alarm were coming from the second sublevel. The loud noise echoed throughout the underground garage. Having to shout on his walkie-talkie, he reported to security that he was leaving his post for a moment to investigate a car alarm on level B.

Jogging down the next ramp, he saw a middle-aged woman with blond hair that almost matched her mink coat. She stood at the front door of a silver BMW, struggling with the device on her key ring. She wore thin, brown leather gloves that matched her high heels.

He was only a few steps away from her when she finally found the right button to shut off the alarm.

"Do you have it under control now?" he asked.

Grimacing, she nodded. "I'm so sorry. This is my sister's car, and I'm not used to this stupid alarm thingee."

"It's okay, ma'am," he grunted.

She gave him a wave as she climbed into the front seat of the BMW.

The parking attendant was about to turn and head up the ramp when he noticed the green Saturn farther down the same row of cars. Its interior light was on.

He recognized the vehicle, which belonged to Janice, from the gift shop. He knew, because she was cute, and every night, when she got off at seven, she'd stop at his booth, show her employee parking card, make a little small talk, then say "Ciao!" as she drove off.

The parking attendant glanced at his wristwatch: 9:25.

Janice should have said "Ciao," and left nearly two and a half hours ago.

Frowning, he moved toward the green Saturn. As he approached the car, he saw why the interior light was on. The driver's door had been left open.

The woman in the BMW pulled out of her spot and started up the ramp. The attendant decided she'd just have to wait a couple of minutes.

He pulled open the front door to Janice's car. "What the hell?"

Opening the door wider, he reached inside the car for what he thought was a white handkerchief draped over the bottom of the steering wheel.

But it wasn't a handkerchief at all.

He was holding a pair of woman's panties in his hand.

Chapter 10

"Excuse me?" Tess whispered.

The nurse at the front desk to the Intensive Care Unit was on the telephone. She had a pretty face, and a dark, olive complexion. Blond streaks highlighted her long, straight dark brown hair, pulled back with a silver clip. Tess had plenty of time to study that clip, because the nurse kept her head down as she continued to talk on the phone.

"Well, the acoustics in that place suck," she was saying. "I went to the worst concert there . . ."

Tess cleared her throat.

The nurse glanced up for a second, her index finger raised as if to indicate that she'd be with Tess in a moment.

Her arms folded, Tess waited by the desk. She was wearing her red kimono and slippers. She'd become accustomed to walking around the hospital in the kimono. She was overdressed—compared to most of the other patients.

She'd already done her share of waiting around today. She'd spent an hour—reading a boring book—in the third floor lounge. And she'd killed another couple of hours in the cafeteria. Those were the two places she'd usually met Neil. She'd thought for certain she would run into him today. She wanted to explain why she hadn't shown up for their semi-date last night. Obviously, she'd gotten his directions wrong. But mostly, she just wanted to see Neil one last time, and wish him well.

A harmless little crush on a married guy was one thing, but meeting him in a remote, secluded spot for a Chinese dinner together—that was plain wrong. And while his wife was in a coma, no less. What was she thinking?

So—she wanted to see Neil and say good-bye.

"Oh, that place makes the best Margaritas," the nurse was saying into the phone. "Last time I was there, Jake and I got so wasted. He had three Margaritas, and I—"

"Excuse me," Tess said, loudly. "If you're on a break here, is there someone else who can help me?"

The nurse glared up at her for a second. "Listen, Heather, I have to put you on hold," she said into the phone. She pressed the hold button, then put down the receiver and sighed. "Yes?"

"Sorry to interrupt," Tess said, forcing a smile. "I'm looking for a man named Neil. I don't know his last name, but his wife is here in the ICU. She was in a traffic accident five or six days ago. She's in a coma—"

The nurse was shaking her head. "There's nobody here like that." She reached for the phone again.

"Just a minute, please," Tess said. "Before you go back to getting wasted away in Margaritaville, could you just check and see if there's a Mrs. Neil Something-or-other listed as one of your patients?"

"I don't have to check," the nurse said. "There isn't anyone like that here."

"Maybe she moved to another unit yesterday or—"

"I doubt it," she cut in. "Anyway, she isn't here. Try checking with the registration desk downstairs. Okay? I'm very busy right now."

"Oh, I can see that." Tess frowned at her. "I guess when they talk about the 'intensive caring' in this place, it's not a requirement for the idiot at the front desk, huh?"

"What?"

"Never mind," Tess said. "Thanks for nothing."

She turned and walked away. She could hear the nurse get back on the phone with her friend again. "Sorry, Heather. I had this crazy patient screaming at me . . . Oh, I don't know. She's probably mad at the world. She had this creepy strawberry mark covering half of her face. Hah, probably here for some plastic surgery. Anyway, about Friday night . . ."

Tess kept walking. She'd overheard comments like that ever since she was a child. Sometimes she managed to let them roll right off her; other times, she couldn't. Tess told herself to let it roll.

And she told herself this was a sign regarding her bittersweet-romantic plans to see Neil one last time. They didn't need closure. There was never anything to close. She really didn't need to see him again.

As she rang for the elevator, Tess wondered what had happened to Neil's wife. Maybe they'd moved her to another part of the hospital. Or maybe she'd taken a turn for the better. Whatever the case, Neil was probably with her right now, where he belonged.

The elevator arrived, crowded with people. Tess stepped on board, squeezed between a man in a wheelchair and the wall, then she pressed the button for the third floor.

She didn't admit it to anyone, but she often prayed—never aloud, never in church. She didn't want to be associated with her crazy, always-on-her-knees mother. Tess did her praying in her head.

So on the crowded elevator, Tess said a silent prayer for that handsome man she was letting go—and for the woman in his care, fighting for her life.

He thought he heard her screaming.

He knew it was his imagination playing tricks on him—or maybe just the wind. Still, it almost sounded like her voice. She'd been crying out earlier. He'd heard her through the trap door, yelling at the top of her lungs: "OH, GOD, PLEASE, SOMEBODY HELP ME!"

There was no one around to answer her muffled, pathetic cries. She could scream until her throat was raw. It didn't matter.

Her voice could carry only a few feet from that trap door. He certainly couldn't have heard her from where he now stood—outside the house, beside his car.

The wind continued to howl. It was dusk. He had a long trip ahead—to Sherita Williams's place.

He climbed into the driver's seat, started up the car, then noticed something on the floor of the passenger side. He smiled. Rolling down his window, he picked up the withered yellow rose and threw it outside.

Then he drove off.

"Her name was Janice Dineen, and she worked in the gift shop," Harlan said, frowning. "I remember her. She was very pretty. I hear she was only twenty-seven."

"Excuse me, Mr. Shaw," Sherita interjected. "But the police are emphasizing that Janice is 'missing.' She isn't assumed dead. You might not want to talk about her in the past tense."

"Well, they're pretty damn sure Rembrandt has her," Harlan retorted, turning in his chair to glare at Sherita in the bathroom doorway. "I'd say if she isn't dead already, she soon will be. Now, are you done in there? Because I'd like to be alone with my wife."

"Harlan," Claire said under her breath. She was sitting up in bed. "Sherita's my friend. Please, don't talk to her like that."

"It's okay." Sherita sauntered toward the door. "I was about to scram anyway. My shift's over."

"You might want to say your good-byes now," Harlan suggested. He turned toward Claire again and smiled. "I've cleared it with the doctors—and the police. You'll be on your way home first thing in the morning. It's been two and a half weeks, the sutures are out. And frankly, I don't think it's safe for you here anymore. Between the photographers getting at you and this woman in the gift shop who's missing, the security in this place is a joke. The guy in charge, this Tim Sullivan character, I'd like to string him up." Harlan sighed, then he seemed to work up a smile, and took hold of her hand. "Anyway, you're going home, sweetheart."

Dumbfounded, Claire stared at him.

Sherita paused at Claire's bed and touched her shoulder. "Well, congrats, hon. You're bustin' out of the joint. I can't miss that. I'll be here early. See you in the A-M." She smiled at Harlan. "G'night, Mr. Shaw."

"Good night," Harlan replied. He waited until Sherita stepped outside and closed the door after her. "I wish we were getting you out of here tonight," he muttered. "Some security they have in this place. Right under their noses he was. When the cops told me about that girl in the gift shop, I just about lost it. She helped me pick out flowers for you."

"Are they sure—this—Rembrandt has her?" Claire asked.

Sighing, Harlan nodded. "They found her panties in the front seat of her car. I guess it's part of his signature, his calling card, or whatever. They've kept that detail out of the newspapers. But when he abducts them, he always leaves behind some undergarment."

"Did they say where they found my panties?" she murmured.

"I asked them the exact same thing tonight," he replied. "They never found any of your clothes." He squeezed her hand. "Anyway, I'm glad we're getting you out of here, sweetheart. You'll be home tomorrow. Aren't you excited?"

Claire gave an uneasy shrug. "I just keep thinking of that poor girl."

"Think about coming home instead."

"It won't seem like home without Brian."

Harlan kissed her. "He'll come back to us, Claire. You'll see . . ."

Wanting like hell to believe him, she kissed Harlan back.

The window in Sherita's breakfast nook had a broken latch. He was inside the kitchen of her town house within five minutes. The place smelled a bit like stale coffee. He switched on the stove light, and saw a bag of Pepperidge Farm cookies on the kitchen counter. Helping himself to a cookie, he studied the photos and Post-its covering her refrigerator door. Sherita's boyfriend was in several of the pictures. He was stocky with a goatee and not a single hair on top of his head. He had pale skin for a black guy. They looked very happy together.

He wondered which one of these photos the boyfriend would give the mortician after Sherita's death tonight. Someone else would get to play Rembrandt with her.

He studied the Post-its, many with names and addresses or phone numbers scribbled on them. But "Claire" wasn't there. He went through the darkened town house, straining his eyes as he checked the desk and bureau drawers. He found old receipts, business cards, and scraps of paper. But none of those bits of paper had the name, "Claire," written on it. If he hoped to learn anything about Claire, he'd have to get it out of Sherita herself.

Returning to the kitchen, he switched off the stove light. He knew Sherita's schedule by now. She'd be home within the next ten minutes.

He stepped into the laundry room, a converted closet just off the kitchen, near the back door. The windowless room was so dark he couldn't see his hand in front of his face. After groping around for a moment, he found the dial on the dryer, gave it a twist, and a little light went on above the operation panel. It beat waiting in the dark.

He'd heard a story about a murderer hiding in a basement

laundry room. Apparently, the guy waited until he knew the woman was alone upstairs, then he set off buzzer on the dryer. When she came down to check it, he was on her in an instant.

He'd use the same method on Sherita Williams. He had the tiny bottle of chloroform in his jacket pocket, a few feet of rope tied around his waist, and a hunting knife in a sheath strapped around his leg—just above the ankle. Sherita wouldn't give him much trouble.

She would tell him everything he needed to know about "Claire." Then he would slit her throat with his hunting knife.

A few days ago, he'd planned to carefully hide her body— so no one would find it for weeks, months even. But it didn't matter any more. They knew he'd been hanging around the hospital. They were probably looking for Janice right now.

He heard a car pull into the driveway. He reached down toward his ankle and took out his hunting knife. Then he twisted the dial on the dryer, so the light switched off. He waited and listened as outside, the car engine gave one last purr, then a door shut. Just a single car door. She was alone.

He heard her come through the front door. "Shit," she muttered. "Bills, bills, bills." She plopped something down on a table—or in a chair, probably her coat and purse. The kitchen light went on. He saw the strip of light along the bottom of the laundry room door. He stayed perfectly still.

There were a couple of beep tones, then a mechanical voice announced: *"You have two new messages."*

He heard some rustling. It sounded like the bag of cookies. There was another beep: *"Hi, Sherita. It's Naomi. I need to tell you about this awful date I had. Call me."*

That impersonal voice dictated the time and date, then another beep followed: *"Hi, Sherita. It's Claire. You're probably not home yet. But I wanted to apologize for the surly way Harlan was acting tonight. Anyway, I'm sorry. I meant it when I said you're my friend. I'll see you at the hospital tomorrow. Take care."*

He was leaning toward the crack in the door. He knew

that voice. Was this the "Claire" they were talking about? It didn't make any sense.

He listened to Sherita munching on a cookie and moving around the kitchen. It sounded as if she were opening up her mail.

He didn't have the patience for this right now. He had to know if that was really Claire Shaw from Deception Island. He wanted to listen closely to the message again. Did she make reference to "Harlan?" Had he heard right?

Tightening his grip on the knife handle, he blindly felt around for the dryer's timer dial. He was about to set off the buzzer, when he hesitated. He heard her walk out of the kitchen, then up the stairs.

He turned on the little light over the dryer's control panel, and waited. He heard her stomping around upstairs for a few moments. Then the water pipes seemed to moan, and he realized she'd stepped into the shower.

With the knife clutched in his hand, he opened the door and crept out of the laundry room.

Sherita turned off the shower, and the pipes let out a surrendering squeak. She quickly dried off, then reached toward the hook on the back of the bathroom door for her panties. But they weren't there. She could have sworn she'd taken out a fresh pair and hung them in the bathroom. At least she hadn't forgotten her bathrobe, thrown across the top of the hamper. Sherita put it on, then wrapped the towel around her head.

Emerging from the bathroom, she heard a noise. Sherita paused, and listened. She figured it must have been the cheap plumbing in her place. The pipes were always making these weird moaning, knocking, and tapping sounds. It was as if the town house was haunted.

In the bedroom, she put on a clean pair of panties, then wiggled into her comfortable jeans. While adjusting her bra, she heard the damn noise again. Only this time, the sound seemed to come from downstairs.

For a moment, she didn't move. She heard it, a creaking noise, footsteps. Then abruptly, the footsteps stopped—almost mimicking how she'd halted in her own tracks. She realized, this wasn't bad pipes. This was someone else in her town house.

Sherita quickly grabbed the smock she'd worn to work today. Clutching it in front of her, she moved toward the top of the stairs and glanced down at the front hall. The light from the kitchen spilled into the foyer. At first, Sherita didn't see anyone. Then a shadow swept across the hallway floor. She heard the floorboards creaking again.

"Owen, honey? Is that you?" she nervously called.

In response, she heard a muffled grunt.

She figured Owen was in a bad mood, or he had food in his mouth.

"Let's order pizza, okay?" she yelled, heading back into the bedroom.

Sherita didn't hear him answer, but then, Owen almost always said yes to pizza. She switched on the radio in her bedroom, and ducked back into the bedroom. Taking the towel off her head, she worked the blow-dryer over her damp hair for a couple of minutes.

Once she shut off the blow-dryer and put it away, Sherita could hear him again—past the music on the radio. He was coming up the stairs. She returned to the mirror, and put on some lipstick. The bathroom door was open. She saw him behind her—a blurred figure in the mirror. He'd just stepped into the bedroom.

She was too busy with her lipstick to focus on him.

"Think I'll go with your basic no-frills cheese tonight," she said, reaching for a Kleenex.

He stopped in the bathroom doorway.

Owen still had his jacket on. "What are you talking about?" he asked.

"The pizza," Sherita explained, applying a bit of mascara to her eyes. "I'm going for plain cheese. What do you want on your half?"

"Oh, we're ordering pizza tonight?" he asked.

"Duh, yeah." She squinted at his reflection. He was taking

off his jacket. "Didn't you hear me earlier?" Sherita asked. "I said, 'Let's order pizza.' "

"Earlier?" Owen asked. "You mean, this morning?"

"No, just a few minutes ago. I called down to you."

"You didn't call down to me, baby." He tossed his jacket on the bed. "I just got in. I heard the hair dryer and came upstairs."

Slowly, Sherita turned toward him. "You mean, you weren't in the kitchen earlier?"

Owen shook his head. "I just came in the front door a few seconds ago." He caressed her arm with a cold hand. "Here, feel. It's getting chilly out."

Indeed, Sherita felt something. She felt her skin crawl.

When Owen and Sherita searched the town house, they discovered the back door open. Nothing was missing. But the contents of her purse had been spilled across the breakfast table. The wallet was untouched. But her address book was open to the "S" section.

"Whoever it was, he wasn't looking for money," Sherita murmured. She stared down at the address book.

"I'm calling the cops," Owen announced, heading toward the phone. "First thing tomorrow, we're getting you an alarm system, and I'm changing the locks." He lifted the receiver, but hesitated before dialing. He frowned at Sherita. "If he wasn't looking for money, what do you think he was after?"

"A name," Sherita replied. "An address . . ."

She glanced down at the address book again—at the "S" page. Claire Shaw wasn't listed among the names. But he'd been looking for her there.

Sherita knew he would probably keep looking until he found her.

A report to the Bellingham Police regarding a break-in at the home of Sherita Williams was taken by an operator at 8:53 P.M.

Seven and a half hours later, and approximately 110 miles south of Bellingham, a phone call was made to the police in Auburn, Washington.

The call, logged in at 4:39 A.M., was from Jim Korabik, an engineer with the Burlington Northern railroad night crew. He'd been in the engine of a grain train en route to a plant near Auburn. They were experiencing their third night in a row of rain. Parts of the ravine running parallel to the tracks had become like a swamp.

Visibility was poor, due to the early morning hour and the steady downpour. But Jim Korabik saw something, and another member of the train crew glimpsed it too.

They saw a man in a dark rain slicker. He was weaving through the bushes, the mud, and the tall reeds beside the tracks. Jim's coworker claimed the man was carrying a dead deer. But Jim had done his share of hunting. And that was one hell of a strange way to haul a dead animal.

Except for the way he was staggering though the marsh, that shadowy figure almost resembled a groom carrying his bride over the threshold.

When the police operator pressed him, Jim admitted he didn't get a good look at what the man was holding. "I'm not sure if it was an animal, a human being, or a bag of wet towels," he told the woman on the phone. "I just know, that thing in his arms was dead."

At 5:20 that morning, eight policemen wearing rain gear and boots, searched the ravine by the Burlington Northern tracks near Auburn. They discovered the nude body of Janice Dineen, twenty-seven. She had been missing approximately thirty-two hours. Her throat was slashed—just below a piece of jute that secured a plastic bag over her head. Mud and bits of leaves covered the blue-white corpse. But with that plastic bag, Rembrandt had preserved the work he'd done on his victim's face and hair.

In a strange way, the dead woman almost looked pretty.

Chapter 11

Linda and Ron Castle didn't come with Harlan to the hospital. According to Harlan, the Castles had to go to Everett, and see Linda's mother, who was in a nursing home there.

"You know, she has Alzheimer's," Harlan explained. "They had problems with her last night. Anyway, Linda feels bad they couldn't come today."

Dressed in a blue blouse and khakis, Claire was throwing some of her things in the suitcase, which lay open on the bed. "Is that the truth?" she asked. "Or is this 'sick mom' excuse just another cover story?" Claire shut the suitcase and locked it. "Ever since I called Linda a liar three days ago, she's been incommunicado."

"Her mother's really sick," Harlan said. "And yeah, Linda was hurt. She's been a good friend to both of us, Claire, and all she gets from you is suspicion and sarcasm."

"Is that a quote from Linda?" She sat down in the wheelchair.

"Sweetheart, if it weren't for Linda and Ron, I would have gone nuts the last two weeks. And that's all I'll say on the topic." He grabbed her suitcase and moved it to the door. Then he peeked down the hallway. "I don't see why they have to wheel you out. You can walk on your own. Where's that damn nurse anyway?"

"That *damn nurse* is my friend," Claire said, frowning.

"All right, all right, so you've pointed out on several occasions." He patted her shoulder, then sat down on the bed. "Boy-oh-boy, you aren't even home yet, and already we're fighting. This isn't a good sign."

"Sorry," Claire muttered. The truth was, she'd hoped against hope that Brian would have returned home before her. Now that she realized it wasn't going to happen, she was in a foul mood. And she wasn't particularly looking forward to going back to Deception Island today.

Harlan was on edge too. They'd given him the news this morning, and he'd passed it on to Claire: the police had found Janice Dineen's body. The police weren't sure if it meant Rembrandt was moving on—or perhaps getting closer to Claire. They didn't think it was a bad idea that Harlan was taking her home.

Harlan was right. It seemed like forever, waiting for Sherita to arrive with the hospital release forms.

When she finally breezed in and handed the folder to Harlan, she told him. "After you see the bill, I'll have to wheel *you* out of here. Hah, that's my standard joke. Usually gets a laugh."

"Not this time, I guess," Claire said, sighing.

Frowning, Harlan was looking over the documents.

Claire remembered something Brian had said about her husband: *"He's not the zaniest guy in the world, is he?"*

He carried the suitcase as Sherita wheeled her down the corridor. Tess was waiting in the hallway for them. She was wearing her kimono, and brandishing a bottle of champagne for them. "Here, I paid one of the orderlies to smuggle this in for me." She handed Harlan the bottle. "Pop it open when you get home, and raise a glass for me."

Tess rode down on the elevator with them. They had to take Claire out a side door. News of Janice Dineen had reached the press. So a mob of reporters had gathered outside the hospital's front entrance.

While Harlan fetched the car, Claire reluctantly said her good-byes to Sherita and Tess. Claire felt good standing outside, breathing fresh air again. But she loathed leaving her friends. By the time Harlan pulled up beside them with the car, all three women were crying and hugging each other. Claire climbed into the passenger seat, and rolled down her window.

"Don't forget," Tess said, clutching her hand. "We have a date to go shopping in Bellingham just as soon as I get out of here, day after tomorrow."

Claire nodded and blew them each a kiss.

She was still teary-eyed as they pulled out of the hospital lot. "I'm such an idiot not to have brought along Kleenex for the trip," she muttered.

At the first red light, Harlan handed her his handkerchief. "Thanks, sweetheart," Claire said, wiping her eyes.

The light changed, and they started moving again. Harlan stared at the road ahead. "Your friend in the kimono, what's-her-name, she—"

"Tess?"

"Yeah. She mentioned a shopping trip the day after tomorrow. What's that about?"

Claire dabbed her eyes again. She didn't want to tell Harlan about her plans to hire a private detective to find Brian. Harlan hadn't done a very good job trying to locate her son, but of course, he didn't see things that way. She figured he'd try to talk her out of it.

"Oh, Tess wants me to go shopping with her in Bellingham, that's all." Claire glanced out the passenger window. They were headed toward the freeway on-ramp. "She's been wearing maternity clothes the last few months, and she needs some new things. I told her I'd come along. I figured—"

"The day after tomorrow?" Harlan cut in. "No, that's not a good idea."

Claire stared at him. "What do you mean?"

He merged onto the Interstate. "I don't want you leaving

the island for a while," he said. "After what happened to you, I thought the last thing you'd want to do was go on another shopping trip with another girlfriend. I figured you'd just want to stay put."

"Well, I don't want to stay put," Claire replied. "And I don't remember the other shopping trip. It might do me some good to get out for the day. I want to do this, Harlan."

"I won't allow it," he said, eyes on the road. "It's too dangerous. As long as this psychopath is out there, I don't want you leaving the island. You shouldn't go off anywhere on your own. It's asking for trouble."

Claire frowned. "Harlan, you can't hold me prisoner on this island. You'll have to allow—"

"You'll do what I tell you," he interrupted. "That's it. End of discussion, okay? Tell your girlfriend in the kimono that you'll have to take a rain check. She'll understand. You're not taking any chances, Claire."

She took a couple of deep breaths and gazed at the freeway traffic. She said nothing.

"This Rembrandt task force is planting a couple of their men on the island," Harlan continued. "You'll be safe there, that is if someone new is handling things, and not that cocky asshole in charge of hospital security. Huh, you should have seen that guy, goofing off at his desk while that murderer was roaming around the hospital. When I think of that poor girl in the flower shop . . ." Harlan shook his head. "Well, I'd like to wring that weasely cop's neck all over again."

Lieutenant Elmore shoved a piece of paper across his desk. "That's the ferry schedule," he said. "The last one leaves Anacortes for Deception Island at 8:50 tonight. Be on it. Claire Shaw is homeward bound as we speak. You and Al Sparling will stay on the island, babysitting duty. Might be a few weeks, so pack accordingly."

Tim Sullivan shifted in the chair facing Lieutenant Elmore's desk. He tapped his foot nervously. "I don't mean to second guess you, Lieutenant," he said. "But am I really the best guy for that job? Claire Shaw's husband hates my guts. You were there when the guy practically took my head off." Tim Sullivan frowned at his superior. "Mr. Shaw got some bad information, and he's under the *delusion* that I'm in charge of hospital security."

The younger cop's words hung in the air for a moment. Elmore didn't say anything.

Finally, Tim cleared his throat and shifted in the chair again. "Anyway, I'd just as soon give Mr. Shaw a wide berth. I don't think he wants me on that island either. Couldn't someone else go with Al?"

Hands behind his head, Elmore leaned back in his chair. "Most of the other guys on the team have families. You and Al are single. It won't matter if you're not home for a few weeks."

"It'll matter to me," Tim muttered.

Lieutenant Elmore leaned forward, his eyes narrowed at him. "Gosh, I'm sorry, Sullivan," he said, his tone dripping with sarcasm. "Is this inconveniencing you in any way? Maybe we should draft a letter to Rembrandt and tell him to stop murdering women, because it's kind of putting a crimp in your lifestyle."

He reached for his coffee mug, and sipped his coffee. "Shit, cold," he grunted. He gave Tim a weary sidelong glance and shook his head. "Y'know, you're smarter than most of the other guys around here. You have more on the ball. All the reports you've turned in have been fine, well written, very detailed. You're a great desk-jockey, Sullivan. They told me that about you when you were assigned to this task force. They also warned me that you're a quirky son of a bitch, very aloof, not a team player. You're a snob, Sullivan. You never hang out with the others. You could learn a lot from them too. But you don't want to go the extra mile."

"Excuse me, Lieutenant," Tim said. "But from the minute I clock in every morning until I leave, I'm on the phone or digging through mail with all these leads—most of them crackpots. Then I'm writing up reports at home—usually past midnight. I don't exactly have a lot of time to hang out with the guys and bullshit."

"Well, then," Elmore said, stone-faced. "This babysitting job on a quiet, little island is just the break you need, isn't it?" He nodded at the timetable in the younger cop's hand. "The last ferry for Deception is at eight-fifty P.M."

"Are you okay there, Claire? I can carry you, if you want."

"Oh, how gallant!" she said, with a little laugh. "No, I'm all right. But thank you, Walt."

Claire stepped down from the pier onto Walter Binns's Chris-Craft yacht. Harlan followed with the suitcases.

Harlan had used a company vehicle to pick up Claire at the hospital. Chemtech had three cars at the Anacortes dock for business use on the mainland. As the chemical plant's manager, Harlan got away with utilizing the cars for personal errands.

Harlan's best friend, Walter Binns, had volunteered to take them home on his boat. Walter had also put in several years at Chemtech, but he'd retired early after inheriting a quarter of a million dollars from his father. There was another inheritance—sixty thousand dollars—when Walter's wife, Tracy, died. She'd been best friends with Harlan's first wife, Angela. They'd died together in an auto accident, driving home from a sorority sister's wedding in Portland.

Apparently, the whole gang had attended the wedding: Ron and Linda, Harlan and Angela, and Walter and Tracy. Four of them had flown down, but Walt and Tracy had driven to Portland in the merlot Mazda Miata convertible he'd just given Tracy for her thirty-fourth birthday. After the wedding, Tracy and Angela had decided to stay on an extra day and drive back together. They'd never even made it out of Oregon. With Tracy at the wheel, they'd slammed into the back of a Pepsi truck on the Interstate.

The way Claire heard it, Linda Castle looked after both widowers for several months, taking on their household chores and cooking for them. Claire imagined Harlan and Walter choking on Linda's godawful casseroles. There was still a magnet on Harlan's refrigerator, showing a cat dangling from a rope ladder, and it said, *"Hang in There!"* That was something from Linda—along with *"Footprints in the Sand,"* which she'd copied on parchment paper with a calligraphy pen, then framed. Never mind the misspellings *("That was when I caried you . . ."),* it was still hanging in Harlan's breakfast nook. In fact, when she first moved into Harlan's house, Claire felt as if she were taking over Linda's kitchen, not Angela's.

She figured Linda absolutely relished playing part-time wife to Harlan and Walt. After all, both widowers were very handsome men she'd known most of her life: Harlan with his chiseled features, and salt and pepper hair; and Walt, lean, and still boyishly cute with curly brown hair, brown eyes, and a endearingly crooked smile. And there was Linda, married to a guy who looked like Bob of Bob's Big Boy.

Linda still had a key to Walt's house, and insisted that he come over to dinner at least once a week. Perhaps that was why Walt spent so much of his time sailing, or working with The Guardians, a local civic men's group that did good deeds for the community.

Ron was also a Guardian. Harlan did work for them too, but he wasn't an official Guardian yet. They helped establish parks on the island, coached little leagues, oversaw teen centers and art fairs, and provided funding for local families who had fallen on hard times. The Guardians threw a pancake breakfast for the community every other month.

When Claire had first come to the island, she'd hoped to start painting again. She'd imagined selling her work at the harbor art fairs and craft shows. She'd also been very optimistic about Brian turning his life around. The Guardians sponsored all those activities for local teenagers: whale-watching expeditions, kayaking, camping, and sports activities. With Harlan as a father-figure role model, and The Guardians keeping Brian busy, Claire had hoped her son would stay out of trouble on Deception Island.

Now, as she boarded Walt's yacht to sail back there, she felt such an aching emptiness inside her. Deception Island was 34.9 square miles, with a population of 3,100. If Brian was on the island, someone would have spotted him. Claire was heading home—to what seemed like an empty nest.

The smell of fish and salt water filled the air, and gulls swarmed overhead. Claire settled below in the cabin. At Walt's urging, she sat with her feet up on the built-in sofa. He set her bags in the bedroom. Up on the deck, Harlan was an adept first mate, untying the mooring lines and getting the boat ready.

Before going topside to join his friend, Walt paused at the step-ladder stairs to the deck. "I'm sorry I didn't visit you in the hospital," he said. "I wanted to come, but Harlan said you weren't up to having visitors. Did Linda bring you the flowers I gave her?"

Claire nodded. "Yes, thanks, Walt. You're very sweet."

And he was, staring back at her with those brown eyes and that sheepish look. Claire wondered if he would be a good match for Tess. In that Irish knit sweater he wore, he could have passed as a Kennedy.

Walt sighed. "I was so sorry to hear about the mugging. I hope they get the guy."

She grimaced a bit. "Um, Walt, I guess they didn't tell you. They should have though. You're Harlan's best friend."

He squinted at her. "Tell me what?"

"I wasn't mugged. That's just a story they've been giving everyone on the island. If you've been reading the papers or watching the news on TV, you might know who 'Jane Doe' is."

"You mean that woman who was almost . . ." He trailed off. "The one Rembrandt—"

"Yes," Claire said, nodding. "I'm that woman. I'm 'Jane Doe.' "

Wide-eyed, Walt numbly stared at her.

"I'm sorry," she whispered. "I thought Harlan would have told you."

"Tell him what?" Harlan asked, stepping down from the deck. "We're ready to set sail, folks."

For a moment, no one said anything.

Claire gazed up at him. "Why did you give Walt that stupid cover story? Of all people, why didn't you tell him the truth?"

Harlan seemed embarrassed. Walt just shook his head at him, then turned to Claire again. "I'm really sorry about what you've been through," he murmured. "I—I don't know what to say."

"It's all right," she whispered. "I'm okay now."

He nodded, then brushed past Harlan on the steps.

Harlan touched his shoulder. "Walt, listen, Linda and I were gonna let you know. We—"

Walt didn't even look at him. He continued up to the deck.

Harlan frowned at Claire. "Thanks a lot," he muttered. "I was going to tell him the truth, you know. Eventually."

"Well, why didn't you?" she retorted. "He's your best friend, for God's sakes."

Harlan just sighed, then retreated up the steps.

A few moments later, Claire felt the boat tip and sway a little. They were pulling away from the dock.

She curled up on the couch. She couldn't fathom why Linda and Harlan had kept Walt in the dark about what had really happened to her.

Once again, Claire wondered what horrible thing they were covering up with all their cover stories.

She felt the yacht slow down, and knew they were approaching Deception.

Claire climbed up to the deck, where she saw Walt at the helm. Harlan stood at his side, a hand on his shoulder. He was murmuring something to him. Walt didn't seem too happy, but he was nodding.

Claire couldn't hear them past the boat's motor and the rushing water. It was cold up on deck, and her chestnut brown hair fluttered in the wind. She turned up the collar of her jacket. Sitting near the edge of the boat, Claire gazed out at the island, its hills covered with trees—so many of them vibrant with red, orange, and yellow leaves. Most of the island was forest.

Deception was one of the many San Juan Islands. Looking at the islands on a map, Claire always thought they resembled dozens of stepping-stones across the Strait of Juan de Fuca—from the peninsula off mainland Washington state to Vancouver Island. She remembered her first ferry ride there, and Harlan telling her about his hometown.

He'd grown up in Platt, the commercial and residential area along the south coast of the island. To the north was Alliance, a fifteen-minute drive through forests, or twenty-five minutes by coastal road. That was the location of Chemtech's large chemical plant and the industrial harbor. Nothing else was there, except for a few trailer homes, a gas station, and the Two Squares Diner, a dive, open only for breakfast and lunch. Harlan had stopped eating there after finding what he suspected was a pubic hair in his fried-egg sandwich.

In contrast, the south end offered a beautiful harbor, quaint shops, a couple of restaurants, parks with breathtaking views, B&Bs, two churches, one minimall, a bowling alley, and a grade school.

There were many retired couples on the island, along with weekend and summer residents, who owned cabins in the woods and on the beach. After the chemical plant, tourism (especially in the summer) and fishing were the other big industries on Deception Island.

"It's the kind of place where no one locks their doors at night," Harlan had told her.

Deception had one sheriff and two deputies. Ferry service

ran three times a day during the week and twice daily on weekends. Charter boats were also available.

Claire remembered trying to entice Brian with the news that he wouldn't be catching a bus to school on Deception. He would be catching a charter boat to Anacortes, where the high school students attended classes. After a while, the novelty wore off. On occasion, he'd miss the charter and have to wait for a ferry, then be late for school. Sometimes, he'd miss the last ferry home, and Claire would ask Walter Binns to sail out and pick him up. Walt never seemed to mind, but it irritated the hell out of Harlan.

She watched Walt and Harlan now, as the Chris-Craft approached the south harbor of Deception Island. Harlan took over at the helm.

Walt came and sat down beside her. Claire noticed the occasional strands of gray in his curly brown hair. Still, he looked years younger than Harlan.

"I'm just totally flabbergasted, Claire," he said. "I can't believe everything you've been through. I feel so bad for you."

"Well, I feel bad too," she said. "I hope I didn't screw up things between you and Harlan. I'm sure he had his reasons for not telling you."

Walt shrugged, then rolled up the sleeves of his Irish knit sweater. "Yeah, I guess so," he muttered. "Harlan says you don't remember anything."

She nodded glumly. "That's right. But what bothers me most is that Brian ran away the night before I disappeared, and I have no memory of it. I have no idea where my son is, and it's killing me." She shook her head. "I don't care about these 'Rembrandt' murders or what's happened to me. I just want Brian back."

Claire sighed. "I'm sorry," she muttered. "Listen, Walt. Have you heard anything about what happened to Brian? Anything at all?"

He shook his head. "I'm sorry, Claire. I was in Victoria

the night before you disappeared. I stayed there through the weekend. When I got back, Linda told me about what happened."

Claire frowned. "You mean, she told you that Brian ran away and I was mugged. She was lying about what happened to me. I'm sorry, but I have a feeling she's lying about Brian too."

"Why would she do that?"

"I don't know. I think something horrible happened to him." Claire felt her voice crack. "And no one wants me to know about it. Did Harlan explain why they didn't tell you the truth about me?"

Walt shrugged. "He just said that—for the time being—Linda thought it was best." He glanced toward the coast. "We're heading in," he said, patting Claire's arm. Then he got to his feet and took over the helm for Harlan.

Claire sat alone. "What is that bitch hiding?" she said aloud, but her voice was drowned out by the wind.

Locked inside the trunk of a car, she couldn't see anything. She couldn't scream, because of the duct tape over her mouth. Her hands were tied behind her, but she could kick. So she banged against the trunk's hood with her feet.

They'd come to a stop light. If she pounded loud enough, maybe somebody would hear it, a pedestrian, a driver with his window down, or—maybe, please God—a cop.

One of her sandals flew off, but she kept kicking anyway.

The car lurched forward again. She felt every bump in the road like a jolt, and the tires made a continual, grinding roar. Perspiration covered her body, but she shivered uncontrollably. All she had on—besides the one remaining sandal—were her bra and panties.

Jenny Ackerman was a sophomore at the University of Washington. She had no idea how long they'd been driving, but it seemed like an eternity. Her only hope was another stop—and possibly making enough noise in the trunk so a passerby might notice. Then maybe they'd call the cops or something.

She sensed the car slowing down. Jenny rocked from side to side as they took a couple of turns. The road became bumpier. Her head was swimming. She felt herself gagging from motion sickness. If she threw up, she truly would choke to death. She told herself to just keep breathing.

They started over a gravel road. She heard the pebbles crunching under the tires, and bouncing against the bottom of the car. She tried to brace her body against the side of the trunk to keep from jostling back and forth, but it was impossible. There must have been a dozen curves in the road, one right after another. They seemed to be speeding up instead of slowing down. The pebbles deflecting off the bottom of the car sounded like a hail storm.

Then the car came to a sudden, screeching halt. For a moment, her heart seemed to stop as well. She didn't hear any other traffic. Along with the silence, she became aware of the smell, a strong garbage stench that began to fill her nostrils. Again, she had to fight the impulse to gag.

The trunk's hood popped open. Only for a second did the cold air feel good against her near-naked, sweaty body. Only for a second did she see someone hovering over her. Then all at once, they put a sack over head. Maybe it was a pillow case, she wasn't sure. At least it let in a little light. They grabbed her arms, and pulled her out of the trunk. "Watch her head," one of them muttered.

Jenny didn't struggle. But she stumbled a bit when they set her on her feet again. Somebody slapped her on the butt, not a gentle slap either. It stung. Jenny felt one of them grab her ankle. Her whole body tensed—until she realized they were merely putting her sandal back on for her.

The rancid smell was overpowering—like rotten fruit or sour milk, or both.

One of them had a boom box, and "My Sharona" was blasting over it. They led Jenny down a garbage-laden hill. She was trembling. Goose bumps covered her near-naked body. As they continued down the path, the stench got stronger.

Her head still shrouded in the sack, Jenny kept stumbling, but they held onto her. Then they stopped. The pulsating music abruptly ended.

"Kneel down," someone whispered.

Trembling, she obeyed. Her bare knees hit the cold dirt.

"You're a worthless slut," one of them said.

If the duct tape weren't plastered across her mouth, Jenny would have told her future "sister" to go to hell. At this point, she didn't want to join their stupid, tight-ass, white-bread sorority.

She could have choked to death in the trunk of their stinking car. And oh, if she had, it would have been a great big tragedy—for about a week. The school would talk about how they should outlaw these hazings—until next year's hell night, when a new crop of pledges would get theirs.

"Is that a raccoon over there or a cat?" one of her sisters asked. "I can't tell."

Someone shushed her. Somebody else giggled.

One of them tugged at her wrists, untying the rope. Her hands were free.

All at once, she heard them running away. There was more giggling. Someone kicked at a can. The sound of footsteps faded.

Standing, Jenny pulled the sack off her head. It was a pillowcase after all. She tore the tape off her mouth, and it hurt like hell. But at last, she could breathe. Even with the foul stench, it felt good to breathe through her mouth again. For lack of anything else to fight the autumn night's chill, she wrapped the pillow case around her shoulders.

Nervously glancing around, Jenny saw she was standing in the bowels of some garbage dump. She looked back over her shoulder—at the path her future sorority sisters had taken her down through the mounds of garbage. She couldn't see them up at the top of the trail, no sign of the car either. But if they'd really driven off, she would have heard the car doors shut and the motor start. She had to keep telling herself that. She wasn't alone.

And she wasn't. In the moonlight, she could see parts of the ground were moving. Jenny cringed. She had rats to keep her company.

Clutching the pillowcase around her shoulders, she started up the trail. She couldn't stop trembling. Because of the full moon, she couldn't help noticing some of the things people had thrown away: a broken dinette chair, a huge teddy bear loosing its insides, a computer monitor, an old cash register, a bathroom scale. All these things stood out among the piles of garbage.

Then Jenny saw something that made her stop in her tracks.

A rat scurried across her path. "Oh, shit," she murmured.

Frozen, she followed it with her gaze. The slimy rodent scaled a big trash bag, then moved across the handle of a broken vacuum cleaner. It paused on top of some unidentifiable thing in a plastic bag, poking out amid the other refuse.

"Oh, my God," Jenny whispered.

That thing in the bag was staring back at her.

Chapter 12

Tim Sullivan was in hell.

He and Al Sparling drove together the eighty miles to Anacortes, where they caught the last ferry for Deception Island. Al had driven—and talked—all the way. He'd bragged about some of the more important cases he'd helped solve. To hear him tell it, he was a regular *Dirty Harry.* He'd also recalled his experiences on several different stakeouts, one of them requiring him and his police buddy to hide out and keep surveillance in their parked car for seventy-two straight hours.

And he didn't kill you? Tim had wanted to ask.

At fifty-three, Al was almost twenty years older than Tim. Perhaps that was why he spoke to him in a condescending, I'm-the-voice-of-authority manner. Tim was somewhat reluctant to take life lessons from a slightly dumpy guy with a Grecian Formula comb-over and a clip-on tie.

Tim Sullivan didn't know if he could survive the next few days—maybe even weeks—on this tiny island with Al Sparling.

Boarding the ferry to Deception, Al announced that once they got to the island, "I think I'll find myself a bar where the beer is warm and the women are cold."

He'd made the same joke when climbing into the car, back in Seattle. Tim managed to work up a second curtesy chuckle for the recycled quip, and all the time, he kept thinking, *God, just kill me now.*

During the ferry ride, Al took it upon himself to tell Tim what was wrong with him. The probably-justified accusation, *not a team player* came up again. Al said he was kind of a snob, really. Why didn't he ever want to hang out with the guys after work? They were a swell bunch of Joes. Why wasn't he more sociable? Did he have a second job? It seemed like he had some kind of other secret life.

Al Sparling's questions hit too close to home for Tim, who explained that he didn't mean to come off as antisocial. "I've just been busy lately," he said. "In fact, I still have a couple of reports to write up tonight."

"Well, you can do that after we have a drink or two," Al replied. "We need to talk over this case."

We couldn't have talked it over some time during the last two grueling hours? Tim wanted to ask.

They checked into The Whale Watcher Inn, an L-shaped row of twenty connected, cabin-style units off Platt's Main Street. About two dozen wind-wheelies on poles were planted outside the lobby: sailors, whose arms twirled; gulls with flapping wings; flying fish around a whale; and other caricatures. The small lobby had been decorated with a beach-nautical theme in mind: lamps made out of ship equipment, a fishing net on the wall—complete with starfish, seahorses, and shells, and a sofa with an anchor design on it. Off the lobby was a cozy bar called The Landlubber.

The desk clerk was a quiet, very serious twelve-year-old boy. The kid looked like he knew what he was doing as he checked them in. But he didn't seem to understood when Al mentioned to him that he wanted to check out The Landlubber, for *"some warm beer and cold women."*

Tim had one drink with him. Al explained that they wouldn't be on an actual stakeout on Deception Island. "It's more a babysitting job," he said, nibbling on peanuts and pretzels from a dish on the bar. "We're letting our presence be known here to make Mr. and Mrs. Shaw feel more secure. Tomorrow morning, we'll introduce ourselves to the local cops, then we'll drive over to the Shaws and introduce ourselves to them."

Frowning, Tim nodded. "Yeah, well, he and I have already met."

Once he retreated to his room, Tim closed the drapes and started to work the combination on his briefcase. He'd told Al he had to write up some reports tonight.

But that was a lie.

Al Sparling knocked on his door at two o'clock in the morning. The lights were on in Tim's room, and he was dressed when he opened the door. Al, who had thrown a jacket over his T-shirt and undershorts, looked surprised. "I thought you'd be asleep," he said, still standing in the doorway. "Were you out?"

"No, I was just working on my reports," Tim Sullivan lied.

Al stepped into the room, and glanced at the closed briefcase on top of the powder-blue painted table. All the furniture in the room had been painted the same shade of blue, then lacquered. The carpet was an ugly brown shag. A brown and blue paisley comforter covered the bed, and some bad original art—seascapes and boats—hung on the walls.

"C'mon in," Tim said. Walking over to the table, he locked his briefcase, then set it upright on the floor. "What's going on?"

"Rembrandt got another one," Al announced. "Elmore just called with the news."

Tim slowly shook his head. He sat down at the table. "Where did he abduct her?"

"No, he's already finished with this one," Al said grimly. "Some sorority girl found her in a garbage dump in North Seattle. A bunch of them were there for a hazing. Same MO:

the plastic bag over the head, and the makeup job. This one's throat was slit. She's a Jane Doe right now, unidentified: Caucasian female, approximately thirty years old. Only one distinguishing mark so far, because the body's decomposed. The medical examiner is having a look at her. He thinks she's been dead about two weeks."

"Two weeks?" Tim murmured. "Claire Shaw was left for dead two weeks ago."

Al nodded, then plopped down in the chair across from him. "Yeah, Rembrandt must have been a very busy boy." His fingers drummed on the tabletop. "Anyway, here's the thing Elmore wanted to know. The one distinguishing mark they got on her so far is a retainer with two fake front teeth. Didn't you file a report on a missing person about a week or ten days ago? It was one of those possibly Rembrandt-related cases you always throw his way. Elmore remembers the fake front teeth. Some broad, who was stepping out on her husband, disappeared after meeting with her boyfriend in a downtown Seattle hotel. Elmore said you might remember."

He pointed to Tim's briefcase. "You probably have the report in there. Let's have a look."

"No, it's not in there," Tim said quickly. "Elmore has the report. It's already submitted. I remember, it's from last week. The woman's name was—um, Terrianne Something . . . Terrianne Langley, that's it. She's from Issaquah. Her husband reported her missing, then a friend of hers confessed that Terrianne had been spending the weekend with a married boyfriend."

Al Sparling grabbed a pen and hotel stationary from a plastic display holder on the desk. He started jotting down notes.

"The woman-friend only knew the married guy's first name: Gary or George, I'm not sure, but it's in the report. The friend said Terrianne and this guy were supposed to check into The Westhill Towers on Saturday. The part about Terrianne's fake teeth was in the husband's description. We have a photo of her on file too. If Lieutenant Elmore can't find the hard copy I gave him, he can get it from my computer. It's under my Missing Persons header, then her name, *Langley, Terrianne*. Missing Persons might have a follow-up, but I don't have one. Elmore didn't request it."

"Good boy." Al stood up and glanced at his notes. *"Terrianne Langley.* I'll pass it on. And don't worry about not having any follow-up. There'll be one now."

He headed for the door. "Get some sleep, hotshot. We're gonna have a long day tomorrow."

Claire Shaw walked to the end of the driveway with her stepdaughter, Tiffany. There was a light morning drizzle, and she held an open umbrella over the six-year-old. Claire wore a trench coat over her black sweater and jeans. She didn't mind the rain. It felt good to be outside again. She tilted her head back to feel the cool mist against her face. She actually smiled for a moment.

Then she remembered Brian's empty bedroom, and the smile ran away from her face. His room was in the lower tier of their split level home—just off the TV/recreation area and down the hall from Harlan's work space and the laundry room. She'd snuck down there late last night, hoping to find something that might indicate where he'd gone. She'd discovered a couple of *Playboy*s in the bottom of his desk drawer, but nothing else. However, she noticed some of his regular "knock-around" clothes—along with the Simpsons T-shirt and plaid Joe Boxer undershorts he religiously wore to bed every night—were missing. So was the duffle bag he'd always packed when spending the night at a friend's house. She had to wonder if it was true. Had he really run away?

Brian's bedroom walls were adorned with posters of rock groups, cartoons from *South Park,* a couple of road signs he'd swiped, and some family photos with his father. Harlan wasn't in any of the pictures. The room still smelled a little like Brian. Curling up on his bed and hugging his pillow, Claire sobbed uncontrollably. She had an awful feeling that her son would never occupy this room again.

It had been the only time she'd allowed herself to break down last night. For the rest of the evening, she acted happy to be back. Tiffany had painted a *"Welcome Home"* sign that she'd taped to the front door with some balloons. And Linda Castle had dropped off one of her casseroles that morning—something with pork and a Frito-crumb crust. There was a note with cooking instructions, and a P.S.: *"A good friend is hard to get rid of. Affectionately, Linda."* They'd ordered pizza.

Harlan had been in a festive mood. He'd downed four Bud Lites instead of his usual one-beer-a-night, then fell asleep in his chair in front of the TV. Claire had helped him up to bed, and received a sleepy good night kiss.

He'd apologized this morning for not being more "romantic" her first night back. In truth, Claire hadn't been in a very sexy mood anyway. She was still putting greasy ointment on the ugly wound between her breasts. Besides, Harlan seemed like a stranger to her.

Tiffany had clung to her most of last night. In turn, Claire doted on her. This morning, she'd cooked her pancakes for breakfast, and packed Tiffany's favorite lunch, Spaghetti-O's in a thermos.

They waited at the end of the driveway for the school bus. The house was near the end of a winding cul de sac. The backyard stopped at the edge of a forest. Tall bushes and shrubs along both sides of the front yard isolated them from their neighbors. Across the street was a large house that was still under construction after a year. There had been a legal dispute between the architect and the construction company. The unfinished shell of a house was roped off with yellow police tape. Harlan considered it an eyesore.

"Your raincoat isn't zipped up, honey," Claire said, hovering over Tiffany with the umbrella.

Harlan's daughter handed Claire her school book and

lunch box, then worked the zipper to her coat. She was a cute little girl, with dimples, beautiful blue eyes, and long, slightly frizzy blond hair. "Will you be home when I get back?" she asked.

"I sure will," Claire assured her. "I'm not going anywhere today."

She returned the books and lunch box to Tiffany, then glanced up the cul de sac. "Here's your bus, honey. Have a good day, okay?" She bent down and kissed Tiffany on the cheek.

The bus came to stop in front of their driveway, and the door whooshed open.

Tiffany paused and stared up at Claire. "Will Brian be home when I get back?" she asked.

Claire tried to smile. "I hope so, sweetheart. I hope so."

From the first floor window of the unfinished shell of a house, he watched Claire Shaw. She stood across the street, waving to her stepdaughter. After the bus pulled away, she folded up the umbrella, then wiped her eyes. He couldn't tell for sure, but it looked like she was crying.

He'd always thought it strange how—after finishing with that woman from the hotel gym—he'd stuck her body in a dumpster in Seattle, then they'd found "Jane Doe" in a Bellingham junkyard, ninety miles away.

Until a couple of days ago, he hadn't known he had a copycat. He'd wasted so many days and nights, sneaking around that hospital, trying to learn the identity of a woman—and all the while, he'd never even touched her. Someone else had left Claire Shaw in that Bellingham junkyard. Someone else had tried to kill her, and botched it.

How much was this copycat getting right? Obviously the garbage-dump "resting spot" of his own second victim, Barbara Tuttle, had inspired his imitator to place Claire Shaw in that Bellingham junkyard. But did she have a beauty mark on her cheek? Was her hair done the right way? Did she look pretty—or overly made-up and grotesque?

What bothered him most about this copycat was his sloppiness. People were attributing the bungled attempt on Claire Shaw's life to Rembrandt.

He wanted to show this copycat how to get it right.

Last evening, from this very spot in the half-completed house, he'd glimpsed someone else skulking outside the Shaws' split-level home. Even under the full moon, his copycat managed to remain in the shadows, lurking in the bushes and peeking in the windows. Obviously, his imitator needed to finish the job on Claire, before she remembered him.

He wondered if his copycat was the competitive type. Because now he wanted Claire for himself. The more time he spent watching Claire Shaw, the more it seemed like a courtship.

Across the way at the end of the drive, she pulled a handkerchief from her coat pocket, then blew her nose. Then apparently something caught her eye on the construction site. For a moment, she seemed to stare directly back at him.

He didn't move.

Claire tipped her head back and let the drizzling rain kiss her face.

She looked so pretty.

He watched Claire start back toward the house, and he thought about how he could make her even prettier.

The way Tim understood it, he and Al were on Deception Island as a courtesy to the Shaws. They would provide extra security and conduct any further investigations with locals in the area if deemed necessary. It would have taken Tim twenty seconds to explain this to Sheriff Klauser, a bony, meek-looking, middle-aged man with glasses and thinning gray-brown hair.

Al managed to stretch out their meeting at the police station to two and a half hours. He was oblivious to the fact that—after forty-five minutes—the soft-spoken sheriff appeared utterly annoyed with him. Tim counted three times when the sheriff started to say, *"Well, I've got a lot of work to do today . . ."* And Tim had tried to intervene twice with *"We know you're busy, so we won't take up much more of your time."* Al just kept rambling on about all the stakeouts he'd been on, and he talked more than he probably should have about Terrianne Langley's murder.

"They called me at two o'clock this morning," Al said, leaning back in the chair in the sheriff's office. He had his leg crossed, one ankle resting on the other knee. Between his sock line and trouser cuff was about three inches of exposed hairless white leg.

"They needed our help to identify the victim," he continued. "We had her name on file, and that sped up the ID process for the guys at headquarters. They found the gal last night in a garbage dump in North Seattle, her throat slit. Anyway, they called me again this morning, confirming it. She's number six, Terrianne Langley. Actually number seven, if you count the one who got away. This girl's been dead two weeks. You'll see it on the news tonight."

But Al wasn't all business and police talk, he also asked the sheriff about the best places to eat on Deception. He wanted to know if the Whale Watching Tour was worth checking out. And was there a nice local bar that served free hors d'oeuvres?

"Any place you can recommend?" Al asked. "I'm looking for a spot where the beer is warm, and the women are cold."

Tim just rolled his eyes.

The sheriff finally got a call that he needed to take. Tim figured it was probably a telemarketer. The sheriff put the caller on hold while he bid them a hasty good-bye.

Tim didn't say anything while he and Al drove to the Shaws' house. But he dreaded what was coming.

Al parked in the Shaw's driveway. On their way to the

front door, he mentioned that it was almost noon. "Maybe this Shaw fella will take us out someplace and treat us to lunch."

Tim sighed. "I think when Mr. Shaw sees me, he'll want to treat us to a couple of one-way ferry tickets back to the mainland."

Ignoring him, Al jabbed at the doorbell several times.

"Who's there, please?" a woman called from other side of the door.

"Detectives Sparling and Sullivan," Al said loudly. He pulled out his badge and held it up in front of the peephole. "We called earlier."

Claire Shaw opened the door. She swept her dark brown hair away from her face, and gave Al a cordial smile. But when she locked eyes with Tim, her smile faded.

"We parked in the driveway," Tim said. "Is that all right? Are we blocking anyone?"

"Oh, no, you're fine," she said, opening the door wider. "Please, come on in. My husband's in the bathroom. He'll be right out. Won't you have a seat?"

"How are you feeling, Mrs. Shaw?" Tim asked.

She smiled and nodded. "Still a little weak. But I'm okay, thanks."

She led them into the living room. He and Al sat on the sectional sofa, their backs to the floor-to-ceiling windows looking out to the front yard and the unfinished house across the street. "You don't have any coffee on the stove, do you?" Al asked. "Because I could sure use a cup."

Claire was about to sit in a club chair. "Um, I'll have to make some."

Tim piped up. "Really, you shouldn't bother—"

She locked eyes with him again. "I don't mind. It'll only take a minute." She retreated toward the kitchen.

"Not a bad looking gal," Al whispered. "Not bad at all."

Tim just nodded. She certainly was pretty. She also seemed a bit nervous. From the way she kept glancing at him, he wondered if she might be a little attracted to him. He felt a certain instant connection. Or was it something else? Maybe she hated him as much as her husband did.

He heard her knocking on a door in another part of the house. "Honey, the police are here," she was calling.

Tim heard a response, but the words were muffled. He felt very uncomfortable. He didn't like confrontations, and he knew one was coming as soon as Harlan Shaw saw him sitting on his living room sofa. Tim began to tap his foot.

When Claire returned to the living room, he stood up.

"My husband and the coffee will be with you in a minute," she said. "Please, sit."

But Tim remained on his feet. "Um, Mrs. Shaw. Your husband and I have met already. I don't know if he mentioned it to you. My name's Tim Sullivan. There was kind of a misunderstanding—"

"Hey, hey, pipe down," Al said.

"I just want to clear something up," Tim continued, ignoring his coworker. "Mr. Shaw got some bad information, and he thought I was in charge of security at the hospital—"

"That's enough," Al said forcefully. "She doesn't need to hear this."

"No, *she does* need to hear it," Claire replied, frowning at Al. She turned to Tim. "You had a run-in with my husband, didn't you?"

Tim nodded. "I don't blame him for being angry. But I never had anything to do with security at that hospital . . ."

Tim trailed off as he heard the kettle whistling.

Harlan Shaw stepped out from the kitchen and stopped dead in the foyer. He glared at Tim. The tall, imposing man wore a T-shirt and jeans.

Claire turned toward him. "Harlan, I think there was a big misunderstanding—"

"Kettle's boiling," he grunted. "You gonna get it, honey?"

She patted her husband's shoulder. "Well, simmer down yourself," she muttered, retreating toward the kitchen. "And listen to what Detective Sullivan has to say."

Harlan let out a chuckle and shook his head at Tim. "What do you think you're doing here?"

"Mr. Shaw, I was just telling your wife—"

"That he's sorry," Al interrupted, jumping to his feet.

Harlan gave Al a wary look. "Please tell me this incompetent son of a bitch isn't part of the security team they sent here."

"I'm in charge, Mr. Shaw," Al assured him. "I just brought him along today to apologize to you, and then he'll be on his way."

"Wait a minute," Tim started to say.

"The door's right there, bub," Harlan said.

Al pulled out the car keys, and handed them to Tim. "I'll call you at the hotel, and you can come pick me up—"

"It's okay," Tim sighed. "I'll walk. It's only a mile or so."

Harlan opened the front door—just as Claire came out of the kitchen. "What's going on?" she asked.

"I am sorry, Mr. Shaw," Tim muttered. He nodded. "You too, Mrs. Shaw. Take care." He ducked outside.

"Wait just a second," Tim heard Claire Shaw say. Then the door slammed shut after him.

Tim locked the door to his room, then closed the drapes. The hotel maid had cleaned already, and the place smelled like Windex.

He set his briefcase on the table, worked the combination, and clicked open the lock.

He told himself it was probably the best thing that could have happened. Now he had a little reprieve from Al. For the next hour or so, he could be alone. They'd probably pull him from this assignment on Deception, which was fine. Maybe he could get his life back. Hell, maybe they'd even take him off the Rembrandt case. He could go back to his mundane paper-pushing, desk-jockey job. Or was that too much to hope for?

He'd never asked to be on the Rembrandt task force. He'd

never even had high aspirations to stay in law enforcement. His degree was in graphic design, but jobs there were scarce. At his father's funeral, a friend of his dad's said he could get Tim into the police academy. It was supposed to be a temporary job. He knew computers pretty well, so they stuck him behind a desk. That was okay by him. He'd proven himself above average on the practice range, but had no desire to pack a gun. For the most part, they left him alone, and kept giving him pay increases. He was doing all right, and helped put his kid brother through college. He hadn't planned on sticking with it for ten years. He had other ambitions.

Tim opened his briefcase, and took out a long sheet of cardboard-like paper that had a tissue cover. He pulled back the tissue. Two of four square panels on the cardboard sheet had been filled with detailed drawings. The first panel showed a cartoon of a slick, handsome man wearing a hat and forties-style suit. He was talking with a woman who looked like Veronica Lake. In the bubble caption over his head it said, *"I'M TELLING YOU, LOLA. THAT EVIL PROFESSOR SHRUBB IS OUT TO TAKE OVER THE WORLD! HE HAS TO BE STOPPED!"*

Tim's cartoon, *THE ADVENTURES OF PRIVATE EYE GUY,* ran in *The Seattle Sounder,* a popular weekly. The comic strip had gained a small cult following. Though set in the forties, the exploits of Private Detective Guy Kaplan were full of current social and political parodies. Weekly newspapers in Portland and San Francisco had picked up the comic strip last year. Recently, there was even an independent film producer interested in acquiring movie rights, but nothing ever came of it.

Tim used the nom de plume, Tim Timster, for his comic strip. He was proud of his creation, but kept it secret from his coworkers on the force. He still needed his day job. He couldn't have lived off the money he was making on *Private Eye Guy.* For several years now, he'd managed to do his ho-hum civil servant job, and afterward, he'd go home and work on the comic.

Tim gave Guy Kaplan a better love life than he had himself. Most of Tim's relationships were short-lived. He turned a lot of women off when he told them he was a cop. The ones turned on by that revelation were often disappointed he didn't fit their vision of a gun-toting macho hero. Some women just didn't understand his dedication to a comic strip. His last girlfriend, Charlotte, left him after nearly a year, because he wouldn't abandon *The Adventures of Private Eye Guy* in favor of a steady job with her father's advertising company. It seemed his devotion to the comic strip was constantly being put to the test.

Last month at work, they stuck him on the Rembrandt task force. It wasn't routine. He'd always felt like a phony at the job, but it didn't really matter until now. He couldn't just punch a clock and coast along sorting data. Lives were at stake. They were trying to stop a serial killer.

He kept hoping they'd wise up and fire him. Or maybe that film producer would get in touch with him again—and miracle of miracles—he'd have a movie deal for his comic strip, then he could just quit. He wanted out. He couldn't handle all the responsibility.

He thought about Claire Shaw, and her husband. Hell, he deserved to be booted out of their house. He may not have been the one who screwed up the security at her hospital, but his lack of initiative warranted Harlan Shaw's contempt just the same.

With a sigh, Tim pulled out his drawing pens. He started working on the third panel of his comic strip.

The telephone rang.

"Oh, crap, it's Al already," he muttered.

Tim pulled himself away from the table and grabbed the phone. "Hello?"

"Detective Sullivan?" a woman asked.

"Yes?"

"It's Claire Shaw," she said. "I'm awfully sorry about what happened."

"Well, so am I, Mrs. Shaw. But you shouldn't apologize. It's no one's fault. It's just a misunderstanding. I'm sure Al—um, Detective Sparling explained it all to you and your husband—"

"No, he didn't," she said. "He didn't say anything to clear your name. It would have meant admitting to my husband that he'd been misinformed. My guess is, someone higher up in the chain of command was responsible for hospital security, but they blamed you for whatever went wrong. You have nothing to do with hospital security. Am I right?"

"Well, you're pretty damn close," Tim admitted.

"In other words, they're lying." Tim heard her sigh on the other end of the line. "Detective Sullivan, since I started getting my memory back, that's all I've heard: lies and cover stories. I was told my son ran away the night before I disappeared. Then the next day, I was supposed to have gone shopping with a friend in Seattle and spend the night there. Well, detective, I don't think I'm Mother of the Year or anything. I haven't always been there for my son, but . . ." Her voice cracked a little. "But what kind of mother goes off on a weekend shopping spree in a city a hundred miles from home the day after her only son has run away? What kind of mother does that?"

"Why are you telling me this, Mrs. Shaw?" he asked guardedly.

"Because you're nice," she replied. "When you came into my house and asked how I was feeling, I could tell you really cared. I know it's silly, but you also asked if it was okay to park in the driveway. Shows you're considerate. And you didn't want me to go to any bother making coffee. But your friend couldn't have cared less. He's down in the living room, talking with Harlan right now. I think he expects me to fix him lunch."

Tim couldn't help grinning. He wondered how long it would be before Al used his "warm beer, cold women" line on Harlan Shaw.

"He keeps hinting about how hungry he is," Claire went on. "I just got out of the hospital yesterday. I've been gone three weeks. There's nothing in the house. I wonder if he likes pork and Fritos. There's this casserole I want to get rid of."

"It's worth a shot," Tim said, shrugging. "Does he know you're talking to me right now?"

"Oh, God, no. Neither does Harlan."

"How did you know to call me here?" he asked.

"Your friend said he'd call you at the hotel, and there's only one hotel in town." She paused. "So do you think you could help me?"

"Help you—how, Mrs. Shaw?"

"I don't think my son ran away, Detective Sullivan. I'm pretty sure something else happened to him and no one wants to tell me the truth. This friend I supposedly went shopping with, her name is Linda Castle. I think she's lying. I wouldn't have gone off on a weekend shopping spree while my son was missing."

"Why haven't you said anything to the police about this?" he asked.

"You're the police, aren't you?" she asked.

Tim didn't answer her.

"I think I can trust you," she continued. "I felt it the moment I met you. Won't you please help me, detective?"

He hesitated. "I don't know, Mrs. Shaw. I may get pulled off this island tonight."

"But if you stay on, could you ask around for me? My son's name is Brian. Brian Ferguson. His father died a few years back. He didn't take Harlan's name. In fact, he didn't take to Harlan. Anyway, could you look into it for me, Detective Sullivan? Please? No one will tell me the truth."

"Well, I—" He glanced at the unfinished comic strip on the table, then sighed. "I'll need some more information from you. Then I'll see what I find out, Mrs. Shaw."

"Thanks," she said. "Call me Claire, okay?"

"Claire," he said into the phone.

Chapter 13

"Well, I'm on a tight schedule right now," Dottie Herrmann said, opening her front door for him. She let out a labored sigh as Tim stepped into the foyer.

"I promise not to take up much of your time, Mrs. Herrmann," Tim said.

Dottie Herrmann was in her forties, with short, auburn hair, careworn blue eyes, and a trim figure. She was pale, and rather pretty, despite the crow's feet around her eyes and laugh-lines around the mouth—which, at the moment, appeared more like frown lines. She wore jeans and a blue sweatshirt.

Tim followed her to the kitchen, which was incorporated with the breakfast nook and a large family room. The kitchen counter and sink divided the areas. As Mrs. Herrmann cleared a couple of plates off the breakfast table, Tim noticed her hands were shaking.

"Excuse the mess," she said, moving to the sink. She put on rubber gloves, and turned on the water. "It's been crazy today. I should have had these dishes done hours ago. I really wish you would have phoned ahead of time, detective." She started washing the dishes. "You said you're from Seattle?"

"That's right," he replied, sitting at the table, which still had three place mats on it. Behind him was a breakfront cabinet with plates on display—and one shelf full of framed family photos. "My partner and I are here investigating what happened to Claire Shaw," Tim explained. "I was talking with Mrs. Shaw today. I understand her son, Brian, ran away the day before she was abducted in Seattle. And on that same day, your son, Derek, suddenly left for Europe."

"It wasn't so sudden," she said, not looking up from the sink.

"Well, before walking over here from my hotel, I called the principal at Derek's high school in Anacortes. He said no one told them about Derek's backpacking trip to Europe until *after* he'd left. He said they'd marked Derek absent for three days before the school secretary called you and—"

"Yes, yes," she cut in. "There was a misunderstanding, but we cleared it up. What does any of this have to do with Claire Shaw?"

"Brian and Derek were best friends. Is that correct?"

"They knew each other," she allowed, scrubbing away at a pot.

"If Brian was planning to run away, do you suppose he might have said something to Derek?"

"I wouldn't know."

"And now, Derek is incommunicado for the next few weeks," he said.

"That's right," she sighed. "You know, I've already had this conversation with Claire Shaw. I'm sorry about what happened to her in Seattle, and I'm sorry her son ran away. But there's nothing I can do about it. I hope—for Claire's sake—that Brian comes home. He's run away before, and he's always come back."

"Has Derek ever run away?" Tim asked.

She stopped her work for a moment, but kept staring down at the sink. "I don't see how that can be Claire Shaw's or anyone else's business," she said finally. She rinsed out some glasses.

Tim glanced at the framed photos on the breakfront. There were pictures of Dottie Herrmann and her husband, and apparently, a daughter, who looked about twelve years old in the most recent snapshot.

Getting to his feet, Tim picked up the picture of a dark-haired, slightly smarmy-looking young man. It was a high school portrait. With the framed photo in his hand, Tim moved toward the sink. "Is this Derek?" he asked.

Dottie Herrmann barely glimpsed at the photograph—before her gaze met Tim's. Then she quickly looked down at the sink again. "Yes, that's Derek," she murmured, shutting off the water.

Tim noticed on the kitchen counter, beneath the telephone on the wall, the Herrmanns had an office "In" box. It was full of bills and scraps of paper. Tim noticed what was on top of the pile. He set Derek's picture down on the counter, and stared at a form receipt from San Juan Island Charities Pick Up Service.

"THANK YOU FOR YOUR DONATION," it said across the top of the yellow slip. From where he stood, Tim couldn't read the smaller print, but there was a blank after the boldly printed line: *"YOUR ITEMS WERE PICKED UP ON . . ."* The date filled in was from earlier in the week. Someone had also scribbled at the bottom of the receipt: *"Six bags—Clothing."*

"Would you please put my son's picture back where it was," Dottie Herrmann said. She peeled off the rubber gloves.

Tim returned the frame to its spot on the breakfront shelf. "Do you know if Derek kept a journal, a diary?"

"No, but if he did keep one, I think he would have brought it to Europe with him, don't you?" A tiny smile flickered across Dottie Herrmann's face for a second. Tim could tell she was proud of her answer.

"Well, Brian Ferguson kept a journal," he lied. He had no idea whether or not Claire's son actually had a diary. "It's a spiral notebook," he went on. "Brian told his mother he left it here. He hid it under the carpet in your son's bedroom. Do you mind if I have a look?"

Mrs. Herrmann stared back at him. She hesitated before answering.

"It would be really helpful," Tim continued. "Mrs. Shaw thinks Brian might have written in this journal something about his plans to run away."

"Well, I'm terribly busy right now." She grabbed a sponge and wiped the counter. "I'll look for the diary later. I'll call you if I find it."

"It'll take less time with both of us looking," Tim suggested. "Couldn't we look now? It'll only take a minute."

Drying off her hands, Dottie frowned at Tim. "His room's upstairs."

Tim followed her up to the second floor.

The walls were bare in Derek Herrmann's room. Tim could see discoloration outlines where posters and pictures had once hung. Three moving boxes sat in the corner, on the floor. No doubt, they contained items plucked off the near-empty bookcases.

"We—we're about to paint in here," Dottie explained.

The closet door was open. Tim noticed some shoe boxes on the shelf, and about a dozen dresses on hangers. Nothing else.

"Pretty interesting wardrobe for a teenage boy," Tim observed.

"Those are mine," Mrs. Herrmann snapped. "Derek took most of his clothes to Europe with him. And I needed the closet space."

"That must be one big backpack he's lugging around," Tim said. "Looks like he didn't leave anything behind."

Tim knew what had happened to Derek's clothes. They'd been given away to charity. The Herrmanns weren't expecting their son to come back—ever.

Dottie Herrmann closed the closet door. "Didn't you want to look under the carpet?" she asked.

Tim went through the motions of checking along the

baseboards for loose spots in the beige carpet. He found some areas where he could lift the carpet edge; but nothing was hidden there. He didn't expect anything.

"Have you seen enough?" Mrs. Herrmann asked. "I don't mean to be rude, but you've already taken up too much of my time, detective."

"I apologize," Tim said, dusting off his hands as he headed out of Derek's bedroom. "Thank you for your patience, Mrs. Herrmann. I appreciate your cooperation."

Dottie Herrmann led Tim down the stairs to her front door, then she opened it for him.

Outside, a teenage girl came up the walkway, carrying a graffiti-covered canvas book bag. In the collection of family photos on the breakfront, Derek's younger sister didn't have a magenta streak in her brown hair and heavy, gothic makeup around her eyes. But Tim still recognized her. He guessed she was about thirteen. She wore a ratty black pullover and jeans.

Tim hesitated on the front stoop. Behind him, Mrs. Herrmann still held open the screen door.

Derek's sister stopped in her tracks. She squinted at Tim, and then at her mother.

"Hi, I'm Tim Sullivan," he said to the girl. "I'm a cop—from Seattle. You're Derek's sister, aren't you?"

A look of horror swept over the girl's face. She took a step back.

"Amy, dear," Mrs. Herrmann said. "Mr. Sullivan was here about Brian. Mrs. Shaw sent him. He's just leaving."

Amy Herrmann let out a sigh and nodded. Tim wondered why she seemed so relieved.

He managed to smile at her. "You don't know what happened to Brian, do you, Amy?"

She quickly shook her head. Brushing past him, she hurried into the house. The screen door shut behind her.

Tim glanced over his shoulder. He could still see them on the other side of the screen door. Mrs. Herrmann gave her daughter a strained, reassuring smile, then said something under her breath. Amy kept shaking her head, then she covered her face with her hands. Mrs. Herrmann put her arms around the girl, and patted her on the back.

When Mrs. Herrmann glanced up, her gaze met Tim's. She stared at him with unveiled contempt. Then she reached over, and shut the door.

According to the San Juan Islands phone book and a map Tim had picked up at the Deception Visitor's Center, it looked like Ron and Linda Castle lived approximately a mile from the Herrmanns.

Tim glanced at his wristwatch: three-forty. He figured Al was probably back at the hotel by now, wondering where the hell he was.

Despite the fifty-five degree temperature, Tim was perspiring. He felt his calves tightening as he walked uphill on the gravelly shoulder of Evergreen Drive. There were no sidewalks. Every few moments, a car whooshed by in one direction or the other. The speed limit was 45 mph on the two-lane highway, which eventually wove through the forest to the north side of the island and the industrial area of Alliance. Trees and shrubs lined both sides of the road. Every quarter of a mile or so, a winding cul de sac branched off the thoroughfare, cozy residential inlets with names like Pirate's Cove Way, Sea Merchant's Lane, and Smuggler's Pass Road.

Linda and Ron Castle lived on Barnacle Way. Tim surmised that the folks living on Barnacle Way were in a higher tax bracket than most of their Deception neighbors. As he walked down the snaky cul de sac, he noticed the manicured, sprawling lawns. The large colonial-style homes looked as if they'd been built in the eighties and nineties. They had spectacular views of the harbor, the water, and the other islands in the distance.

Ron and Linda Castle's two-story, yellow, colonial-style home had an old-fashioned park bench under a Japanese maple tree in their front yard. Two squat gnome figurines stood guard on the stoop to their front door. Tim didn't see a car in the driveway.

As he started up the front walk, an attractive, older Latino woman came around from the back of the house. She had her hair in a bun, and wore khakis and a denim jacket. She stopped halfway down the driveway and stared at Tim.

"Are you Mrs. Castle?" he asked, cutting across the lawn toward her.

"Oh, God no," she said, with a little laugh.

He pulled out his wallet and showed her his badge. "My name's Tim Sullivan. I'm a cop, and I here to—"

"Oh, yeah," she nodded. "You're the good-looking one."

"I beg your pardon?"

"My friend, Sheila, is the housekeeper at The Whale Watcher. She said two cops from Seattle checked in yesterday, and one of them was cute with dark hair and a dimple in his chin."

"Well, thank Sheila for the compliment," he said. "Do you know if Mrs. Castle is home?"

"No, she's at the Platt Gardens Plaza. Today's her day to pitch in, till the soil and become one with nature." The woman said this in such a droll manner, Tim figured she didn't think too much of Linda Castle or her civic activities. She extended her hand. "By the way, I'm her cleaning woman, Yolanda Martinez."

He smiled and shook her hand. "Hi, Yolanda. Are these gardens very far from here?"

"About two and a half miles. Do you need to see her highness about something?"

"Yes, I do." He grinned slyly. "You don't seem overly fond of your employer."

"Actually, she's not so bad." Yolanda glanced toward the street, where a pickup had stopped at the end of the driveway. "Did you walk here? Do you need a ride to the gardens?"

She introduced Tim to her brother-in-law, Virgilio, who was driving the pickup. There was no room up front, so Tim rode in back with a lawn mower, yard equipment, and big plastic bags full of yard waste. They passed through the commercial area down near the harbor, then continued up another hill. The houses weren't as stately as in the Castles' neighborhood: modest cedar bungalows, weather-beaten Cape Cods, and a few ramblers from the fifties.

The pickup pulled into a small parking area near the top of the hill. In one direction, through some trees, Tim could see the water, and the horizon—growing a bit darker as dusk approached.

In the other direction was the park. A sign had been posted by a rock garden entrance:

CITY OF PLATT GARDENS PLAZA
Established In 2002 By The Platt Guardians
For the Enjoyment of the Residents and Visitors
of Deception Island, Washington

Tim climbed off the back of the pickup, then came up to the passenger window and thanked them for the lift.

Rolling her window halfway down, Yolanda nodded at the black BMW in the parking area. "There's the royal coach. She's still here." She smiled at Tim. "So are you paying for the ride?"

"Oh, you—want some money?" he asked, surprised.

"God, no," she said. "I want the dirt. Why do you want to talk with her? Does it have to do with Claire Shaw?"

Tim hesitated, then nodded. "Yes, it does."

"Nice lady, Claire Shaw," Yolanda said. "You know, ever since she disappeared on that shopping trip a couple of weeks ago, things have been pretty damn tense at the Castles' castle."

"What do you mean?"

"Well, I work for them three days a week," Yolanda replied, rolling the car window down even further. "And let me tell you, every one of those days lately, it's been nuts there, just awful. The mister and missus have been so edgy, snapping at each other, snapping at me. They've practically been climbing the walls."

"Well, I'm sure they've been worried about their friend," Tim said.

"That's just the thing," Yolanda whispered. "Last week, when I heard they'd found Mrs. Shaw, I thought old Ron and Linda would chill out a bit. I mean, their friend's okay, time to lighten up, right? But you know something?" She hesitated. "And promise not to quote me, officer."

"Okay, I promise."

"Ever since Claire Shaw was found, things at the Castles' house have only gotten worse. Much worse."

Tim stared at her. "Do you—have any idea why that is?"

Yolanda shook her head. "You're the police detective, Maybe you can find out. Like I say, just don't quote me." She smiled and started rolling up the window. "Good luck, officer."

Then she said something in Spanish to Virgilio, and the pickup began to pull away. Tim watched the truck go down the hill, then disappear around a curve.

"What's the last thing you remember before waking up in the hospital?"

"Oh, God, the doctors asked me that same question so many times, and it never worked. I'm sorry. I can't remember the 'jumping off point.' " Claire shook her head at Dr. Moorehead.

They sat across from each other in his office, which was above a florist just off Main Street. Dr. Linus Moorehead, psychiatrist, had his diplomas displayed—along with a couple of Monet prints—on the sea-foam green walls. There was a fake ficus tree behind his desk, and another by the file cabinet. He'd given Claire a choice where to sit: the cream-colored sofa or one of the two tan club chairs facing each other. She'd chosen a club chair.

The doctors at the hospital had recommended these sessions, and Harlan had scheduled this one before she'd even come home. Linus Moorehead was the only psychiatrist and therapist on the island. Claire had never gone to Dr. Moorehead before. But for a while, at Harlan's urging, they'd sent Brian to him.

Brian had gone to him three times before begging his mother, "Please don't make me go back to that dork. I promise I'll never get into trouble again."

Apparently, in their last session, Dr. Moorehead had given Brian a homework assignment. He'd wanted him to buy a poster board and tape, then cut words and photos from some old magazines. "He wants me to make a collage of my life," Brian had complained. "How bogus is that?"

Moorehead reported to Harlan and Claire that Brian had been *"guarded, hostile, and uncooperative."* The psychiatrist hadn't had much luck with Derek Herrmann either, and the Herrmanns had sent their son to him for three months.

Claire figured Dr. Moorehead wasn't very adept with teenage boys. She'd hoped he would fare better with her, and he wouldn't make her do any collages.

Moorehead certainly had an edge with women. He was in his late thirties, with wavy, sand-colored hair and a goatee. He had a penchant for turtlenecks and tweed jackets, which made him look like a sexy English professor or author.

Sitting across from Claire, he studied her with a slightly pained look. "So you have no memory whatsoever of that time?" he asked. "No fragments or images that you can recall?"

Claire sighed. "One memory keeps coming back to me. I'm with Linda Castle in the front seat of this car, and someone is coming at us from outside. He has a gun. I'm terrified, and Linda's nervous too. She tells me to pray. That's all I can remember."

"Did you talk about this with Linda?"

Claire nodded. "She said it never happened, and I must have dreamt it. But I don't believe her."

"Why not?"

"Because it's the one memory I have, the one real thing that I can hold onto. Everything else seems—manufactured. Linda and Harlan are filling in the blanks, and I don't believe them."

"I'll ask you again, Claire," he said, leaning forward. "Why? What have they done to deserve your mistrust? Is there an incident or time when Linda Castle hasn't been a loyal friend to you? Hasn't Harlan been a good husband?"

Sighing, Claire squirmed in the chair. "I can't explain it. But they're like strangers to me now. I feel so lonely and lost here without my son. I miss him. Believe it or not, I almost wish I were back in the hospital. I made a couple of friends there, another patient, a woman named Tess, and this nurse, Sherita. I could really talk to them. I miss them very much."

"Is there anyone here on the island you feel close to?" he asked.

Claire shrugged. "My stepdaughter, Tiffany."

"I mean, someone you can talk with, someone you can trust."

"There's one person—maybe," Claire replied, glancing down at the tan carpet. She couldn't look at Dr. Moorehead. She didn't want to tell him about Tim Sullivan. She wasn't totally certain she could even rely on the young cop. She'd asked for his help based on a hunch—and a little hope—that he was a decent guy. If he couldn't help her, she'd be all alone.

"Can you tell me about this person, Claire?" the psychiatrist asked.

She bit her lip, then shook her head.

"Why not?" he asked.

Claire crossed her arms in front of her. "I'm sorry," she murmured. "I don't want to jinx it."

There weren't many flowers blooming in the cool of November, but the Platt Gardens Plaza had plenty of interesting plants and trees. Tim was pretty certain Linda Castle had selected the gnome statues, old-fashioned park benches, and bird baths situated just off the brick path winding through the gardens.

He saw a young woman coming out of the greenhouse, and asked where he might find Linda Castle. She pointed to someone kneeling in front of some neatly trimmed hedges. A spade in her gloved hand, the woman had a box of tulip bulbs at her side. She wore a sailor hat with the brim turned down, jeans and a lavender pullover that had *'HOE, HOE, HOE!'* written on the back.

"Mrs. Castle?" Tim said, approaching her from behind.

"Yes?" she replied, not look up from her work.

"I'm Tim Sullivan. I'm a policeman—from Seattle." He had his wallet out to show her his badge, but she didn't turn around.

Linda hesitated for a moment. Then she went back to digging with the spade. "Are you one of the officers they sent over here as insurance—or extra protection, or whatever?"

"Yes, I'm here for whatever," Tim said, putting away his wallet. "I stopped by your house, and ran into your cleaning woman, Yolanda. She said you might be here."

"Tim Sullivan," she mused aloud. "Aren't you the young officer Mr. Shaw had some words with not too long ago? You must be a glutton for punishment to come around here."

Linda finally glanced up over her shoulder to smirk at him. She wiped the sweat off her forehead with the back of her glove.

"That incident with Mr. Shaw was just a misunderstanding," Tim explained, squatting so he was at her eye-level. "It's all cleared up now."

"Well, isn't that nice?" she said, turning away and going back to her gardening.

"Speaking of misunderstandings," Tim continued. "There are some things I don't quite understand about your Seattle shopping trip with Mrs. Shaw two weeks ago. I was hoping you could help out with a detail or two."

Linda sighed. "I've already been through this with you

people—ad nauseam—last week. I can't believe you want me to go over it again."

"Well, this is kind of off the record," Tim said. "We already have the facts. What I'm really after here is your perspective, your honest opinion."

She stopped digging, and gave him a dubious look. "My opinion?"

Nodding, he smiled. "For starters, I was wondering what you really think of Claire's son, Brian."

"He's an obnoxious brat, a delinquent," she replied. "Is that honest enough for you?"

"Yes, thank you," Tim said, numbly staring at her.

"Do you know what he and that worthless friend of his, Derek Herrmann, did one night this summer? Those little bastards broke in here, and stole my French gnome . . ." She pointed to a figurine with her spade. "In its place, those two bastards planted a toilet. Yes, a toilet! They desecrated this beautiful park. And do you know where the police finally found my gnome?"

Trying to keep a straight face, Tim shook his head.

"In the men's room at Lyle's Stop and Sip Gas Station, that's where. I suppose they thought it was very funny."

"Wow, that—that's really awful," Tim managed to say. "I guess you must be glad Derek's off in Europe now. He left rather suddenly, didn't he?"

"Suddenly, but not soon enough." Linda said, turning toward the garden again.

"And now Brian's gone too. I guess your gnomes are safe for a while."

"Is that all you wanted to ask me about, Officer Sullivan?" she asked.

"No, I wanted your opinion on something else too. I really appreciate your honesty so far, Mrs. Castle. Do you—" He hesitated. "Do you think Claire Shaw is a good mother?"

She glanced over her shoulder at him for a moment. "I suppose Claire has tried her best with Brian."

"Don't you think it's a little odd that she'd go out of town on a shopping spree the day after her only son has run away from home?"

Linda's eyes narrowed at him.

"I can't imagine her going away like that," Tim said. "If she was really and truly worried about him, wouldn't she have stayed home?"

"Claire didn't want to take the trip," Linda answered, an edge in her tone. "That's in my statement to the police. I persuaded Claire to go, and I don't feel too good about it, considering what happened to her while we were in Seattle."

Linda tossed the spade in the box of tulip bulbs. "I feel partially responsible for what happened. And I get sick when I think about it too much—or talk about it."

She straightened up and faced him. "How's that for 'honest'?" she asked coolly. "Now, do you have any other questions?"

"Not so much a question as an observation," he said carefully.

Linda pulled at the Velcro on the back of her knee pads, and took them off. "Go on, I'm listening."

"You'll probably see it on the news tonight. They found another victim of the Rembrandt murders. Her name was Terrianne Langley. I submitted a Missing Persons report to my superior about Terrianne last week. They estimate she was abducted around the same time you lost Claire Shaw in the department store."

Linda took off her gardening gloves. "I'm sorry to hear about this—Terrianne person. But I don't understand what any of this has to do with me."

"Terrianne was married," Tim continued. "She was meeting a boyfriend—also married—at the Westhill Towers in Seattle two Saturdays ago. To keep her husband in the dark, Terrianne had a cover story worked out with her best friend . . ."

Linda was shaking her head. "I still don't see how any of this—"

"The cover story was," Tim talked over her, "that Terrianne was joining her friend in Seattle for the weekend, and they were going shopping. Doesn't that strike you as an odd coincidence? The best friend's cover story is almost identical to yours."

She gave him a wary sidelong glance. "You're right, officer. It's an odd coincidence. I don't know this Terrianne woman, and I don't know her friend. Our stories may be somewhat similar, but there's one major difference. The other story was a lie. My story really happened. It's the truth."

Tim didn't say anything, but he smiled and shook his head at her.

"I'm really not sure what you're insinuating," Linda said. "In any event, this conversation is over, Officer Sullivan. I don't want to be *off the record* with you any more." She tossed her gloves and knee pads into the tulip bulb box, then scooped it up. *"For the record,* now I realize how you rubbed Harlan the wrong way. And I totally agree with Harlan's first impression of you. I'll be sure to tell him so. My husband and I are having dinner with Harlan and Claire tonight. In fact, you can bet I'll tell them about this entire conversation."

She swiveled around and started to walk away.

"Even the part where you called Claire's missing son an obnoxious brat and a bastard?" Tim said to her back.

It was a stupid thing to say, but he needed to get at least one dig in. Tim figured it was his last shot. Within the next twenty-four hours, Linda Castle's and Harlan Shaw's complaints would reach the powers that be in Seattle

As he left the Platt Gardens Plaza. Tim figured he hadn't done a damn thing to help Claire Shaw.

All he'd done was insure for himself a one-way passage off the island.

Chapter 14

Tim doodled a cartoon character on his paper place mat. He pretended to listen to Al, seated across from him. Al was chiding him for "almost blowing it" during their visit to the Shaws' house the previous day.

Apparently, Al hadn't gotten a call yet about Tim's disastrous discussion with Linda Castle at the Platt Gardens. Tim figured this was his last day on Deception, and this breakfast, his last meal here.

The morning rush had already quelled at the Fork In The Road Diner. Except for a view of the water from one side of the restaurant, the atmosphere—like the food—was a small step above Denny's quality. The Fork In the Road was named for its location, where Main Street merged with Harbor View Lane. For years, the island's Parks, Roads, and Utilities Committee had turned a blind eye, allowing the restaurant to keep a yellow eight-foot-long fork painted on Main Street, directly in front of the sixties-chic, glass and white-brick, oblong structure.

Tim and Al shared a booth and sipped their coffee. They had just ordered their breakfast.

"You have to learn how to handle people," Al was saying. "You need to use finesse with them. You can't just go in there, half-cocked—like you did yesterday. What you said made the whole task force look bad. Hell, if I hadn't stayed on and chatted it up with Harlan and his missus, they'd probably have your ass transferred back to the mainland by now. You owe me one."

Tim just kept doodling and nodding tiredly. He hadn't told Al about the phone call from Claire Shaw—and his follow-up talks with Dottie Herrmann and Linda Castle. He assumed Claire probably didn't want the older cop in on it. After all, when she'd telephoned him at the hotel asking for help, Al had been sitting in her living room. If she wanted Al involved, she would have told him herself.

Al probably would have dismissed her as paranoid and a bit hysterical. Tim imagined pleading Claire's case to Mr. Warm-Beer-Cold-Women, and it seemed pointless.

"Are you listening to me?" Al asked.

"Yes, Al," Tim said, raising his coffee cup. "I'll try to have more finesse—like you."

Their waitress, Roseann, came to the booth and set their breakfast plates on the table. Al got pancakes and a side of sausage. She placed an order of toast in front of Tim, along with his milk and a bowl of Rice Krispies.

"Excuse me, I didn't order any toast," Tim told her.

"That's the cinnamon toast," Roseann said. "My treat." She smiled at Tim, then patted him on the shoulder. Roseann was in her midforties, and lanky, with short, light-brown hair and cat-eye glasses.

"Well, thanks a lot," Tim said.

"How come I didn't get a freebee?" Al piped up.

"Because you're not as cute as he is, ace," Roseann answered. "Enjoy, officers." She started to turn away.

"Hey, wait a minute," Al said. "What makes you think we're cops?"

Rolling her eyes at him, Roseann leaned against the table. "It's a small island. Word gets around. You guys are from Seattle and you're staying at The Whale Watcher down the street. You're here because Claire Shaw was abducted and shot by that Rembrandt character. I guess you guys are worried he might come after her again. And I don't mind telling you, the idea of him prowling around this island gives me a the heebie-jeebies. I for one am locking my doors and sleeping with a baseball bat by my bed tonight." She tapped the table top a couple of times. "Anyway, eat up. Your breakfast is getting cold." She sauntered away from the table.

"Well, how do you like that?" Al muttered. Then he started wolfing down his pancakes.

Tim was having his second wedge of cinnamon toast when Roseann returned to the table to refill their coffees.

"So—does everybody on the island know about Claire Shaw and Rembrandt?" Tim whispered.

Roseann's mouth twisted up while she pondered his question. "I'd say about twenty-five percent know. By the weekend, it ought to be more like fifty."

"Do you have a minute?" Tim asked. "Or are you really busy?"

"Actually, it's kind of dead," she said. "How can I help you, handsome?"

Tim smiled. "Thanks. You seem to know a lot. What's the general consensus on Claire's son, Brian? I hear he ran away the day before she was abducted."

Roseann nodded. "Yeah, I've heard that too."

"Do you believe it?"

"Well, he's run away before." Roseann put the coffeepot down on their table. "He's had some brushes with the sheriff too. But I never had any trouble with Brian. He's always been a sweetie pie to me. A good tipper too."

"What about his friend, Derek Herrmann?" Tim asked. He ignored Al, who was glaring at him.

"Derek?" She let out an abrupt laugh. "Oh, talk about screwed up. Whenever he stepped into the joint, I used to lock up the cash register. But I'll tell you something about that kid. As much as he's rubbed me the wrong way, I've always kind of felt sorry for him."

"Are you gonna eat?" Al asked, his mouth full.

"In a minute," Tim said distractedly. He didn't take his eyes off Roseann. "Do you really think Derek went on a back-packing trip through Europe? It was pretty sudden, wasn't it?"

Roseann shrugged. "Well, that's the story we got. I guess you're right though. It came out of nowhere. Suddenly, he was gone. No one wants to question it, I guess. Would be like looking a gift horse in the mouth. I know Sheriff Klauser's grateful for the break."

"I gather that," Tim said. "I spoke with Linda Castle yesterday. I don't think she's going to miss him either—or Brian for that matter."

Roseann cracked a smile. "Oh, you spoke with Linda, huh?"

Tim nodded. "She seems very involved in a lot of things with the community. How long has she lived here?"

"Oh, Linda, Harlan, and Walt Binns all go way back. They grew up on this island, then went to college at Western. It's always been up for grabs which one of the two Linda thought she'd end up marrying. For my money, I think she always had it bad for Walt Binns. Have you met him yet?"

"No, not yet," Tim answered.

Hunched over his breakfast, Al wasn't paying attention.

"Nice guy," Roseann said. She glanced around the restaurant for a second, then turned to Tim again. "Anyway, from the get-go, neither one of those guys was ever interested in Linda—except maybe to pal around with. In fact, when they were seniors, both Harlan and Walt fell for Angela Leffert. She ended up marrying Harlan. Two months later, Walt got hitched to her best friend, Tracy." Roseann shook her head. "I don't think Linda ever forgave Walt for that. It was like a one-two punch in old Linda's bread basket, losing them both to other women. Then she suddenly hooked up with Ron Castle, her consolation prize." Roseann let out a little laugh. "Old Linda went right from Park Place and Boardwalk to Baltic Avenue—without passing Go. But I guess she got some bucks out of the deal."

Tim nodded. "Yeah, I saw their house."

"Not a shabby setup, huh? Not that you'd guess Ron was loaded, no siree, not around here. You know how some people figure a tip by doubling the tax? Ron figures the tip by taking all the paper money from his change and leaving the coins. Talk about cheap. Yet he's this big wheel around here with the Guardians."

"I've heard of them," Tim said. "What are they?"

"Oh, sort of a do-good organization for the community. They throw pancake breakfasts, art fairs, picnics, that kind of thing. Walt and Harlan are involved too. It's strictly stag. But Linda always manages to keep her hand in it. She likes to think of herself as *The Guardians' Angel.* I've heard her use that on more than one occasion." Roseann made a sour face. "Cute, huh?"

"I gather you're not one of Linda's biggest fans," Tim said.

Roseann sighed. "Actually, I kind of feel sorry for her. I think the happiest time in her life was after Harlan and Walt's wives were killed in a car wreck together. She had the boys all to herself again—for a while. Then Harlan met Claire."

Roseann smiled at Al. "How are you doing there, partner? Let me heat up that coffee." She topped off his cup.

His mouth full, he grumbled, "Thank you."

"What about Walt?" Tim asked. "Did he ever remarry?"

"No. The rumor is that he's carrying on with this woman in Victoria," Roseann's voice dropped to a whisper. "A married lady. But little Linda still has her hooks in old Walt. She tries to run his life. He doesn't seem to mind. When Linda gets to be too much for him, he sails off someplace, usually Victoria Island."

Suddenly, Roseann seemed distracted by something at the front of the restaurant. She grabbed the coffeepot off the table. "Oh, crap, I'm getting the stink-eye from my boss. Gotta go. Eat the rest of your toast before it gets cold."

Tim glanced over his shoulder. A pale, paunchy, balding man with a mustache stood at the register. He was scowling at Roseann as she approached him. Then for a moment, he directed his hostile gaze at Tim.

"What the hell was that all about?" Al murmured.

Tim turned forward, then poured milk over his Rice Krispies. "I heard some rumors yesterday," he said. "I was just wondering if they were true. How are your pancakes?"

Al was staring toward the front of the restaurant. "Shit, he's really chewing her out."

Tim looked back at the register again. Roseann's boss was growling something under his breath at her. He stabbed his finger at the air, almost poking her in the chest.

"This is what I mean about you going off half-cocked," he heard Al whispering. "You ask a lot of questions that are none of your business, and you're gonna piss people off, hot-shot."

". . . and your BIG MOUTH!" the manager said, his voice suddenly raised.

"Oh, pound sand up your ass, Wayne!" Roseann retorted. She retreated to the kitchen with the coffeepot.

Tim turned toward Al once more. He started eating his cereal.

"See? Look what you started," Al whispered.

Tim ate his breakfast. He didn't say anything. He glanced over at the manager, who stared back at him.

The pale man with the mustache muttered something. Tim couldn't hear it across the restaurant, but he could read the manager's lips.

The man had looked at Tim and said, *"Son of a bitch."*

"I'll meet you here in an hour, sweetheart," Harlan said.

"Thanks, honey." Claire kissed him on the cheek. She opened the passenger door and climbed outside. She waved to him, then stepped into the foyer. Halfway up the stairs to Linus Moorehead's office, she stopped.

Claire had no intention of going up there.

She'd lied to Harlan about having an appointment today.

Her session with Moorehead wasn't for another couple of days.

Claire listened to the car pulling away, then she crept down the stairs. Peeking out the window in the door, she didn't see Harlan's Saab. Still, she decided to wait another minute and make sure he was really gone.

She needed this hour away from him. Last night, they'd gone out to dinner with Tiffany, and Ron and Linda. Marrazo's Villa was a family Italian restaurant and steakhouse with red-and-white checkered tablecloths, and candles in old Chianti bottles as centerpieces.

She usually liked Marrazo's, but didn't have a good time last night. Over her minestrone soup, Linda told Harlan: "I met up with your favorite cop. You know, that arrogant son-of-a-so-and-so you had a brush with last week? He came around the Gardens while I was working there, and he started asking me all these prying, personal questions." She turned to Claire. "Mostly about you, Claire, and *what happened.*"

"Honey, little ears . . ." Her husband, Ron, whispered, with a look at Tiffany.

Linda frowned at him. "I know. Don't nudge me. I didn't say a thing. Anyway, in addition to being incompetent, this cop was rude to me."

"I'm sure he was just doing his job," Claire piped up. "Can we talk about something else, please?"

But when they returned home, Claire couldn't wait to talk about it. While Harlan settled in front of the TV downstairs, she tucked her stepdaughter in bed. Then she crept into their bedroom, picked up the phone on the nightstand, and dialed.

"Good evening, Whale Watcher Inn," the hotel operator answered.

"Yes—" Claire fell silent. She stared back at Harlan in the bedroom doorway. She hung up the phone.

"Who were you calling?" he asked.

"My friend from the hospital, Tess."

Nodding, Harlan began to unbutton his shirt. "The kimono woman with that red mark on her face." Staring at her, he cocked his head to one side and rubbed his hairy chest. "Why'd you hang up so quickly?"

"Oh, it was just going to be girl talk," Claire said, a little nervously. She remembered that look from Harlan. She could always tell when he wanted to make love.

Claire managed a coy smile. "But I can always call her later."

Tossing his shirt on the floor, Harlan moved toward her. He caressed the side of her neck with his fingertips, then leaned in and kissed her.

Claire wrapped her arms around him. He smelled of musk and Cool Water, and his skin felt warm. For a man with such a hairy chest, his back was smooth and flawless. She'd always liked Harlan's body. He was rubbing his pelvis against her, and she felt him growing hard.

Claire kissed him deeply. His whiskers scratched at her face.

Holding onto him, she felt a rush of excitement, but a panic overwhelmed her at the same time.

When he began to unbutton her blouse, Claire pulled away. Her friend, Tess, had her mark. And now she had her own. At the hospital, they'd told Claire that she no longer needed to put a bandage over her chest wound. But they'd recommended applying an antibacterial ointment to the area. The scarred piece of flesh only looked worse with the greasy salve over it.

She didn't want Harlan to see. She wore a T-shirt while they made love. She tried to ignore the television set downstairs, and the loud laugh track of some comedy show. When he was inside her, she remembered the only one-night-stand she'd ever had. It had been a year after Charlie's death. She remembered wanting the guy to hurry up and leave so she could relax and breathe right again.

Harlan was her husband, but he felt like a stranger. And this stranger wasn't going away.

She faked her orgasm. She wanted Harlan to feel good about their reunion sex. What was the point of him knowing that she'd been uncomfortable most of the time? She knew he was making his best effort for "normalcy" too.

Claire told him that it was wonderful.

That wasn't the only lie she'd told last night. She'd also invented this appointment with Dr. Moorehead for 1:00 P.M. Harlan had said he would drive her into town.

Claire stood at the bottom of the stairwell to Moorehead's office. She stared out the window in the door.

Ever since last night, she'd been anxious to talk with Tim Sullivan. She was so grateful to have someone helping her. He'd talked to Linda for her, had even ticked her off. The last time she'd made Linda mad, she'd been digging at the truth. Maybe Tim had been doing the same thing. Maybe the truth was within their grasp after all.

She stepped outside, and turned up the collar to her trench coat. A chilly breeze came from the harbor, and the sky was gray. Claire cut across the street, and walked half a block to The Fork In The Road Diner. She kept glancing over her shoulder to make sure Harlan wasn't still around.

She headed into a phone booth outside the restaurant. From her purse, she fished out a couple of quarters, along with a piece of paper on which she'd scribbled the number of the hotel. She got The Whale Watcher Inn operator, and asked for Tim Sullivan's room. The phone rang and rang.

The hotel operator broke in and asked if she wanted to leave a message. Claire hesitated, said, "No thank you," then hung up.

All at once, someone slammed into the side of the booth. Claire swiveled around.

"Fucking bitch!" yelled the town drunk, Vernon Gutterman. He seemed to ricochet off the glass. Though in his forties, Vernon looked like an old man. Years of heavy drinking had ravaged his face and cost him his job at the plant. Usually, he just loitered around Main Street, hitting folks up for money. But on rare occasions, the dipsomania turned him bitter, and he'd weave along the sidewalk, screaming obscenities at people.

A hand on her heart, Claire stared at him through the glass.

Vernon Gutterman stared back at her, seemingly just as startled. "Oh, I'm sorry, Mrs. Shaw!" he yelled, his speech slurred. "I didn't know that was you." He continued down the street. "Mrs. Shaw isn't a bitch!" he announced loudly. "She's a very nice lady . . . pretty lady . . . Mrs. Shaw . . ."

Claire hurried out of the phone booth and headed in the opposite direction. She didn't need anyone calling attention to her at this moment.

The police station was half a block away. She wanted to go to there, and make sure a Missing Persons report had been filed for Brian. She wondered how much it would gel with the story Harlan and Linda had given her.

She headed toward the police station, about two blocks away. Then Claire saw something that made her stop dead. A man in a stocking cap stepped out of the alley across the street—between the florist and a travel agency that was closed. As soon as Claire spotted him, he ducked back into the alley, and disappeared. Claire didn't get a good look at him. The only thing she was sure of was the gray stocking cap and an army jacket. Was he wearing sunglasses? She couldn't tell in the distance.

Had he been watching her?

A chill raced through Claire's body. He didn't look like Harlan. He didn't look like anyone.

She hurried toward the police station.

Ever since her return to Deception two days ago, Claire's main concern had been her son's whereabouts and the block of time she'd lost.

Now, she had a new concern. That faceless stranger in the alleyway had brought it on. For first time since coming back to the island, Claire thought about this serial killer on the loose.

She knew he wasn't through with her.

*   *   *

He'd told Al that he had diarrhea.

It was the only way he could avoid going with him on a Whale Watching cruise. Al had been looking forward to this cruise since they'd arrived on the island the day before yesterday. He'd been insisting Tim come along. Al must have figured he wouldn't get in so much trouble if they *both* played hookey that afternoon. Tim couldn't fathom any other reason why the older cop wanted him along. He was pretty sure Al disliked him as much as he loathed Al. In any event, old Al couldn't argue with a case of diarrhea.

So Tim holed up in his hotel room, and worked on his comic strip. Even with a delivery deadline looming, he had trouble staying focused. He kept thinking about Claire Shaw and her missing son. She was right. It was too much of a coincidence that Brian and his friend had both disappeared within 24 hours of her own disappearance. What were Derek's parents and Claire Shaw's friends covering up?

Tim remembered Derek's younger sister, Amy, looking so panicked when he'd told her that he was a cop. And then she'd broken down and cried with her mother.

He thought about tracking Amy Herrmann at the school, then talking with her. There was a good chance he could get the truth from her. But at what cost? The idea of preying on some eighth grader—and intimidating her with a bunch of questions—made him sick. How much could she know anyway? Amy's parents probably kept her in the dark about certain things.

Tim had no idea what his next move would be. He almost hoped they would ship him back to the mainland. Then he could advise his replacement about Claire Shaw's concerns, and let a real detective handle it.

He retreated into his comic strip, where he was safe and *Private Eye Guy* knew how to dig out the evil villains and save the girl. This particular installment wasn't among his best. But he'd submitted worse.

In the right hand corner of the final comic strip frame, Tim signed his pen name, Tim Timster. He packed his work in a padded Express Mail envelope, then walked to the post office on Main Street, not far from the Fork In The Road Diner.

As he stepped out of the post office, Tim passed by the police station, and spotted Claire through the big, plate-glass window.

She sat at a gray, metal desk, studying some paperwork. Her trenchcoat was thrown over the back of her chair, and she wore a pretty green pullover sweater. Her chestnut hair was pulled back in a bun. Claire hadn't noticed him yet.

But the deputy behind the counter was staring at him. Tim had briefly met him yesterday when Al and he had visited Sheriff Klauser. Tim waved at the deputy, then he stepped inside the police station.

Claire glanced up from the papers. For a second, she looked so happy to see him. Tim gave her a cordial smile. "Hello, Mrs. Shaw."

Her eyes shifted to the deputy, then back to Tim. She nodded. "Officer Sullivan."

"Hey, you're back," the deputy piped up.

Tim couldn't remember his name. The deputy was tall, about thirty years old, and good-looking. He had a thin face and brown hair that fell across his forehead.

Moseying out from behind the counter, he shook Tim's hand. He seemed a bit cocky, and Tim imagined him flirting with just about every woman he pulled over for speeding or running a stop sign. This close, Tim could see his name tag above the badge on his gray shirt: Deputy Troy Landers.

"The sheriff's not in," he told Tim. "Anything I can do for you?"

"No, thanks," Tim said. He turned toward Claire for a moment. "I saw Mrs. Shaw in here, and just wanted to say hello."

"How about some coffee? I was about to make a new pot."

"Sounds great, thanks." Tim was hoping maybe they'd be rid of him for a couple of minutes. He watched Deputy

Landers saunter behind the counter again, toward a room in back.

Except for the quaint store-front look, the police station was a stark, charmless big room. Maps of Washington State, the San Juan Islands, and Deception were tacked to the dirty, yellow walls—along with about a dozen "Wanted" fliers. A row of six connected black bucket-style seats, the kind found in airports desperately needing a remodel, was set against the wall. On the opposite wall, between the counter and the stairs, there was also an old, beat-up metal drinking fountain, with a pail beneath it to catch a leak. The jail, Tim had been told yesterday, was downstairs.

Someone as lovely as Claire Shaw seemed so out of place in such an ugly, colorless room. "I've been wanting to talk with you," she whispered. "You met with Linda Castle yesterday?"

"Derek Herrmann's mother too," Tim said in a low voice. "I didn't get much from either one of them. I'm pretty sure Derek's never coming back. Either the family sent him away for good, or maybe he's dead. We might find out more from his kid sister, Amy. But I wouldn't count on it." Frowning, Tim shook his head. "The people around here are very guarded when it comes to talking about you, and Brian and Derek."

Tim shot a cautious look toward the back room, behind the counter. "What are you doing here anyway?"

She glanced down at the stack of files on the desk and sighed. "I wanted to look at the Missing Person report on my son."

Tim squinted at the stack of papers in the file. "How many years worth of Missing Persons do you have there?" he murmured.

She checked a bulletin on the bottom of the stack. "About four years."

"Must be fifty people here." Tim came around the desk and glanced over her shoulder. He looked at several of the sheets. "That's an awful lot of Missing Persons for one little island."

He kept checking photos of the missing. Most of them were teenagers, like Brian and Derek. He stopped and studied the bulletin on top of the pile.

From the black-and-white photo, Brian Ferguson looked like a handsome, fairly unaffected teenager. No strange haircut, gothic eye makeup, or weird piercings. Tim checked the statistics listed under his name:

DOB: 9/3/86 Age: 17
Ht.: 5'10"　Wt.: 151 lbs.
Hair: Light Brown　Eyes: Green
Date Missing: 10/24/03　From: Platt, WA

Report made on 10/26/03 by victim's stepfather, Harlan Shaw, 142 Holm Drive, Platt (Deception Is), WA. Victim is a runaway, who has run away from home on two previous (unreported) occasions within the last year. Missing from wardrobe, (and might be seen in) brown suede jacket, blue jeans, black sneakers.

"Not much to go on," Tim murmured. He remembered what Roseann had said about Brian having had a few brushes with the local police. Had it been for stunts like stealing Linda Castle's gnome, or was Brian a more serious repeat offender?

Deputy Landers came from the back room with a couple of mugs full of coffee. He gave one to Tim. "There you go, sport. Hope you like it black."

"That's great, thanks," Tim said. He showed him Brian's "missing" bulletin. "Could I get a copy of this?"

Deputy Landers nodded over his coffee cup. "We have a Xerox machine in back. No sweat."

"Also, I'm wondering if you have any other police records on file for Brian. I understand he had a few brushes with the law."

Deputy Landers glanced at Claire, who squirmed a little

in her chair. She seemed to muster up a smile, then nodded at the deputy.

Troy Landers shrugged. "Sure, I can show you a file on him."

"I'd also like to see what you have on Brian's friend, Derek Herrmann. I understand he raised some hell from time to time. Do you have a file on him too?"

The deputy hesitated, then nodded. "Sure, I guess I can show you that too. Anything for our Seattle buddies in blue."

Troy took them behind the counter to a claustrophobic, windowless back room. Four file cabinets stood against the wall, along with fax and copy machines. Pushed against the other wall was a long table with three folding chairs. A mini-refrigerator, a microwave, and a Mr. Coffee coffeemaker were crammed in the corner.

The deputy pulled a couple of files from the cabinet.

"My son has his own police file?" Claire asked, grimacing a bit.

"It's the sheriff's own system," Troy explained, setting the folders on the table. "Any more than three offenses—no matter how minor—and the perpetrator gets a file."

Tim sat down at the table, and started sorting through the reports. Brian had five "incidents" on record.

In the outer office, the phone rang, and Troy excused himself to answer it. Claire plopped down in the chair beside Tim. "Why do you need to see Brian's police record?" she whispered.

"I want to find out if he and Derek have ticked off anyone else besides Linda Castle."

"Oh, her seventh dwarf, or whatever it was." Claire sighed. "She told you about that?"

Nodding, Tim cracked a smile.

"To make up for it, Brian worked in that garden three days a week all summer long. And Linda still hasn't forgiven him. I know he's gotten himself into some trouble, but deep down, he's really a nice boy."

"There's nothing very serious here," Tim murmured, pouring over Brian's rap sheets. He noticed the typical pranks of a teenage boy. His worst offense was "borrowing" a small yacht from the harbor, and sailing it to Anacortes.

"That was the last time he ran away," Claire explained. "The boat belongs to Phil Gannon, who works with Harlan at the plant. Anyway, it's a long story, but Harlan got Phil to drop the charges, and he covered the cost for Brian mooring the boat in someone else's spot."

She put her hand on Tim's arm. "I know it's sounds like I'm making excuses for him," she whispered. "But he and Harlan didn't always get along. I'm afraid I didn't—well, I . . ." Her voice cracked a bit. "I never took Brian's side. I kept thinking, *'Why can't you get along with him? You're going to blow it for us, kiddo.'* I didn't want to lose Harlan. He'd really rescued us. I'd been so broke, and miserable and lonely before he'd come onto the scene."

"It's okay," Tim assured her. "You don't have to explain." He glanced at the police report again. "Was this Phil Gannon pretty forgiving?"

"I don't think he's a huge fan of Brian's, but he's very nice to me. He and Harlan are still friends."

Tim glanced at Derek Herrmann's file: busted twice for possession of marijuana; caught shoplifting three times; driving under the influence (license suspended); driving without a license; car theft; drunk and disorderly. There were over a dozen reported incidents, and most of the time, it appeared the Herrmanns had managed to get the charges dropped.

"Compared to Derek, your son is St. Francis of Assisi," Tim muttered. He glanced at a report from August 8, 2001, when both boys—along with a third named Frank Killabrew— were arrested for trespassing, drunk and disorderly, and indecent exposure. The three of them had gotten drunk, and gone skinny-dipping in the pond at Falls Park, a nature area closed to the public after ten-thirty at night.

"That was our first summer here," Claire explained.

"Who's Frank Killabrew?" Tim asked.

"I think his family came here on vacation and rented a cabin for a week. The woods are full of rental cabins. They get a lot of business in the summer."

"That name *Killabrew* is familiar," Tim muttered, almost to himself. He sipped his coffee.

"Well, I don't think I ever met him—or his family." Claire glanced at her wristwatch. "Listen, Harlan thinks I'm seeing this therapist right now. He's supposed to pick me up outside the doctor's office in about five minutes. I should go. But I want to tell you something that happened when I was walking here. Please, don't think I'm paranoid, but I'm pretty certain someone's following me—and watching me."

Tim started to reach out to her, but hesitated. "Did you get a good look at him?"

Claire shook her head. "He was too far away, and he ran off the moment I spotted him. He could be a reporter or photographer, like the ones trying to get at me in the hospital. But I can't help thinking maybe Rembrandt has tracked me down on this island. I don't know. Maybe I'm overreacting."

Tim frowned. "No. I'm glad you told me."

Glancing at her wristwatch, Claire got to her feet. "Damn, I've got to go."

"Promise me, you won't go anywhere by yourself," he whispered, standing up with her. "If you're alone at home, keep the doors and windows locked. You should have someone with you at all times, Claire."

She nodded distractedly. "I'll call you at the hotel later," she said in a low voice. "Thanks for everything, Tim."

She headed toward the front of the police station, and almost bumped into Deputy Landers in the doorway.

"You okay?" he asked. "Find what you needed?"

"Yes, thanks," Claire said nervously. She walked around the counter. "Bye, Troy." As she opened the door, Claire turned back and looked at Tim. "Nice running into you, Officer Sullivan," she said. Then she stepped outside.

Tim came to the front window, and watched her cross the street.

"She's a bit of all-right, if you know what I mean," the deputy said. "I guess she's got a big hole in her chest now, but what the hell? I still wouldn't mind trading places with Harlan Shaw for a night or two."

Tim saw Claire stop under the awning of the flower shop, just off Main Street, about half a block away. She glanced toward him, and gave a little, secretive wave.

Tim waved back. "Do you have any records of off-islander people who have rented cabins here during the summer?" he asked, his eyes still on Claire. Raindrops began to slash against the police station window.

"Yeah, the folks leasing out cabins have to submit a list of occupants if they're staying over three days." Deputy Landers slurped down some coffee. "I don't know if it has to do with taxes or keeping track of local tourism or what the hell it is. Anyway, they have all that stuff at the City Hall office. Second floor."

Tim watched a Saab pull up near the flower shop. Claire stepped up to the passenger side and opened the car door. She glanced back at him for a fleeting moment, then ducked inside the car.

Rain continued to slash at the police station window. Unblinking, Tim gazed at the car as it drove away. "City Hall, second floor?" he asked.

"That's right, sport." Troy Landers replied.

"Thanks, deputy," he said.

"The name is Killabrew, and they rented one of the cabins around the second week of August 2001," Tim said.

The large, middle-aged woman behind the counter wore a white pullover sweater that had a photo of a kitten on it. Nodding, she scribbled on a piece of paper. She took off her bifocals, leaving them to dangle from a chain around her neck, then she waddled over to a file cabinet.

Tim noticed three desks in the drab, little office, but she was the only person there. The Platt City Hall of Records was in a stately old building on Main Street. The first floor was a historical museum, open to the public Thursdays through Saturdays.

The woman shuffled back to the counter with a half-sheet of paper. "Let's see now, *Killabrew*," she said, adjusting her bifocals and studying the document. "Five occupants. Rented the Miller place from August third through the ninth, oh-one. That's one of the bigger cabins, a three bedroom. Belongs to Mr. William M. Miller in Seattle. But Chad Schlund manages the place. You want the address?"

"Yes, please," Tim replied. "And a phone number for Mr. Schlund too—if you have it."

"Easy-breezy," she said, scribbling on an index card. "Chad manages about a dozen of the cabins, all owned by off-islanders. He rents them out, hires the maid brigades, makes sure the water and electricity are running, fills out all the paperwork."

"Do you know if he has the Killabrews' year-round address?" Tim asked. "And maybe the names of the five people who stayed there?"

"Oh, I have that right here, officer," she said. "Want me to write it down for you?"

Tim nodded. "Yes, thank you. Thank you very much."

" '*Mr. and Mrs. Francis G. Killabrew,*' " she said aloud as she wrote. " '*Twelve-oh-three Laramee Drive, Wenatchee, Washington.*' Hmm, looks like they brought the whole family," she said lightly. " '*Nancy Killabrew, Frank Killabrew, and Phoebe Killabrew.*' "

"I really appreciate this," Tim said. He drummed his fingers on the countertop. "Do you know if the public library here has old *Seattle Times* or *Post-Intelligencers* on file?"

The library had microfiche files for *The Seattle Times* since 1995. At the front desk, Tim had filled out a form requesting issues dated: 11/19/02 and 11/20/02. He knew the first date very well. Most everyone on the Rembrandt task force knew it. But Tim couldn't remember if *The Times* had run the story on November 19, or the next day.

The library was a big, slightly weather-beaten old, white house. The inside had a certain seedy grandeur, with a big chandelier and a fake fireplace in the main room. There were a couple of stuffed sofas and a long, mahogany study table with old, mismatched chairs. Two cubicals with microfiche machines interrupted the row of bookcases against one wall.

Tim started up the microfiche reader. It made a humming noise. He slipped in the file for November 20 and started scanning.

Tim found what he was looking for, an article on page two. He stared at the headline:

BODY OF SLAIN WENATCHEE WOMAN FOUND
Shooting Victim Has Been Missing Two Days

> *Two days after her husband reported her missing, the body of Nancy Hart, 23, a newlywed from Wenatchee, was discovered Monday morning in a ravine near Marina Drive in Everett. She had been shot in the chest.*
>
> *Hart was last seen by her husband when she left their home to go jogging early Saturday morning . . .*

Tim knew the rest. Nancy Hart never returned from her morning run. The police were able to keep out of the news-papers the bizarre details regarding the discovery of her corpse. The article didn't mention that a heavy dose of makeup had been applied to Nancy's face, and the cosmetic work was protected from the elements by a clear plastic bag that had been pulled over her head and tied around her neck. At the time, the police didn't know what to make of it.

Nancy had been Rembrandt's first.

Tim scanned the article until he reached a paragraph near the end:

James and Nancy Hart had been married for only two months. Nancy Hart is also survived by her parents, Mr. and Mrs. Francis Killabrew of Wenatchee, a younger brother and sister. "Nancy was so happy," according to her mother, Arlette Killabrew. "She and Jim had been dating since high school. Marrying him was a dream come true for her. I've never seen anyone so full of life and so in love as Nancy . . ."

Hunched over the microfiche machine, Tim slowly shook his head. "My God, she was here," he whispered to himself. "She was here. This is probably where he first set eyes on her."

Chapter 15

"Don't you see the significance of this?" Tim asked Al.

He kept his voice down to a whisper. The Fork In The Road was in the middle of its breakfast rush, and the place was crowded. They didn't get a booth this morning, and there were people within reaching distance at tables on both sides of them.

Al nibbled at his cinnamon toast. "So she took a vacation here with her family," he said. "Doesn't mean anything. That was over a *year* before she was killed."

"Yes, but Nancy Killabrew Hart was the first," Tim argued. "Rembrandt could have met her here—or at least seen her. He may be a local, or maybe he rented a cabin in the woods near where her family stayed."

"You're saying he was obsessed with her for over a year? Give me a break."

"Al, some obsessions last a lifetime. And it's just too much of a coincidence that two of Rembrandt's victims have spent time on this tiny island."

"That's just what it is," Al said, over his coffee cup. "A coincidence."

The waitress, a forty-something woman with limp black hair and a flat nose, stopped by to refill their coffees. There wasn't a name tag on her brown uniform. "How are you guys doing?" she asked.

"Great, thanks," Tim said. "Um, is it Roseann's day off?" He'd been hoping to ask her some more questions about Brian and Derek.

"Roseann's out sick today," the waitress said. "I'm filling in. Something wrong with your pancakes?"

Tim glanced down at the stack of blueberry pancakes in front of him. A pile of blueberries sat on the side of the plate by a big mound of melting butter. "Oh, I'm sure they're great," he said. "I just haven't dug in yet."

"Well, eat up before they get cold." Coffeepot in hand, she sauntered away from the table.

Tim picked up his fork, but hesitated. "You know, I remember a theory that went around the office a while back. It was about Rembrandt being two people—or maybe one guy with an accomplice, a disciple."

"Yeah, I heard that too," Al grunted. He finished his scrambled eggs.

"Well, I keep thinking about Brian Ferguson and Derek Herrmann, and how they both suddenly vanished when the attempt on Claire Shaw's life was botched. What if Claire Shaw's memory lapse is some kind of unconscious way of shielding herself from the truth about her son and his friend?"

"Y'know this cinnamon toast your girlfriend was pushing yesterday is okay, but not exactly filling." Al pointed to Tim's plate. "Are you gonna eat those flapjacks or what?"

Tim pushed the plate toward him. "Go ahead, knock yourself out. Are you even listening to me?"

"Yeah, you're saying Claire Shaw's kid tried to knock her off." Al dug into the blueberry pancakes. "And he's Rembrandt or working for Rembrandt. I'm sure she'll love hearing that."

Tim sighed. "I hope I'm wrong. But Derek and Brian knew Frank Killabrew, that's a fact. It's in a police report. Chances are they knew his sister, Nancy. I think we should drive to Wenatchee and talk to Mr. and Mrs. Killabrew. They might remember someone stalking Nancy while they were vacationing here. Or maybe—"

"Now, hold on, hotshot," Al said. His fork made a clanking sound as he set it down on his plate. "You aren't talking to anyone else with your cock-a-mamie theories. In fact, I wasn't going to say anything to you. I wanted to give you another chance. But I got a call last night from Ron Castle. He was out for blood. He said you were rude to his wife the day before yesterday."

Tim shook his head. "Al, listen—"

"No, you listen," the older cop said, picking blueberries off his plate and popping them in his mouth. "You were harassing the wife of a VIP around here. This Ron Castle is one of the head honchos in this men's club, the Guardians, which I guess is a big deal around here. And you pissed him off."

"I'm sorry," Tim muttered.

"Well, I smoothed his ruffled feathers, and told him that I'd give you a talking to. But I think I'll do my talking to Lieutenant Elmore, and recommend you be shipped back to Seattle." He popped another couple of blueberries in his mouth. "You're a loose cannon here, and I can't keep making excuses for your screw ups."

"Listen, Al, I'll be honest with you," Tim said. "The last thing in the world I wanted to do was come to this island. But now, I believe we have a shot at actually catching this killer— or at least, finding out who he is. All we have to do is just keep digging. Don't you think it's worth a try? I want to stay, Al. I'm pretty sure Claire Shaw wants me to stay too. All you have to do is ask her. And she's the reason we're here, right?"

Al was shaking his head. "I wouldn't bet on Claire Shaw being in your corner once you tell her that her kid is the Rembrandt killer."

"That's just a theory, Al. I'm hoping it's not true. I want the chance to prove myself wrong. Hell, wouldn't that give you some satisfaction, proving me wrong? C'mon, Al, don't say anything to Elmore for another twenty-four hours, and if by then—"

"Sorry," he cut it. "My mind's made up. It's nothing personal. You're just a liability here."

Disgusted, Tim sat back and stared at Al, who was wolfing down his pancakes. "Yeah, and you're a real asset," he grumbled. "Taking whale watching cruises, while Rembrandt runs around free to kill again."

Al kept on eating. Tim wondered if he'd even heard him, and for a moment, he hoped he hadn't.

Al didn't look up. He simply paused before shovelling another forkful of blueberry pancakes in his mouth. "Checkout time at the hotel is twelve noon," he said, finally. "I suggest you pack up, hotshot."

"Anyway, I don't think our private detective shopping venture will happen," Claire said into the phone. "I can't come to Bellingham, Tess. Harlan has laid down the law. I'm not allowed off the island. It's like Alcatraz."

Claire refilled her coffee cup, then sat down at the kitchen table. It was a round, stained oak table with four matching chairs that Claire never found very comfortable. The ceramic jack-o-lantern centerpiece was leftover from Halloween, three weeks ago, before she'd disappeared. Claire was still in her bathrobe, and hadn't yet cleared off the breakfast dishes. She'd seen Harlan off to work, and Tiffany off to school. The stove clock read eight-thirty, but it might as well have been eight-thirty at night. The sky had turned dark gray within the last half hour. It looked like a bad storm was looming. Claire reached over and switched on the light in the pantry.

"In fact, Harlan wouldn't have left me alone here this morning," Claire continued. "Only Linda Castle is stopping by within the hour. We're spending the day together. That apparently makes everything all right, which is pretty ironic when you stop to consider what happened the last time I spent the day with Linda Castle."

"She's your best friend on that island," Tess said on the other end of the line. "Yet you hate her guts, don't you?"

"I just don't trust her, that's all."

Tess laughed. "Yeah, well, if you can't mistrust your best friend, then I don't know what."

"I haven't always been like this," Claire replied, rubbing her forehead. "It's just, ever since I've come back from the hospital, I've felt so *estranged* from Linda and Harlan. It's like they expect me to live in their little world here, and believe everything they tell me. And I'm not supposed to miss my son."

"Do you think maybe that's why Brian ran away?" Tess asked gently. "Is it possible he's always felt the same resentment you feel now, coming to this island, living in Harlan's house?"

Claire didn't respond. She remembered all the times she'd told her son to try getting along with Harlan, all the times she took Harlan's side in their squabbles.

"Claire? Listen, I'm sorry, that was tactless—"

"No, it's very true," she murmured. "You've got my number. You're a helluva lot better than the shrink I'm seeing here. You know, he's another one on this island I don't really trust."

"Ha, color me shocked."

"Okay, enough about boring me," Claire said. "What's going on with you, Tess? How are you doing?"

"Well, I'm still a little sore, still a little depressed. But at least I don't have to go back to work for another week. Hmmm, let's see, what else? I've become totally hooked on bad daytime TV, and I'm thinking about getting a cat. Could I possibly be any more pathetic?"

"What's wrong with owning a cat?" Claire asked. She heard a break on the other end of the line.

"Oh, just a sec," Tess said. "I have Caller ID. It's work, the Seattle office. I should probably grab this, Claire. Want me to call you back?"

"I need to clean up and get ready for Linda. Let's talk tomorrow. Okay?"

"You bet. Say hi to your *best friend* for me."

"Smart ass. Take care, Tess."

After she hung up, Claire tried Tim at the hotel—her third attempt this morning. They rang his room, but again, no answer. She didn't leave a message.

Claire cleared the table and washed the dishes. She switched on another light. Outside, the wind was kicking up. Through the sliding glass doors in the pantry, Claire watched leaves scatter across the lawn. She saw tree branches swaying in the wooded area that bordered their backyard. She remembered what Tim had told her about locking all the doors and windows while alone in the house.

She finished the dishes, dried off her hands, and started checking the windows and doors.

She hadn't told Tess about Tim Sullivan. It was a conscious omission in their phone conversation just now. She didn't want to admit to Tess—or herself—how much she'd come to depend on this good-looking cop. And yes, his good looks had a lot to do with her feelings for him.

While checking the living room windows, Claire gazed out at the half-finished house across the street. Tiffany called it the "face house," because she thought the upstairs windows looked like eyes, and the front door, a nose. Claire knew what she meant. There were times when she felt that house was staring back at her.

The phone rang, and gave her a start.

She still thought of Brian, every time it rang. She hated getting her hopes up, but couldn't help thinking it might be him. Claire grabbed the receiver before the answering machine clicked on. "Hello?"

No response. But she could hear someone sigh. It sounded like a man.

"Yes, hello?" she repeated, her hope turning into something else. "Who's there?"

This was no wrong number. The person was still on the line. She thought of the man who had been watching her in the alley yesterday. Did he like to listening to her as well? Claire swallowed hard. "I can hear you," she said evenly. "Who's there?"

There was a click. The line went dead. Frowning, Claire disconnected for a moment, and tried star-six-nine. A disembodied voice told her the number was blocked.

She hung up the receiver. "Relax, it's nothing," she muttered to herself.

Still, she took one last cautious glance out the sliding glass doors before retreating upstairs. It was so dark, she needed to turn on the second floor hallway light, then another one in the bedroom. Claire grabbed a black pullover and a pair of jeans from the closet, then laid them out on the bed.

Claire didn't linger in the shower. She's seen *Psycho* one too many times, and felt nervous enough being alone in the house right now. Even with the bathroom door locked, she faced the shower curtain and rushed through the ritual.

After drying off, she donned her bathrobe and opened the bathroom door a crack. She switched off the vent, and the sudden quiet was a bit eerie. A steady drip from the showerhead echoed in the tiled bathroom.

She ran a towel over her head, then pulled the hair dryer out from under the sink. Claire plugged it in, and a spark suddenly burst from the outlet. An electric, nerve-wrenching jolt surged up her arm, and she recoiled. Claire screamed. For a moment, she thought she was being electrocuted. The lights flickered. Smoke spewed from the outlet.

All at once, the lights went out.

"Oh, Jesus," she whispered. She couldn't stop shaking. "Jesus, calm down, Claire. You're okay . . ."

But she wasn't. Her heart was racing. As much as she tried to steady herself, the tremors wouldn't go away. She could hardly walk without falling on her face. It felt as if every joint and muscle in her body had been seared.

She managed to open the bathroom door all the way, letting in some light. She kept talking aloud, assuring herself that she was okay. In the bedroom, she fanned her right hand. Little phantom electric jolts still resonated through the nerve ends.

Claire teetered down the dim hallway, then she took the stairs one step at a time. "You blew a fuse," she said aloud, between deep breaths. "And you scared the ever-lovin' crap out of yourself. But you're okay . . ."

She could have used the phone in the bedroom. But she'd had an inexplicable urgency to be on the first floor. Maybe she didn't want to be trapped upstairs—by someone, or something, even if it was just the dark.

She was still trembling. She needed to call someone. The first person who came to mind was Tim.

She picked up the phone in the pantry. After three failed attempts to connect with Tim this morning, she still dialed The Whale Watcher Inn one more time.

Claire took a few deep breaths. She didn't want to sound crazy and shrill on the phone. When the hotel operator came on the line, Claire calmly asked for Tim Sullivan's room. Counting the ring tones, she turned toward the sliding glass doors.

Outside, the leaves continued to scatter across the lawn. And at the edge of their yard, where the woods started, a man stood alone, watching her.

He was back, the man in the gray stocking cap and army fatigue jacket. Even with the darkened, ominous sky, he still wore his sunglasses.

Claire froze.

"Hello?" she heard someone say on the other end of the line.

"Tim?" she gasped, turning away from the glass doors. "Tim, is that you?"

"Claire? Listen, I—"

"Somebody's in the backyard!" she whispered. "And I'm alone here. It's the man I saw yesterday . . ."

Claire turned around again. She didn't see him. He'd disappeared.

"Okay, I'll be right there," Tim said. "As soon as we hang up, call the police. Make sure the doors are locked. I'm leaving right now. Okay, Claire?"

"I don't see him now," she murmured. "I—I don't know . . ."

"I'm on my way. Call the police."

She heard a click on the other end of the line.

With a shaky hand, Claire pulled down on the phone cradle. She had to do it twice, before she got a dial tone. She glanced out the glass doors again. Something caught her eye, just on the other side of the glass, near the door handle. Claire gasped and hung up the phone.

It took her moment to realize that it was merely a piece of newspaper that had gotten swept up in the wind. It fluttered away.

Claire ran to the pantry closet, and dug out a baseball bat. Harlan coached little league, and the closet was crammed with sports equipment. The bat clutched in her hands, she went from window to window on the first floor.

She didn't see anything. But Claire kept looking outside, knowing all the while he was somewhere out there, looking in.

Tim stepped into Al's room and found the older cop, sitting on the floor at the foot of his bed. Al had his kicked off his shoes and pants. He still wore his undershorts, black socks, and lime-green short-sleeve shirt. He had pulled the knot of his clip-on tie down to loosen his collar button, and the tie was flapped over his tie clasp like a long, knotted tongue. Al's color was so sallow, Tim thought he was going to pass out.

The older cop had just used the bathroom. It was obvious from the wall of stench that hit Tim when he opened the hotel room door. He could hear the toilet tank still refilling.

Al had first felt queasy when they'd stopped by the police station following breakfast. Tim had known it was serious when Al cut short his bull-session with the sheriff after only an hour. They'd hurried back to the hotel. Tim had gone to his own room to fetch something for Al's stomach.

That was when he'd gotten the call from Claire.

He was grateful Al hadn't locked his door. He couldn't afford to wait. Every second counted.

"Al, listen, here's that Pepto-Bismol," Tim said hurriedly. He handed the bottle to him. He tried not to breathe in the foul air. "Keep it. I need the car. There's an emergency at the Shaws' house. Where are the keys?"

Al pointed to his rumpled pants on the floor. "Shit, I'm dying," he moaned. He guzzled from the Pepto-Bismol bottle like a drunk beginning a bender.

Tim frantically hunted through the trouser pockets until he found the keys. "I'll phone you from the Shaws' house," he said, rushing out the door.

Tim ran to the car. Once inside, he peeled out of the hotel lot. Clutching the steering wheel, his knuckles turned white. He pressed hard on the accelerator, and sped most of the way toward the Shaws' house. Leaning on the horn, he passed two cars, and ran a red light. Every minute in the car was grueling. He didn't think he'd reach Claire on time. She'd sounded so scared on the phone.

It started drizzling, and he switched on the windshield wipers. But he didn't slow down.

The car tires screeched as he turned down Holms Drive, then wound along the cul de sac. He didn't see a single police car in front of the house. And the place looked so dark, not one light was on.

He pulled over to the curb, and jumped out of the car.

Please, God, let her be okay, he thought, running up the driveway. He didn't know what he'd find in that house. Did Rembrandt have time to make her over? Or maybe she'd been abducted again, and all Tim would find was a pair of discarded panties.

He pounded on the door, then tried the knob. Locked. He kept banging against the door, thinking all the while he was too late.

Tim stepped back, and glanced around. There had to be another way into the house. How had Rembrandt gotten in?

He stepped down from the front stoop. Just then, the door

opened. Claire stood at the threshold with a baseball bat in her hand. She wore a blue bathrobe, and her hair was in tangles. "Oh, Tim, thank God," she whispered.

She dropped the baseball bat, then rushed into his arms. Startled, Tim held onto her. He could feel her trembling.

"Are you okay?" Tim asked. "Where is he?"

"I'm all right," she said in a small voice. She was crying. He felt her tears against the side of his neck. After a moment, her soft lips brushed against him there. Almost involuntarily, Tim held her tighter. He stroked her damp hair.

Eyes downcast, Claire pulled away. "Sorry," she murmured, touching her mouth. "I—I just saw him for a second, out by the woods in the backyard. I think he ran off."

"Did you call the police?" Tim glanced past her, at the open front door and the darkness inside. "What happened to the lights?"

Claire wiped the tears from her eyes, and let out a sad, little laugh. "Do you know how to change a fuse?"

Claire watched him through the sliding glass doors.

She'd run upstairs and quickly thrown on her clothes. Linda was due over at any minute. It wouldn't have looked so good with her in her bathrobe and nothing else, and this handsome young cop paying a visit.

While pulling her damp hair back into a ponytail, she gazed out at the backyard. Like Tim, she carefully studied the woods for a sign of her secret admirer. She didn't see anyone amid the trees and wild, overgrown shrubbery. Then again, that army fatigue jacket probably camouflaged him very well.

Tim stood at the edge of the forest area. He glanced her way, then gave a little wave.

Claire waved back.

She couldn't believe she'd actually kissed him. It was only on the neck, but it was a kiss just the same. She'd been so caught up in the moment, and so relieved to see him, she wasn't thinking. Still, if Sheriff Klauser or Deputy Landers were coming to her rescue, she wouldn't have hugged or kissed them. It was just plain inappropriate.

Tim probably thought she was crazy, calling him up and screaming that someone was in her yard. She wondered if he really believed her about the stocking cap man.

Claire put on her trenchcoat, and grabbed an umbrella, then she stepped out the sliding glass door. She started across the lawn. Tim had been looking down at the ground, but now he glanced up at her.

"Do you have a camera I could use?" he called.

She stopped, and nodded.

"And a ruler or a yard stick?"

Claire retreated back into the house. She found a plastic ruler in the kitchen junk drawer, along with a disposable camera that had come free with a box of Crest White Strips. She brought them out to Tim. "You can keep the camera if you want," she said. "It was free and hasn't been used yet. Did you find something?"

"Yeah, footprints," Tim said, pointing to the muddy ground.

Claire gazed down at the tracks. At least, she wasn't crazy.

"I need to take pictures before the rain washes away these prints," Tim explained. "Al might want to get a team over here to comb through these woods. This guy could have tossed away a cigarette butt, a gum wrapper, or something."

Numbly, Claire watched Tim set the ruler by the footprints in the mud. She held the umbrella over his head while he took photos of the tracks.

Back inside, Tim tried to phone Al at the hotel. But the hotel operator didn't answer.

He called Sheriff Klauser and reported that Claire had spotted someone in the backyard. "Possibly a prowler," Claire heard him say into the phone. "Possibly Rembrandt." He passed along the description she'd given him of the stocking cap man. "I think he might still be in the general vicinity," Tim reported.

After he hung up the phone, Tim told her that the sheriff would patrol the area for her elusive stalker.

Upstairs, in the bathroom, Tim used a pair of rubber-handled pliers to unplug the hair dryer. He found exposed wires in the cord, near the plug, but couldn't tell if the damage had been done before or after the dryer short-circuited.

"So this might not have been an accident?" Claire asked apprehensively.

He caught her reflection in the bathroom mirror.

"Do you think my husband set it up?"

He shook his head. "I really don't know, Claire. I can't tell."

He wrapped the cord around the hair dryer handle. "Let's look at the fuse box. Where is it? In the basement?"

A flashlight in his hand, Tim started down the dark basement stairs. They couldn't ignore the possibility that the stocking cap man had climbed through one of the basement windows and was waiting down there.

In the darkness, Claire hovered behind Tim. She kept one hand on the railing, and the other on his shoulder. Reaching the bottom of the stairs, Tim shined the light along the wood paneled wall. He directed the beam to an easel with one of Claire's paintings on it. "What's that?" he asked.

"It's nothing." She nodded toward a door at their right. "The fuse box is there in the furnace room."

Claire clung to his arm as they entered the darkened room. The flashlight's beam cut through the blackness. Again, Tim aimed it along the wall, and the shadowy nooks behind the furnace. Claire showed him the fuse box.

He gave her the flashlight, and she directed it on the panel while he fiddled with a couple of switches. Claire kept her other hand on his shoulder. She was so afraid of being separated from him in this blackness.

Maybe it was the darkness and being scared that brought it on. But suddenly, Claire remembered lying across the backseat of a car. It was night. Her hands and feet were tied. Someone had slapped a piece of heavy tape across her mouth. She remembered breathing through her nose, and listening to the constant purr of the car engine. She'd been drugged, and couldn't struggle or fight. All she could do was lie there. She watched fractured fragments of light coming through the side and rear windows—headlights from passing cars, and illuminated street signs. But most of the time, she was engulfed in darkness.

Tim flicked a switch. Claire noticed a dim light filtering through from the other room. It came from the kitchen upstairs. She moved into the rec room and turned on the overhead. "You fixed it," she announced.

Tim stepped into the paneled rec room. Tiffany's doll house was in one corner, along with some other toys. Claire's paintings occupied the other corner. The one on the easel was a half-finished rendering of a woman sitting alone at a bus stop. Tim stared at it. "God, this is really good," he murmured.

"Thanks. It's been sitting there a few months," Claire admitted. "That poor woman's been waiting for the bus forever."

Tim noticed a group of paintings leaning against the wall, one in front of the other. "Can I have a look?" he asked.

She nodded. "I was going to sell those at the local art fairs. The first couple of months, I actually sold a few to some tourists, another that's now hanging in my dentist's waiting room, and two more to Harlan's friend, Walt. But Harlan thought it was a little undignified, and this part-time job opened up in the chemical plant's accounting department. The money's more steady."

"These are fantastic," Tim said, sifting through the pile of canvases. "I can't believe your husband made you quit."

"Well, he didn't exactly *make* me," Claire heard herself say. She remembered thinking at the time that it wouldn't kill her to go along with what Harlan wanted for a while. She had tried the same reasoning with Brian.

"You know, I'm an artist myself." Tim shrugged. "Well, actually a *semiartist*. I do cartoons."

"What kind? You mean like political cartoons?"

He shrugged. "Well, sometimes they're political. I have a comic strip that runs in a little Seattle weekly newspaper—and in a couple of other cities. It's called *The Adventures of Private Eye Guy.*"

"You mean in *The Sounder?* That's you? You're Tim Timster?"

He nodded. "None of the guys on the force know. I can't believe you get *The Sounder* here."

"Oh, when we were living in Seattle, Brian got hooked on *Private Eye Guy.* He subscribed to *The Sounder,* and had it mailed here." She pointed to a half-open door at the other end of the rec room. "He's got copies in his bedroom, right there. *Tim Timster.* I can't believe that's you." Claire let out a little laugh. "Now, I know why I felt this connection with you." She started to reach out and touch his arm, but hesitated.

He was gazing at her, and she could tell, he wanted to reach out to her as well.

"I—I guess we should go upstairs, huh?" she whispered.

He nodded, but didn't move. "Claire?" he said finally. "I felt a connection too. But you're married, and I—"

The doorbell rang.

Claire sighed. "That must be Linda."

She gave Tim a sad smile, and gently put her hand against the side of his face. "Thanks for—being such a gentleman, Tim."

The doorbell rang again. Claire turned and started up the stairs.

Linda frowned at Claire, then at Tim. "Did you call Harlan at the plant and tell him what happened?"

"Not yet, Linda," Claire replied. "We phoned Sheriff Klauser. All this happened less than ten minutes ago. In fact, Tim—Officer Sullivan and I were just downstairs getting the electricity turned back on when you rang."

Linda gave Tim a wary sidelong glance as Claire mentioned him by his first name.

Claire waved her friend into the kitchen. "C'mon in and pour yourself a cup of coffee. I think it's still warm. The power wasn't out that long. I'll call Harlan right now, if you'll excuse me." She picked up the phone in the breakfast nook, and started dialing.

Linda poured a cup of coffee. She leaned against the counter and glared at Tim. "Lucky you just happened to be passing by," she muttered.

Tim shook his head. "No, it's like Mrs. Shaw told you. She called me, and I drove over from the hotel."

"Funny that she'd call you, and not the police or her husband," Linda said.

"I *am* the police," Tim replied. "My partner and I are here specifically for Mrs. Shaw's protection. It's not so funny, Mrs. Castle."

Claire kept the conversation with Harlan brief. Tim overheard her say—three times—that she was all right. Claire hung up and announced that Harlan was on his way.

Sheriff Klauser arrived before Harlan did. He said he hadn't seen anyone suspicious in the area. Linda started to make a fresh pot of coffee while the sheriff got on the phone with his deputy.

Tim decided he didn't need to stick around any more. He gathered up the hair dryer and the camera. Claire gave him a plastic bag for them, then walked him to the door.

"I'll take these with me to Seattle," he said. "I don't know how useful those footprint photos will be," he said. "But I'm sure someone on the task force will be able to tell if your hair dryer was tampered with or not."

Claire stared at him. "You're going to Seattle?"

Tim nodded. "Yes, I'm leaving this afternoon. They'll be sending someone to replace me."

"But why?"

He sighed. "It just didn't work out. I rubbed too many

people the wrong way, I guess. My partner says I lack finesse." He managed a smile. "Anyway, you'll probably be getting a detective with a lot more experience, Mrs. Shaw."

"Claire," she whispered.

Tim glanced past her—at Linda, leaning against the arched kitchen entryway. "Nice to see you again, Mrs. Castle," he said.

Linda nodded. "You too, officer."

Claire gave him a wistful smile, and put out her hand. "Thank you for everything, Officer Sullivan," she whispered.

He shook her hand. "I hope you find your son, and that he's safe and healthy." He held onto her hand for another moment. "Take care, Mrs. Shaw."

As he drove away in Al's car and headed up the cul de sac, Tim felt a pang in his gut. He didn't want to leave her. Never mind that he was falling for her. She was a married woman. But she was also very much alone there. Someone was stalking her, maybe Rembrandt, maybe not. He didn't want to say anything, but that business with the hair dryer didn't seem like an accident. Someone was trying to kill her. The first person Claire suspected was her husband. Tim didn't have the heart to tell her that perhaps her son might somehow be involved in the Rembrandt murders. He still hoped he was wrong about that.

He hoped he was wrong about another hunch. He had an awful feeling that once he left this island, Claire would die.

Tim turned the corner onto Main Street. Past the rain-beaded windshield and wipers, he noticed the emergency lights in the distance, two blocks away. An ambulance was in front of The Whale Watcher Inn.

Tim pressed harder on the accelerator, and didn't slow down until he reached the hotel lot. He parked Al's car, then jumped out and ran around the corner to the front of the Inn. Huddled under umbrellas, some on-lookers blocked the sidewalk. He brushed past them in time to see the paramedics loading Al into the back of the ambulance. The older cop was in his T-shirt, and a gray blanket covered him from the chest down. One of the medics had strapped an oxygen mask on Al's face. His eyes were half-closed. He looked dead. Tim only caught a glimpse of him before they shoved the stretcher into the back of the ambulance and shut the door.

"Aren't you his partner?" the inn keeper asked. He was the yuppie father of the twelve-year-old who had checked them in.

Dazed, Tim stared at him and nodded. The stocky, forty-ish man huddled under an umbrella. Behind him, all the folksy pinwheel creations by the hotel entrance were whirling in the wind and rain.

"We didn't know how to get a hold of you," he said. "Your buddy's real sick. He threw up all over the room. He called us. By the time the ambulance got here, he was having convulsions."

"Where are they taking him?" Tim asked, a little out of breath.

"To San Juan Island by emergency charter boat. From there, they'll probably airlift him to the hospital in Bellingham." The inn keeper shrugged. "At least, that's what the paramedics were saying."

The rain soaking him, Tim stared at the ambulance as it pulled away. The siren started up. He slowly shook his head. "I just left him a little over an hour ago. I thought the worst that could happen was he might need a doctor to prescribe him something for diarrhea."

"No, your buddy's pretty sick," the inn keeper said grimly.

Tim just kept shaking his head. He watched the ambulance head for the harbor, then disappear around a curve in the road.

Chapter 16

Someone had forgotten to buy tortilla chips and margarita mix. So Kimberly's roommates elected her to run down to the 7-Eleven at the last minute. The four Western Washington University juniors had been sharing an apartment off campus since the school year started, and this was their first party.

Kimberly Cronin didn't mind walking the five blocks to the store. The rain had let up a little, and it wasn't quite dark yet. She needed to get out of the apartment anyway. With the party starting in an hour, her roommates were all on edge, snapping at each other and fighting over bathroom time.

Kimberly still needed to change for the party and do something with her hair. At this moment, she wore jeans and her WWU sweatshirt. Her long blond hair was in a ponytail. Her head was getting damp from the rain, so she put up the hood to her sweatshirt.

Glancing around, she didn't see anyone else on the street. The rain and the slight cold snap were probably keeping people inside.

The neighborhood wasn't the best in Bellingham. But then, how else could college students afford apartments there? The houses were a bit run down. Lawns were neglected, and trash cans and recycling bins became permanent fixtures near the end of just about every driveway. The place was a borderline slum.

Still, Kimberly rarely worried about wandering alone there late at night. That was when the neighborhood, often called Sorority Row, was hopping. But not now. It was twilight, and most everyone was inside, getting ready to go out.

She was thinking about Larry Blades, a cute senior, who was supposed to come to the party. The tall, lanky business administration major had shown interest in her lately. So Kimberly had a mission tonight—besides picking up the extra chips and margarita mix. She was determined to ask Larry out.

About two blocks from the 7-Eleven, she heard a baby crying. The infant's screams came from an alleyway just ahead. Kimberly pulled the hood away from the left side of her face so she could get a better look at a young dad outside his SUV, parked near the mouth of the alley. He was having a hell of a time, trying to open the back door, while holding an umbrella, a big tote bag, and keeping the infant—swaddled in a Care Bears blanket—close to his chest.

Kimberly smiled and took pity on him. The baby wouldn't stop crying. "Oh, c'mon, kiddo," the dad was saying. "Give your old man a break."

Awkwardly, he reached for the door handle to the backseat, but the umbrella started tipping to one side. "Shit!" he hissed.

Kimberly stepped into the alley. "Do you need some help?"

He looked over at her. He was cute, with glasses and a crooked smile. "You're a life-saver," he said, readjusting the swaddled baby in his arms.

"You look like you could use an extra hand," Kimberly said, grinning.

"Thanks a million." He held out the tote bag. "If you could just open the car door, then put this on the floor back there, I can do the rest."

"No sweat," she said, taking the tote bag from him. It was a bit heavy. She turned and opened the back door. "So how old is he?" she asked, over the baby's cries.

"Two months," the man replied.

Kimberly bent over and set the bag on the floor. Then she noticed something very strange. There was no infant seat in the back. She didn't see anything to hold a baby in the front passenger seat either.

She heard the baby fussing, the same cries over and over again.

"Can you take him?" she heard the young dad ask.

Still half-inside the SUV, Kimberly started to turn toward him.

He rested the swaddled infant on the backseat. Kimberly reached out for the baby, but hesitated. There was nothing in the Care Bear blanket but a lump of clothes and a small tape recorder. The infant cries reverberated inside the car.

Suddenly, she felt the man grab her arm and twist it. He swiveled her around so she was lying across the backseat— on top of that pile of clothes.

Kimberly struggled. She opened her mouth to scream.

He pulled back his hand, clenched in a fist.

It felt like a hammer-blow to the side of her face, Then she didn't see anything, just blackness. As she slipped away from consciousness, the last thing Kimberly Cronin heard was a baby crying.

"I took photos of the footprints," Tim said. He was using one of the pay phones in the corridor by the hospital's emergency room. "They're in a disposable camera. I have the hair dryer too."

"Fine, fine," Lieutenant Elmore said on the other end of the line. "Box everything up, and send it overnight mail. I'll have our boys take a look-see."

"I think Al has a brother in Boulder, Colorado," Tim said.

"Maybe somebody ought to notify him about Al's condition."

"Will do. I'll get someone on it. Listen, Tim. Sounds like the doctors have it covered. There's nothing you can do for him. So why don't you head on back to Deception Island and hold down the fort, okay?"

"Well, I'll need backup. Someone's stalking Claire Shaw, and I—"

"Yeah, but it could be another one of those goddamn reporters. Just go back, and keep us posted on anything else that happens." Then he added—almost as an afterthought, "You're doing a great job, Tim."

"Well, thanks, but I really could use some help. I don't think this hair dryer short-circuiting was accident. And then what happened to Al—"

"Oh, c'mon," Elmore interrupted. "You've seen the way Al eats, and *what* he eats. He's like a human garbage disposal. Sooner or later, he was bound to chow down on something that didn't agree with him."

"For chrissakes, he was poisoned!" Tim argued. "He was having convulsions . . ."

Elmore didn't say anything.

Tim rubbed his forehead and listened to the silence on the other end of the line. Earlier, he'd packed up Al's clothes and belongings from his hotel room, which still reeked of vomit. Among Al's things, Tim had found two *Penthouse* magazines, and another one called *Boobs, Boobs, Boobs*. He'd decided to hold onto Al's cell phone and his gun, both of which belonged to the department.

He'd loaded Al's suitcase in the trunk of his car, then caught the ferry to Anacortes. From there, he'd driven up to the hospital in Bellingham. Al didn't have a room yet, but an orderly took his suitcase off Tim's hands.

He'd figured out—long before the doctor said anything—that Al had salmonella or some other kind of food poisoning. Tim kept thinking back to this morning's breakfast at the

Fork In The Road Diner. He remembered the waitress with the limp black hair and the slightly flat nose. *"Something wrong with your pancakes?"* she'd asked. He'd given his breakfast to Al. Tim could still see the older cop, sitting across the table from him, popping blueberries in his mouth.

"I'm almost certain he was poisoned by someone at the restaurant where we had breakfast this morning," Tim continued. "I think it was meant for me. Al ended up eating my breakfast."

"So now you think there's a conspiracy on the island, and someone's trying to kill *you*," Elmore said. "Do you know how paranoid you sound?"

Tim just sighed.

He'd already told Elmore about Rembrandt's first victim, Nancy Hart, vacationing with her family on Deception fourteen months before her murder. Elmore's response on the "coincidence" had been the same as Al's: *"That was over a year before she was killed."* Apparently, the force's statute of limitations on killers obsessing over their victims was twelve months or less.

Tim knew they didn't take him very seriously on the force. But he'd thought these new revelations—and what had happened to Al—would at least give his concerns some credence.

"Listen, Tim," Elmore went on. "This is your first time in the field, and you've come across what might seem like a couple of hot leads. You've also had a bad shake up with Al getting sick. It's natural for you to be a little overeager and extra cautious. But don't bust my ass here. I have a lot on my plate right now. Go back to the island, maintain a low profile, and we'll send you reinforcements in the morning. Are you clear on that?"

"Yessir," Tim grunted.

After hanging up, he checked in with the nurse at the emergency room desk. She didn't have any updates on Al's condition. Yes, she had the police lieutenant's number in Seattle and Tim's cell phone number. And yes, someone would call them and keep them informed of Mr. Sparling's status.

It was still raining when he stepped outside. Walking to Al's Ford Taurus, Tim figured at least one good thing came of this. He was staying on Deception Island. There was a chance he could help Claire.

As he opened the car's front door, Tim saw someone out of the corner of his eye. It was a man in coveralls, a few cars down the row across from him. He seemed to duck behind a minivan as soon as Tim turned in his direction.

Tim stood there for a moment. Finally, he climbed inside the car. He sat and stared at the minivan, waiting for the man to reappear. But there was no sign of him anywhere. Tim started up the car. Was Lieutenant Elmore right? Was he paranoid?

With each stop light on the way to the interstate, Tim felt something wasn't quite right with Al's car. Of course, he wasn't used to driving it, and the roads were slick with rain. He checked all the gauges on the dashboard and didn't see any problems. He told himself to take it easy, make concessions for the weather conditions, and enjoy the ride.

In fact, it was kind of pleasant driving alone, not having to listen to Al's constant chatter. "I'm going straight to hell," Tim muttered, thinking of Al in the hospital. He felt guilty, but went ahead and switched the radio from Al's favorite, annoying Country Gospel station to an FM rock station.

Tim was listening to Bruce Springsteen as he turned onto the freeway entrance. He tapped the brake to slow down for the interstate's curved on-ramp. Nothing happened. Tim felt every muscle in his body tighten. He pressed down harder on the brake, but it didn't seem to make any difference.

White-knuckled, he maneuvered the steering wheel and veered around the curve, almost grazing the guard rail. The wheels let out a terrible screech. For a moment, he thought the car might tip over. "Jesus Christ!" he muttered. He kept pumping the brake—to no avail.

The on-ramp straightened as he came closer to merging on Interstate 5. Tim didn't dare touch the accelerator. He couldn't stop, and he couldn't get off the road. In his rearview mirror, he saw another car barreling down on him. The driver honked his horn.

Shaking, Tim felt around the dashboard for the hazard flasher light switch. He finally found the button and pressed it. But the other car was still right on his tail.

Tim veered off the freeway, driving on the shoulder instead. He prayed Al's car would slow down on its own. But this section of the interstate was a winding downhill run. He peered over the side of the low guard rail. It looked like a hundred-foot drop. He was glancing down at treetops. Cars in the right lane honked their horns, and swerved to get clear of him.

"God, please, please," he whispered. He tried shifting to second gear, and heard something snap. Then there was an awful clanking sound as if he was dragging something under the chassis. After a few moments it was gone, and he heard the clanking in the distance behind him.

Al's Taurus hadn't slowed down at all. In fact, the hill only made the car go faster. Up ahead, Tim saw an abandoned vehicle on the shoulder. "Oh, shit!" he cried. He tried the parking brake. Nothing happened.

He checked the side mirror, and grimaced at the steady stream of cars in the right lane. They were still honking at him. "Goddamn it, somebody give me a break, please," he whispered. He was charging toward the abandoned car, almost on top of it.

Tim jerked the wheel to the left. Another horn blared, and he heard tires screaming. He had to accelerate for a moment, the last thing he wanted to do. It was either that or possibly kill someone.

Passing the abandoned car, Tim veered back onto the shoulder. He took his foot off the accelerator, then wiggled the steering wheel—from side to side. He couldn't tell if the maneuver was working—or if the road was on an incline, but the car started to slow down to thirty miles per hour.

Tim tried to ignore all the cars that wouldn't stop honking at him. He still had no way of pulling off into a ditch on the other side of the shoulder. The drop was still too sheer.

He remembered that man in coveralls hiding behind a minivan in the hospital parking lot. He must have sabotaged the brakes in Al's Taurus.

Hunched close to the steering wheel, Tim stayed on the freeway shoulder. He didn't see any signs for an exit up ahead. If only there was a way he could drive off the freeway without killing himself or someone else.

Wide-eyed, he studied the road in front of him. The windshield wipers slashed back and forth, and Tim noticed something in the distance. "Oh, no," he whispered. "Oh, Jesus, please, no . . ."

He was looking at the orange cones up ahead. They began on the shoulder, then lined up to block off the far right lane. He also saw a traffic jam. All those red taillights, the cars were at a standstill. Directly in his path stood a construction team, and a truck unloading tar.

Tim swerved into the right lane to avoid hitting an orange-colored construction-zone sign. A car horn blasted, and tires squealed. Despite his efforts, Tim hit the sign anyway. He winced as the big placard bounced off his front fender and flew over the guardrail into the treetops.

Stiff-armed, his back pressed against the driver's seat, Tim saw the gridlock ahead, and the cones in the right lane. Cars were slowing down, but a few idiots were picking up speed in their attempts to get ahead of one or two other vehicles.

Suddenly, a pickup darted in front of Tim. Panic-stricken, he automatically leaned on the horn and slammed on the brake, forgetting for a second that it didn't work. The pickup's taillights went on. The son of a bitch was stopping.

Tim couldn't avoid him. There were construction workers

on the shoulder, and a station wagon on his left. He careened toward the back of the pickup.

For a second, he thought he'd stopped safely. He didn't feel an impact. But then he heard a screeching noise, and the crunch of metal. All at once, it felt as if someone punched him in the face. Tim realized that the air bag had activated. That was why he didn't feel anything. The horn had gone off too. The blaring noise pierced his eardrums.

As the air bag deflated, a burning, gassy smell filled the car. Past a crack in the windshield, and the crumpled hood, Tim looked for smoke, but didn't see any. Then he realized the smell was coming from whatever had filled up the air bag.

The pickup in front of him inched forward. Its back bumper was bent in one place, and a taillight was broken. He didn't see any other damage to the pickup.

Yet Tim could tell without even stepping outside to look, Al's car was totaled.

But at least it wasn't moving anymore.

Beep.

"Hello, Lieutenant Elmore. This is Tim Sullivan calling at around seven-fifty. I'm waiting for the last ferry to Deception Island. I'm driving a loaner car, because Al's Taurus got totaled. Or at least the mechanic at the auto place thinks it is. He also thinks the brakes were sabotaged. I agree with him, but then, I'm paranoid. Right? And by the way, I don't know if you've heard from the hospital yet. But they called me an hour ago. Al's in a coma. I've got his cell phone if you need me. Or you can reach me at the hotel. Bye."

Tim stopped by the front desk of The Whale Watcher Inn to ask for his messages. The innkeeper's wife, a petite, sweet-looking redhead named Beven, was on duty. She said a woman had called, but left no message. "She asked if you were still checked in, and I told her, yes. I hope that's okay."

Tim nodded. "That's fine, thanks." He figured it was Claire, wondering if he'd left yet.

"Officer Sullivan?" Beven's voice dropped to a whisper. "They're saying that he's on the island. Claire Shaw saw him. Rembrandt's here on Deception. Is it true?"

"I can't say for sure," he replied.

Behind the counter, the door to the innkeeper's quarters was open. Tim could see her husband, sitting in a recliner, watching TV. But the man was also looking at his wife.

"This is the kind of place where you feel your kids are safe," Beven said, her eyes tearing up. "No one locks their doors here at night. Now, I'm hearing that this maniac is out there somewhere. What are we supposed to do? My husband's going crazy with worry. And I'm pretty scared myself."

Tim didn't know what to tell her. "Well, you should lock your doors, and be extra cautious. But you need to keep living your life. You can't let something like this—paralyze you."

She nodded. "That's exactly what I've been telling my husband," Beven whispered. She gave Tim a pale smile. "You look pretty tired—and hungry. Did you have dinner yet? The Fork In The Road is still open." She winced a bit. "Then again, after what happened to your friend, I guess you might not want to go back."

"No, it's okay," he said soberly. "I need to stop by there anyway. Thanks." Tim started toward the lobby door. "Take care."

"G'night, officer," she called to him.

The only waitperson on duty at the Fork In The Road was a haggard-looking woman with short brown hair, too much makeup, and bad skin. She briefly glanced at Tim as he stepped inside the restaurant. "Sit anywhere you want," she called. "I'll be right with you."

The place wasn't very crowded. Tim took a booth. He didn't have to wait long before she shuffled over to the table. He saw the name tag on her brown uniform: Darla.

"We're out of the special, so don't bother asking," Darla announced, handing him a menu. She set down a too-full glass of water, which immediately made a puddle on the Formica tabletop. Then she slapped down the paper place mat in front of him—along with a paper napkin and the silverware.

"Anything besides water to drink?" she asked.

"A Coke, please," Tim said. "And I have a question. I promise, it's not about the special. Do you have a minute?"

Nodding, she leaned on the table. "Shoot."

"There was another waitress working here this morning. She had dark hair and—"

Darla let out a disgusted laugh. "Huh, you mean that bitch who left right before the lunch rush? Don't get me started on her. I had to come in early, because of her. Talk about a screw up."

"So—she doesn't ordinarily work here?" Tim asked.

"No, thank God."

"And you don't know her?"

The waitress shook her head. "Never laid eyes on her, and I hope I never do. Otherwise, she'll have a hard time removing my boot from her ass." Darla sighed. "One of the cooks said her name was Ronnie. She came in to work for Roseann."

"Yeah, I heard Roseann was sick," Tim said,

"Real sick. Like Mount Saint Helen's, if you get my drift."

"Must have come on pretty suddenly. Do you know what happened?"

Darla shrugged. "To hear the cook tell it, she was in ship-shape when she came in first thing this morning. She had a couple of cups of coffee, waited on a few customers, and suddenly went down for the count. About an hour later, this Ronnie yo-yo showed up. I guess she's supposed to be Roseann's cousin or something. Anyway, she lasted about three hours, then poof, she disappeared. So—I've been here on my feet since ten-thirty this morning. Any other questions?"

"Then this Ronnie isn't a local?" Tim asked.

"Like I say, no one here knows her. I'm guessing she's from out of town. Roseann's the one you should be talking to."

"You don't happen to have Roseann's phone number, do you?"

Darla planted a hand on her hip and squinted at him. "Are you kidding? I may have a big mouth, but I don't give out coworkers' phone numbers to complete strangers."

"My name's Tim Sullivan," he said. "Now we're not strangers. Roseann will probably remember me. Does that help?"

Darla shook her head. "Not really."

Tim pulled out his police badge. "Would this?"

She nodded. "That would do it. I'll get your Coke—and Roseann's phone number." She shuffled away from his table.

Tim sat in a stupor. Everything he'd been through today suddenly hit him: the morning with Claire, then Al becoming so violently ill, and finally, surviving that car wreck. He was so overwhelmingly tired.

As much as he wanted to go back to the hotel, take a shower, then go to bed, he knew the night was far from over. If Rembrandt was on this small island, then Tim would have to do his best to track him down.

Most of the Deception residents knew each other. He wondered where an outsider would hide if he wanted to stay close to someone and not be seen.

Tim pulled Al's cell phone out of his jacket pocket. He remembered Al making a big deal in front of Sheriff Klauser about adding the sheriff's phone number to his speed dial. Tim pulled up the menu function, and pressed Klauser's number.

"Sheriff speaking," he answered on the third ring.

"Hi. This is Tim Sullivan. How are you doing?"

"I'm about to go out of my goddamn mind, that's how I'm doing," the sheriff replied. "I don't know how the hell Linda Castle and her big mouth did it, but since that incident at the

Shaws' house this morning, it's gotten all over the island that Rembrandt is *here among us*. My phone's been ringing off the hook. I've got worried housewives and husbands calling me, and false alarms up the wazoo. The whole community is in an uproar. And today of all days, when I'm short a man—"

There was a break in the connection. "Oh, crap, some other nut is calling. Hold on."

While Tim held, Darla returned to his booth with a Coke and Roseann's phone number scribbled on a napkin. "There you go, officer. Did you decide on dinner?"

"Um, thank you. Could I have another minute?"

"Take two, they're free, ha." She sauntered toward another table.

Tim heard a click on the line. "Yep, another concerned citizen wanting to know if Rembrandt is really here on the island," the sheriff said. "Par for the course today. You still there? Where was I?"

"You were short a man," Tim said.

"That's right. Troy had the day off. Couldn't get a hold of him either, because he went out of town."

"You mean Deputy Landers?"

"Yeah. He won't be back until tomorrow night. Until then, it's just you, me, and my other deputy, Ramon. So what can I do for you?"

"Well, I was going to ask if you'd tracked down that mystery man in the army fatigue jacket and stocking cap, but you already answered my question. Is everything okay with Mrs. Shaw? Any more scares?"

"Nope. I gather Harlan has the place locked down tight for the evening. Ramon will be patrolling the area on and off until dawn tomorrow."

"I'm here at Fork In The Road about to order dinner," Tim said. "After I eat, I'd like to sit down and talk with you for a few minutes. Is that okay?"

"Hell, get your food to-go, and come down the block to the station," the sheriff replied. "That's where I am, filling out my umpteenth response report for the night. Do me a favor, will ya? Bring me a large coffee and a piece of blue-berry pie."

"I'd skip the blueberries if I were you," Tim said. "How about apple?"

After hanging up with the sheriff, Tim waved down Darla, who was behind the counter.

She shuffled over to the table. "F-Y-I. I don't wait on people while they're on their stinking cell phones."

"Good rule," Tim said. "Sorry. It was kind of a police emergency."

"So what are you gonna have, officer?"

Tim ordered a cheeseburger deluxe, an apple pie, and a coffee, all to-go. Darla wrote it on the guest check as she wandered back behind the counter.

Tim glanced at the napkin with Roseann's phone number scribbled on it. He reached for the phone again, and dialed. Her machine picked up: *"Hi, this is Roseann, and this is Einstein."* A dog barked twice. *"Neither one of us can come to the phone right now. So leave us a message after the tell-tale beep."*

"Hi, Roseann . . . Einstein," Tim said, shifting a bit in the booth. "You might remember me from yesterday morning. I'm Tim Sullivan, one of the cops. The cinnamon toast guy? Anyway—"

There was a click on the other end of the line. "Hi, I'm sorry, I'm screening," she said, sounding groggy. "I've been sick all day."

"I know," Tim said. "That's why I'm calling. The other cop I was with yesterday, Al, he got sick this morning too—after eating here."

"Where's here?"

"Fork In The Road. He had the blueberry pancakes, with a bunch of blueberries on the side. He ate up the whole damn thing. An hour later, he was brutally ill. And now, he's in a Bellingham hospital in a coma."

"My God," she murmured. "The poor guy. And I thought I had it bad."

"I hear you were fine when you came to work this morning. Did you eat any blueberries?"

"No, all I had was coffee. But it tasted funny, so I threw out the pot after my first cup."

"Was there someone you didn't know working in the kitchen this morning?" he asked.

"Nope. Same old, same old."

Tim glanced over toward the unmanned register. "What about that man from yesterday?" Tim asked. "The balding guy with the mustache, the one who yelled at you for talking to us. I think you said he was the manager—"

"That's Wayne, the owner," she said.

"The owner?" Tim chuckled. "I heard you talking to him. You told the restaurant *owner* to pound sand up his ass?"

"Yeah, well, Wayne owns the restaurant. But he doesn't own me."

"Was Wayne here this morning?"

"Nope. He doesn't come in on Fridays. Why? Do you think someone tried to poison me or something?"

"Well, it's possible," Tim said. "Look what happened to my friend. Did you leave your coffee cup anywhere someone could have gotten at it?"

"Sure, I left it on the counter."

Tim looked over at the lunch counter—and the eight empty stools lined up in front of it.

"Were any strangers sitting at the counter?" he asked.

"Nope. Like I say, same old, same old. There was Bill Comstock. He's always the first one in. Then Rachel Porter and Tom McFarland, Ron Castle, and old Richard Boswell with the bad breath. He's there practically every—"

"Did you say Ron Castle?" Tim interrupted. "Linda Castle's husband?"

"That's right," Roseann said on the other end of the line. "He's a regular. Only he usually sits at the two-top in the corner by the window. But this morning, he took a counter seat."

Tim glanced across the restaurant at the empty table for

two in the corner by the window. "Was someone in his usual spot?" he asked.

"No. But I have a question for you."

Tim pulled a pen from his jacket pocket and scribbled down on the place mat: *"Ron Castle—switched tables—no reason."*

"Are you still there?" Roseann asked.

"Yes. You have a question. Go ahead."

"You mentioned earlier that your partner had a big pile of blueberries by his pancakes. Did I hear you right?"

"Yes, he had the blueberry pancakes. I ordered them, but he ended up eating them."

"That's funny, because I've worked in that dump for seven years. I must have served up a few thousand plates of blueberry pancakes, and never—not once—have any of the cooks dished them out with berries on the side. Who was waiting on your table?"

"Your cousin," Tim said.

"My cousin? Honey, I have two cousins, and they both live in Evanston, Illinois. What are you talking about?"

"Well, Darla said she thought this woman was your cousin or something," Tim explained. "Her name's Ronnie. She's in her late forties with black hair, and sort of a flat nose. You must know her. You got her to fill in for you."

"I don't know anyone named Ronnie," Roseann said. "I couldn't find anyone to take my place. I called the other girls, including Darla, and none of them could take my shift. Who's this Ronnie character?"

"I don't know," Tim replied. "I was really hoping you could tell me."

Tim didn't realize how hungry he was until he sat down in the police station and unwrapped the cheeseburger. Except for a Nestle's Crunch bar from a vending machine in the hospital, he hadn't eaten anything all day. He'd skipped lunch, and Al had gobbled up his breakfast, which of course, had come from the same kitchen as this cheeseburger now making him salivate.

He watched the gaunt, wizen-faced sheriff at the desk across from him, gorging on the apple pie. Tim decided to take a chance on the burger. While they ate, and between phone calls from concerned, terrified islanders, Tim told the sheriff about "Ronnie."

"Nobody at Fork In The Road knows who she is," Tim explained, picking at his fries. "She punched in on Roseann's time card and lied about being her cousin. Roseann never laid eyes on her, never talked to her. Yet this woman knew Roseann was sick. Who told her? Who sent her?

"I think we need to question the other employees at Fork In The Road while this 'Ronnie' was there. Maybe we can track down some of the other customers she waited on. Someone might know her."

Sheriff Klauser nodded grimly. "I'll start asking around over there."

Tim sighed. "Before 'Ronnie' came on the scene, somebody must have dosed Roseann's coffee with something. I made a list of the customers Roseann remembers being there when she opened this morning—before she got sick." Tim pulled a folded-up napkin from his shirt pocket, and handed it to Sheriff Klauser. "One of those guys might be in cahoots with this 'Ronnie' woman—if that's really her name, and I doubt it."

The old sheriff squinted the names scribbled on the napkin. He shook his head. " 'Bill Comstock, Tom McFrarland, Ron Castle, Richard Boswell . . .' I know all these fellas. None of them could be involved in anything shady."

Tim shoved his half-eaten dinner aside. "There have been three 'accidents' today. Accounting for two of them, someone poisoned my breakfast, and the brakes in my car were sabotaged. It's pretty obvious, someone wants me dead."

"Why?" the sheriff asked, giving Tim back the list.

"Because I'm asking a lot of questions that are making people uncomfortable, questions about the disappearance of

Brian Ferguson and Derek Herrmann, questions about Rembrandt and what happened to Claire Shaw. That's where the third *accident* comes in. There's something fishy about Claire Shaw's hair dryer going haywire this morning. I think somebody wants Claire Shaw dead too—before she starts to remember certain things."

"So you think Rembrandt broke into the house and rigged up the hair dryer?"

"Maybe," Tim allowed. "Maybe someone else."

"Well, who, buddy?"

Sighing, Tim reached for his cheeseburger again. "I don't know. But it's more than one 'someone,' I can tell you that. No way could just one person be responsible for setting up all those *accidents*. Obviously, it's someone who doesn't want it to look like murder. My guess is they want to avoid having this island crawling with investigators and cops. So—they've tried setting up a death by electric shock, a food poisoning, or an auto accident. Freak mishaps, minor investigations, case closed."

Tim was about to take another bite out of his cheeseburger, but frowned at the sandwich, and set it back down.

His head cocked to one side, the old sheriff stared at him. "So you think someone on the island is working with Rembrandt? Somebody who's afraid you're getting too close?"

Nodding, Tim pointed to the napkin with the list of names. "Maybe it's one of these guys."

"Well, buddy, you won't find your stalker in the stocking cap there."

"What makes you so sure?"

"Because," the sheriff said. "An islander wouldn't need a disguise to walk around on Main Street in the middle of the day. Why do that? He'd only be calling attention to himself. It would be just as easy to stalk her without wearing some getup." He took his last fork-full of apple pie, then sipped his coffee. "Trust me, buddy. This stalker, this guy whose shoe print you photographed this morning, he's an outsider. In a place like Deception, where everybody knows everybody else, this character has to remain anonymous—and unseen."

"Do you think he might have slipped away on one of the outgoing ferries this afternoon or earlier tonight?" Tim asked.

The sheriff winked at him. "Great minds thinking alike. I had Ramon check both outgoing ferries today for any strangers." He sighed and shook his head. "No one suspicious."

"So chances are, this outsider's still on the island," Tim said. "You think maybe he's stowed away on one of the bigger boats in the harbor? Or maybe in one of those cabins in the woods?"

The sheriff nodded. "A definite possibility. I—"

The phone rang again, and he rolled his tired, old eyes, and grabbed the receiver. "Island Police, Sheriff Klauser speaking . . ."

Tim tossed what was left of his cheeseburger and fries in the bag. He wasn't paying much attention to the sheriff's phone conversation. He only caught the end of the discussion. "Well, Estelle, I'm sure Rolo is barking at a squirrel or a raccoon," Sheriff Klauser said. "Give him a dog biscuit, and maybe he'll shut up . . . I wouldn't worry about Rembrandt, Estelle. He goes after younger gals . . . Oh, all right . . . I'll swing by. Give me a few minutes . . . Yeah, hmmm, bye."

He hung up the phone and sighed. "Crazy old biddy," he grunted. "She's sixty if she's a day, and as ugly as a muddy picket fence, and she thinks Rembrandt's peeping in her windows. Hell." He got to his feet and stretched his bony body. "Poor old Estelle doesn't seem to realize she's no college girl anymore, and never was anywhere near as pretty as Claire Shaw. I need to head over there."

Tim stood up too. "I'd like to take a drive in the woods, and start checking some of those cabins, sheriff. Maybe after you drop by this Estelle's house—"

Giving him a dubious gaze, the sheriff shook his head. "There are almost a hundred little cabins in those woods. And getting to some of those places is a major pain in the ass. We couldn't hope to tackle the job tonight. Hell, not even in three nights."

Sheriff Klauser sauntered behind the counter, then pulled his jacket from out of the back room. "Besides, I got the phone ringing off the hook, and I can't be stuck out where God lost his shoes. I need to be close by when people like Estelle want me on a house call. And I'm not taking Ramon off patrol-duty by Claire Shaw's house. Damn it, I wish Troy was around."

Tim followed him to the station's front door. "Do you mind if I drive out to some of the cabins by myself?"

"Tonight?" Sheriff Klauser paused in the doorway. "What are you, nuts? You can't go in any of them. They're locked up. We need to get the keys from the managers or the owners, and we'll need permission—or search warrants. It's a major project, buddy. Wait until tomorrow. I'll get the Guardians in on it, and we can organize a regular search party—instead of some half-assed one-man or two-man job."

"Well, would you mind if I just drove around the woods and had a look?" Tim asked.

With a sigh, the sheriff lumbered back inside the station, and opened a bottom drawer to one of the two metal desks. He pulled out a flashlight, and handed it to Tim. "Here, buddy, have yourself a good time. Just remember, some of those cabins are occupied, and people are scared. They have guns. Don't get your head blown off."

"Thanks," Tim said, testing the flashlight. He followed Sheriff Klauser out the door.

"I still think you're better off waiting until tomorrow," the old cop said. He locked the station door, then headed to his police car. "But you do what you gotta do. Thanks for the pie, buddy."

He ducked into the patrol car, then shut the door. He started up the emergency flashers on the car roof.

Tim watched him drive away in the night.

* * *

He didn't know where the hell he was.

It was so dark in this part of the forest, Tim felt as if he were driving in a tunnel. The headlights in front of him were the only thing that pierced the blackness. All he could see was about forty feet of narrow road ahead. The trees were merely ink-colored shapes and shadows looming over him. They played havoc with his radio reception. So Tim drove in silence.

He glanced at the clock on the dashboard: 10:50 P.M. He'd already spent an hour at the Platt Harbor. He'd gone from boat to boat, shining the sheriff's flashlight into galley windows, looking for a stowaway, and finding no one.

Tim had a feeling this trip into the woods would be just as fruitless. The headlights played tricks with shadows racing along the tree trunks. Tim half-expected to catch sight of a man in stocking cap lurking amid those trees.

He'd brought along Al's gun, but he'd never fired one at a human being before.

The farther he drove from civilization, the more he worried about the loaner car. Earlier he'd parked it in the hotel lot while he'd been at the restaurant and the police station. The brakes seemed to be working all right for now, but Tim couldn't help feeling wary.

He still wasn't certain about the cheeseburger he'd eaten either. He remembered Al's diarrhea kicking in about an hour after breakfast. If that cheeseburger was laced with something, he didn't want to be lost in these woods when the first pang of nausea hit.

Tim had a map, but still didn't know where the cabins were. He kept trying to ignore the voice in his head telling him: *Maybe this isn't such a good idea.*

Up ahead, he saw a turnoff on his right. He steered onto an unmarked dirt and gravel road, and he felt the car vibrate over the bumps and divots. Pebbles crunched under the tires as Tim followed the coarse, winding path. After a few moments, he realized he was driving like an old man, leaning close to the windshield, hands clutching the wheel.

He went over a big stone in the road, and felt the car suddenly drop. "Jesus!" he cried. The sheriff's flashlight rolled off the passenger seat and onto the floor.

His stomach in knots, Tim kept driving. He didn't know where he was, but in the distance, he saw a break in the trees, and the silhouettes of a couple of squat cabins against the dark horizon. As Tim drove closer, he didn't see a single light on in either of the cabins. He didn't notice any cars parked in the area either. Then again, he was only about three or four miles from the Shaws' house. It was a long hike for Claire's stalker, but not so terribly far.

Tim pulled up in front of the first cottage, a typical one-story log cabin with a front porch. He started to circle around the bungalow, directing the flashlight into the windows. Except for some old furniture, the place looked empty and dusty inside, uninhabited.

Moving around to the back, he tore his trouser leg on a nail sticking out the side of the cabin. Looking down to inspect the tear, he noticed his shoes were covered in mud.

He was in back of the cabin when he heard something in the bushes behind him. Swivelling around, Tim directed the flashlight toward the trees and shrubbery. "Who's there?" he called.

For a moment, he felt paralyzed. He didn't see anyone. Slowly, he took Al's gun from his jacket pocket.

Tim kept shining the light toward the woods. He heard twigs snapping underfoot, leaves rustling. They seemed to be getting closer. "Who's out there?" he called again. "I have a gun. Who—"

A raccoon crawled out from behind a bush and lazily looked up at him. Its eyes were momentarily illuminated by the flashlight. Tim sighed, then let out a little laugh. "Okay, paws in the air," he muttered.

He watched the animal moved on.

Tim put the gun back in his jacket. He glanced over his shoulder at the deserted cabin, and started to move onto the one next door.

"One down, about ninety-nine left to go," he muttered. "Shit."

It took Claire a moment to realize she was alone in the queen-size bed. The digital clock on the night stand read 1:23 A.M. She'd been sleeping for about an hour.

Pulling back the covers, she got up and padded to the bathroom. The door was closed, and a strip of light showed at the threshold. Harlan was awfully quiet in there. She was about to knock and ask if he was all right, but Claire hesitated. She tiptoed away from the door, and retreated to the darkened hallway. Feeling a chill, she rubbed her arms as she looked in on Tiffany. Her step-daughter was asleep.

Claire ducked into the bathroom across the hall, then closed the door after her. The color scheme in there always reminded her of Good & Plenty candy. The tub, sink, and toilet were white, but the rest of the bathroom was painted pink. Harlan's first wife, Angela, had done the decorating. Claire wasn't crazy about it. The towels were white with a pink rose pattern. The same rose pattern was on the shower curtain, tissue dispenser, toothbrush holder, and tumbler.

At the sink, Claire started to reach for the tumbler with the pink rose pattern on it. She remembered the last time she'd drunk from that tumbler, she'd been crying. In the mirror in front of her, she'd seen her reflection, the blotchy skin, and the tears in her eyes. She'd looked at Harlan's reflection too. He'd stood in back of her, asking over and over what had happened. *"He's run away again,"* she'd told him. *"I don't know what I'm going to do . . ."*

Claire gazed at the pink rose-patterned tissue dispenser. On that night, she'd gone through several Kleenex. She'd been crying, practically hysterical. What word had Linda used to describe her behavior? *Bonkers?*

Claire drank some water, then stared at her reflection. She looked pale. She wondered if Harlan and Linda had been telling the truth about that night.

She went back into the master bedroom, and saw the bed was still empty. She withdrew to the hallway again, then down the stairs. Her eyes adjusted to the darkness, and in a way, she almost felt safe without any lights on. At least, no one outside could look in and see her.

She passed by the sliding glass doors in the pantry. Harlan had left the back lights on, and the yard was illuminated—right up to the woods at the edge of the lawn.

Claire didn't need to turn on any lights to dial the phone. She didn't have to look up the number either. At this point, she knew it by heart. But a machine answered at The Whale Watcher Inn. A recorded voice told her that the switchboard was closed after eleven P.M. The recording provided an emergency contact number, but Claire hung up before this disembodied voice read it to her.

She stared out at the backyard. Her nightgown was a bit flimsy, and she crossed her arms in front of her, partly to keep warm, but mostly for modesty.

She didn't see a soul in the backyard. Yet Claire still felt someone's eyes taking in every inch of her.

It was a beautiful, chilly fall night. The rain clouds had moved on, and he could see stars in the sky. Huddled in his jacket, he sat in a lawn chair and sipped brandy.

It was two o'clock in the morning. It had been a long day. But he felt good. He smiled. Someone—unlike himself—might have felt lonely and insignificant sitting alone under the dark, celestial skies.

But he wasn't alone. She was close by. In the stillness of the night, he could hear her muffled cries. She was screaming the same things as all the others before her. She begged for help, for someone to come to her rescue. Her parents had money and would pay him to let her go. Could anyone hear her? Was anyone there?

Her name was Kimberly Cronin. He'd looked at the driver's license in her purse. It wasn't a flattering picture.

He would make Kimberly prettier.

He gazed up at the night sky, and smiled. No, he wasn't alone. And he was far from insignificant.

Chapter 17

It sounded like the maid was trying to unlock his door.

Tim had double-locked it when he'd gone to bed a few hours ago. He'd been dead tired, but still alert enough to take the extra precaution. After all, there had been two attempts on his life within the previous twenty-four hours. What would stop them from trying again while he was asleep?

He'd checked several different cabins in those woods, and didn't come across anything except more raccoons. He almost got stuck in the mud outside the eleventh bungalow. He took that as an omen to call it quits for the night.

On the way back to the hotel, Tim turned down Holm Drive and parked near the end of the cul de sac for a few minutes. The Shaw house was dark. He didn't see anyone lurking about the grounds. When a patrol car came by, and Sheriff Klauser's other deputy, Ramon, shined the side-door high-beam in his face, Tim introduced himself. He was glad to see the young cop vigilant in his patrol duty. Tim went back to The Whale Watcher Inn feeling Claire was safe.

There weren't any messages from the hospital, so he assumed Al's condition was unchanged. As he got ready for bed, he switched on the TV. Tim didn't pay much attention to the infomercial for some miracle, fat-reducing, easy-clean cooker. It was just background noise to keep him from feeling too lonely on a Friday night, alone in a strange town—in a slightly cheesy motel. And yes, he was a little scared too. Hearing the has-been, still-pretty actress from an eighties hit TV show ramble on about weight-loss and heathy cooking practices was just what he needed to take his mind off his worries. He almost hated turning off the television.

Tim had fallen asleep moments after his head hit the pillow.

Now, he heard what sounded like a key in the door, and a strange grinding. He had no idea of the time. The thick blue and brown paisley drapes were closed, and the room was dark. He didn't bother rolling over to look at the clock. He kept his eyes shut and called out: "Could you come back later, please? I'm still sleeping, okay? Thank you!"

She didn't respond, but at least she stopped fiddling with the door.

Tim shifted under the covers, and went back to sleep.

He didn't know how long he was out. But he was awakened again by someone knocking on the door. The room didn't seem quite as dark as before. Tim sat up in the bed, then squinted at the clock-radio on his nightstand: 6:20 A.M.

"Officer Sullivan?" he heard, during a pause in the knocking. "It's Gabe Messing, the innkeeper. Are you okay?"

Rubbing his eyes, Tim crawled out of bed. He staggered to the door in his boxer shorts. Unlocking the door, Tim opened it a crack and looked at the yuppie innkeeper. "Morning," he muttered.

"Didn't you hear?" Gabe asked. "We had an attempted break-in."

"You did? Oh, I'm sorry. I was out late last night, and just woke up. No one told me about it—"

The innkeeper was shaking his head. "No, they tried to break into *your* room. You didn't hear any noise?" He pushed the door open wider.

Tim gazed down at the doorknob, so dislodged it was

nearly hanging out of the door. Someone had scraped away at the woodwork around the lock area.

"The maid hasn't started her rounds yet, has she?" Tim said numbly.

"No, she doesn't even clock in until seven. Why do you ask?"

Frowning, Tim shook his head. "No reason," he replied.

"Island Police, Sheriff Klauser speaking."

Tim was sitting on the bed with the receiver to his ear. He'd shaved, showered, and dressed, and would have paid fifty bucks to crawl back into bed right now. "Hi, Sheriff. It's Tim Sullivan calling. Have you been up all night? Are you okay?"

"Oh, I'm fine as frog's hair," he answered. "I actually caught a couple of hours' sleep on one of the beds in the jail downstairs. If I never hear the name Rembrandt again, I'll be a happy man. I asked around at Fork In The Road this morning. And nobody knew this 'Ronnie' character, never saw her before. Did you find anything in the woods last night?"

"A few raccoons," Tim admitted. "I don't know if Gabe here at The Whale Watcher told you or not, but someone tried to break into my room last night—while I was here, sleeping."

The sheriff didn't say anything.

"Hello? Are you still there?"

"I wish to God I weren't," Sheriff Klauser said on the other end. "That's another report I have to fill out."

"I can come over and help," Tim said. "Also I want to follow up on that idea about searching through some of the weekend and summer cabins."

"Sure, come on by," the sheriff said. "Could you do me an enormous favor and stop by Fork In The Road? That bowl of fiber cereal I had this morning didn't do the trick. Pick me up a large coffee and a bacon and egg sandwich. And get something for yourself. My treat."

* * *

"We won't be able to get this search party together until later this afternoon." the sheriff admitted, between bites of his breakfast sandwich.

They were sitting and eating again at the same ugly metal desks where they'd sat and eaten last night. Roseann had handled Tim's carry-out order at the Fork In The Road, so he figured the sheriff's bacon and egg sandwich and his own order of cinnamon toast were safe.

The station phone kept ringing, interrupting them. While the sheriff took calls, Tim typed up the police report on the attempted break-in. There wasn't much to investigate, but the hotel needed a report for insurance purposes. Tim was more concerned about starting the cabin-to-cabin search in the woods.

"I got Walt Binns to organize this thing," the sheriff continued. "He's a good buddy of Harlan Shaw's, and knows those woods as good as anybody. He should be able to enlist some of his pals with the Guardians to help out. This needs to be a tight little group. We have too many nutcases with guns who see this as an excuse to go hunting off-season. A lot of those cabins will be occupied today by weekend residents. I don't want anybody getting shot."

"Is there something I can do?" Tim asked.

"You can help Walter Binns in the woods," the sheriff answered. "But that won't be until this afternoon. If you have something going on this morning, go do it, buddy. No use in hanging around here."

Tim nodded. "Okay, I'll get out of your way."

The sheriff grinned. "You aren't in the way. In fact, you're a big help, buddy. I don't mean to speak ill of the ill, but I'm glad it's you I'm dealing with here instead of your windbag partner. How's he doing anyway?"

"I was wondering if you've heard from the hospital about Al," Tim said. He was on the cell phone, unpacking his suitcase. They'd decided to change his room at The Whale Watcher.

"Nobody called you?" Lieutenant Elmore asked on the other end of the line.

Tim stopped unpacking for a moment. "No, why?"

"Al died last night around eleven o'clock."

Tim sat down on the edge of the bed.

"You did everything you could," Elmore said. "The state police will be handling the investigation," Elmore said. "Health code violations and salmonella cases are their baili-wick. I'm sure they'll have some questions for you."

Tim swallowed hard. "Lieutenant, this isn't a health code violation, it's a homicide. Al was poisoned."

"Well, the state police will have to determine that. In the meantime, sit tight. You'll be on your own for a while. We're all working overtime here. Rembrandt has another one, a student up at Western Washington."

"What?" Tim whispered.

"He nabbed her early last night. Her roommates say she took off to buy some last-minute stuff for a party, and never came back."

"Are they sure it's Rembrandt?" Tim asked.

"Positive. He left his calling card. Two of the roommates went looking for the girl, and found her panties hanging on a No Parking sign by an alley near their apartment. That was twelve hours ago, and the clock is ticking."

"She was a student at Western Washington in Belling-ham?"

"That's right. The girl's name is Kimberly Cronin."

"Al was in Bellingham," Tim said. "It's where someone sabotaged my car brakes. Maybe he's following me—"

"Oh, please, Sullivan," Elmore groaned.

"Could you at least fax me her photo and stats?" Tim asked.

"Fine, fine," Elmore grumbled. "I'll shoot something off to your local police there."

"And with your permission, I'd like to go to Wenatchee

today," Tim said. "I want to talk with Nancy Hart's parents about their vacation here. Maybe they'll remember something we can—"

"No, no, and one more time, no," Elmore interrupted. "Leave them alone. Stay put, and sit tight. Okay?"

Tim hesitated.

"Listen," Elmore said. "For every minute I'm on the phone placating you, that's time you're taking me away from Kimberly Cronin's case. And that girl doesn't have a lot of time. Get my drift, Sullivan?"

"Yessir." He barely got the words out before he heard a click on the other end. Then the line went dead.

"I'm just calling to make sure that you and Mrs. Shaw are doing okay," Tim said. He'd hoped against hope that Claire would answer the phone. And of course, he'd gotten Harlan—interrupting his breakfast, no less.

"Well, we're fine, thanks," Harlan answered tersely.

"Also just to let you know, I'll be your contact here. I have some bad news. My partner, Al, died last night—from food poisoning."

"Oh, no. That—" Harlan paused. "I heard he'd gotten sick. That's too bad. He seemed like good people."

"Yes, well, anyway," Tim said awkwardly. "If you need to reach me, you can call Al's cell. The number is—"

"I have it right here by the phone," Harlan said. "I appreciate the call, officer. And speaking for my wife, we both appreciate your quick response to the emergency here yesterday morning."

"No problem," Tim said. He figured this was the closest Harlan Shaw would come to apologizing for kicking him out of his house three days ago.

"Sorry about your friend," Harlan said. Then he hung up.

*   *   *

"Oh, my God, that's horrible," Claire said.

She'd started to clear Tiffany's plate from the breakfast table, but now she set it down, and sank back into her chair. Numbly, she stared at Harlan.

He hadn't been on the phone with Tim very long. Claire had tried not to seem overanxious about the call. But she hadn't had a chance to talk with Tim since yesterday morning.

Harlan put his napkin back in his lap, then sipped his coffee. "Yes, it's too bad," he muttered. "Food poisoning of some kind. Ron mentioned on the phone last night that he'd gotten sick."

"I can't believe it," she continued. "He was just here Wednesday morning, and now . . ." Claire glanced over at Tiffany within earshot in the family room. She was lying on her stomach in front of the TV, and her favorite Saturday morning cartoon line up.

"How was Tim handling it?" she whispered. "Did he sound okay?"

"Tim?" Harlan scowled at her. "You call him *Tim?"*

"Oh, for God's sakes." Rolling her eyes, Claire stood up, grabbed Tiffany's plate, and moved around to the other side of the kitchen counter. "I can't call him by his first name?" she asked. "I heard you calling his partner, *'Al'* ten minutes after he walked into this house."

"That's different," Harlan argued. "I don't understand all your concern for this guy. It's his partner who died."

Claire took Harlan's plate from the table. She glanced over at her stepdaughter. "Tiffany, if you want me to help you wrap Courtney's present for the birthday party, I need you to get it for me during the next commercial. And start thinking about what you want to wear."

"Okay," Tiffany called back, her eyes still glued to the TV screen.

Claire started to wash the dishes. She looked over at Harlan, seated at the breakfast table. He went back to reading the newspaper he'd set aside for Tim's call.

"Did Tim—I mean, did *Officer Sullivan* say whether or not Al had any family?" she asked.

"No, he didn't," Harlan replied, not looking up from his paper.

Claire stood over the sink, and started washing the dishes. The truth was, she called Tim by his first name because she liked him—and trusted him.

Now the lack of trust she had for her husband seemed mutual.

She was tempted to ask him about last night—or rather, early this morning, when she'd woken up in bed alone at one-thirty.

Claire had come back to the bedroom around two. The bed was still empty, and the bathroom light still on. She knocked on the door, but Harlan didn't answer. She opened the door.

No one was in there. Claire figured he was on the computer in his workroom down in the basement. He did that in the middle of the night sometimes. But why the charade with the bathroom door?

She crawled back into bed. While listening for him, Claire drifted in and out of sleep. She was also thinking about her recollection, the memory flash from that night, when she'd told Harlan about Brian running away. Had she been wrong not to trust Harlan?

When she finally heard him creep up the stairs, Claire stole a look a look at the clock: 4:20 A.M.

Then something occurred to her. What if it wasn't Harlan coming up the stairs? She feigned sleep and held her breath as she listened to the footsteps in the hallway. They were drawing closer. Through the slits in her eyes, she recognized her husband's silhouette in the bedroom doorway. Harlan was wearing a T-shirt and jeans.

She wanted to sit up in bed, switch on the light, and ask him where the hell he'd been for the last two-plus hours. Instead, she kept pretending to be asleep. He turned off the bathroom light, stepped out of his jeans, and crawled into bed next to her.

To her relief, he didn't touch her. Within a few minutes, she heard him snoring.

She might have asked him about it before breakfast. But Claire hadn't said anything.

And she didn't say a single word about it now.

Instead, Claire washed the breakfast dishes, and talked about coordinating their schedules for the day. Harlan needed to put in a few hours at the plant. Tiffany had a birthday party. Claire had to see Dr. Moorehead—for real, this time. Then she was supposed to spend the afternoon doing volunteer work at the Garden Plaza with Linda.

Claire wanted to steal some time alone, so she could see Tim. Someone had poisoned his partner. She had a feeling Tim was in trouble, maybe in even more trouble than her.

She pretended to listen as Harlan talked about dropping her off at Dr. Moorehead's, then taking Tiffany to her party. All the while Claire stared at him and thought he'd taken the news of Al Sparling's death pretty easily. The two of them had been talking like old friends in the living room just a couple of mornings ago. And now the man was dead, poisoned. She wanted to ask Harlan how he could be so nonchalant.

But she didn't say a single word about it.

Not far from the ferry terminal on the mainland, Tim found an auto repair shop. He had them inspect his loaner car to make sure nothing had been tampered with. While he sat in the waiting room, Tim checked a Washington state map for the best route to Wenatchee.

Lieutenant Elmore had told him to sit tight. But he couldn't. And he couldn't understand how they'd just dismissed it as a coincidence that two of Rembrandt's victims had spent time on this tiny island in the San Juans.

He'd telephoned Nancy Killabrew Hart's parents from the hotel, and asked if he could come see them regarding the ongoing investigation. Mr. Killabrew had seemed reluctant at first, but finally agreed to meet him. He'd given Tim directions to their house in Wenatchee.

Tim hadn't noticed anyone tailing him from the hotel to the ferry terminal. He hadn't seen anyone suspicious on the ferry either. Still, he'd decided not to take any chances with the car.

The auto mechanic stepped into the waiting area and gave Tim's loaner car a clean bill of health.

From the map, Tim figured he had a three-hour trip to Wenatchee ahead of him, some of it over a mountain pass. And most of the way, he would be checking his rearview mirror.

"Do you remember anything before—or after—that moment you were in Tiffany's bathroom talking to Harlan?" Linus Moorehead asked.

He was looking rather dapper today, with a tweed coat over his black knit shirt. He and Claire sat across from each other in his matching club chairs.

Harlan had dropped her off at Moorehead's office. Linda was supposed to pick her up later and take her to the Garden Plaza. The Whale Watcher Inn was only about four blocks away. But Claire couldn't hope to break away and see Tim.

She shifted a bit in the chair, and gave Dr. Moorehead an apologetic smile. "Sorry. I just remember standing in the bathroom and telling Harlan that Brian had run away again. And I was crying."

"How did Harlan seem to take this news?" Dr. Moorehead asked.

"He was surprised, and concerned for me. I—" Claire hesitated.

"Go on."

She sighed. "I was going to say, I feel bad for not trusting him more, for not—believing what he and Linda told me about that night. I thought they were lying, but all this time, I've been lying to myself." Frowning, Claire slowly shook her head. "I didn't want to think that Brian really ran away, and chose to *stay* away. I was hoping—and sort of dreading—there was some other explanation. But I guess it boils down to the fact that I must be a lousy mother. I'm not a very good wife to Harlan either."

"Aren't you being a little hard on yourself?" he asked.

"No," Claire replied. "Because I still don't completely trust Harlan. Nor Linda for that matter."

"Quit beating yourself up, Claire," Moorehead replied, with a warm smile. "You've been through a hell of a lot, and you can only remember little bits of it. What other people are telling you doesn't make sense. It will take a while before anything makes sense. It's only natural for you to be wary of everyone and everything around you. Finally, most importantly, you miss your son."

Claire just nodded. Everything he said made sense.

"I don't blame you for being a little suspicious," he went on. "And I'd be a bit angry too—if I were in your place. You've lost a couple of weeks of your life. You should be allowed some emotional baggage from that. If your husband and your friends don't understand that, then the hell with them. Tell them to come see me."

Claire smiled and let out a surprised little laugh.

In a couple of sessions, her opinion of Dr. Moorehead, the "dork" with the collages, had turned around. A part of her wanted to tell Linus Moorehead about Tim.

But she did what most of the therapists she'd seen over the last two weeks told her not to do.

She held back.

Arlette Killabrew showed Tim a framed photo of the family in front of their vacation cabin on Deception Island. "Nancy was engaged at th-th-the time, and we figured this was our last vacation as a family," she explained. "And it-it-it was, but not in the way we th-thought."

Tim studied the picture. Rembrandt's first victim was a beautiful young blonde. They were a good-looking family.

He hadn't expect Nancy Killabrew Hart's parents to be so young. With his curly blond hair, chiseled good looks, and sporty long-sleeve T-shirt, Mr. Killabrew could have passed for one of those rugged great outdoors–men, paddling down the rapids in a beer commercial. His wife was a pale, natural beauty with shoulder-length red hair. She wore a yellow pullover and jeans that hugged her trim hips. Their daughter, Nancy, would have been twenty-four if she were alive today. Tim guessed Mr. and Mrs. Killabrew were in the late-forties, but they looked much younger.

At the door, Frank Killabrew had given Tim a bone-crunching handshake, and invited him into the family room. When Arlette Killabrew had offered Tim a cup of coffee, he'd noticed her slight stutter.

The Killabrews' family room had a big, stone fireplace, a TV and stereo, and a couple of dozen framed family photos on the wall. There was a blank spot from the picture Arlette Killabrew had taken off the wall to show Tim.

He'd admitted to them he was the only person on the investigation task force who thought their weeklong vacation on Deception Island might have been a factor in Nancy's murder fourteen months later. He explained about Claire, a Deception Island resident who had survived Rembrandt's attack.

"It's such a small island," Tim concluded. "And two of his victims have spent time on it—Nancy on your family vacation, and Claire Shaw as a full-time resident. He waited until both women were off the island, before he went after them."

The Killabrews agreed that it was an awfully strange coincidence.

"We never got to meet Mrs. Shaw," Frank Killabrew explained. He sat upright in a recliner across from Tim. "But we met her son, Brian. He got into some trouble with Frank Junior and another boy, Derek Somebody."

"Derek Herrmann," Tim said. He was sitting beside Arlette Killabrew on the blackwatch-plaid sofa. "I'm wondering if you remember anything else about that vacation, specifically anything that happened to Nancy. Did she go out with anyone while she was on the island?"

Frank Killabrew shook his head. "No, Nancy didn't have any dates," he said. "As Arlette told you, she and Jim were engaged at the time."

"Yes, of course," Tim said. "But I think Nancy's first encounter with this man was on Deception Island. I'm looking for some sort of early warning sign—if you know what I mean. Was there anything unusual that happened? Anything Nancy might have shared with you?"

Frank Killabrew sighed. "Well, she caught that Derek Herrmann kid outside the cabin looking at her through her bedroom window one afternoon. Nancy told me, and I gave the little pervert a talking-to. That's about it."

"There was something witha-witha-witha policeman," Arlette Killabrew said over her coffee cup. "He st-stopped Nancy for not using her indicator, or something s-s-silly like that, and-and-and then he flirted with her. I remember Nancy telling me, and we laughed about it."

"Did she mention this policeman's name or what he looked like?" Tim asked.

Mrs. Killabrew thought for a moment. Frowning, she patted back her red hair. "Sh-she said he was good-looking. His name was—um . . ."

"Troy?" Tim interjected. "Troy Landers?"

She nodded emphatically. "Th-that's right. I remember Nancy saying, he was—he was cute, but-but he gave her the creeps."

"Did she mention anything else about him?" Tim asked. "Did she have any other kind of contact with him?"

Arlette Killabrew shook her head. "No, that was it."

Tim once again picked up the framed photo of the Killa-brews in front of their cabin on Deception Island. He focused on Nancy's image. She was laughing, and had her arm around her kid brother's shoulder.

He wondered if—when this photograph was taken—she'd already met the man who would kill her.

Kimberly was naked, strapped down on a massage table. She couldn't speak or scream, because of the tape over her mouth.

He quickly covered her from the neck down with a white sheet. On either side of the massage table, he'd set up bright lamps on tripods—like lights for a movie set. They were blinding. Kimberly didn't see anything on the white-painted walls. A sheet hanging from a clothesline sectioned off the rest of the room from this little windowless area.

At her right was a tall, narrow cabinet on wheels, one of those portable chest-of-drawers hair-cutters and beauticians have near their workstations.

Squinting in the lights, she tried to focus on him. She couldn't see his face. He wore a surgeon's mask, hair-bonnet, and apron. He had on the thin rubber gloves too.

"I'm not going to hurt you, Kimberly," he explained behind the mask—in a calm, oddly personable tone. "I'll be letting you go soon. That's why I made you wear the hood when I took you out of your room. It's why I'm wearing this mask. After I let you go, I don't want you telling the police what I look like—or where you were. Would I take these precautions if I was going to kill you? Now, don't squirm, okay? This isn't surgery, Kimberly."

He reached into the narrow cabinet and pulled out a bottle of astringent and some cotton balls. "You're a very pretty girl, Kimberly," he said. "I just think you could be prettier."

* * *

"She's very pretty. Is she your girlfriend?"

The young female clerk at the Foto Finish in Wenatchee's Valley River Mall handed the photos to Tim. One was an original, and two were copies she'd made for him in three minutes.

The photo was a college graduation portrait on loan from Mr. and Mrs. Killabrew's family room. Tim had promised to return it after making the copies. He wanted to show the picture of Nancy Hart around Deception Island. Maybe Roseann or the sheriff would remember seeing her with one of the locals—or with a stranger.

He would add the photo to his own Rembrandt file, a green folder with sleeves holding data he'd gathered so far. It had everything: copies of Derek Herrmann's and Brian Ferguson's police records; paperwork from the auto wreck place; copies off the library microfiche of *The Seattle Times* article on Nancy Killabrew Hart; and notes jotted on napkins. So far, none of it came together to make any sense.

The girl behind the counter smiled at Tim as she handed him his change. "Well? Is the girl in the picture your sweetheart?"

Tim just shook his head.

He'd left the Killabrews about a half hour ago. They'd given him a couple of leads: Derek and his window-peeping and Troy Landers on the make. Was it just a coincidence Rembrandt had abducted another woman on Troy's day off?

Tim pulled into the Killabrews' driveway. As he came up to the house, the door opened. Arlette Killabrew stepped outside and gently closed the door behind her. She met Tim on front stoop. She had a handkerchief in her hand, and her eyes were bloodshot. "Glad I—I caught you before you rang," she said in a quiet voice. "Frank's taking a nap."

Tim handed the photo of Nancy to her. "Thank you. I hope my visit didn't upset you."

She gave him a sad smile and shook her head. "It-it-it's all right. After you left, Frank and I started talking about that vacation. Like I—I said, it was our last trip together as a-a-a family. It was a very happy time. We both had a good cry."

"Well, thank you again for you help, Mrs. Killabrew."

"Arlette," she said. She held out her hand.

When Tim shook it, she didn't let go.

Tim stared at her. Mrs. Killabrew looked as if she wanted to say something, but couldn't form the words.

"What is it?" he asked.

"Something d-d-did happen," she whispered. "I remembered it after you left. I never t-t-told Frank, never told anybody. I think Nancy did—see someone on the island. She didn't say anything to me. She was engaged to Jim." Mrs. Killabrew let out a tiny laugh. "Th-they were high school sweethearts. Nancy never—never even went out w-w-with another boy. I know that was on her mind during the vacation."

Mrs. Killabrew glanced down at the ground. She rubbed her arms from the chill.

"Go on," Tim said.

"Nancy used to t-t-take long walks alone in the woods on Deception. She always came back before dark. But one night she-she-she almost missed dinner. We—were barbecuing outside, and I—I saw her slip into the house. I found her in her—room, and she was crying. I asked what was wrong, and she shook her head and answered th-that she was fine. She said, *'I—I almost did something really stupid, Mom, but I'm okay.'* I could, I could see she was—upset, clearly. Then she went into th-the bathroom, and washed up. Nancy didn't say anything about it again."

"Do you think she'd been attacked?"

Mrs. Killabrew's mouth twisted into a frown, then she shook her head. "Nancy's clothes looked clean. But wh-what I remember is her face was—all made up. I remember the mascara running when she was crying. I'd never seen her all-all-all made up like that before. Sh-she even had a beauty mark painted on . . ."

Chapter 18

Linda wore her sailor hat with the brim turned down, her orange HOE-HOE-HOE sweatshirt (she had it in three different colors), and her gardening gloves that matched her knee-pads.

Since picking up Claire at Dr. Moorehead's office, Linda had mentioned twice—perhaps as a conversation filler: *"I can't believe you didn't bring gloves or anything, Claire. What you've got on I'd wear to go* shopping, *not gardening."*

What Claire had on were jeans, an olive-colored pullover, and a windbreaker, and she didn't see what was wrong with the outfit. They'd found some gloves and a knee pad in the greenhouse. Even with a hole still healing in her chest and the *wrong outfit,* she seemed to keep up with Linda in the number of tulip bulbs they were planting.

Molly Cartwright, the third member of their horticultural party, was a bit slower. Though dressed appropriately in a baseball cap, gardening gloves, and knee pads, Molly still wasn't planting the bulbs correctly, according to Linda. A plump, fortyish blonde with bangs and a sweet smile, Molly took Linda's criticism in an obliviously good-natured way. Then she went back to talking about what a hunk Dr. Moorehead was.

"Oh, there's something so sexy about him," Molly said, digging into the soil with a spade. "I'd act crazy just for a chance to sit and talk with him for an hour. Don't you think he's sexy, Claire?"

She paused over her work. "Kind of intellectual-sexy. I didn't think much of him at first, but I'm getting to like him. I think the visits are doing me some good."

"Molly, dear, could you get some more mulch from the greenhouse?" Linda asked. "I'll be your slave for life."

Linda waited until Molly Cartwright got to her feet and started toward the greenhouse. She stared at Claire. "You're starting to remember things?" she asked in a hushed voice.

Claire shrugged. "Not much, just fragments."

"Like what?" Linda pressed.

"I remember being tied-up, and I was in a car." Claire started digging at the soil again. "And there was a conversation with Harlan. I told him that Brian had run away again. I was crying."

"So—you remember that now? See? I wasn't lying, Claire. At the hospital, you accused me—"

"Yes, I know," she said. "I'm sorry, Linda."

"Do you remember anything else? Or is that all?"

"That's it, except for that episode with you and me in the front seat of Ron's Jeep. I told you about it already. There was a man outside the car, and he had a gun. You told me to pray."

Linda shook her head and went back to gardening. "That just plain didn't happen, Claire. Like I told you, I think you dreamt that one up."

Molly returned, lugging a five-pound bag of mulch. "You know what we should be planting?" she said, plopping the bag on the ground. "Violets."

"They're not outdoor plants, dear," Linda sighed, busily digging away.

"Too bad," Molly said, getting down on her knees at the edge of the garden. "I thought it might be sweet. You know, because of Violet Davalos?"

Linda stopped digging. Her eyes narrowed at Molly. "Are

you joking?" she asked. "Because what you're saying is hardly appropriate."

Wide-eyed, Molly gazed back at her and shrugged. "I wasn't joking," she said innocently. "I just thought it might be a nice tribute to Violet. We could plant some violets in her honor. Maybe in the greenhouse—"

"Well, I think it's in bad taste." Linda sighed, then went back to work.

"Who's Violet Davalos?" Claire asked.

"Oh, that's right, it happened before you moved here," Molly said. "The Davalos family used to live here. Their house was on this very spot at one time—along with a vacant lot. And oh, it was just a mess, a regular eye-sore. I don't really blame Violet for letting the place go—"

"Molly, you're not digging deep enough again," Linda interrupted. "I told you how to do it. You're almost as bad as my poor mother, and she has Alzheimer's. That reminds me. Do you know what she did the other day?"

Linda told a story about her mother in the rest home in Everett. It was obvious she didn't want to talk about Violet Davalos.

A half hour and a dozen tulip bulbs later, Molly got a call on her cell phone. Her daughter needed to be picked up from a friend's house.

"Could I hitch a ride to the Shermans?" Claire asked. "Tiffany's at a birthday party there. If you'd drop me, Tiffany and I will get a ride home from one of the other mothers. Harlan ought to be back from work by then."

She turned to Linda. "Do you mind? I don't mean to poop out on you, but I'm feeling a little tired. This is the first real exercise I've had since . . ." She shrugged. "Plus I'm a bit clammy. Y'know, Linda, I think you were right. I didn't dress appropriately. Will you be okay here by yourself?"

Linda looked a bit confused. But she nodded. "Well, I suppose so."

*   *   *

"So—who is Violet Davalos?" Claire asked.

She sat on the passenger side of Molly Cartwright's station wagon. Molly was at the wheel, watching the road.

"Gosh, did you see how Linda got all bent out of shape when I suggested we plant something in Violet's honor?" Molly asked.

"Yes, I wondered what that was about," Claire said. "You were saying earlier that Violet Davalos's house used to be where the Garden Plaza is."

Eyes on the road, Molly nodded. "That's right. Well, it all happened before you came here, Claire. Hugh and Violet Davalos had a house on the property. And there was a vacant lot beside it. No one in their right mind would want to live next door to the Davalos family. They just let the place go to pot, which by the way, the two teenage sons were growing in their backyard. Not that you could see it—past all the overgrown grass and trash they tossed out on that lawn. And don't get me started on those two boys."

"They were bad news, huh?" Claire asked.

"Well, let's put it this way," Molly said. "They were just like their father, and he'd been in jail. He was alcoholic, and violent. We always knew something awful would happen to that family. Poor Violet."

"What happened to them?"

"Hugh got drunk and crazy one night," Molly said, eyes on the road. "It's really sad. He—well, he shot Violet and the two boys, set fire to the place, then turned the gun on himself."

"My God," Claire murmured. "When did all this happen?"

"About three years ago. It was the Fourth of July. I remember, because at first, they thought some fireworks had gone off. The place burned to the ground. The bank owned the property. Hugh and Violet were in debt up to their elbows. Anyway, the Guardians got together, and bought up the land—along with the lot next door, and they turned it into the Garden Plaza."

Claire just shook her head.

"I can't believe you've lived here two years, and never heard about it," Molly said. "Huh, then again, I guess people would like to put it behind them. Still, you'd think there would be a plaque or a memorial birdbath or something in the Garden Plaza. I mean, Violet wasn't a bad sort. Was I crazy to want to plant a violet or two in her honor? I don't know why Linda got so snippy."

"Me neither," Claire murmured, staring at the road ahead.

"Wouldn't that be a sweet idea though? A couple of violet plants, maybe in the greenhouse?"

"Claire, the phone's for you." Kira Sherman brought the cordless receiver to her.

When Claire had arrived at Courtney Sherman's birthday party she'd volunteered to help. Courtney's mother, Kira, had put her to work in the kitchen.

Claire set down the dish towel, and took the phone from her. "Thanks, Kira," she said, a bit mystified that someone was calling her there. "Hello?"

"Hi, Claire. I'm just calling to make sure you're all right. You left so suddenly, I was concerned."

"Oh, Linda, hi. I'm fine, just a little tired. Sorry we deserted you."

"Do you want me to come get you and Tiffany at the Shermans?" Linda asked on the other end of the line. "I can take you home. You really shouldn't be alone, Claire. Harlan wouldn't like it."

"Oh, I'll get a lift from one of the mothers here. Harlan should be back by the time we get home." Claire had already told Linda all this at the gardens. Was Linda really that concerned? Or was she checking up on her for some other reason?

"So what did you and Molly talk about in the car?" Linda asked.

"Um, the gardens, mostly," Claire answered. "Molly thought

it could use another birdbath, and maybe a violet plant or two in the greenhouse." She paused. "Listen, Linda, one of the kids here needs to phone her mom, I should hang up. Let's talk later tonight, okay?"

There was no one waiting to use the phone. Once Claire clicked off with Linda, she asked Kira if she could make a call.

Courtney's mother opened the basement door. They were assaulted by ear-piercing squeals and screams from the party-goers down in the recreation room. Kira waved and nodded tiredly. "While you're at it, call a paddy wagon to take me away in a straight jacket!" She headed down the stairs.

The remark milked a laugh from a couple of the other mothers who were helping out. Claire stepped away from them as she dialed The Whale Watcher Inn. She got the operator, and asked for Tim Sullivan's room. There was no answer. The operator broke in, and asked if she'd like to leave a message.

"Um, yes, please. I don't have a phone number for you. But please tell him—a fellow artist tried to get a hold of him. And she'll try again. No emergency. Got that?"

"Fellow artist . . . she'll try again . . . no emergency. I got it."

"Thank you," Claire said.

One of the other mothers gave Claire and Tiffany a ride. But Claire had her drop them off at the library.

She left Tiffany to browse in the Children's Section, then Claire repaired down to the basement, where the old periodicals and newspapers were stacked. The place smelled musty, and for a library, it was poorly lit. The overhead fluorescents were staggered so pockets of darkness broke up the big, gray room. The floor was unpainted cement. Rows of tall metal shelves were loaded with bound periodicals, stacks of yellowing newspapers, and dusty magazines. Claire didn't see any place to sit, except for a metal mini-stepladder with a grooved rubber antislip surface. They probably didn't want people lingering unobserved down in the basement for too long. If that was the ploy, it worked. At the moment, Claire was alone.

She wandered up and down a couple of aisles until she found where old copies of *The Islander* had been shelved. *The Islander* was a thin weekly that came out every Thursday, covering news and events for the San Juan Islands.

Claire pulled up the little stepladder, then sat and started thumbing through the old newspapers. She was looking for an issue dated around July 4, 2000, when the Davalos house had burned to the ground.

She wouldn't have been all that interested if Linda hadn't bristled at Molly's mentioning the name, Davalos.

Claire's hands became dirty as she shuffled through the pile of weeklies from three years ago. All of a sudden, she heard a noise in another part of the basement. It sounded like a door closing—or perhaps the furnace starting up. At the same time, she felt a chill. Claire turned toward the maintenance area door, with a chain in front of it and "No Entry" stenciled on a frayed, faded placard. The door was closed.

She waited a moment, listening for another noise. She heard footsteps, but that was upstairs. With a sigh, she went back to the newspapers. She found an issue of *The Islander* dated July 6, 2000, and paged through it. According to Molly, the Davalos fire was an arson, triple-homicide, and suicide. It should have made the headlines.

But Claire couldn't even find anything in the "Police Beat," a report of police emergencies, incidents, and what passed for crime on the quiet little islands. Brian's gnome-stealing incident had been reported in a "Police Beat" last summer. Fortunately, they didn't mention any names in their bulletins.

Unfortunately, they didn't mention any names—or any

fire—in the July 6 installment of "Police Beat." Claire even tried the obituary page, but found nothing about the Davalos family.

She pulled out the July 13 issue, and thumbed through it. Then she heard another noise, and suddenly froze. It sounded like a magazine had fallen off one of the shelves in the next aisle. For a few seconds, Claire didn't move. If someone had come down from the main floor, she would have heard them on the old, rod-iron spiral staircase.

Slowly, Claire got to her feet. Clutching the newspaper, she crept to the end of the aisle, and peeked past the row of shelves, Nothing in the next aisle, not even a magazine on the floor.

Biting her lip, she warily glanced down one more aisle. Again nothing. But the overhead light on the other side of the room was out, and she couldn't tell for sure whether or not someone was there in the shadows. There was a dark alcove in the corner too. "Hello?" she said.

No response. She wondered if the library basement had rats.

Rats or Rembrandt, either way, she wasn't staying down there.

As she started to move toward the spiral staircase, Claire heard a rustling noise. She stopped to listen for only a second, then bolted for the stairs. Claire raced up the old wrought-iron stairway so fast, she was out of breath when she reached the top. She'd made some noise too. The librarian—and two people in the main room were staring at her.

Her head down, Claire quickly walked to the long study table, and sat in one of the mismatched chairs. Catching her breath, she once again started to page through *The Islander* for July 13, 2000. Claire kept looking over at the railing at the top of the spiral staircase to the basement. No one had come up from the cellar yet. Maybe they did have rats down there. After all, it was an old building, and near the water.

She glanced toward the Children's Section, where Tiffany

was parked on a sofa, reading a Christmas book with a cartoon crocodile on the cover.

Claire kept paging through *The Islander.* She finally found something on page seven: *"JULY 4TH TRAGEDY ON DECEPTION ISLAND: FOUR DEAD AS FAMILY VIOLENCE ERUPTS IN GUNFIRE, ARSON AND SUICIDE."*

For such a sensational headline, the article was surprisingly brief. Claire had already gotten the gist of it from Molly. The story pointed out that Hugh Davalos had been arrested three times for assault, twice during domestic disputes, and once for attacking a police officer, who had stopped him for driving while intoxicated. He'd also served jail time for auto theft. The sons, Dean, 19, and Rodney, 17, were barely mentioned. There was a quote from a neighbor about Violet:

> *"For someone whose home life wasn't very easy, she always kept a brave face and a positive attitude. Violet never complained. We'll never know what she really went through. We only know that Violet's passing is a sad loss for many people."*

At the end of the article, they mentioned: *"Violet Davalos is survived by her brother, Steven Griswald of Bremerton, Washington."*

Claire turned the page, and saw a photo of Ron Castle in a chef's hat and apron. He was smiling and brandishing a spatula. The article was about the forthcoming Platt Guardian-sponsored "Summerfest Scramble" pancake-and-eggs breakfast. It received more coverage than the Davalos murders, suicide, and fire.

Claire pulled a pen and piece of paper from her purse and scribbled a note to herself: *Steven Griswald—Bremerton, Washington.*

"Mom?"

With a start, she looked up at Tiffany. "Yes, sweetheart?"

Tiffany handed her a book, called *The Christmas Crocodile.*

"Can you check this out for me?" she asked. "I didn't bring my library card. Then can we go home? Because I have to go to the bathroom."

"You mean—like—number two?" Claire whispered.

Tiffany nodded.

"Well, we have to walk home. It'll be eight blocks. Can you last that long? I can guard the door for you here."

"I'll last, I promise."

Claire returned *The Islander* to the front desk, and checked out Tiffany's book.

"Sure you're not rushing the season a bit?" Claire handed Tiffany the Christmas book as they stepped out of the library together. A gust of cool air hit them. "It's not even Thanksgiving yet."

Tiffany pointed across the street—at the Santa Claus display in the hardware store window. "It's Christmas there," she said. She turned to the building next door to the library. "And it's Christmas there too . . ."

Claire looked at the bunted string of Christmas lights—not yet illuminated—along the top of the squat, one-story locksmith shop. Her gaze followed the lights along the side of the little building, toward the back.

Claire suddenly gasped. She saw someone dart behind the locksmith shop. He seemed to have come from the back of the library. Claire only caught a fleeting glimpse of him, but she saw the army fatigue jacket.

"Honey, get back inside," she whispered urgently. She gave Tiffany a gentle push toward the library's front entrance. "Hurry, I'll be right there."

Claire waited until her stepdaughter ran inside the building. Then she crept toward the back of the locksmith shop. At the same time, she stayed a safe distance from the building. She didn't see anyone in back of the shop. Nobody was hiding behind the garbage cans or the old, abandoned, rusty shell of pickup truck parked back there. A high wooden fence sliced through some overgrown shrubs, and the gate was half-open, still swaying a bit. Beyond the fence was an alley.

Claire stood there, trying to get her breath. She decided to back away. She didn't want to leave Tiffany alone while chasing after some phantom stalker. And what did she think would happen once she caught up with him?

A wind blew in off the water, and the chill cut through her. As she retreated toward the library, Claire smoothed back her hair. Beads of cold sweat covered her forehead.

Near the back of the library, she noticed an outside stairwell leading to the cellar. Her heart was still racing. Claire stopped and glanced down the cement steps. The door—one of the old kind with peeling gray paint and a fogged window that had chicken-wire in it—was open.

She looked around to make sure the man with the army fatigue jacket had moved on. Had he just come from down there?

Biting her lip, Claire took a couple of steps down the cement stairwell. She hesitated a moment, then moved on to the door. Peeking past the entry, she saw a dark, little alcove. The cellar door was below ground-level, yet she still felt the chilly wind kissing the back of her neck.

There were lights past the shadowy area. Taking another step forward, Claire saw the shelves full of bound periodicals and old newspapers. Some of the papers ruffled slightly from the draft—and the open door behind her.

Swallowed up in darkness, Claire saw the mini-stepladder, where she'd been sitting just minutes before. Claire shuddered, because she knew.

She knew he'd been watching her just a few minutes ago—from this very spot.

Chapter 19

Tim came in from the ferry deck to take the call on Al's cellular. It had been blustery out there, and his dark hair was in a disarray. He sat at one of the tables in the passenger area, near a heater duct.

From the window, he had a view of the choppy gray water, and the other islands in the distance. The ferry wasn't crowded, but someone had let their two kids run up and down the aisle. They were squealing and laughing.

"I got a fax from your boss in Seattle," Sheriff Klauser was saying over the phone.

Tim had to put a finger in his free ear. "Yes, I asked him to send it," he said. "Is there a picture?"

"Uh-huh, very pretty gal too. Kimberly Cronin. According to this fax, Rembrandt abducted her around six o'clock last night—in Bellingham. I hate to say it, but everyone here is taking a big sigh of relief."

"What do you mean?" Tim asked, hunched over the table.

"Well, it means he's not on the island any more. He isn't stalking Claire Shaw. He's moved on. We can call off that cabin search."

"I wouldn't do that just yet," Tim advised.

The kids moved to another part of the ferry, and Tim took

his finger out of his ear. "I'm on my way back from Wenacthee," he said. "I talked with the parents of Rembrandt's first victim, Nancy Hart. Nancy and her family spent a week vacationing on Deception a year before she was killed. Her mother told me Nancy used to go for long walks in the woods by herself."

"What does this have to do with—"

"Just listen, please," Tim said. "One night, Nancy came home from a walk, and her mother found her in her room. She said Nancy's face was all made-up, and she had a beauty mark. Rembrandt always gives his victims a beauty mark."

"I'm not reading you," the sheriff said. "What are you getting at?"

"I think Nancy might have been meeting someone during these walks in the woods," Tim said. "And on this particular night, he must have tried to put makeup on her."

"What do you mean?" the sheriff asked. "How?"

"Maybe he talked her into a make-over," Tim said. "Maybe he tied her up and started painting her face, I don't know for sure. But he did *something* to scare her, because she ran away. And she was crying when her mother found her."

"So you're saying this guy—if there really was a guy— was Rembrandt?" the sheriff asked. "But you don't know for certain, do you? I mean, so far, all this is just a theory, right?"

"Yes. But don't you think it's worth pursuing?"

"How do you want to pursue it, buddy?"

"Well, for starters, by searching those cabins in the woods— especially the ones near where the Killabrews stayed. Maybe we can find out who was renting the neighboring cabins at the time."

He heard the sheriff sigh on the other end of the line. "Listen, buddy . . . Tim. I called your boss after I got that fax. I wanted to thank him. I mentioned this cabin-to-cabin search you wanted to launch, and he shot it down—but pronto. The idea went over like a pregnant pole-vaulter. He said all it would do is cause a lot more panic. And I'm sorry, I have to agree with him. He said you should just sit—"

"Sit tight, I know," Tim cut in. "But don't you see? Between Nancy Killabrew Hart and Claire Shaw, there's a chance Rembrandt's a permanent—or at least, a part-time—resident on Deception. He may own one of those cabins, or he's renting it, or maybe just stowed away there. Think about it, Sheriff. Wouldn't one of those remote cabins out there in the woods be an ideal place to hold someone captive? Kimberly Cronin could be somewhere on Deception Island right now."

"I'm sorry, buddy," the sheriff replied. "But yesterday evening—while Rembrandt was abducting that gal in Bellingham—you had me convinced he was here on the island. Well, if he ever was here in the first place—and I'm beginning to have my doubts—I think he's long gone by now."

"So—I'm on my own if I want to search cabins," Tim said grimly.

"Well, you can always call Walt Binns, and see if he'll still help out. I won't stop you, buddy. But aren't you going against your boss's orders?"

"Yes," Tim admitted.

"Then I don't want to know about it," the sheriff said on the other end of the line. "And for chrissakes, don't scare any of the weekend residents while you're out there in those woods tonight."

The man standing on the front porch of the three-bedroom cabin looked a bit scared. He was about thirty, and lanky with red hair. He'd obviously dressed in a hurry. His flannel shirt was half-unbuttoned, he'd forgotten to zip the fly to his jeans, and he stood in his stocking feet. The front door was open behind him. "Can I help you with something?" he asked.

He must have been alarmed to see two men driving up to the cabin, where he and his family were staying for the weekend.

It was the same cabin the Killabrews had rented two summers ago. The current occupants probably had no idea that in one of those bedrooms there had slept a woman who was murdered by a serial killer.

"Hi. We didn't mean to bother you," Tim said.

He and Walt Binns stopped in front of Walt's Range Rover, parked on the dirt road. They'd already checked three other cabins in the vicinity, all unoccupied. Walt had procured the keys from Chad Schlund, who managed about a dozen of the cabins. Walt had volunteered to be Tim's driver and guide through the island's woods.

"I'm your neighbor," Walt called to the man, giving him a friendly wave. He stepped up to the front porch, and Tim followed. The red-haired man still looked a bit apprehensive.

Walt shook his hand. "Walt Binns. I have a cabin a couple of miles from here, closer to the coast. My buddy here is a cop."

Tim shook his hand. "Tim Sullivan, hi."

"Rob Schilling," the man said, still visibly wary. "Is there something I can do for you?"

"We were wondering if you've noticed anyone—hanging around here," Walt said.

"He was last seen wearing an army fatigue jacket and a stocking cap," Tim piped up. "Um, his family's looking for him. He's—harmless, just not all there, if you know what I mean. He wandered off. His folks are worried."

Rob Schilling shook his head. "No, we haven't seen anyone." He frowned at Tim. "I'm here with my wife and two kids. You say this guy's harmless?"

Tim hesitated. He was thinking of Rembrandt. At the same time, he didn't want to start a panic. "Yes, but if you see him, you should phone the police or you can call me. Give him a wide berth. He—he scares easily. And just so he doesn't scare you, I suggest you lock your doors tonight."

Tim gave the man Al's cell phone number, and Walt gave him the number at his cabin. As they were leaving, Walt shook Rob Schilling's hand again. "Don't forget, I'm just down the road a piece. If you folks need anything, give me a holler."

They climbed back into Walt's Range Rover. Tim whispered to him, "Give you a *holler?*"

"I was trying to sound folksy," Walt replied, scooting behind the wheel. "You know what I'd like to do? I'd like to check out my own place. I haven't been there in a few days. I bet you'd like to see it too, wouldn't you?"

Sitting on the passenger side, Tim shrugged. "Sure, I guess."

Walt started up the car. "Oh, don't try to act so casual about it," he chuckled. "You want to take a look at my place. I'm a suspect, aren't I?"

Tim tried to laugh. In fact, he didn't want to consider Walt Binns a potential suspect. Harlan's best friend was an easygoing guy, who looked years younger than his buddy and had a better sense of humor. Tim had been driving around with Walt for nearly an hour now, and he liked him.

Tim had already shown him the photo of Nancy Killabrew Hart. Without hesitation or a false note, Walt had said he didn't recognize her. Tim had believed him. Or maybe he'd just wanted to believe him.

"If I'm not a suspect, I ought to be," Walt went on, driving up the dirt road. "If this serial killer is on Deception, he'd have to own or lease one of these cabins. He couldn't keep his victims anywhere in town."

"That's what I was thinking," Tim admitted, rocking a bit as they drove over some bumps on the dirt road.

"Well, I have a cabin, very isolated," Walt volunteered. "And this guy would need a boat too. He has to be free to come and go to the mainland to do his abducting . . ."

"And his dumping—once he's finished with them," Tim said soberly. "That means smuggling dead bodies back to the mainland at all sorts of weird hours. Even with his car, he couldn't do that on the ferry running only three times a day."

His eyes on the road, Walt nodded. "So our guy would need his own boat. I have a boat."

"Should I read you your rights now or later?" Tim asked.

Walt chuckled. "Oh, later, please. You have to hear my alibi first."

"Go ahead, I'm listening," Tim said.

"Seriously, that weekend Claire was abducted down in Seattle, I was on Victoria Island. If you want, I can dig up a receipt from the hotel. In fact, they dated and stamped these one-third-off-your-next-stay coupons. They're yours if you want. I get a corporate rate at this place. Take your girlfriend up there for the weekend on me."

"That's very generous of you."

"Consider it a bribe, officer," he said. "I'm going thirty miles an hour, and the speed limit here is twenty. I'm hoping you'll look the other way."

"Were you all by yourself on Victoria?" Tim asked.

"I was afraid you'd ask that," Walt muttered. "I was seeing someone. But I'd appreciate it you didn't contact her—unless it becomes absolutely necessary. This someone happens to be married. We occupy a very small part of each other's lives. I only see her one weekend every few months. That was Suzanna's and my weekend."

"So—you don't know anything about Harlan's stepson running away."

Frowning, Walt shook his head. "Just what everyone has told me. It's a shame too. Claire's been through enough. She doesn't need to be tearing her hair out, wondering where Brian's gone off to. He's a good kid, but kind of a screw up."

"Do you think it's possible Brian got himself into some real serious trouble, and maybe that's why he ran away?"

"Like what kind of trouble?"

"Rembrandt trouble," Tim said. "Brian and his friend, Derek Herrmann, both disappeared at the same time the attempt on Claire's life was botched. They also knew Nancy Killabrew Hart's brother. Mr. Killabrew told me that Nancy once caught Derek peeping into her bedroom window."

"Why does that put them in 'Rembrandt trouble'?" Walt asked.

"There was a theory circulating around the task force for a while that Rembrandt wasn't working alone, that he could have a partner, or maybe a young disciple or two."

"And you think Derek Herrmann and Brian fit the bill?" Walt said. He frowned. "Maybe Derek, which is a real stretch. But not Brian. He'd never intentionally do anything to hurt his mother. He and Claire have something special. Harlan recognizes that. It's why he tolerates Brian. Hell, it's why I kind of have a soft spot for the kid."

Walt turned onto a gravel path. Up ahead, Tim noticed a clearing in the woods, and a chalet-style cabin. Through the open window, he heard gulls in the distance, and water lapping against the shore.

Walt pulled over beside the house, and shut off the engine. "I like Claire Shaw a helluva lot," he said. "Harlan hit the jackpot his second time around. I don't mean to bad-mouth my late wife's best friend, but Angela could be pretty cold." He seemed to work up a smile. "You've spent some time with Claire, haven't you?"

"Yes," Tim answered a bit cautiously.

"Then you know what I mean. Claire's an amazing woman. That's why I'm here, helping you out. We need to make sure this maniac doesn't get near her again. Harlan's looking after her, but I can't help worrying. Maybe it's because of what happened to his first wife—and my wife. I've become a fatalist."

He let out a sad laugh, then glanced at Tim. "Hell, I'm worried about her now. Isn't that nuts? What do you think she's doing right now?"

"I'm sorry, there's no answer in Mr. Sullivan's room," said the operator at The Whale Watcher Inn. "Would you care to leave a message?"

Claire was using the phone at the librarian's desk. By

now, she was pretty certain the hotel operator knew her voice and was sick of hearing it. "No message," she whispered. "Thank you."

She asked the librarian if she could make another call, then dialed home. She got the machine. "Harlan, are you there screening?" she asked, after the beep tone. "It's me. Pick up. I just had another little scare. Are you around? Okay, it's a little after four, and I'm at the library with Tiffany. We need a ride home, honey. I—I'll try you at work. Bye."

She hung up, then asked the librarian for one more call. She called Harlan at work, and his machine picked up.

"Hello, you've reached the office of Harlan Shaw, Plant Manager, Chemtech Industries. I'm away from my desk at the moment. Please leave a message after the beep. If this is a plant emergency . . ."

Claire knew the message, and there were about five emergency contact numbers Harlan would rattle off before the beep.

She smiled across the room at Tiffany, who sat stiffly in an oversize chair with her library book in her lap. Claire didn't feel safe walking home. They needed a ride, and they needed it quickly. Tiffany still had to go to the bathroom.

Claire had tried to persuade her to use the library restroom. She'd guarded the door for her. But after five minutes, Tiffany had emerged, tearfully announcing that she couldn't go—but still had to go. "I need to poop at home!" she'd whimpered.

". . . the Chemtech 24-hour-emergency hot-line," Harlan's recording went on. *"Or press zero for the operator. Thank you."*

Just as Claire heard the beep, she saw Dr. Linus Moorehead step into the library. A book under his arm, he headed for the front desk. But he didn't seem to recognize Claire until she waved at him. She hung up the phone.

"Well, hi, Claire," Dr. Moorehead said, setting the book in the return slot. "We meet twice in one day. This is a nice surprise."

She let out a sigh. "Divine intervention is more like it," she whispered. "Do you have your car with you?"

He nodded. "It's parked over by my office. Why? Can I give you a lift someplace?"

Claire nodded. "Yes, thanks . . ."

The following is a transcript of a recorded emergency call to a 9-1-1 operator in Skagit County, Washington, on Saturday, November 15 at 4:12 P.M.:

9-1-1 OPERATOR: Police Emergency.

CALLER: Yeah, I'm on my cell. I got a flat tire here on Highway 20, just East of Sedro Woolley—

9-1-1 OPERATOR: Sir, for roadside assistance, please dial 206—

CALLER: I don't need roadside assistance, god-damn it. I know how to change a fucking flat tire.

9-1-1 OPERATOR: Sir, what's your emergency?

CALLER: I'm trying to tell you! I pulled over to the side of the road, and saw it down by the river. It's right out there in the open—just a few hundred yards from where I'm standing. There's a naked woman down on the rocks, at the river's edge. She's dead. I can see it from here. She has some kind of bag or something wrapped around her head . . .

"Why do you think he does it?" Walt Binns asked. He was feeling along the top of the door frame for a hidden key to the seemingly deserted cabin.

"Rembrandt?" Tim shrugged. "There are all sorts of theories."

"Nothing here, try under that flower pot, will you?" Walt pointed to a dead plant in a clay pot at the front stoop. He checked along the window sill and flower boxes.

This was the fifteenth cabin they'd visited—not counting Walt's. Tim had been impressed by Walter Binn's little chalet, a very cozy two bedroom. According to Walt, it was the only cabin that had a phone hooked up. With all the other modern conveniences, stylishly "rustic" furniture, and shelf after shelf of books, it was the perfect weekend retreat. Tim had also noticed one of Claire's paintings—a rainy, Seattle street scene—hanging over the fireplace in the living room. Walt had taken him outside, where he'd cleared away some trees for a backyard with a tool shed, barbecue pit, and patio. Tim could see the water through the trees.

He envied Walt—for about a minute. Sure, Harlan's friend had youthful good looks, money to burn, and all the freedom and independence a guy could want. But he was also in his midforties, widowed, childless, and living on a small island. The best life had to offer was weekly dinners with Ron and Linda Castle, a crush on his best friend's wife, and every couple of months a weekend with yet another man's wife. Walt had mentioned having his own boat, and the freedom to come and go. But in reality, he seemed trapped on that little island. Hell, here it was, Saturday night, and he'd volunteered to show Tim around the woods.

Tim didn't want to be like Walt Binns in ten years. Yet he wondered if he was on his way to the same life—only without the money and the boat.

"I found the key, never mind," Walt announced, plucking the key from the window flower box. He unlocked the door.

With his flashlight, Tim followed Walt inside. Decorated in Early Fire Sale, the place was dusty. The electricity had been shut off. Tim opened the refrigerator, and he got a waft of rancid, rotten fruit on the shelf.

Obviously, no one had been in this cabin for at least a couple of weeks.

They were out of there and driving down the dirt road

within five minutes. Dusk had set in, and Walt switched on the headlights. "So I bet you guys on the force have a lot of theories about Rembrandt," Walt said, his eyes on the road. "I've heard he puts the clear plastic bags over their heads, and semisuffocates them in order to get-off. Y'know, reach a sexual climax? Do you think that's true?"

"It's possible," Tim allowed. "But none of the women actually died from suffocation." He was uncomfortable talking motives and modus operandi with civilians—especially in casual conversation. The police had withheld certain details about Rembrandt from the press and public. They weren't supposed to talk about Rembrandt's penchant for leaving behind his victim's panties, or the beauty mark he drew on each woman's cheek. There were several other details they kept secret.

"So—what theory do you subscribe to?" Walt asked.

"I think he's making them up to look like someone," Tim answered.

"You mean—like his mother, or an ex-girlfriend?"

Tim nodded. "Or a high school crush or Marilyn Monroe or someone who has become his obsession. I think he uses the plastic bag to preserve his work, and keep the victims looking like this woman for as long as possible. I agree with what they say in the newspapers. He wants his victims found before they start to deteriorate." Tim shrugged. "There are details to back up this theory, but I really can't talk about them, Walt."

They pulled up to another cabin, one for which Chad had given them the key.

"You know, if it's some kind of personal obsession for Rembrandt," Walt said, unlocking the cottage's front door. "Why would he have disciples working with him? Why share it? And what's in it for the accomplice?"

Walt continued to talk and speculate while they checked out the cabin. The bungalow was small enough that they could hear each other from different rooms without having to shout.

Tim went down to the cellar, a potentially perfect spot for

Rembrandt to imprison his victims. One of the other cabins had had an old bomb shelter. But with all the cobwebs and dust, Tim had figured no one had been down there in months. This place only had a laundry and storage room in the basement, no potential dungeons.

Upstairs, Walt was still talking. He really didn't think Brian Ferguson's running away had anything to do with Rembrandt. It probably had more to do with Deception Island, and restlessness. Walt admitted that as a teenager, he'd run away a couple of times himself.

Tim came up the basement stairs.

"You know, Harlan ran away too," Walt told him. "Harlan must not remember. Otherwise, he'd be a little more patient with Brian."

As they started back toward the car together, Tim thought about all the runaways and missing persons he'd noticed in the police files. Most were young men. Walt and Harlan had both come back to the island. Brian had returned on two previous occasions. So—why, after three weeks, was he still gone? And where was Derek Herrmann?

If they weren't tied in with Rembrandt, what part did Brian and his bad-seed friend play in the attack on Claire? Their nearly synchronized disappearances were just too much of a coincidence.

Walt suggested taking a dinner break. Heading down Evergreen Drive, Tim noticed a nearly hidden dirt road on the right side of the street.

"Are there any cabins down there?" he asked, pointing ahead.

"Yeah, just one." Walt eased up on the accelerator. "I don't have a key. Did you want to check it out?"

"Yes, please," Tim said.

Walt turned onto the narrow, muddy road. He slowed down and used his high beams to navigate the winding, bumpy trial. A couple of low-hanging tree branches scraped against the car roof.

They approached a clearing in the woods, and Tim could

see the cabin, a small, slightly decrepid, cedar shaker. All the windows were dark. "Do you know whose place this is?" he asked.

"A middle-aged couple from Lynnwood named Logan," Walt answered, navigating toward the house. "They're kind of nuts. You know Roseann at Fork In The Road? She said they brought in their own silverware when they ate there once. Then they walked out with the restaurant's salt and pepper shakers. Huh, you go figure."

Walt pulled up to the side of the bungalow. "The Logans come and use the place a few times during the summer, and that's it. They don't rent out to anyone."

They couldn't find a key hidden anywhere near the front of the house. Tim went around to the back, and discovered the kitchen door unlocked. He called to Walt, who met him at the back door. Tim tried the light switch and the kitchen overhead went on.

"Wait a minute," Walt whispered. "This isn't right. The last time the Logans were here was early September. They wouldn't have left that door open. They're totally paranoid. It's part of their craziness. And they're cheap too, tight as a bull's ass in a snowstorm. They wouldn't have left the electricity on."

The chairs at the kitchen table were mismatched, and there was a framed sampler on the wall with a little crack in the glass: *"God Bless This Kitchen."* Tim recognized a pair of salt and pepper shakers from the Fork In The Road.

Walt moved to the refrigerator and opened it. "Look at this," he whispered.

Tim saw a bag of fresh grapes on the shelf, along with some Cokes, cheese, packaged cold-cuts, and milk. He sniffed from the container of milk. Still good. The expiration dates on the cheese and meat weren't for another month.

Walt started sifting thought the trash pail under the sink. "I found something," he announced. He showed Tim a receipt, dated five days ago. "It's from the Handi-Hut Food Mart," he said.

"Where's that?" Tim asked in a hushed voice.

"About halfway between here and Alliance," Walt explained. "It's a grossly overpriced, mom-and-pop store, one of the only places on Deception Island where you can go shopping without someone recognizing you. It caters mostly to summer-cabin-renters and people coming to and from the plant. In high school, I used to pedal my bike out there to buy *Playboy*. If I needed groceries, and I didn't want to be seen, I'd go to the Handi-Hut."

Tim peeked in the bedroom, off the kitchen. The bed was rumpled, like someone had been sleeping on top of it.

He and Walt crept into the living room. The furnishings were cheap and sparse, seedy secondhand stuff—right down to the water-stained, early American oval rug. Tim noticed some papers on the old, battered wood desk. On top of the stack was a flier. *"MISSING,"* it said, over the slightly-blurred photo of a smiling Claire Shaw. Below the picture was an explanation: *"Last Seen 10/25/03—Nordstrom Downtown Seattle—Wearing Blue Suede Shirt-Jacket, Black Pullover, and Jeans."* This was followed by a description of Claire and a contact number for the Deception Police.

"What is this?" Tim murmured.

"Two days after she disappeared, Harlan had those made," Walt said. "He posted them all over the Island—and in parts of Seattle too. I helped him. So did Linda and Ron Castle."

Tim heard something outside, and he put down the newspaper. "What was that?" he whispered, moving to the front window. He hid behind the old, dusty curtain and peered outside. He couldn't see anything in the darkness, just outlines of the trees and bushes.

Walt crept to the side window. "Something's out there," he whispered. "It's a guy. I can see him. He just ducked behind a tree."

Tim felt his heart racing. He moved over to the side window with Walt. He stared out at the woods, but didn't see anyone. "Did you get a look at his face?"

"No, but it's a big guy," Walt whispered. "I couldn't tell if he was armed. Listen, I have a gun in my car. I'll go out the front, and you sneak out the back. We might throw him off if we come from two different directions. We'll meet up at the Range Rover, and I'll get the gun."

Tim nodded. "Okay. See you by the car."

He ducked below the window, and scurried into the kitchen. At the door, he glanced back at Walt, by the front entrance. Slowly, he opened the door, then stepped outside. He kept his eyes on the forest, the same dark, dense area where they'd been looking earlier. Tim didn't see anyone, but he heard twigs snapping underfoot.

He crept around the side of the house. He could see Walt at the other end of the decrepit cedar shaker. He was looking out at the woods as well. Suddenly, he turned toward Tim: *"Jesus, Tim, get down!"*

Tim heard the gunshot, and at the same time, he felt something dart past him. Within a second, he was on the ground. The shot was still echoing in the woods when another loud blast went off. It seemed to come from that thick, shadowy area in the woods. Tim could actually hear the bullet cutting through the air, coming at him. A mound of dirt exploded just inches from his leg.

On his belly, he scuttled toward the car. Walt already had the door open. He was reaching into the glove compartment.

"Who's out there?" Walt called, grabbing a semiautomatic. "I have a gun! I've got you in range. C'mon, out, goddamn it! I see you!"

Tim ducked behind the car, and tried to catch his breath. He could hear twigs breaking again.

"I said come on out!" Walt shouted.

There was a silence. Then someone cleared his throat. "Walt? Is that you?"

Fred Maybon swore up and down that he'd mistaken Tim for a deer. Fred was a tall, overweight, tow-head in his late thirties. With his bulky frame, he could hardly be the man in the fatigue jacket whom Claire had seen darting in and out of alleys and woods.

"What the hell were you doing?" Walt asked him, his voice raised. *"You're not allowed to hunt in this area. And what idiot shoots at something directly outside a house, a house with lights on, no less?"*

Fred apologized to Tim. Tim asked if he'd stored any food or reading materials in the Logans' cabin. Fred said he hadn't set foot in the Logans' cabin—ever.

Although Tim had almost been shot, he seemed quicker to forgive Fred his transgressions than Walt was. Tim sat on the front stoop of the Logans' bungalow, and dialed the sheriff. Walt and Fred stood in the forest clearing—just far enough away so Tim only heard an occasional word or phrase from the still irate Walt: *". . . be so stupid? . . . careless . . . could have killed both of us . . . you're just lucky . . ."* Through it all, Fred kept rolling his eyes and shrugging.

Once he got Sheriff Klauser on the line, Tim told him about the stash of recently bought food and reading materials in the Logans' cottage. He asked the sheriff to assign one of his deputies to stake out the place.

"Well, I'll talk to Troy Landers," the sheriff said glumly. "He's back from the mainland. He won't be a happy camper spending his first night back on a stakeout. But that's his tough luck. Anything else?"

"Yeah, thanks," Tim said. "If you can get him here ASAP, I'd sure appreciate it. We can't stick around. The way I figure, since this stalker isn't here, where he's set up camp, then he must be at Claire Shaw's house."

Harlan snatched up the cordless phone on the second ring. He'd been sitting at the pantry table with his one beer for the night. Nearby in the family room, Tiffany was ensconced in front of the TV and her umpteenth viewing of *Finding Nemo*. Claire stood in the kitchen, cooking dinner.

"Yes, hello?" Harlan said into the phone. "Oh . . . Uh-huh . . . Yeah. . . ."

Claire caught his eye, and she silently mouthed to him: "Who is it?"

Harlan turned his back to her. "So—is that where you're calling from now?" he asked. He stepped closer to the sliding doors, and Claire couldn't hear him any more.

She glared at him—though he was oblivious. Things had been a little strained ever since Harlan had come home at five o'clock to find her sitting in the living room with Linus Moorehead.

She and Dr. Moorehead had gotten Tiffany home—and to the bathroom—in the nick of time. Once she emerged from the bathroom, Tiffany showed Dr. Moorehead her drawings and her doll collection. "I think I'm more of a hit with your stepdaughter than I was with your son," Dr. Moorehead whispered to Claire.

Then Harlan walked in. He waited until Linus had left and Tiffany had taken her dolls and drawings upstairs, before he started in on Claire. What was she thinking going off to the library without anyone besides Tiffany to keep her company? Why didn't she stay with Linda like she was supposed to?

"Because I got tired of gardening, okay?" Claire snapped. "It wore me out. I've been in the hospital, for God's sakes. Where were you this afternoon? You said you'd be in your office. I called from the library around four—and again when I came home. Both times, I got the machine."

"Well, I must have been in the file room." Harlan sighed, and gave her a kiss on the cheek. "Anyway, you're okay now. So let's just drop it. I need a shower."

Claire listened to the pipes squeaking upstairs, and she knew Harlan was in the master bathroom. She tried Tim at The Whale Watcher once again. Big surprise, still no answer in Tim's room.

After hanging up, Claire pulled out a piece of scrap paper from the pocket of her jeans. She picked up the phone again, and dialed Directory Assistance. "What city, please?" the operator answered.

"Bremerton, Washington," Claire said.

"Go ahead."

"Do you have a listing for Steven Griswald?"

She was lucky. Violet Davalos's surviving brother still lived in Bremerton. While Claire was dialing the number, she heard a click on the upstairs connection. "Hello?" she said.

"Oh—" Harlan said on the upstairs phone. "Who are you calling?"

"Linda," Claire lied. "Who are *you* calling?"

"Um, work," he answered. "I was going to leave myself a message."

"Well, go ahead, honey. I can wait," Claire said, then she hung up.

She listened to the pipes humming upstairs. He had the shower on, yet he was using the phone. He wanted her to think he was still in the bathroom. Obviously, he was making a secret call of his own. But to whom?

Claire didn't ask.

Ten minutes later, freshly showered, Harlan came down to the kitchen. Claire had just put the chicken on the stove. She glanced over at him. "Hey, you know, at the Garden Plaza today, Molly Cartwright started talking about the Davalos family," she said, ever so casually. With a fork, she pushed the chicken around the saute pan. "I had no idea there used to be a house on that spot."

"Molly Cartwright has a big mouth," Harlan muttered. He opened the refrigerator door.

"How's that?" Claire asked, though she'd heard him.

"What did Molly tell you?"

"Not much," Claire lied. She gave a little shrug. "Just that this family of four used to live in a house there. What happened to them?"

"They all died in a fire," Harlan grunted. He sat at the breakfast table with his beer. "It's not very pleasant conversation before supper. So let's just drop it. What are you cooking up there anyway?"

"Chicken and pasta in a cream sauce," Claire replied. She worked over the stove, and stole another look at Harlan. Frowning, he gazed out the sliding glass doors.

What happened to the Davalos family was a triple-homicide, arson, and suicide. It wasn't just a fire. Harlan's aversion toward discussing the tragedy seemed to echo Linda's sentiments.

"Not very pleasant conversation before supper." This from a guy who at the dinner table last month went into grisly detail about a plant worker getting his arm eaten down to the bone by some chemical. Claire remembered telling him to change the subject, because he was upsetting Tiffany.

Yet he didn't want to talk about the Davalos family.

And at the moment, he didn't want her to know who was on the phone.

When it had first rung, Claire immediately thought of Tim. But now, she watched Harlan with his back to her, muttering into the cordless, and she wondered if it was the person he'd been secretly calling a few minutes before.

"All right, come on over," he said. Then he hung up.

"Are you going to tell me who that was?" Claire asked.

"Your cop friend, Tim Sullivan," Harlan said, turning to stare out the sliding glass door again. "He and Walt think they've found where your stalker's been hiding out. They're coming over to check around and make sure he isn't here—just as a precaution."

He stuck his head in the family room. "Tiffany? Baby, turn off the TV, and come in here."

Harlan closed the blinds in the family room. He took Tiffany by the hand, and led her toward the front of the house.

Claire turned off the stove, then followed them into the living room. She sat down on the sofa with Tiffany, and stared out the window. Dark clouds were racing across the night sky, and for a moment, the moonlight briefly illuminated the unfinished house across the way, the "face house," Tiffany called it.

Harlan shut the drapes. Then he went downstairs to his workroom, where he kept a gun.

"I'll get to the bottom of this, and find out what the hell's going on," Walt Binns said, studying the road. He sped along Evergreen Drive, toward the Shaws' cul de sac. "The whole time I was talking to Fred Maybon, he kept giving me this look like I had a screw loose, like it was *unreasonable* for me to be upset he'd just shot at you—*at us.*"

"Do you know him very well?" Tim asked. Nervously tapping his foot on the floor of the passenger side, he glanced over at the speedometer on the dashboard. Walt was going sixty on the dark, narrow winding road.

"Fred's with the Guardians, this local men's group I belong to. But he and I aren't exactly close. I don't know what his problem is." Walt shook his head. "Fred said he shot at you because he thought you were a deer."

"Maybe he should get his eyes fixed," Tim offered.

"Maybe you should, pal," Walt replied. "Didn't you get a look at the Colt M-16 Conversion rifle Fred had slung over his shoulder?"

"No, why?" Tim asked, gazing at Walt's profile.

Walt was frowning. "Because," he said. "That's not a gun for deer hunting. It's a gun for people hunting."

Walt switched off his headlights as they turned down the cul de sac. They parked about half a block away from the Shaws' house, then walked. Tim shined his flashlight in the bushes, then toward the half-constructed house across the street. Walt carried his gun in his jacket pocket.

They came up the Shaws' front walkway and rang the bell. After a moment, Harlan Shaw opened the door. He gave his friend a very stalwart hug, then punched his arm. "Don't let Tiffany know what's going on," he whispered. Then he nodded curtly at Tim, and invited them both in.

"Hi, Uncle Walt!" Tiffany squealed. Jumping off the sofa, she ran to him, and threw her arms around his legs.

Tim glanced over at Claire, seated on the couch. Their eyes met, and she gave him a wistful, furtive smile.

"Tiffany, baby," Harlan was saying. "Uncle Walt needs to talk with Dad and this other gentleman. So—why don't you go back to your movie, okay? Claire will watch it with you."

When Tiffany was out of earshot, Harlan told them about Claire's brush with her stalker at the library. "I want to get this son of a bitch," he whispered. But begrudgingly, Harlan relinquished to Walt and Tim the job of searching the woods behind the house. He stood guard outside the sliding glass doors while Claire and Tiffany watched a movie in the family room.

Tim ventured into the forest with a flashlight as his only defense. He'd left Al's gun in the hotel room—locked away in the briefcase that held the materials for his comic strip. He felt like a sitting duck. He was just waiting for someone else to take another potshot at him. The near-fatal mishap from Fred Maybon made four times he'd almost bought it within the last two days. They'd tried poison berries, sabotaging his car, breaking into his hotel room at night, and just an hour ago, what might have been a "hunting accident."

Trudging through the woods, Tim thought back to what he'd first suspected a couple of days ago. Certain people on this island were involved in a cover-up. But it didn't make sense that Fred Maybon, Linda Castle, Dorothy Herrmann, a "waitress" calling herself Ronnie, and maybe several others in Deception were all connected to a serial killer. If the cover-up—or conspiracy, or whatever it was—had nothing to do with Rembrandt, what were these people hiding?

Walt said he would *"get to the bottom of this."* Tim hoped Harlan's friend would have some answers—before the next *"accident"* fell upon him.

After a half-hour, in which Tim had scraped his face on a

couple of low hanging branches, and stepped ankle-deep in a mud puddle, he heard Walt call to him: *"Hey, I don't know about you, but I'm hungry, and I have burrs on my socks. Let's wrap this up!"*

When they got back to the house, Harlan agreed that if anyone had been out in those woods, they'd probably been scared away—at least, for the night. Their shoes covered in mud, Tim and Walt didn't step back inside. Claire came to the sliding glass door, and asked them to stay for dinner.

Harlan turned to his wife, with a pinched smile. "Honey, I'm sure Officer Sullivan has work to do—"

"That's right," Tim quickly chimed in. "But thank you anyway."

Walt said something about needing to take Tim back to the inn. Harlan gave his buddy another stalwart hug. Claire kissed Walt on the cheek.

Tim was surprised he got a warm smile, a handshake, and a "Thank you," from Harlan Shaw. Claire thanked him as well, calling him "Officer Sullivan." As she shook his hand, he felt something in her palm, a folded-up piece of paper.

Tim took it, then shoved his hand in his pocket.

He and Walt walked around the side of the house. Harlan's friend asked if he wanted to grab dinner at the Fork In The Road. Tim was tired and frayed. He needed a shower more than anything else. Right now, the idea of sitting in his hotel room by himself, ordering a pizza, and watching bad TV was somehow strangely appealing. He asked Walt if he could take a rain check, and suggested they meet for lunch tomorrow.

They approached the Range Rover. As Walt moved toward the driver's side, Tim reached into his pocket and furtively pulled out the note Claire had slipped to him. Tim quickly unfolded the piece of paper, and shined the flashlight on it:

I'LL CALL YOU TOMORROW, EARLY A.M. WE NEED TO LOOK UP POLICE RECORDS FOR

*DAVALOS—HUGH, VIOLET, DEAN & RODNEY—
ANY ARRESTS BEFORE 7/4/00. THEY'RE ALL DEAD.*

By 9:35, the dinner dishes were done, Harlan had nodded off in front of the television, and Claire had sent Tiffany to bed.

She used the phone in the bedroom to call Steven Griswald in Bremerton. It rang twice, before a machine picked up: *"Hi, you've reached Steven and Sherry Griswald,"* a woman chirped on the recording. *"And Trevor!"* a little boy piped in. *"We can't come to the phone right now . . ."* the woman continued.

Claire hung up. What she wanted from Steven Griswald wasn't something she could ask on an answering machine.

She dialed The Whale Watcher again. This was her last chance before the switchboard closed for the night. She asked the operator for Tim Sullivan's room.

"I think you're in luck this time," the operator said.

Tim answered on the third ring. "Hello?"

"Hi, it's Claire," she said.

"Thank God," he murmured. "I didn't think I'd get a chance to talk with you tonight. How are you doing?"

"I'm okay," she said. "I must have tried you a dozen times today."

"Well, I have Al's cell phone," Tim explained. "Your husband has the number. Didn't he give it to you?"

"No. Just a second, let me grab a pencil." Claire found a pen and pad on the nightstand by Harlan's side of the bed. She got back on the line, and Tim read off the number to her. Claire scribbled it down, then tucked the piece of paper in her jeans.

"I can't understand why Harlan didn't give you that number," Tim said.

"He's a little jealous of you. And it's not totally unfounded," she admitted. "I think that's why he didn't want you staying for dinner tonight."

"Yeah, I definitely caught that."

"Did you read my note?" she asked.

"Yes. I stopped by the police station after Walt dropped me off here. It's all locked up with an emergency number on the door. I forgot, one of the deputies is out of pocket, because he's watching the Logan cabin—in case your stalker shows up tonight. So—who are the Davaloses anyway?"

Claire told him about working at the Garden Plaza with Linda Castle and Molly Cartwright today and how when Molly mentioned the Davalos family, Linda bristled, then quickly changed the subject.

"Harlan had the same reaction earlier tonight, when I asked about them," Claire explained. She recounted for Tim what she'd learned from Molly and from the story in that old *Islander* she'd found in the library.

"You sure it's not just a civic pride thing?" Tim argued. "A triple-homicide, suicide, and arson aren't exactly great for the tourist trade. Maybe that's why they don't want to talk about it."

"Tim, I've lived here for two years, and today is the first I've heard of the Davalos family. This is more than some little skeleton in the town hall closet. It's a cover-up. There's more here than we know." She sighed, then her voice cracked a little. "I keep thinking about the Davalos's two teenage boys—always getting into trouble—and I wonder what really happened to my son—and Derek."

"Okay, Claire," Tim whispered on the other end of the line. "Tomorrow morning, I'll see if I can find something in the police records. Will you be home tomorrow?"

"No. There's an after-church art show and breakfast at Tiffany's school. It's a mother-daughter thing. Linda's going with us. Harlan has to work again. It's all planned out so I won't be alone for a minute. I don't think I'll have a chance to break away and see you."

"Well, you can call me on the cell phone—anytime you feel like it."

"Thanks, Tim," she whispered. "I don't know what I'd do if you weren't here."

"Try to get some sleep," he said. "Good night, Claire."

That night, before going to bed, Tim double-locked the hotel room door, and checked the windows. He put Al's gun under the extra pillow beside him in bed.

He hoped to get through the night without needing it.

Chapter 20

Claire stood between Tiffany and Harlan in a pew near the front of St. Mark's Church. Claire wore a navy blue print, wrap-around dress, and Harlan had on a suit and tie. People still dressed for Sunday morning services on Deception Island.

St. Mark's was a small church with chalky-white walls, polished wood trim, and a red carpet. The square, little stain-glass windows depicted the Stations of the Cross. The altar was white marble with red-and-gold trim.

Ron Castle, looking a bit pinched inside his blue suit, stood at the pulpit and gave the Reading. He fluffed a couple of lines, but at least his toupee was on straight. The reverend, seated on the other side of the altar, didn't seem to notice. In fact, he looked as if he was sleeping.

Claire sympathized. She'd felt herself almost nodding off a few times during the service. She hadn't slept well last night. She kept waking up and checking to see if Harlan was in bed with her. He was.

If he'd slipped away during the night again, she hadn't noticed.

Before church this morning, while Harlan was in the bathroom, Claire snuck downstairs and tried Steven Griswald's number again. She'd just finished dialing when Harlan stepped into the pantry—half dressed. Claire hung up, and muttered something about trying to call her friend, Tess, in Bellingham.

"Why don't you do that later?" he'd said, frowning. "We'll be late for church."

They weren't late. In fact, they'd arrived the same time as Ron and Linda Castle. Linda now sat in the pew in front of them.

Ron read off the Special Intentions, which he always had a hand in writing. Every time Ron was a reader, Claire could count on hearing some sort of semipolitical prayer. *"For the continued guidance and inspiration of our country's great leaders in the war against terrorism. Let us pray to the Lord."*

The congregation responded, *"Lord hear our prayer."*

"For the sick and recently departed of our community, especially my mother-in-law, Josephine Bowland, who is struggling with Alzheimer's. Let us pray to the Lord."

"Lord hear our prayer," everyone replied.

"And now, if anyone has a special intention they would like to share . . ." Ron said solemnly.

There was a silence among the congregation.

After a few moments, Ron once again leaned toward the microphone on the pulpit. He took a deep breath.

"For my son," Claire heard herself say.

Ron stared at her from the pulpit.

"For Brian Ferguson, who has been missing for over three weeks," Claire continued, speaking loudly—so everyone in church heard her. *"For his safe return home."*

Frowning, Linda glanced back at her.

Claire defiantly met her gaze. *"And for Brian's friend, Derek Herrmann, that God keep him safe during his travels through Europe. Let us pray to the Lord."*

That was Ron's cue to step up to the microphone and lead the congregation in the response. But he didn't move. His mouth slightly open, he stared at Claire.

There was a strange silence for a moment. Some people

cleared their throats or shuffled their feet. It seemed only half of the churchgoers replied with, *"Lord hear our prayer."*

Claire noticed that Harlan, Ron, and Linda weren't among them.

"Not a creature was stirring last night around the Logan cabin, according to Troy," Sheriff Klauser reported. "I don't think he likes being stuck out there, but hey, tough titty said the cat to the kitty."

Between bites of his bacon and egg sandwich, Klauser fetched all the police records for Hugh, Dean, and Rodney Davalos—along with the report on their deaths. The account of the shootings and fire didn't waver from what Claire had told Tim. In addition to his jail time on the mainland, Hugh Davalos had kept the island authorities busy with arrests for assault, driving while intoxicated, shoplifting, and drunk and disorderly, among other minor infractions. The sons followed in their dad's crooked footsteps. Both Dean and Rodney had chalked up a number of arrests, and seemed well on their way to becoming career criminals—until July 4, 2000.

"Everyone saw that one coming, buddy," the sheriff said, sitting at his desk, finishing up his sandwich. "Hugh Davalos was a real hothead, darn-right combustible, if you know what I mean. And talk about the fruit not falling far from the tree, those boys were a pair of junior-league assholes."

"Something tells me that you didn't give the eulogy at their funeral," Tim said.

"Well, Violet wasn't a bad sort," Klauser allowed. "But I'd be hard pressed coming up with anything nice to say about the rest of them." The sheriff sipped his coffee. "Say, what do they have to do with your investigation anyway?"

"I'm not sure yet." Tim said, studying the arrests records for Dean and Rodney.

"Something your boss has cooked up for you?" the sheriff asked.

"He doesn't know about this," Tim replied.

Lieutenant Elmore didn't know a lot. He didn't know about the intruder in the Logans' cabin, or about Tim almost getting shot outside the place. Nor had Tim told his boss about Nancy Killabrew Hart returning home from a stroll in the woods, crying, with her face made-up.

Tim had come upon these discoveries by flagrantly disobeying Elmore's orders. He didn't see any point in talking to Elmore again—not until he had something absolutely concrete linking Rembrandt to Deception Island.

Sifting through the records on Dean and Rodney Davalos, Tim noticed a section at the bottom of each form that showed police or court action in connection with the violation:

> *"Juvenile released in custody of parent (mother). Counseling recommended . . ."*
>
> *"Warning issued. Counseling recommended . . ."*
>
> *"Juvenile Offender assigned six weeks of community service, and required to see professional counselor . . ."*

"Who's the professional counselor around here?" Tim asked.

The sheriff had his nose in the newspaper. "There's only one, Linus Moorehead," he replied. He slurped down some more of his coffee.

"Did they enforce these recommendations for counseling? Did the Davalos boys actually go see Moorehead?"

Eyes still on the newspaper, Klauser nodded. "Not that it did any good."

Tim remembered Claire mentioning that Brian and Derek had both seen Moorehead at one time.

"The runaways and missing persons you have on file," Tim said. "Do any of them have police records?"

"Some do," Sheriff Klauser replied. "A lot of those runaways had problems. I mean, it just shows to go ya."

"Could I take a look at some of those records?" Tim asked.

*   *   *

The Mother-Daughter Art Show and Breakfast was held in the school gymnasium. The mothers had their choice of coffee or tea, and there was milk for the girls. With only fruit, stale scones, or coffee cake on hand, it wasn't much of a breakfast. Then again, it wasn't much of an art show either; all of the artists were under fourteen years of age.

But Tiffany obviously relished having a venue for showing off her watercolors. She even had one painting of a boat at sunset framed and displayed on an easel. She was oblivious to the fact that some of the other moms weren't talking to her stepmother.

Claire kept busy in the small kitchen off the gym, helping clean up after the meager breakfast. Kira Sherman stacked coffee cups by the sink, while Claire washed them out. Kira grabbed a tray, and went back out to collect more cups, saucers, and spoons. Claire was momentarily alone. Then Linda stepped into the kitchen.

"I didn't want to say anything in front of Tiffany," she whispered. "But what exactly did you think you were accomplishing with that little show you put on at church?"

"You mean when I said a Special Intention for Brian and Derek?" Claire asked, still standing over the sink.

"Yes. Ye Gods, talk about embarrassing. To make an announcement like that about your runaway son—and—and—and bringing up Derek Herrmann . . ." She shook her head, then clicked her tongue. "Honestly, Claire, you didn't succeed in anything, except maybe making some people feel uncomfortable."

Claire turned to stare at her. "So—what are you saying, Linda?" she whispered. "Do you know something I don't? Are you telling me that it won't do any good to pray for my son—and Derek?"

Police records showed twelve runaways and five persons "missing" from Deception Island in the last two years. Brian was one of them. Among the total of seventeen, none had been found yet. Fourteen of them had police records.

Tim pored over the documents for two hours. As it got closer to noon, he phoned Walt Binns and left a message on his machine, canceling their lunch appointment. He had a lot of profiles to read. Most of them were of teenagers. Their infractions ran the gamut from typical drunk and disorderly teenage fare to grand theft auto, drug dealing, and attempted rape. The more serious offenders served time at juvenile correctional facilities on the mainland, but a few got by with warnings, or community service time *"on the condition that the above party agrees to psychological counseling."*

"A lot of these kids went to Dr. Moorehead," Tim said, hunched over the ugly metal desk with the files in front of him.

"Uh-huh," the sheriff nodded. Sitting across from Tim on the edge of the other desk, he was momentarily distracted by the fax machine phone.

"Who determined all these—recommendations for counseling?" Tim asked.

"Judge Ward Fanning. He does the whole judicial kit and caboodle around here—handles marriage licenses, hears arguments for traffic tickets, trial judge. You name it, Judge Fanning resides over it."

"He must be pretty tight with Linus Moorehead," Tim said. "He sure sends a lot of business his way."

The sheriff ambled over to the fax machine behind the counter. "I'm not sure exactly how buddy-buddy they are. They're both with the Guardians, I can tell you that. But Moorehead doesn't charge for most of the juvenile offender cases, especially the hard-luck ones."

"You mean he counsels these JDs out of the goodness of his heart?" Tim asked.

"That's what the Guardians are all about," Sheriff Klauser explained. He paused in the doorway to the back room. "Working for the good of the community. Sure makes my job easier."

He stepped into the back room.

"Do you know how I can get a hold of Judge Fanning?" Tim called.

"You can't," Klauser answered from the back room. "He always goes on vacation with the wife the week before Thanksgiving. Palm Springs. It's a smart move, considering how shitty the weather gets here this time of year. In fact, we're expecting a mother-of-a-storm here tomorrow. Did you—"

Tim glanced up from the police records. " 'Did I'— what?" he called. "Sheriff?"

Klauser emerged from the back room, staring at a piece of paper in his shaky hand. He stopped behind the counter, and after a moment, he finally looked up from the fax. His old, weary eyes met Tim's. "It's from your boss," he said in a flat, toneless voice. "That gal who got abducted yesterday, Kimberly Cronin, she's dead. Someone found her by a riverbank near Sedro Woolley yesterday afternoon. Lord, twenty years old. Poor kid."

Sighing, he walked around the counter. "She had the plastic bag over her head and the makeup job, same MO as the other Rembrandt victims." He placed the fax on the desk, in front of Tim. "Son of a bitch shot her in the chest—twice."

"My God," Tim muttered, staring at the fax. He felt responsible. If Rembrandt was on the island, then he should have been able to stop it.

"He's out of control," Tim whispered. "He's killing them practically one after another. He—he isn't holding onto them as long as he was before. It's like his appetite for killing has become insatiable."

Tim gazed at the police reports on the missing and runaway teens. What was he doing? What did any of this have to do with Rembrandt?

On one of the forms, that phrase caught his eye again: *". . . recommend psychological counseling."*

"How long has Linus Moorehead had his practice on the island?" Tim heard himself ask.

"Oh, about nine years now, I think," the sheriff answered.

"Are a lot of adults sent his way too? I mean, for weird little infractions—like indecent exposure, lewd behavior, stalking, or Peeping Tom type of stuff?"

Sheriff Klauser nodded. "The perverts. Yeah, Judge Fanning refers those types to him from time to time."

"So—a high percentage of people who have gotten into trouble on this island have ended up seeing Dr. Linus Moorehead?" Tim said.

"I guess you could say that. Why?"

Tim didn't want to say it out loud. But if Rembrandt had spent any significant time on the island—and gotten into any trouble—chances were he'd been required somewhere along the line to unburden himself on Dr. Linus Moorehead.

Tim knew the psychological profile on Rembrandt. And maybe—just maybe—Dr. Linus Moorehead knew the man.

The answering machine clicked on at the Shaws' house, but no one was home to hear it.

"This is Tess calling for Claire. Hi, Claire. I'm in the car. Can you tell? I'm now one of those people I used to hate, a cell-phone driver. I'm probably screwing up traffic right and left, but I'm oblivious. How are you? I've been thinking of you a lot. I'm actually in a pretty good mood this morning. I head back to work tomorrow. Anyway, listen, I was thinking of setting Tuesday aside so I could come see you on the island. How do you like me inviting myself over? So—call me, and let me know what your schedule's like. Okay? Take care!"

Tess turned down the driveway, and parked by the back door. The three-bedroom brick Tudor she'd gotten for herself and the baby was in a family neighborhood. She'd liked the size of the backyard too: small enough so mowing the lawn wasn't a problem, and big enough for a swing set and slide. Now, without a baby, the yard looked too damn big.

And suddenly the house seemed too big as well, even if she turned Collin's nursery into an office.

But she'd made up her mind to spend the winter there. Come spring, she'd move somewhere more practical, a place for a single woman, instead of a single mom. Maybe a condominium, she'd figure it out later.

For now, she would treat herself, little rewards to make it through each day. Yesterday, she got a pedicure. Later today, her friend Mary Lou would be passing through from Vancouver on her way back to Seattle. They'd planned on having dinner together, like old times. Tuesday, she hoped to see Claire. And to cover her ass so she wasn't alone on Thanksgiving, she'd already volunteered to help serve up turkey dinner at the Homeless Shelter.

At the moment, Tess had her Italian Roast coffee, chocolate chip muffin, and *New York Times*. She carefully unloaded them from her car. It was going to be a long, leisurely, self-indulgent morning before she started cleaning up for Mary Lou.

She unlocked the kitchen door, then carried in her paper, coffee, and muffin. She set everything on the kitchen table. Her morning of leisure needed music, so she went into the living room and popped an Enya CD into the player. Tess kicked off her shoes, sat down at the kitchen table and took the lid off her Italian roast.

Past Enya, she thought she heard a muffled humming noise somewhere in the house. It seemed to come from the first floor—or maybe the basement.

Tess got to her feet. Suddenly, she heard a buzzer go off. After a moment, she realized it was the clothes dryer in the basement. She hadn't done any laundry this morning.

Tess moved toward the basement stairs. "That's the damndest thing," she muttered. She wondered if the dryer had been doing that off and on while she'd been gone.

The buzzer stopped—so did the humming noise.

She switched on the light at the top of the stairs. Parts of the house were still a bit strange to her, and the cellar was one of them. She hadn't done anything to it yet, except store some boxes down there, and hook up the washer and dryer. Not much light came through the small windows, which were five feet above the cement floor. The walls were painted a dingy beige color. Exposed pipes and a few too many cobwebs hung overhead.

Tess took a deep breath, and started down the creaky wooden staircase. Past the bannister, she could see the washer, dryer, and laundry sink. The dryer's operator panel was illuminated.

Tess hesitated halfway down the stairs. On top of the washing machine, she saw several footprints. She looked up at the small window above the washer and dryer. The glass was broken, and the frame was stuck out slightly. Whoever had crawled through hadn't shut it all the way.

"Oh, my God," she whispered. For a second, Tess couldn't breathe. Her hand gripped the bannister. She just kept gazing down at the basement.

His footprints were all over the cement floor.

Tess swiveled around and started to race up the stairs.

All at once, the light went out. She was swallowed in darkness. Tess could only see a light ahead—from the kitchen doorway at the top of the steps.

Then he stepped into that doorway, blocking her path. She could only see his silhouette. "Hello, Tess," he whispered.

She stopped dead. She still couldn't see his face in the shadows. But she recognized his voice.

"Don't you remember me, Tess?" he asked in gentle tone. "Don't you remember me from the hospital?"

Thirteen-year-old Amy Herrmann wasn't a bad artist. Some of her pencil drawings were copied from punk rock CD covers. A couple of her original sketches showed dead angels—seminude young men with wings—shot down and pierced with arrows. Amy had used a red pencil for the blood. The drawings were crude, but disturbing.

"You're very good," Claire said. "I mean it."

Fiddling with the magenta strand of her brown hair, Amy sat at the desk, guarding her art work. Her classmates were ignoring her. With the gothic makeup around her brown eyes, Amy gave Claire a wary look. She snapped her gum, and kept twirling her hair around her finger.

"Where's your mom?" Claire asked.

"She's not here," Amy muttered. "She dropped me off."

Claire glanced at the sketches again. "These certainly don't look like they were done by an eighth-grader. Then again, I remember Brian saying you were one of the *oldest* thirteen-year-olds he'd ever met. I think he meant that as a compliment." She turned and stared into those overly made-up eyes. Her voice dropped to a whisper. "You know where he is, don't you, Amy?"

The girl let out a stunned, little laugh, then she glanced to her left and right. "I don't know what the fuck you're talking about," she said, her lip curled. "You gotta be crazy. You should go back to the hospital."

"Brian was a good friend to your brother," Claire whispered. "Even when Derek didn't deserve it. He was pretty nice to you too, wasn't he, Amy? You liked him, didn't you?"

Amy shrugged. "He was okay, I guess," she muttered. But tears started to well in her eyes.

"Where is he, Amy?" Claire asked quietly. "Where's Brian? And where's your brother?"

"Shit." Her head down, Amy wiped her eyes. "Not here," she said under her breath. "I—I'll meet you on the stage, behind the curtains. Five minutes. Now get the fuck out of here, Mrs. Shaw."

Claire turned away, then browsed a couple of other eighth-grade art exhibits. Linda came up to her side.

"What*ever* were you talking about with that little freak?" she asked.

"I just wanted her to know that I said a Special Intention

for Derek at mass today," Claire answered, trying to look interested in some watercolors.

Frowning, Linda sighed. "And what did she say to that?"

"She said, '*So frigging what?*' " Claire shrugged. "Or at least, that's the PG-version of it."

"Yes, quite the mouth on that little brat." Linda shook her head. "I'm telling you, she's no better than her older brother. She'll end up just like him."

Claire turned to her. "You mean, in Europe?"

Linda seemed stumped for a second, then she put on a phony smile. "No, I mean, she'll end up getting into trouble all the time. Did you see her art work? Talk about psycho."

"Well, it's provocative," Claire replied with a shrug. She glanced back, and saw Amy had left her exhibit desk. "Listen, I need to phone home, and check my messages," Claire said. "I'm expecting a couple of calls."

She stepped away before Linda had a chance to respond. Claire headed toward the stage—at one end of the gymnasium. Beside the raised platform and heavy, red curtain was the stage door. But she didn't want anyone following her in there.

She'd helped with a couple of Tiffany's pageants, and knew the layout. Claire hurried out to the hallway, and walked around the corridor, where there was a janitor's closet and a second door. It was the door backstage, and it wasn't locked.

Claire ducked through the doorway, then climbed up a short flight of stairs. Her eyes were still adjusting to the darkness. A slice of light peeked through a line where the heavy curtains didn't quite meet. On the other side of those curtains, the chatter from the mothers and daughters seemed to echo through the gym.

Someone must have had a meeting on the stage recently, because eight folding chairs had been arranged in a semicircle, with one chair facing them. Her head down, Amy Herrmann sat alone in the dark, in a chair at the end of the semicircle.

Claire took the lone folding chair, opposite her. "Derek isn't backpacking through Europe, is he?" she said.

"That's where my parents say he is," Amy murmured. She

stared down at the stage floor and snapped her gum. "Only they're fucking liars."

"How do you know?"

"Because my brother never said shit to me about a trip to Europe. All of the sudden he's gone, and that's the story I got. I looked at my mom and dad's checkbook. They didn't take out any money for him, not a goddamn dime. And Christ knows, Derek never had much cash. Last week, they gave away most of his stuff to charity." Her eyes welled up with tears again. "They wouldn't even let me keep some stuff of his that I wanted."

"What do you think happened to your brother?" Claire asked.

"He's dead," Amy whispered. "They killed him. My mom and dad aren't saying anything, because they're scared. They're ashamed Derek was always getting into trouble. He pissed a lot of people off."

Claire moved over to Amy, then sat in the folding chair beside her. "Who killed him?" she asked, a hand on the girl's shoulder. "How?"

"Why don't you ask your husband?" Amy sneered. "Or maybe your girlfriend with the stick up her butt? They know."

"I've asked them," Claire replied. "We're in the same boat, Amy. All I'm getting are lies. They're telling me that my son ran away the same night Derek disappeared. Do you know what really happened to him?"

"Brian ran away?" Amy let out a sad little laugh, then stood up. "For my money, he and Derek got about as far as Silverwater Creek. I don't think either one of them ever made it off this fucking island. Brian's dead."

Shaking her head, Claire stared up at her.

"I gotta go now, Mrs. Shaw. I'm really sorry about Brian. If you have any more questions, talk to your husband and your gal pal. And you can tell them for me, I hope they die and rot in hell."

Amy Herrmann hurried toward the door backstage. She disappeared in the shadows.

Claire closed her eyes, then heard the stage door slam. She bent forward. It felt as if someone had just punched her in the stomach. That tough-talking little girl didn't tell her anything she hadn't already suspected. Yet hearing actually someone say those words devastated her. *Brian's dead.*

"Well, it's an interesting theory, Tim," Dr. Moorehead said, sitting on the edge of his desk.

"I know it's a stretch," Tim admitted. "But it's all I have to go on for now."

He'd phoned Linus Moorehead from the police station, and left a message. Within fifteen minutes, Dr. Moorehead had called back, saying he'd meet him at his counseling office.

Tim had expected the stereotypical old professor of psychology, a hunched over, bespectacled, white-haired Freud knockoff. After all, the guy's name was *Linus.*

He was surprised when a sandy-haired man with a goatee hopped out of his BMW near the office entry by a florist. He wore a sweatshirt and khakis, and gave Tim a hearty handshake.

Tim had also expected very little cooperation from the psychologist. Once he explained his theory that Rembrandt may have spent time on Moorehead's couch, Tim figured the good doctor would balk, then give him a lecture on doctor-client privilege.

Instead, Moorehead asked him to sit down, and offered him a bottle of Evian water from a small refrigerator by the file cabinet. Then he listened intently as Tim told him about Nancy Killabrew Hart, Claire's stalker, and the various attempts on his life.

"I wouldn't say it's so much of a stretch," Moorehead finally said. "But there are a few 'assumings.' You're assuming Rembrandt is on this island. You're assuming he might have gotten himself into some trouble while here, and I counseled him. Finally, you're assuming I've kept records on everyone I've seen since starting work here nine years ago." He sipped his Evian water and smiled. "On the last one, Tim, you assumed right. If I saw him, I'll still have the file."

He sighed. "This is a small island, but I've provided therapy to hundreds of people in the last nine years. It's a rather formidable task you're setting up for me."

"If it's any help," Tim said. "The Rembrandt task force has him as a white male, single, between the ages of twenty-five and forty. He lives alone . . ."

The doctor laughed. "That could be me."

Tim shrugged. "Me too. Listen, I'd be willing to look through some of the files with you—if you'll let me. Rembrandt could be one of the teenagers you saw in your first few years here. He might have been showing symptoms back then. He might have a history of abuse in his family—like the Davalos brothers. You counseled them, didn't you?"

Moorehead frowned a little. "How did hear about the Davalos brothers?"

"Claire mentioned them to me. I was looking at their police records just now. Either one of those boys—if they weren't dead—would be a perfect candidate for Rembrandt."

Dr, Moorehead nodded soberly. "So we're looking for someone with a history of violence, possibly retarded sexual development . . ."

"That's right," Tim agreed. He couldn't believe Moorehead seemed so willing to work with him on this. He had to keep his enthusiasm in check. "Rembrandt's probably a voyeur. We know he stalks his victims. Barbara Tuttle, the second victim, told friends that she thought someone had been following her. That was two weeks before they found her in a garbage dump.

"So when Rembrandt came to you—or *if* he came to you, he might have been in trouble for voyeurism, you know, Peeping Tom stuff. It's not unusual with serial killers. As a teenager, Ted Bundy used to sneak out at night and watch women undress in their windows. Once he disabled a woman's car, just so he could watch her while she was stranded and vulnerable."

"Sounds like a few of the ones I've had in here," Moorehead said pensively. "I'll look into some of the sadists too, the dog and cat killers. Any other tips from the Rembrandt task force?"

"Yes. It sounds weird, but try shoplifters too. Rembrandt steals these women and makes them his. He seems to get a real thrill from almost getting caught, and teasing the police. It's like a game with him."

Tim listened to himself spouting off like an expert on Rembrandt. Among his coworkers on the force he felt as if he didn't know a damn thing. Suddenly, he was tapping into everything he'd read and heard while behind that desk in the office. Maybe all he needed was someone to take him seriously.

"This might be a long shot, But I think it's worth taking—if we can save a life."

Moorehead smiled. "Looks like I have my work cut out for me," he said. "I better get started right now."

Tim sat up in the chair. "Can I help?"

The doctor shook his head. "Not right now. If I work through most of the night, I'll be finished sometime tomorrow afternoon." Moorehead climbed off his desk. "Now, scram. I have a lot of work to do. I need to call Fork In The Road and order lunch with extra coffee, then start digging into that file cabinet. Call you tomorrow, Tim."

Tim shook his hand. "Listen, I don't know how to thank you," he said.

Moorehead slapped him on the shoulder. "No sweat," he said, leading him to the door.

Tim thanked him again, then headed out.

Letting out a long sigh, Moorehead glanced toward his file cabinet. He picked up the phone on his desk and dialed.

"Hi, it's Linus Moorehead," he said into the phone. "I'm calling from my office. . . . Yeah, I have an order for you . . . You listening? Good. I want this cop dead within twenty-four hours. No screw ups this time. The son of a bitch was just in here asking about the Davalos family, for Christ's sakes. Claire Shaw told him. We need to do something about her too—but fast. She's starting to remember things . . ."

"What in the world has gotten into you today, Claire?" Linda said, taking her eyes off the road for a moment to glance at her. "You look positively catatonic. I mean it."

Claire kept her fist against her mouth. She was trembling with rage. For weeks now, she'd tolerated Linda's lies, because a part of her still wanted to believe it was true that Brian had run away on his own. At least, then it meant he was all right.

But an eighth-grader with a dock-worker's vocabulary had given her a wake-up call. Derek and Brian were dead. Her husband and "friend" weren't just covering it up either. They'd played a part in those deaths.

Now Claire couldn't even look at Linda, she was so full of utter contempt for her. It made her sick to be in the car with her.

"Are you okay?" Linda asked, hands on the wheel. "Claire?"

"I'm fine," she muttered evenly. "I just need to get home." She couldn't say anything with Tiffany in the back seat. Biting down on her lip, Claire stared straight ahead. They rode in silence until Linda turned down the cul de sac.

"Huh, I don't see Harlan's car in the driveway," Linda announced. "He must still be at work. Well, don't worry. I'll keep you company."

"No thank you," Claire said.

"Nonsense!" Linda replied, pulling into the driveway. "Especially if you're not feeling well, Claire. Plus Harlan would absolutely strangle me if I left you two alone."

The car came to a stop. Claire swallowed hard. "Tiffany, honey," she said. "Could you go wait by the front door? I'll take in whatever paintings you can't carry."

"Okay," Tiffany said, opening the back door. "I think I got'm all."

"Good girl," Claire said, staring forward.

"Claire, what in God's name is wrong with you?" Linda whispered. She turned off the car.

"My son is dead," she whispered.

"What?"

"I know he is," Claire muttered, tears welling in her eyes. "I know, Linda. So quit lying to me, goddamn it. I'm sick of your lies."

Linda let out a stunned laugh. "Listen, you're wrong, Claire. I'm coming in, and we're having a nice little talk—"

"I'm through talking with you." Claire opened the car door, climbed outside, then slammed it shut. "And you're not setting foot inside the house," she said through the open window. She was trembling.

"Oh, for God's sakes, Claire . . ." Linda started to open her door.

"No, Linda," she said evenly. "I swear. If you get out of that car, I'll fucking kill you."

Linda froze, then stared at her, wide-eyed.

Claire glared back at her.

"I—I—" Linda shook her head. She quickly closed the door, then fumbled for the ignition. The car's tires screeched as she backed out of the driveway too suddenly.

Still trembling, Claire retreated up the walkway, then stepped inside the house with Tiffany. Her stepdaughter asked if she was sick.

"It's just a headache, sweetheart," she managed to say. She worked up a smile. "I was very proud of you today. Your watercolors were just about the best in the whole first grade." Claire gave her a hug. After a few moments, she pulled back and wiped the tears from her eyes. She wasn't shaking so much any more. "Listen, Princess, why don't you put your watercolors away in your room, and change your clothes? Meanwhile, I'll see what we can make for lunch."

Once Tiffany scurried upstairs with her paintings, Claire glanced over at the phone in the pantry. The message light was blinking.

She rubbed her forehead, and wandered over to the answering machine. She pressed the message button. *"You have one message,"* the automated voice announced.

Claire sighed, and waited.

"This is Tess calling for Claire. Hi, Claire. I'm in the car. Can you tell? I'm now one of those people I used to hate, a cell-phone driver. I'm probably screwing up traffic right and left, but I'm oblivious. How are you? I've been thinking of you a lot . . ."

Claire smiled. Just hearing her new friend's voice made her feel a little better.

If for nothing else right now, she could at least thank God for Tess.

"Tess?"

Mary Lou Cadwell knocked on the front door, then tried the doorbell again. "Tess? Are you in there?" she called.

She and Tess had been friends since their junior year at the University of Washington. Mary Lou was passing through Bellingham on her way home to Seattle. She and Tess had a dinner date tonight.

She'd phoned to tell Tess she might be late, but never got an answer—not even from the machine. She'd passed through U.S.–Canadian customs rather quickly, and was actually on time.

But Mary Lou didn't see Tess's car in the driveway, and no one was answering the front door. It wasn't like Tess to stand up a friend. She'd just gotten out of the hospital after losing her baby not long ago. So Mary Lou was extra concerned.

She walked down the driveway, toward the back of the house. Mary Lou stopped dead at the kitchen door. With darkness falling, the temperature had dropped. It was too cold to leave the door wide open—even with the outer screen door closed.

She peeked through the screen. The wind was blowing,

and a couple of newspaper pages fluttered along the kitchen floor.

"Tess?" she called. "Tess, honey, are you okay?"

She hesitated, then opened the screen door and stepped inside. "Oh my God," she murmured, staring at the mess in the kitchen.

A cup of carry-out coffee had spilt across the breakfast table, and the brown liquid soaked part of the newspaper. The kitchen phone was off the hook. Mary Lou could hear the pulsating alarm tone from the receiver.

The dish draining rack had been knocked over. Silverware, broken dishes, and glasses were scattered across the floor. Mary Lou noticed Tess's purse amid the rubble—along with her cell phone, which had been smashed.

There was a handprint of blood smeared on the white refrigerator door.

Near the refrigerator was a thick, wooden chopping block table with what looked like a small crumpled, white napkin hanging from it. Frowning, Mary Lou stepped toward chopping table. Glass crunched under her feet.

A butcher knife stood on the block, its pointed tip buried in the wood. This close, she could see she'd been wrong. It wasn't a white napkin pinned to the butcher block. What she saw made her shudder.

A pair of panties were stuck under that knife.

Chapter 21

Tess woke up shivering.

Her head throbbed, and she felt sick.

For a moment, she thought she was back in the hospital. But she still had her clothes on. They were clammy and damp with cold, dried sweat. Only something was missing. She touched the front of her jeans. They were unfastened at the top. She wasn't wearing any panties.

She opened her eyes to utter blackness.

"What's happening?" she whispered. "Is somebody there?"

She was lying on a thin uncomfortable cot. She could feel the canvas material stretched across poles on either side of her. She clung to a heavy, itchy blanket for warmth.

Wherever she was, it smelled dank and dirty. The air was so stagnant, she could hardly breathe. Had someone stuck her down in a cellar?

She was too scared and disoriented to make a move. If only she could see something—a crack of light somewhere, a shadowy outline amid all the blackness.

Tess touched her forehead. It was sore and bleeding.

He'd hit her. She remembered now. She'd put up a struggle. She'd tried to rush past him at the top of the basement stairs. She'd seen his face, and yes, she'd recognized him from the hospital. But that hadn't stopped her from fighting him. Even then, amid all the confusion and shock, Tess had known she was fighting for her life.

In the darkness, Tess reached out and fanned at the air until her hand brushed against something. She discovered a table at her side, and heard something roll on top of it. Blindly patting the tabletop, she found a light-weight, plastic flashlight, and quickly switched it on. The beam of light cut through the darkness, and gave her a tiny bit of comfort.

Tess sat up, and moved the light across the cement floor, then up the walls, which were covered with cheap, imitation-wood paneling. One wall hadn't been paneled yet; a plastic tarp shrouded whatever lay beyond it. Tess wondered if she'd find a door or window back there. She didn't see a way out anywhere else.

But on the ceiling, paneled with the same cheap wood-board, she noticed a trap door. No stairs or ladder, only a portal—just out of her reach.

Crawling off the cot, Tess felt dizzy. When her bare feet touched the icy cement floor, she flinched and pulled back.

With the flashlight, she searched for her shoes, but didn't see them. She figured he must not have bothered with her shoes and socks after putting her jeans back on. She wondered why he'd taken her panties. Was he doing something with them right now?

Tess got to her feet. But she stood up too fast, and started to teeter. She reached out for the little table, then took a couple of deep breaths.

Getting her balance back, Tess aimed the flashlight on the table. He'd left her some supplies: six large bottled waters, three boxes of army K-rations (Beef Stew, Chili with Macaroni, Tuna and Noodles), a box of Kleenex, and two towels. On the floor, by the make-shift nightstand was a stainless steel pot with a lid. He must have expected her to use it for a toilet.

Tess's teeth started to chatter. She wrapped the blanket around her shoulders, then padded over to the plastic sheet.

Peeling it back at one side, she found a solid dirt wall. A few strategically placed wood slats seemed to hold it up.

At least, now she had some idea where she was—underground, in an unfinished room. Perhaps it was part of someone's basement, or an expanded crawlspace beneath a garage or a barn. "God, help me," she whispered.

She shined the flashlight at the base of the dirt wall. Behind the plastic tarp was a rumpled pile of women's clothes, discarded shoes, and handbags. Tess picked up one of the purses. The wallet was still inside. The money was missing, but all the credit cards were still there—as well as the woman's driver's license.

Tess shined the flashlight on the plastic card. She recognized the face and name. The woman had been on the news yesterday. Her name was Kimberly Cronin, and she'd been abducted near her college apartment in Bellingham.

They were saying that she could be Rembrandt's latest victim. Someone on the radio mentioned that several church services this morning included prayers for Kimberly's safe return.

But Tess knew the girl was dead. Rembrandt had finished with her. He'd discarded her as he had these clothes. The coats, dresses, jeans, tops, shoes and bags—they all belonging to dead women.

Tess suddenly realized this place had been dug out of the earth for a very specific function. She wasn't standing in someone's basement or a storm shelter or a crawl space.

She was in a waiting room.

All she wanted to do was sneak down to Brian's room in the basement, curl up on his bed, and cry.

But Claire had to fix lunch for Tiffany. Unlike her dad, Harlan's daughter adored Brian. Claire wondered how she would tell Tiffany that her stepbrother was dead.

She wouldn't. At least, not now.

So she made a grilled cheese sandwich and heated up

some chicken and stars soup. While Tiffany ate her lunch, Claire managed to put on a smile and they talked about the art show. She kept busy washing out the soup pot, frying pan, and utensils.

Tiffany didn't quite finish her lunch. Inspired by the art show, she ran back up to her room to paint. Claire picked at the rest of her grilled cheese sandwich. After a couple of bites, she felt too nervous and upset to eat any more.

She tried to phone Tess back, but there was no answer. The machine didn't even pick up. She tried twice, without any luck.

Claire sank down in one of the chairs at the breakfast table, and stared out the sliding glass door for a moment. She start to cry—deep, uncontrollable sobs. The tears streamed down her face. For the first time after nearly a month of wondering and worrying, she finally grieved for her dead son. Yet there was no relief, no outlet—just utter hopelessness, and the feeling that some part of her guts had been cut out with a dull knife.

When Julia had died, Claire's arms had ached. This time she felt the pain in her heart, and in her chest, where she'd been shot.

She cried and cried for her sweet boy. All the while, she knew Harlan would soon come through the front door. She expected him any minute.

No doubt, Linda had already called him. Claire imagined Linda on the phone with Harlan—and perhaps others: *"She threatened me . . . She was acting absolutely bonkers . . . She knows . . ."*

Claire wiped her eyes with a napkin. She was kicking herself for losing her composure with Linda. As long as she didn't remember that night Brian had "run away," as long as she pretended to believe their cover stories, she was safe. But less than an hour ago, she'd told Linda she knew about the lies, and she knew Brian was dead.

She'd just dug her own grave by saying that. She was forcing them to deal with her.

Well, fine. She didn't give a damn. Her son was dead. Let them come after her.

Only, who was *them?*

"Why don't you ask your husband?" she remembered Amy Herrmann saying. *"Or maybe your girlfriend with the stick up her butt? They know."*

Amy had said Derek and Brian never left the island. They'd gotten *"about as far as Silverwater Creek."* It was a campsite in the woods, about a twenty-minute drive away. Harlan and some of the Guardians sponsored camping trips for teenagers at Silverwater Creek. Was that where Derek and Brian were killed? Were their bodies buried there?

Claire wondered how this thirteen-year-old girl could know so much. Or was what happened to Brian and Derek an open secret among the islanders?

In church this morning, Claire had noticed a lot of people looking uncomfortable when she said the Special Intention for her son and his friend. She might as well have been saying a prayer for the Davalos family.

Claire reached over for her purse—on one of the other chairs at the breakfast table. She started fishing through it, and dug out a few items until she found the piece of paper with Steven Griswald's number on it.

Her hand was shaking as she dialed the number of Steven Griswald in Bremerton. A man answered on the first ring. "Yeah, hello?"

Claire hadn't thought about what to say to him. She hesitated.

"Hello?" he repeated.

"Hello, is Steven Griswald there?"

"Who's calling?" he shot back.

"Um, my name is Claire Shaw. Are you Steven Griswald?"

"Is this a telemarketer? Because if it is, you can stop now—"

"I'm not a telemarketer," Claire said. "I live on Deception Island. Did you have a sister named Violet?"

There was a silence on the other end of the line.

"Mr. Griswald?"

"What the hell do you want?" he whispered.

"I—" Claire hesitated. She heard the front door opening. *"Claire? You home?"* Harlan called.

Panicked, she quickly hung up the phone.

Peeling off his jacket, Harlan stepped into the pantry area. He wore jeans and a flannel shirt. He never dressed up for work on the weekends. "What are you doing here alone?" he asked.

She gave a casual shrug. "Oh, Linda and I sort of had a blow up." she said. "I got mad and sent her home. I'm surprised she didn't call you. She—"

Before Claire could finish, the phone rang.

She grabbed the receiver. "Yes, hello?"

"Listen, why did you just call me?" she heard Steven Griswald ask. He must have dialed star-six-nine on her. "I want you to stop bothering my family. Understand?"

The receiver to her ear, Claire glanced at Harlan. He was staring at her. "Um, yes . . ." Claire said into the phone.

"What exactly do you want from me?" Steven Griswald asked.

"I'm—sorry," Claire said carefully. "But thank you anyway."

She hung up, and smiled at Harlan. "Stupid telemarketers," she muttered. She prayed Steven Griswald wouldn't call back again.

"Where's Tiffany?" Harlan asked.

"Upstairs in her room, painting."

"I don't like you and Tiffany being here alone," he said, moving toward the refrigerator. "What did you and Linda fight about anyway?"

Claire shrugged. "Um, my Special Intention at mass this morning. She didn't think it was appropriate."

"Oh, that," Harlan said, rolling his eyes. He pulled a Coke out of the refrigerator. "Sometimes I wish Linda would mind her own goddamn business," he muttered. He sat down at the breakfast table.

Claire couldn't help smiling a bit. At the same time, she was so wary of him. "Um, can I fix you a sandwich or something?" she asked.

"That would be great. Thanks, sweetheart."

Claire stole a glance at the phone, then she headed over to the refrigerator. She pulled out some deli meat, and started making her husband a sandwich.

"Where's Harlan now?" Tim asked.

"He's in the shower," Claire whispered on the other end of the line. "I can't talk much longer."

Tim was on the cell phone, leaning against the car in a turnaround area off Evergreen Drive.

He'd been checking some of the other cabins in the forest when Claire had called. Tim missed having Walt Binns for a guide. He hadn't come across anything. He'd checked around the Logans' cabin again, and found Troy Landers, parked along a path in back of the dilapidated cedar shaker. The deputy had been sleeping in his patrol car, and wasn't too happy to see the man responsible for his current situation. "You're the first two-legged creature I've seen out here," Troy told Tim, with a curled lip.

Tim sort of knew how he felt. Searching through those woods was a lonely, frustrating experience. But after a couple of hours, Tim realized he might not be completely alone. At one point, he'd noticed a dark blue Honda Accord following him at a distance on the narrow, winding roadway. It disappeared for a while. But he'd spotted it again, a half-hour later, when Claire had called.

Now, as he stood outside the car, Tim couldn't see the Accord. It was as if the blue Honda had just vanished. He figured it must have turned off onto one of the dirt trails. But he kept a lookout through the trees while talking with Claire.

"Amy Herrmann didn't leave any room for doubt?" Tim asked gently. "She said both Derek and Brian were—"

"Yes, she said they're dead," Claire finished for him. "And

Linda, Harlan, and I-don't-know-who-else are all involved
in it."

"Did she tell you anything else?"

"She said Derek and Brian never made it off the island.
'*They got about as far as Silverwater Creek.*' I'm not sure
what she meant. But I want to go out there. If I can get away,
will you drive me tomorrow? Maybe I'll remember something that happened there. Maybe that's what I'm blocking."

"Of course," Tim answered. "In the meantime, do you
think you're okay in the house with Harlan? I wonder how
can you stand it."

"I've stood it for the last few days," she said. "I guess I
can hold on for another night. I don't think he'll try anything
with Tiffany here."

"Just the same, I'll park across the street from your house
tonight, and sleep in the car. If you need me, I'll be close by."

"Oh, Tim, I'd feel so much better if you did that. You
don't mind?"

"Not at all. I haven't slept in a car since college," he said.
"It'll be my first stakeout. Be sure to tell Harlan I'm out
there. It might keep him on his best behavior. I think maybe—"

Tim heard a call-waiting beep on the line. "Claire? Hold
on a minute. Okay?" He clicked the call-waiting button.
"Hello?"

"Tim? Sheriff Klauser calling. Your boss in Seattle just
sent another fax."

"I'm talking on the other line. But I'm in my car. I'll
come pick it up in about ten minutes. Is that okay? Are you
at the station?"

"Sure am, buddy. See you in a bit."

Tim clicked back on the line to Claire. "Are you still
there?" he asked.

"Yes, but I think Harlan's done with his shower," she
whispered. "I need to hang up soon."

"All right. Just, please, be careful. I keep thinking of the
other day with the hair dryer. He may try something that will

look like an accident—like you slipping in the bathtub, or another electric shock—"

"Huh, you're scaring me." She laughed nervously. "Listen, I should go."

"Okay," he said. "I'll be parked outside your place tonight."

"Thanks, Tim," she whispered. Then she hung up.

He climbed back into the car, and started up the engine. Pulling out of the turnaround, he veered onto Evergreen Drive. In a strange way, he almost looked forward to spending tonight in his car, parked outside Claire's house. At least, he'd be close to her.

He hadn't meant to frighten her about "slipping in the bathtub" or some other "accident" that could transpire tonight in her home. But he didn't know what Harlan Shaw had in mind for his wife. She could break her neck, falling down a flight of stairs. Didn't Harlan work in a chemical plant? Did he know about poisons that couldn't be detected? Or maybe in the middle of the night, Harlan would just happen to mistake her for a prowler, and shoot her.

Clutching the steering wheel, Tim glanced in the rearview mirror. He spotted the blue Honda Accord in the distance behind him. It was about ten car lengths back. Tim squinted in the mirror. It was the same car, he was almost positive. "What the hell?" he murmured.

He wanted to get a closer look at the driver. Easing off the accelerator, he slowed down to thirty-five miles per hour—ten below the speed limit. Tim checked the mirror again to see if the blue car was gaining on him.

But the other vehicle lingered a safe distance behind.

Tim noticed another turnaround on his right, Quickly, he pulled over. Gravel crunched under his tires as he came to a stop in the bay area. He glanced back for the other car.

Tim didn't see it. He stuck his head out the window and gazed back at the two-lane thoroughfare. It was as if the blue Honda had just vanished.

The other driver must have ducked down a side street.

Tim continued to stare out his window, scrutinizing the trees and dense foliage along both sides of the road. He still didn't see anything.

An SUV came up Evergreen Drive, then passed him.

Tim waited another minute before pulling back onto the road. He kept checking his rearview mirror for the blue Accord, but it wasn't behind him.

As he drove closer to town, Tim began to wonder about the fax from Lieutenant Elmore. It was too soon for Rembrandt to have abducted another victim. They'd just gotten the news on Kimberly Cronin's death this morning. Tim tried to think optimistically. Maybe they'd finally analyzed those photos of the footprints he'd sent, or they'd inspected what was left of Claire's hair dryer.

Tim turned down Main Street, and headed toward the heart of town. Dusk was looming over the harbor. Most of the weekend visitors had already caught the afternoon ferry back to the mainland.

Tim switched on his headlights for the last few blocks. He glanced in the rearview mirror again.

"Jesus, what's going on?" he whispered.

There it was again, about two blocks behind him on the nearly deserted street. The blue Honda Accord had reappeared as quickly and inexplicably as it had vanished just a few minutes ago. Its headlights weren't on. But Tim could tell it was the same car.

Scowling at the rearview mirror, he didn't notice the old man on the bicycle until he was almost on top of him. The headlights came so close to the man that he was just a glaring white shape in front of the car.

Tim slammed on the brakes. The car tires let out a screech. The cell phone and a flashlight flew off the passenger seat.

His heart racing, Tim clutched the wheel and stared at the old man, who merely glanced over his shoulder and peddled on down the road.

Tim caught his breath, then looked in the rearview mirror

again. No sign of the Honda Accord. "What the hell?" he said to no one.

The speedometer never went over fifteen as he drove the remaining few blocks to the police station. He kept checking the rearview and side mirrors for that elusive car.

It was like a specter, darting in and out of Tim's view. The driver had to know these roads, the shortcuts and escape routes. He seemed to be making a game of it. Tim couldn't help thinking about Claire's stalker—and Rembrandt.

"Do you know someone in town who drives a blue Honda Accord?" he asked the sheriff. He was still a bit shaken as he lumbered into the station.

Sheriff Klauser shrugged. "Hell, these new cars all look alike to me." He retreated behind the counter. "Guess I'm getting to be an old fart. Half the time, I need to read the name off the back of a car before I can write out a traffic ticket. I have your fax back here. He got another one."

Tim frowned at him. "What do you mean?"

"Rembrandt," the sheriff said, handing Tim the fax sheets. "He's going into overdrive, I guess. Nabbed up another woman in Bellingham. They think it happened this morning. This one's a little older than the last."

Tim glanced at the grainy photo of Rembrandt's most recent prey. She was thirty-five, according to her stats. She looked pretty in the photograph. At first, Tim thought the shadowy patch on one side of her face was a flaw in the fax. But in the description, it said she had a large birthmark on her left cheek and neck.

Her name was Tess Campbell.

Chapter 22

She'd finished crying.

She'd drunk a little water, then used some more to clean the cut on her head.

She'd pulled the cot beneath the trap door in the ceiling, then stood on it. But she still hadn't been able to reach the damn trap door.

She'd screamed for help until her throat felt raw. It hadn't done any good.

Now she tried to figure out a way to defend herself.

Tess had no idea how long she'd been trapped in this make-shift dungeon. But any minute now, her abductor could open that trap door in the ceiling and come down to get her. She wouldn't let him.

Crouching down behind the plastic tarp, she started going through the purses and coat pockets of the women who had been there before her. Dead women. Perhaps he'd missed something. Maybe one of them hadn't had time to reach for her pepper spray or a nail file.

Using the flashlight, Tess continued her search. She found some Fruit Stripe gum in one of the coat pockets. She didn't know which victim it had belonged to, but she was grateful. The gum took away the sour, gritlike taste in her mouth.

For a crazy moment, she hoped against hope to find a cell phone. That was a laugh. Like she'd get through to anyone. And what could she tell them? *I'm underground somewhere.* She didn't know if she was in Canada or Portland. She could be at a farm or under someone's suburban garage. Still, she would have welcomed the sound of another person's voice.

Sifting amid the pile of clothes, Tess tried to remember how many women Rembrandt had killed so far. Eight? Certainly the police had enough clues from all those murders. Maybe they were close to identifying this monster.

She felt a strange affinity with these women as she searched through their pockets and bags. Her predecessors were no longer photos of victims that she'd seen in the newspaper and on TV. Barbara Tuttle had a Blockbuster card, a Seattle's Best Coffee punch card, and a photo of someone's baby in her wallet. In Kimberly Cronin's purse, she found a postcard of Barcelona that a friend had written her, and a picture of Matt Damon. A tiny Bart Simpson figurine was attached to her key chain.

Tess went though the whole pile. All she'd come up with were some nail clippers—with a tiny, sharp file, and a box of Altoids.

Sighing, she stood up and shined the flashlight on the wooden slats against the dirt wall. She yanked at one, then another, and another. They didn't budge. She needed to knock him over the head with something. She wondered if any of the others had tried to defend themselves—or escape. Or had they just gone willingly?

She aimed the light on the wall of dirt and noticed a large crater at eye level. One of the women had tried to dig her way out. Tess placed her hand in the cavity, about a half-foot deep and a foot wide. The earth felt solid. But she managed to claw out a handful of dirt.

How long had that poor woman been digging with her bare hands to get this far? And to what end?

She could dig and dig, only to find herself beneath a cement foundation. At the same time, Tess had to admire her predecessor. At least she'd made an effort. She hadn't just sat and waited for Rembrandt to take her.

Tess shined the light once again on the pile of clothes at her feet. She found two pairs of high heels. One pair looked new and expensive. They were sturdy too. *Amalfi's*. The owner had been a woman of good taste.

Tess took a deep breath. With the heel of Connie Shafer's shoe, she began to tap away and loosen the dirt in the crater.

She wasn't going to sit and wait.

It was ten o'clock, and the lights were still on inside the Shaws' house.

Tim had been sitting in the parked car for less than an hour, yet it seemed like an eternity. He'd liked the idea of being close to Claire. But the idea and the reality of it were two different things. He was bored out of his mind.

He'd told the sheriff what he was doing. Then he'd stopped by Lyle's Stop and Sip Gas Station for some bottled water, magazines, and candy bars. His last stop had been The Whale Watcher for his toothbrush, toothpaste, and the paperback he'd been reading. He'd also gotten Al's gun. There had been two messages waiting for him at the hotel, both from Walt Binns. Gabe and Beven's twelve-year-old son read them off to Tim: *"First, at eleven-fifty this morning, he said 'no sweat' about missing lunch. The second message at three-twenty, he was 'sorry I missed you again,' and he'll 'call back later.'"*

On his way to the cul de sac where the Shaws lived, Tim had kept a lookout for the blue Honda Accord again. But he hadn't seen anything.

Watching the house, and the surrounding area, he sat in the car and ate a KitKat bar for dinner. As bored as he was, Tim felt nervous too. He had the window cracked open, but the doors were locked.

He hoped Claire might come to one of the windows and

wave at him. But he didn't see anyone yet. He knew if he saw her, he'd feel better, and the night would go by more quickly.

Instead, what he saw was a pair of headlights in the rearview mirror. Someone was coming up the cul de sac. Tim wondered if it was the blue Honda Accord again. He reached under the car seat for Al's gun.

The car was advancing—until the lights in the mirror were blinding and the interior of Tim's car became illuminated. He turned and squinted at the car pulling up behind him. He clutched the gun, and felt his heart racing. Then the headlights went off, and Tim recognized Walt Binns's Range Rover.

Walt climbed out of the car and waved to him. He was wearing an Irish knit sweater, and carried a small shopping bag.

Tim slipped the gun back under the seat, and climbed out of the car.

"Hey," Walt said, grinning. "I bought you some stuff to help pass the time. *Sports Illustrated, GQ, Playboy,* and chewing gum." He handed the bag to Tim. "I also put those coupons in there for that hotel in Victoria."

"Wow, thanks," Tim said. "How did you know I was here?"

"I called Harlan about a half hour ago, and he told me you were parked outside the house for the night." Walt leaned against the car. "I don't know why the hell my buddy won't invite you in."

"I'm all right out here," Tim said.

"I guess you got my messages," Walt said. "In lieu of lunch today, I had another talk with my trigger-happy, dim-witted pal, Fred Maybon. He had a whole new story for me. Y'see, he thought you were Rembrandt."

"Oh, really?" Tim said, deadpan. "Amazing."

"Isn't it though?" Walt replied, continuing his mocking tone. "See, Fred heard the rumors, and that's why he was tramping through the woods with his assault rifle." Walt shook his head. "Have you ever heard such a crock of shit? Anyway,

I don't know what he's up to. But I'll ask around, and find out what's really going on."

"Thanks, Walt. I appreciate it." Tim glanced back at Walt's car. "Listen, you don't happen to know someone who drives a dark blue Honda Accord, do you?"

Walt let out a surprised laugh. "Well, yeah. Fred Maybon. Why? Did you see him today?"

Tim nodded. "Yeah, off and on. He's been following me. And I don't think he was trying to catch up with me and apologize for yesterday."

"That's just crazy. We really ought to talk to the sheriff."

Tim frowned. "Well, I don't want to jump the gun."

"Why not? Fred did." Walt sighed. "You know, I always thought Fred was a moron. I've never taken him too seriously. Even after yesterday, I figured, hell, it was just Fred being an idiot again. But this is really disturbing. He was following you?"

Tim nodded pensively. He glanced at his wristwatch. "It's after ten. I'll talk to the sheriff tomorrow."

"Listen, do you want some company tonight?" Walt asked. "Fred's not about to try anything while I'm here."

Tim nodded toward the Shaws' house. "I don't think he'll try anything in front of them either. You don't have to stick around, Walt. I'll be all right." He hoisted the bag. "I'll catch up on my reading."

A few minutes after Walt left, Tim saw something out of the corner of his eye.

Someone darted up the Shaws' front walk toward his car. He realized it was Claire. She wore a gray sweatshirt and jeans, and she was carrying a folded-up blanket. Tim rolled down the window. As she came closer, she looked so pretty. Her brown hair was swept back, and slightly wind blown.

He started to open the door. But she shook her head. "I can't stay," she whispered. "Harlan's getting ready for bed, and I only have a minute." She handed him a Tupperware container. "I brought you some apple cobbler. It's not bad if

I say so myself." Then she passed the blanket to him through the window. "And here, take this. By midnight, it'll be freezing out here."

"Thanks." Tim set the blanket and Tupperware container on the passenger seat. "Listen, I wanted to tell you. If you need me and can't get to a phone, just blink the lights on and off. Is everything okay in there?"

She nodded. "I'm all right." Hovering near the window, she smiled apologetically at him. "I'm sorry you're stuck out here."

"I don't really mind so much," he replied shyly. "At least I got a chance to see you today."

She placed her hand on his cheek. "Thank you, Tim," she whispered. "Thank you for everything."

Then she leaned forward and kissed him on the mouth.

It took Tim by surprise. He just started to kiss her back when she pulled away. Yet he could still feel her soft lips against his. Tim stared at her.

"I've been wanting to do that ever since I first set eyes on you," she whispered. Then Claire turned and ran toward the house.

Dazed, he watched her. She let herself inside, and a moment later, she came to the living room window. She gave him a furtive, little wave.

Tim blinked his headlights on and off.

She nodded, then moved away from the window, out of sight.

His cell phone rang, and it gave him a start. He clicked it on before the second ring. "Yes?"

"Tim, it's Walt."

"Oh, hi." He'd been hoping for Claire.

"I just wanted to let you know," Walt said. "I drove by Fred Maybon's house a few minutes ago. His blue Honda Accord is parked in the front driveway. And guess what? I don't know how in the world it happened, but the two back tires are flatter than pancakes. Imagine that."

"What?" Tim laughed. "You mean, you . . ."

"Fred ain't going anywhere tonight, pal. You can rest easy. Call me if you need anything."

Tim thanked Walt Binns. After hanging up with him, he sampled Claire's apple cobbler. On top of everything else, she could cook. He took only three bites. He'd save the rest for later.

Tim figured he could make it though the night now.

He searched for a magazine to read. Among the things he'd brought along was his green folder, full of Rembrandt-related data. He found the fax from Lieutenant Elmore.

Tim glanced at the photo of Tess Campbell, the Bellingham woman Rembrandt had abducted today. "Poor thing," he whispered.

Tess stood on the cot, scooping earth, rocks, and dirt out of the crater. Her hands were raw, and her fingers were bleeding.

The first high heel had lasted about a half-hour before it broke. Then she'd turned it around and started chipping away at the dirt with the toe.

When the ground got too hard, she dowsed it with water, then kept digging. With the stainless steel pot he expected her to use as a toilet, she scooped out the soil. A large mound of earth had collected at the bottom of the plastic tarp.

Tess could stick her entire arm into the hole she'd burrowed. It was over two feet deep. She was exhausted, and had worked up a sweat. On the bright side, at least she wasn't cold anymore.

Tess caught her breath. "At this rate, you ought to hit that concrete foundation by Christmas," she muttered to herself.

But she couldn't quit. She knew who Rembrandt was. She could identify him. She was the only one who could put a stop to the murders. If she didn't escape, he'd go on killing.

With her muddy, swollen fingers, Tess touched her pale

green pullover and jeans. She didn't want them to end up in the pile of discarded clothes near her feet.

Tess grabbed the pot and started digging again.

Please, Brian, be home. Please, be home.

She remembered speeding in her car up Evergreen Drive, and praying that he would be home. White-knuckled, her hands clutched the steering wheel. The tires screeched as she pulled into the driveway. She was out of breath and crying by the time she opened the front door. *Brian? Brian, are you home?*

Claire sat up in bed.

It wasn't a dream. It was a memory, just as clear as the others.

Claire glanced at the digital clock on her night stand: 1:18 A.M. She was alone in the bed. Frowning, she felt Harlan's side of the mattress. Cold. He'd been gone a while.

She crept out of bed, put on her robe, then checked the bathroom. "Harlan?" she whispered, knocking gently on the door.

It was the same set up as the other night—with the door closed, the light on, and no Harlan.

She tiptoed into the dim hallway, then down the stairs. Harlan wasn't in the pantry or family room. She peeked down the basement stairs. The light was on in the rec room.

Claire crept down the basement steps, then she flicked off the light switch near the bottom of the stairs.

She could see a line of light under the door to Harlan's workroom. He was probably on his computer again. Claire thought of knocking on the door, but decided against it.

Instead, she turned the light back on, and tiptoed up the stairs again. She went into the living room and peered out the window. She had a good view of Tim's car, but couldn't see anyone inside it. Claire gave a little wave.

Nothing happened.

She waved again.

The headlights blinked on and off.

Claire nodded and smiled.

She went back to bed. Funny, how just the sight of those headlights blinking filled her with a warmth and comfort.

She felt herself drifting off. Then it occurred to her. What if Harlan was pulling the same trick down in his workroom that he used in the master bathroom? He could have just put on the light and closed door so she'd think he was in there. He could have snuck off some place, and left her alone in the house with Tiffany. But why would he do that?

Claire told herself not to worry. Tim was right outside. Or was he? How could she be sure he was all right? What if she'd been waving to someone else a few minutes ago?

What if, what if . . .

Claire sat up in bed again.

"Mom?"

She gasped, then stared at Tiffany, standing in the bedroom doorway. "What? What is it, honey?"

In her flannel nightgown, Tiffany fingered her hair as she inched into the room. "I can't sleep," she whimpered. "Can I get into bed with you?"

Claire let out a little laugh. "Of course, sweetheart." She pulled back the covers on Harlan's side of the bed.

Tiffany crawled in, then snuggled up next to her. "Where did Dad go?" she asked.

"He didn't go anywhere, honey," Claire said, stoking her hair. "He's just down in his workroom. No reason to fret. Everything's fine . . ."

Claire thought if she kept saying it, she might believe it.

The digital clock on the dashboard of Ron and Linda Castle's SUV read 1:22 A.M. The radio was tuned to an Easy Listening Station. Sitting at the wheel, Linda sang "Evergreen" along with Barbra Streisand. She was slightly off-key, and quite drunk.

They were parked in the lot by the Anacortes Marina. Ron and Linda's boat, *The Lovely Linda,* was moored at the dock. They kept their SUV parked in the lot for use on the mainland. This was the vehicle Linda claimed to have taken for the drive down to Seattle with Claire.

They had a spot near the edge of the parking lot. Beyond the SUV's windshield, they had a beautiful view of the dark, choppy water, and all the boats gently rocking along the pier. Black clouds passed over the moon.

" 'Like a rose . . .' " Linda sang. Then she forgot the rest of the words, and started humming. She'd gotten dolled up for this clandestine meeting. She'd taken off her windbreaker, so he could admire the purple silk blouse, unbuttoned just enough. The color went well with her frosted, light brown hair, and the garnet earrings she wore.

He handed her the pint of Jim Beam, and she drank from the bottle. She scowled at the gloves covering his hands, then laughed. "When did you put those on?" she asked,

"Just now," he answered.

"Ye gods, why?"

He smiled. "Fingerprints."

She laughed again. "What did you give me earlier? I feel so—giddy."

He reached over and switched off the radio. "Just a Valium—to take the chill off."

"You naughty boy," she purred.

"You've known for a while now that I can be very naughty."

"Well, I'm no tattle-tale. I haven't breathed a word to any-body about your—artistic side." She giggled for a moment, then seemed to consider what she was saying. Her smile waning, Linda bit her lip. She took another swig from the Jim Beam bottle.

"Still you relish holding it over me," he said. "You've kept me under your thumb with that bit of knowledge."

"I'll keep you under my thumb—and fingers." Linda giggled. She placed her hand on his thigh, and slowly inched her way toward his crotch. "Is this okay? Or are you still worried about fingerprints?"

Gently, he turned her hand over. "Here," he said, setting a gun into her open palm.

She laughed. "Ye gods, where did you get that?"

"From *The Lovely Linda.* It's yours, the one you keep on the galley shelf behind the Ritz crackers." Gingerly, he guided her finger along the trigger. "Careful. The safety's not on."

"What the hell are you doing?" she asked, still giggling.

"I'm making this look like a suicide," he said.

She didn't resist as he guided the gun in her hand. He moved it up toward her face. "Close your eyes, Linda," he whispered. "And open your mouth a little."

She stopped laughing, and numbly gazed at him. "Why?"

"I want to kiss you," he said. "C'mon . . ."

Her eyes closed, Linda tipped her head back slightly.

He kissed her on the mouth, then pulled back.

Her lips were still parted, wanting more.

He guided the gun barrel into her mouth.

Linda opened her eyes. Gazing at him in horror, she tried to recoil and scream. Linda started to struggle, but she was too late.

With his finger over hers, he squeezed the trigger.

Chapter 23

Claire waited at the end of the driveway with Tiffany. The school bus was due any minute.

She'd thrown a trench coat over her sweater and jeans. On the radio this morning, the local station advised islanders and coastal residents to brace themselves tonight for severe wind and rain storms, possible flooding and power outages. The skies above looked gray and slightly ominous, but that wasn't unusual for seven-forty on a November morning.

Tim had moved the car across the street. Claire gave him a little wave. Smiling, he waved back.

"Mom, who's that man?" Tiffany asked.

"He came over last night with Uncle Walt, remember?"

"What's he doing?"

"He's a policeman," Claire said. "He's just watching over us, making sure we're all right—kind of like a guardian angel."

Claire squatted to adjusted the collar on Tiffany's jacket. "Promise you'll be a good girl at Andrea's house tonight."

Tiffany wore her backpack. It was pink and almost as big as she was. She had an afterschool meeting with the first grade Christmas pageant committee, and one of the mothers had volunteered to take them out to dinner, then host a sleep-over.

"Are you gonna be home when I get back tomorrow?" Tiffany asked, with a worried pout.

"Of course, sweetie," Claire whispered. "What's wrong?"

Before Tiffany answered, Claire realized why her step-daughter seemed worried. The last time Tiffany had slept over at a friend's house, her stepmother and stepbrother had disappeared. It was one of the only things Claire could re-member about that day: Tiffany had been at a sleepover.

The school bus drove up the cul de sac. Claire kissed Tiffany on the cheek. "Listen, it's supposed to storm tonight. If you get scared or homesick or anything, call and we'll come pick you up. Okey-doke?"

Tiffany nodded. "Okey-doke."

The bus pulled up to the end of the driveway, and the door opened with a whoosh.

Claire straightened up, then stroked her stepdaughter's hair. "Have fun tonight," she said. "And I'll be here tomor-row."

"Okey-doke," Tiffany said again. "Bye, Mom." Then she stepped on the bus. The door closed after her.

Claire watched the bus maneuver the turnaround at the end of the block, then pass by again. She waved to Tiffany in the window, and wondered if she really would be around to see her tomorrow.

In her discussion with Tim last night, she'd said Harlan wouldn't let any harm come to her—as long as Tiffany was around. Well, now Tiffany would be gone for the next thirty-four hours.

Claire shivered. It was colder than she thought. She gazed across the street at Tim's car. She couldn't quite see him, be-cause of a reflection on the window. She started toward the car.

"Claire?"

She swiveled around.

Harlan stood on the front stoop, the door was open behind him. "C'mon in, sweetheart," he called. "I need to talk to you."

She could see Tim looking back at her now. She waved at him, very matter-of-fact, nothing furtive or flirty about it.

With a sigh, she turned and headed up to the walkway.

Harlan wore a blue shirt, khaki pants, and an ugly tie Linda had given him. He pushed the door open wider for Claire. "I don't know how we'll work this out today," he grumbled, stepping inside after her.

"I just got off the phone with Ron," Harlan continued, following her into the kitchen. "He's not sure when Linda can make it over. She took the boat to the mainland last night. Another emergency with her mother. Anyway, she's not back yet. I don't want to leave you alone here, but I have a meeting at ten-thirty, and I can't miss it."

Claire started making Harlan his breakfast. "Well, just go," she said, cracking a couple of eggs. "It's not like I'm here alone. Officer Sullivan is right outside. In fact, honey, I think it would be nice—decent of us—if we invited him in to use our bathroom and maybe have some breakfast."

"I'm not leaving you alone with him," Harlan said, pouring himself a second cup of coffee.

"Why not?" Claire said. She set the egg-soaked bread on the frying pan. "He's a cop. The reason he's here on the island is to look after me. So let him do his job. And in the meantime, would it kill you to be nice to him? The poor guy has been sitting out in that car all night—just to protect me. The least we could do is offer him a warm breakfast."

Harlan had a third cup of coffee as he watched Tim, seated at their breakfast table, eating French Toast.

If Harlan had had his way, Tim would have been allowed to use the powder room for three minutes before being exiled to his car with a cup of coffee and a sweet roll to go. But

Claire had insisted they let Tim take a shower in Tiffany's bathroom. She'd even found a disposable razor and a fresh bar of soap for him.

Harlan had reluctantly agreed to leave her under Tim's watchful eye, but he'd insisted on Tim staying outside the house.

"I'd feel better if you didn't go out today, sweetheart," he told Claire.

She stood at the kitchen sink. "Well, I thought I'd go to town for some candles and batteries in case the storm knocks out the power."

"We have enough emergency supplies on hand. I'd rather you stay put."

"Tell it to Dr. Moorehead. I have a five-thirty appointment."

"I can drive you, Mrs. Shaw," Tim piped up.

Harlan frowned at him over his coffee cup, then glanced at Claire. "I might be home early, then I can take you. I'll call and let you know."

Tim seemed to rush through his breakfast during the uncomfortable silence that followed. Claire reached over and switched on the radio to the twenty-four-hour news station. At least someone was talking.

But no one seemed to be listening—until the newscaster mentioned the name Rembrandt:

> *Bellingham Police, working with the "Rembrandt" task force, are investigating yesterday's disappearance of a thirty-five-year-old Bellingham woman. The identity of the woman is pending notification of her family. The "Rembrandt" killer is believed to have murdered at least seven women in the Western Washington area in the past eighteen months. The latest victim, Kimberly Cronin, a twenty-year-old college student at Western Washington University in Bellingham, was discovered only yesterday . . .*

Claire reached over and switched off the radio. Tim had stopped eating.

Harlan cleared his throat. "It looks like the guy we're worried about is otherwise occupied." He turned to Tim. "If you're finished, I'd like a little time alone with my wife before I go off to work. And I'd appreciate it if you stayed outside in your car today—unless there's an emergency."

"Of course, Mr. Shaw," Tim said, getting to his feet. He took his plate and handed it over the counter to Claire. "Thank you for the good food."

Harlan walked him to the door.

Claire stayed in the kitchen, washing the breakfast dishes. "That was kind of rude," she muttered, when Harlan returned to the pantry. "He's doing us a huge favor, and you're treating him like crap."

"I don't want him in this house while I'm not here," he said.

"Why, for God's sakes?" Claire asked. "Do you think he'll abscond with the silverware or something?"

"You know damn well why," Harlan replied. He took a last gulp of coffee, then handed the mug to her. "I've seen the way he looks at you, Claire. Do you think I'm blind? Think I don't notice? I've seen the way you look back at him too."

Claire just shook her head.

The telephone rang.

Frowning, Harlan sighed, then reached for the receiver. "Yeah? Hello?"

As she finished up the dishes, Claire watched him muttering into the phone. He turned his back to her.

She didn't know what to say to him about Tim and her. *Nothing happened?* That wasn't quite true. She'd kissed Tim last night. And she couldn't deny that she had feelings for him. Obviously she'd done a poor job concealing them.

For a moment, she thought about turning the tables on Harlan and asking what he'd been doing in his workroom until four-thirty this morning. She'd pretended to be asleep when he'd crept into the bedroom. Then he'd crawled under the covers with her and Tiffany. No one had said a thing about it this morning.

Claire stared at him as she dried off her hands.

Harlan hung up the phone. "That was Fred Maybon," he announced. "He needs a ride to the plant. He's stranded. Some joker slashed his car tires last night."

Claire followed Harlan to the front hall closet. He pulled out his jacket, then put it on. "Make some calls," he said. "See if one of the girls can come over today. Meanwhile, I don't want him in this house. Am I clear on that?"

Claire nodded. "Yes, but you have the wrong idea about—"

"We'll discuss it later tonight," he said, cutting her off. Harlan opened the door, then glanced back at her. "Why don't you try calling Linda in an hour or so?" he suggested. "She should be back from the mainland soon. I'm sure she'll be happy to come over and keep you company."

Claire just nodded again.

He stepped outside, then shut the door.

Danielle had a bone to pick with the owner of that damn black Jetta.

Danielle was twenty-two, and a parking attendant at the Anacortes Marina U-Park lot. The owner of the black Jetta kept parking there without a permit or payment. Sometimes, the son of a bitch left envelopes or a lousy *photocopy* of a parking ticket on his windshield, hoping to throw her off. But Danielle wasn't stupid. She kept track of the cars she'd already ticketed.

This morning, Mr. Black Jetta was parked a bit out of the way, facing the water at the edge of the lot, space number 163. Big surprise, there wasn't any money in the U-Park slot for space 163.

Danielle put her Starbucks latte down on the hood of the black Jetta while writing out the ticket. She stuck the ticket under his windshield, closed her book, then picked up her latte again. She'd left a ring. *Good.*

She noticed a burgundy SUV in spot 159. Danielle was pretty sure they had a permit. Still, she stepped closer to the SUV until she saw the permit tag hanging from the rearview mirror. She also saw something splattered on the windshield. It was on the inside of the car. It looked like blood.

Danielle took another step toward the SUV. "Oh, my God," she whispered. The latte container slipped out of her hand, and splashed on the pavement at her feet.

A woman sat in the car, behind the wheel. She was slumped against the door. Her eyes were open, and her light brown hair was matted with blood.

It looked like half her head had been blown off.

When Harlan Shaw backed out of his driveway, his Saab pulled up alongside Tim's car. Tim nodded and smiled at him through the window. In response, Harlan Shaw glared back and gave him a quick nod. Then he shifted gears and took off down the cul de sac.

If looks could kill, Tim thought. He pulled out Al's cell phone and dialed Sheriff Klauser for an update.

" 'All's Quiet on the Logan Cabin Front,' " the sheriff said. "In fact, I'm taking Troy off the stake out. He's pretty fed up, and I don't like having a man out of commission. He can still check the place every few hours."

Tim figured the sheriff was right. Whoever had secretly occupied that cabin knew enough not to come back.

The sheriff also had some other news. A detective with the state police had telephoned. He'd be arriving on Deception tomorrow morning with an investigating team to make inquiries into the poisoning death of Al Sparling.

"I know you'll want to talk with them," Sheriff Klauser said. "Maybe they can track down that 'Ronnie' gal who was posing as a waitress at Fork In The Road."

"Let's hope," Tim said. "Have you gotten any follow-up on the Bellingham woman, the one Rembrandt abducted yesterday?"

"Nothing yet. But I'll give you a shout the minute I hear anything."

"Thanks, Sheriff."

After Tim hung up with the Sheriff Klauser, he phoned Dr. Moorehead.

"I'm sorry, Tim," Linus Moorehead told him. "I spent five hours digging and digging last night and hardly made a dent in my files. This is going to take longer than I expected."

"Have you come up with anything yet? Any potential candidates?"

"No, not really," the doctor replied. "Listen, why don't I call you later tonight? Is that cell phone number still good?"

"Yes, thanks, Dr. Moorehead," he said.

He switched off the cell phone, then muttered to himself, "Shit."

Tim turned and saw Claire trotting up the walkway. She looped around the front of his car to the passenger door. He quickly cleared off the seat, transferring the magazines, candy bar wrappers, and his green folder with Rembrandt-related information to the backseat. Then he unlocked the door.

Claire climbed inside the car. She smelled nice, part fresh air, part perfume. "Well, wasn't that was a real cheery breakfast?" she said, a little out of breath.

Tim worked up a smile. "Your husband hates my guts, doesn't he?"

Claire nodded. "Pretty much. He knows how I feel about you."

"Are you sure?"

She nodded again.

"Oh, Christ," he muttered.

Claire sighed. "Listen, I don't think we have much time before Harlan gets on the horn and sends one of his buddies' wives over to keep me company. Remember yesterday, I told you about Silverwater Creek? Amy Herrmann said her brother and Brian never left the island, they probably got 'as far as Silverwater Creek.' I need to see what's out there. Could you take me, Tim? Now? I know the way."

The Silverwater Creek campsite was only twenty minutes away by car—a few miles on Evergreen drive, then a long, winding trek on a narrow road through the forest. Tim kept checking his rearview mirror to make sure no one was following them.

For the last mile, the road became a one-lane gravel drive with a few turnouts so cars going in opposite directions could get by each other. The forest was so dark and thick that Tim switched on his headlights. The last mile seemed interminable.

"I was here at night," Claire said, numbly. A fist clenched to her mouth, she stared out the window. "There were other cars."

Tim glanced at her for a moment. She was trembling slightly.

"I remember driving back," she said. "Another car was coming at me, but I made them use the turnout. I didn't even slow down."

The narrow gravel road led to an unpaved parking area and a clearing in the forest. At the edge of the lot was a slightly neglected brick barbecue, an outhouse, and a water pump.

Tim stopped the car, and turned off the ignition. "You said there were other cars," he prompted her. "How many?"

"Five, maybe six . . ."

"Were you with anyone?"

Claire looked so pale. Tears welled in her eyes. "Something horrible happened here," she whispered.

"Was someone with you?" Tim repeated.

"Linda. She and Harlan argued. She—she didn't think I was ready."

"Ready for what?"

Claire squirmed, and shook her head.

"Would it help if we got out of the car?"

"I'm scared."

"I'm here with you, Claire," Tim said. "Come on."

He climbed out of the car, and walked around to open her door. As he helped her out of the car, Claire clung to his arm. He could feel her shaking.

A look of utter panic swept across her face. "Tim, I can't do this . . ."

"What do you remember?" he asked, his arm on her shoulder.

Claire nervously glanced around. Above them, the skies grew darker. They could hear the wind through the trees.

"It's okay, Claire," he whispered.

He felt her whole body stiffen. "Tim, I can't breathe," she said, gasping. "Please, my chest hurts. I have to get out of here . . ."

She broke away from him and ducked back into the car.

Tim hurried around to the driver's side. He started up the ignition.

Claire was shaking her head back and forth. "I can't breathe . . ."

"It's okay," he said. "We're leaving. You'll be all right." Tim turned the car around, and sped down the narrow, gravel road.

Claire rolled down the window. Eyes closed, she kept a hand clenched over her mouth.

"What did you remember?" Tim asked.

"Nothing," Claire said. She seemed to breathing a bit easier. "It—it just *felt* horrible. I'm sorry to be such a baby. I just had to get out of there. I think I had a panic attack."

Watching the road, Tim eased up on the accelerator. "I have chewing gum in a bag back there—if you want some."

Claire nodded. "Thanks. I think that might help." She reached in back for the bag, and found the Wrigley's Double-mint gum. She unwrapped a stick. "You want some?"

"No, thanks." Tim checked the rearview mirror. He wanted to make sure no one was following them. So far, he didn't see anyone.

Claire put the bag on the backseat. "There's a *Playboy* here," she said. "Were you sitting in the car last night—outside my house—reading *Playboy?*"

"I wasn't reading it," Tim said. "I was looking at the pictures."

She let out an uncomfortable laugh. "Sorry. It just strikes me as a little creepy that you brought an 'adult' magazine with you last night."

"Hey, I didn't bring it. Walt gave it to me—along with the gum and a couple of other magazines. Does that exonerate me a bit?"

Claire didn't respond.

Tim turned to smile at her. "Claire?"

She was gazing at his Rembrandt file in the green folder. She began to tremble again.

"What's wrong?" he asked.

Claire stared at the fax, with the photo and description of the Bellingham woman Rembrandt had abducted yesterday.

Tears filled her eyes. "Oh my God, he's got my friend," she whispered. "He's got Tess . . ."

"I don't mean to be a pain," Tim said into Al's cell phone. "But I'd appreciate it if you took me seriously for just five minutes."

Tim had driven Claire back home. She now sat in a stupor at the breakfast table. She had Tim's file folder open in front of her—along with several used, wadded-up Kleenexes she'd gone through.

Tim was making her some tea while he spoke with Lieutenant Elmore. "You never followed up on the footprint photos I sent—along with Mrs. Shaw's hair dryer. You're ignoring the fact that Al was deliberately poisoned—"

"Now, hold on," Elmore said. "First, the state police are handling the investigation into Al's death. They'll be there tomorrow."

"Yes, I know, but—"

"Our boys analyzed the hair dryer, and the results were inconclusive. They couldn't determine if the wire damage occurred before or after the thing short circuited. And—it's right here in front of me—your stalker's footprints are a size ten Doc Marten shoe. They estimate the shoe's owner is a male, approximately six feet tall, one hundred and sixty pounds." Elmore sighed. "This stuff landed on my desk only this morning, Tim. I followed it up. Okay? I'm taking you as seriously as I can."

" *'As seriously as you can?'* " Tim repeated. "What does that mean?"

"It means the way it sounds," Elmore answered. "Now, anything else? Any more theories? Any more attempts on your life?"

"No," Tim coolly replied. "Just what I told you at the beginning of our conversation. Claire knows Tess Campbell. She became friends with Tess while they were staying in the hospital in Bellingham."

Tim glanced over at Claire. She gave him a pale smile, then got to her feet and collected the used Kleenexes. She tossed them in the trash can under the sink, then washed her hands. The tea kettle was boiling. She took the kettle off the stove, and started making the tea.

"I think I could use some reinforcements, some back up," Tim said, moving into the pantry. "There's a lot going on here, and I'm worried about Mrs. Shaw's safety."

"We can't spare anyone right now," Elmore replied. "I wouldn't worry too much about Mrs. Shaw. It's her friend we're concerned about. That's the priority."

"I know, but—"

"Tim, Rembrandt has moved on," Elmore said, cutting him off. "He might have been curious about Mrs. Shaw when she was 'Jane Doe.' Obviously, he hung around the hospital in Bellingham for a while. It's probably where he first got to know both Tess Campbell and Janice Dineen. But we're ninety-nine percent sure he's lost interest in Mrs. Shaw."

"Why? What do you mean, he's *'lost interest?'* Claire's the only person who could identify him."

"Tim, didn't Al tell you? Claire Shaw can't identify Rembrandt—"

"Well, maybe not right now, but once she gets her memory back—"

"She'll *never* be able to identify him," Elmore said. "The closest Rembrandt ever got to Claire Shaw was in that hospital. He's never touched a hair on her head."

"What do you mean?"

"The person who shot Mrs. Shaw and left her for dead wasn't Rembrandt. It was a copycat."

"What?"

"We suspected as much while she was still recuperating," Elmore said. "The evidence was mounting up back then. I called Al—I think it was the day before he got sick, and I confirmed it with him on the phone. Mrs. Shaw was the victim of a Rembrandt-copycat. Al didn't mention it to you?"

"No," Tim numbly replied. "I don't think he said anything to Mr. and Mrs. Shaw either."

"Who didn't say anything to me?" Claire whispered. She set two cups of tea on the table.

Tim glanced at her and pantomimed scribbling something down. Claire retreated to the kitchen, then got him a pen and a memo pad.

"What kind of evidence do they have?" Tim asked. "Why is this the first I've heard about it?"

"We've kept quiet, because we don't want this copycat to know we're on to him," Elmore explained. "As for evidence, the makeup job on Claire Shaw was different from the others. Rembrandt's very meticulous. But with Mrs. Shaw, it was laid on pretty thick, not quite in Tammy Faye's league, but pretty close."

Tim sat down at the breakfast table. He had the pen in his hand.

"The brands and colors of makeup on Rembrandt's victims has always been consistent. The lipstick he uses is a brand that was discontinued fifteen months ago, something called Lady deMilo Scarlet Passion."

Tim scribbled the name down. He'd heard it before. They'd figured out Rembrandt's cosmetics of choice a few weeks ago.

"They analyzed the makeup on Mrs. Shaw's face, and none of it matched with the other victims."

"But she had a birthmark penciled on, didn't she?" Tim said.

"That, she had. But it wasn't on her left cheek, like the other victims. It was a little lower—by her mouth. And then there's Mrs. Shaw's panties. They never turned up. Rembrandt always leaves them where they can be found. About a dozen other little details set Claire Shaw apart from the other victims. No question about it, a copycat did the work on her. He was a good copycat, but a little sloppy."

"If Rembrandt didn't attack Claire," Tim whispered into the phone. "Then why was he hanging around the hospital?"

"Like I said, we think Rembrandt was curious about 'Jane Doe' for a while. After all, his name was linked to hers. When Mrs. Shaw was released from the hospital, we sent you and Al to Deception Island as an extra precaution in case Rembrandt got curious again. But we're pretty certain he's moved on. Kimberly Cronin and Tess Campbell substantiate that."

"In the meantime, what about this copycat?" Tim asked. "He's probably on this island. I'm still concerned for Claire Shaw's safety."

"And that's your job, Tim," he replied, a bit patronizing. "You're there to look out for Mrs. Shaw's well-being. But keep in mind, this copycat abducted her in Seattle, and dumped her in Bellingham. We think he's somewhere here on the mainland, between those two cities. That's why I've been telling you all this time to stay put on the island, sit tight and report anything unusual."

Tim sighed, and put down the pen. He'd only jotted down one note—about the lipstick.

"Okay, Tim?" Elmore said. "Have I answered all your

questions? Because I'd like to get back to work. I'd like to think there's a chance we might track down Mrs. Shaw's friend before she becomes Rembrandt's Victim Number Eight."

Tim's tea was cold by the time he got off the phone with Lieutenant Elmore. He wasn't much of a tea drinker anyway. The Earl Grey just grew colder for the next several minutes as he explained to Claire that she'd been the victim of a Rembrandt *copycat.*

"You know, I remember my first day here," Tim said, leaning back in his chair. "I thought Al Sparling was almost downplaying it too much. He told me this was a *'babysitting job,'* and something about *'making our presence known'* on the island so you and Harlan could feel secure."

He sipped the cold tea. "My boss said he'd confirmed this copycat business with Al a few days ago. I can't figure out why Al didn't say anything to me—or to you and Harlan, or the sheriff, for that matter."

Claire frowned. "I only spent one afternoon with him, but my guess is old Al wanted to keep acting important for as long as he could around here."

Tim just nodded. It made sense. And it made sense now why Elmore had chosen Al and him for the job on Deception. They weren't very important. The task force wouldn't miss them.

Claire opened the green folder on the table. "You know, this doesn't change anything as far as I'm concerned. Rembrandt still has my friend in his—*custody* or whatever you want to call it. And something horrible did happen at Silverwater Creek. I don't know if it's connected to Rembrandt or this copycat. But I'm dead certain something terrible occurred there."

"Something so bad your memory blocked it out," Tim said.

Browsing through Tim's folder, Claire took out the graduation photo of Nancy Killabrew Hart "Why do you—" she trailed off.

Tim put down his tea cup. "Why do I—what?"

She shrugged. "Nothing, for a second, I thought this was a picture of Harlan's first wife, Angela. It looks a lot like her."

Tim got to his feet, then came up to peer over Claire's shoulder. "That's Nancy Hart, Rembrandt's first victim. She's the one who vacationed with her family here on the island— about a year before she was murdered."

"Well, the resemblance to Angela is pretty uncanny," Claire said. She put her finger on the photo—on Nancy Hart's cheek. "All that's missing is a birthmark—right there."

"That's how he does their hair," Tim said, studying the photo of Angela Shaw in a family album. He and Claire stood together at the kitchen counter with the album in front of them.

He'd seen police photos of Connie Shafer and Janice Dineen after Rembrandt was through with them. The way he'd cut and styled their hair practically matched Angela Shaw's hairstyle in these family snap shots. Their bangs were swept over to one side, and the modified shag flipped up on the ends—a couple of inches above their shoulders. All the victims had been given false eyelashes—possibly in an effort to duplicate Angela's dark, exotic eyes. And there was the beauty mark on Angela's left cheek, which had become Rembrandt's second signature.

"I've always thought Angela looked very striking in these pictures," Claire said. "But you know, for a blonde, and with her coloring, that dark eye makeup and deep red lipstick makes her look a bit harsh too."

"*Lady deMilo Scarlet Passion,*" Tim muttered—almost to himself.

"What?"

"It's the lipstick Rembrandt uses on his victims." Tim

reached for the pad of paper he'd left by the ceramic jack-o'-lantern on the breakfast table. "Here, I wrote it down. Did I spell deMilo right?" He showed her the notation.

Claire just stared at it for a moment.

"The brand—or that particular color—has been off the market for fifteen months now," Tim explained.

"So—you can't get it anywhere now," Claire murmured. She gave the little memo pad back to him. "Come upstairs with me, okay? I need to show you something."

Claire led the way up to Tiffany's room. She went into her stepdaughter's closet, and pulled a woman's purse off the shelf. "This was Angela's. Tiffany takes it out from time to time when she plays dress-up."

Claire emptied the purse on the bed. Costume jewelry, a compact, mascara wand, lipstick, and bubble gum Tiffany must have been hording spilled across the pink bedspread.

Claire took the lipstick, plucked off the tortoise-shell top, and twisted the bottom. A flat, nearly depleted dark-red stick poked out over the edge of its silver tube. She turned the tube over and let Tim read what it said on the bottom:

LADY deMILO®
"Scarlet Passion"

Chapter 24

She didn't want to wear out the flashlight battery.

In truth, Tess had worn herself out. She needed to rest—just a few minutes on the cot, under a blanket. She wasn't going to fall asleep, just a little break.

She was exhausted. She'd burrowed out at least three and a half feet of earth. The tunnel ran at a ninety-degree angle toward what she hoped was the ground's surface—and freedom. Standing on the cot, she could fit half her body into the crater. The pile of dirt she'd scooped out was almost enough to make a mound she could stand on. Then it would be easier to crawl into the tunnel and keep working.

But she'd already used up all the shoes to chip away at the harder sections of soil. Three of the six bottled waters were gone. She'd used the two bottles dampening the earth to make it more pliable. She'd gone through the third bottle rinsing the soot out of her eyes and mouth.

Tess had no idea how long she'd been digging nonstop—perhaps four or five hours. To keep up her strength, she'd eaten one of the K-rations, *beef stew*. It wasn't so godawful.

That had been a while ago. And now she was fading. Another K-ration meal wouldn't help. She needed to lie down. With a sweater belonging to one of her predecessors, Tess brushed the dirt off the portable bed. Then she dragged the cot away from the dirt wall, and from behind the plastic tarp. She switched off the flashlight, and set it on the little table.

As soon as she fell back on the cot, she started to cry. It wasn't just fatigue either. Tess lay there in the dark, feeling so doomed.

She'd already gone through all the shoes. The stainless steel pot she'd been using to scoop out the dirt had a rounded edge. It wasn't any good for chipping away at the hard dirt. Her hands were raw, swollen and bleeding. What was she going to do?

She still had to dig through another four or five feet of earth and rocks. She wasn't even halfway done yet.

Tess felt a sharp pebble under her shoulder. Sitting up, she brushed the pebble over the edge of her portable bed, where the canvas stretched over a pole. She fell back on the cot again. Her hand lingered on the canvas-covered pole. What was it, stainless steel, or some kind of aluminum?

Tess reached for the flashlight, switched it on, then climbed off the cot. Kneeling on the cold floor, she tugged at the canvas to expose the seams where the rods joined together. If she could take the portable bed apart, she could use the poles to dig out the earth. Hell, she'd even have something with which she could defend herself.

Tess shined the flashlight on one of the bars, where it joined with the metal legs. The pieces were screwed together.

She remembered the nail clippers she'd found in one of the purses. It had a small file.

Tess reached over and felt along the tabletop, where she'd left the clippers. She grabbed them, and pried out the little file. Then she went to work on the screw adjoining pieces of the portable bed's frame. She held the flashlight between her knees so she could see what she was doing. The screw was actually moving. Her swollen hands trembled as she loosened the screw.

At last, the screw came out, and she pried apart that section of the bed frame. The pole was hollow—with a sharp edge at the end. Tears were streaming down her face, but Tess began to laugh.

Suddenly she heard something overhead. A door rattled, then footsteps. Someone was up there.

She wanted to scream for help. But what if it was him? What if he was coming down to get her?

Tess held her breath, and wondered if the waiting was over.

With a knife, Tim tried to trip the lock on Harlan's workroom door.

Claire stood behind him in the corridor off the basement utility room. "I really don't think Harlan's hiding anything in there," she said.

"Then why does he keep it locked?" Frustrated, Tim pulled at the doorknob and rattled it.

"I told you," Claire said patiently. "He has a couple of guns in there—along with his computer and some work files. He locks the door so Tiffany can't get in."

Claire was reluctant to admit that with Brian's bedroom just down the hall, Harlan had become extra vigilant about locking the door. He didn't trust his stepson near his guns—or his computer.

Tim kept trying to pick the lock with the knife. "I want to check out that computer—and those work files," he said. "Harlan's the manager at that chemical plant over on the other side of the island, right? He must know every inch of the place."

She shrugged. "I suppose he does. Why?"

"I'm hoping he has a map or a blueprint of the plant in here. He must know where there are hidden bunkers, old storage areas, and run-off pits. He could have your friend, Tess, locked in one of those areas right now."

"Oh, no." Claire shook her head. "Listen, Tim. I think I'd know if Harlan was committing these murders. I—"

The telephone rang.

Claire raced up the stairs. She grabbed the phone in the pantry before the machine clicked on. "Hello?" she said, a bit out of breath.

"Claire? This is Bill Klauser. Is Harlan home?"

She glanced over at Tim at the top of the basement stairs. He looked back at her inquisitively.

"Um, Sheriff Klauser . . ." she said. "Hi. I'm sorry Harlan isn't in right now. Is there something I can help you with?"

Claire heard the sheriff sigh. "No, I was hoping Harlan could run over to Ron Castle's house for me. I figure Ron should hear it from a friend."

"Hear what from a friend?" Claire asked.

"The state police just called me. They found Linda Castle in her SUV, parked near the dock in Anacortes. Looks like she had a lot to drink, then she shot herself. They think it happened very early this morning."

The phone to her ear, Claire stared at Tim. "Linda's dead."

"What?" Tim asked.

"Who's there with you?" she heard the sheriff ask.

"Oh, um, it's Tim Sullivan," Claire answered. "He's been outside, guarding the house. He came in to use the bathroom."

"Oh, yeah," the sheriff said. "That's right. I forgot he was there."

"Can I talk to him?" Tim asked.

"Sheriff, Officer Sullivan would like to speak with you. Okay?" Claire handed the phone to Tim. Wandering into the kitchen, she stared at Linda's *"Hang In There!"* magnet on the refrigerator door. She felt numb.

"Hi, Sheriff. It's Tim Sullivan. Can you tell me what happened?" Tim started to pace in front of the sliding glass door. "Listen, could you do me a favor? Let me drive over to the Castles' house and talk to Ron. I think this might have some kind of connection to the Rembrandt murders. . . . Well, I'm not sure exactly . . . But let me talk to Ron. And in the meantime, could you not say anything to anyone about this?"

* * *

"Harlan told you Linda couldn't come over today because she had an emergency with her mother over on the mainland. Is that right?"

Claire nodded. She stood on the other side of the kitchen counter from him. "That's what Harlan said Ron told him. She took the boat over late last night."

"She sailed over by herself? How did she get to her mother's?"

"Linda's a good sailor—or was. They keep their SUV in a lot by the Anacortes dock. Her mother lives in a nursing home in Everett."

"Do you know the name of this nursing home?"

Claire thought for a moment. "Um, Harbor . . . Harborland Nursing Home."

"You don't happen to know Linda's mother's name, do you?"

Claire sighed. "Oh, lord. Ron just gave a Special Intention for her at church yesterday . . . Um, Jenny . . . no, Josephine . . . Josephine Bowland."

"Her name is Josephine Bowland," Tim said into the telephone five minutes later. On the breakfast table in front of him were the Yellow Pages, open to the section for Nursing Homes.

"I'm her son-in-law's brother, Ned Castle," Tim continued. "I heard Josephine took a turn for the worse last night. I think you folks might have called my sister-in-law, Linda Castle. Do you have any record of that call? And could you tell me how Josephine is doing?"

"They never phoned Linda," Tim said. "There haven't been any changes in her mother's condition in the last two weeks. So either Ron was lying to your husband, or Harlan was lying to you. I'm betting on Harlan."

He turned onto Main Street, and surveyed the traffic near the harbor. Claire sat in the passenger seat. She still couldn't believe Linda was dead.

She thought about her "memory," with Linda in the front seat of Ron's Jeep. A man with a gun was coming at them from outside. And Linda told her to pray. Claire wondered if that really was a memory or some kind of vision into what *would* happen. Had it occurred that way last night?

Was the man with the gun Harlan? She'd already told Tim about waking up alone in bed around one-thirty this morning, and thinking Harlan was in his workroom. It was possible Harlan had snuck out of the house. But wouldn't Tim have seen him?

Tim admitted that he'd nodded off for a few minutes last night while on the stakeout. Harlan could have slipped out unnoticed, and walked to a car he'd parked some place. Maybe a company car. He always had them at his disposal. And he had access to Chemtech charter boats at the plant dock—and on the mainland at the Anacortes marina.

Still, Claire had a hard time believing Harlan was a serial killer. She tried to account for his whereabouts when so many of those women had been abducted. According to the fax in Tim's folder, Tess had been taken from her house some time yesterday morning or early afternoon—when Harlan had been at "work."

What about the others? She didn't know exactly when Kimberly Cronin was first reported missing. Had Harlan been "working" at the time? Harlan claimed to have met the girl who worked at the hospital gift shop. He said he'd bought flowers from her. Was he also her executioner? Had he made her up to look like his dead wife?

The first victim, Nancy Hart, certainly bore a striking resemblance to Angela. But Claire remembered looking at all the victims' photos in that tabloid. None of the others—not even that tabloid photo of Nancy—reminded her of Harlan's first wife. And Tess didn't look at all like Angela. So why was Rembrandt going after her?

"I think he likes the challenge," Tim told her. "He's gotten hooked on the make-over, the transformation process. I think that's what excites him now. Nancy Hart was unique. Often a serial killer's first victim provides the spark that sends him in a particular direction. My guess is, since murdering Nancy, it might not matter so much to him what his victim starts out looking like, just as long as he feels he's transformed her into Angela before he kills her."

Little droplets of rain started to hit the windshield. Claire stared ahead at Deception's Main Street.

She wondered if it was true, that her husband was a murderer. Nothing made sense anymore. If Harlan was indeed Rembrandt, why was she the victim of a Rembrandt *copycat?* What had happened to Brian—and to Derek Herrmann? She knew something horrible had occurred at Silverwater Creek. Were they killed there? And so many people on the island seemed involved in a cover-up. She kept thinking about the way no one spoke of the Davalos family and the violent way they'd perished. And now, Linda, another "suicide." Were all these things somehow connected?

"I didn't see anyone following us," Tim announced, pulling into the parking lot of The Whale Watcher Inn.

As they walked to his room, Tim kept glancing around, and looking over his shoulder. "I think you'll be okay here," he said, unlocking the door.

They'd decided his hotel room was the safest place for her. The place was decorated in a gaudy royal blue and dark brown.

Tim seemed nervous about leaving her alone. "Just keep the door locked," he said. "If you get scared, call the front desk, and go sit in the lobby. If you get bored, the TV's right there—"

"I'll be okay, Tim. Thanks." Claire smiled at him.

He moved to the door. "I should be back from the Castles' in about a half hour. Okay?"

"I'll be here," Claire replied, stepping toward the door.

"Lock up after I go," he said. He took her hand, then pulled her toward him, and kissed her.

Claire slid her arms around him, and kissed him back. She didn't want to let go. For a few moments, she forgot about everything else. All that mattered was his touch, and his lips parting against hers. Her head was swimming. She held onto him tightly.

Tim finally pulled back. "I've been wanting to do that ever since I set eyes on *you*," he whispered. He kissed her gently one more time, then reached for the door. "Take care."

Claire put her hand on his shoulder, and it lingered there until he stepped outside. Then she closed the door, and double-locked it.

"Hello?"

Claire couldn't believe he was finally answering. She'd tried calling him twice this morning with no luck.

She sat down on the edge of the bed—with the hotel's ugly blue-and-brown paisley spread. She was using the phone on the nightstand.

"Mr. Griswald," she said. "This is Claire Shaw calling again. Please, don't hang up. I'm sorry to bother you. When I called you yesterday, I didn't have time to explain . . ."

She paused. There was silence on the other end of the line.

"Mr. Griswald?"

"What the hell do you want?" he whispered.

"I—I'm not sure," Claire admitted. "I thought you might know something about the fire."

More silence.

"People on this island seem reluctant to talk about it," Claire continued.

"I'm not surprised," he grunted.

Restless, Claire stood up and carried the phone over to

the desk. "Mr. Griswald, I know your brother-in-law and nephews got into a lot of trouble here. They might have made some enemies—"

"Excuse me," he interrupted. "I still don't understand the purpose of this call."

"I want to find out what happened to my son," Claire heard herself say. "He and his best friend disappeared over three weeks ago. Together, they got into trouble here too, and made their share of enemies. I can't get a straight answer from anyone about what really happened to them. I don't know if there's a connection to what occurred with your sister's family. Maybe I'm just grabbing at straws—"

"So you're on the level?" he asked. "You're not calling to make sure I won't raise a stink again?"

"I don't understand what you mean," Claire murmured.

"Jesus. You don't know a thing about it, do you?"

Claire sat down at the desk. "What are you talking about?"

"A few days before the shootings and the fire on July Fourth, I talked with my sister. Violet told me someone had tried to set fire to their back porch in the wee hours of the morning. It wasn't Hugh either. At the time, he was passed out next to her in bed, and the boys were asleep. Violet said when they called the police and fire department, it took them fifteen minutes to get there. *Fifteen minutes.* By then Hugh, Rodney and Dean had put out the fire themselves—with the garden hose."

"Did they ever find out who started the fire?" Claire asked.

"No, but Violet told me this local civic group was putting a lot of pressure on them to sell their house and move off the island."

"Was this group the Guardians?"

"That's right. I guess they offered to buy the house—on the condition that they left Deception. Hugh tried to milk them for more money. But he never had any intention of budging. I guess they figured that out."

"So—you think someone from the Guardians started the fire?"

"Both fires. I think they shot my sister and her family too. Hugh was a lot of things. But he wouldn't have killed Violet and the boys."

"Did you tell anyone about this?" Claire asked.

"Yeah, I talked with the cops on the island. This deputy told me there was no record of the first fire. As for what happened on that July Fourth, well, with his reputation, Hugh was the obvious scapegoat. All the bullets were from Hugh's gun, which they found in his hand. But I don't believe it. I think the cops, the fire department, and half the people on that goddamn island are lying."

"Couldn't you have gone to someone outside the island?" Claire asked. "Maybe get an outside investigation going—"

"I threatened to do that," he cut in. "I told this deputy I'd talk to the state police, and *The Seattle Times,* maybe even the FBI."

"Was this deputy's name Landers?"

"No. Something Parker. A real asshole too."

"What did he say?"

"He said it was an open and shut case, and I was wasting my time."

"And so you just gave up?" Claire pressed.

"No, I gave up after the tool shed in my backyard mysteriously caught on fire that night. I have a little boy, and I don't want him to end up dead. For the next few days, they sent things to the house."

"What kind of things?"

She heard a brief, cynical laugh on the other end of the line. "The kind of things neighbors send to people who have lost loved ones, flowers and home-cooked dinners. We'd find them on the doorstep, but there were never any cards. Of course, we threw out the food, though something tells me none of it was poisoned. I think it was just their way of reminding me how close they could get to us. They called the house too. The number was always blocked. Sometimes it was a man, sometimes a woman."

"Did they threaten you?"

"No. They were too clever for that. They'd say things like, *'We're sorry about your loss,'* or *'What a terrible tragedy. Don't you agree?'* Then they'd hang up. They didn't have to say anything else. I got the message, loud and clear. They were telling me to leave it alone.

"In fact, when you phoned me yesterday and said that you live on Deception, my stomach did a ninety-degree turn." He let out a sigh. "You see, Mrs. Shaw, I thought you were one of them."

"Well, hello again, handsome." Yolanda, the Castles' cleaning woman, opened the front door wider for Tim. She wore a pale blue smock over her clothes. "His Nibbs is expecting you," she said in a low voice.

"Thanks, Yolanda." Tim said, checking out the Castles' front hallway, a colorless, yet pristine foyer with an imitation white marble floor and a sparkling chandelier hanging overhead.

He'd phoned Ron Castle ten minutes ago to make sure he was home. Tim knew he was semiretired. He'd asked if he could swing by and "discuss a few things about the Rembrandt case." Castle had said he was busy, but could spare five minutes.

Yolanda knocked on the study door, then opened it. "Mr. Castle? The policeman is here." She threw Tim a furtive smile, then sauntered toward the back of the house.

"Come on in," Ron Castle said. He sat at his big, mahogany desk, typing on a computer keyboard. Ron's beady eyes were glued to the computer screen while Tim stepped into the study. Ron just kept typing.

Tim glanced around the room, decorated a bit too heavily in early Americana. There was an American Eagle emblem in the middle of the rug, and busts of George Washington and Abraham Lincoln that had been converted to lamps. A wastebasket by Ron's desk had little pictures of the presidents on it. On the walls were framed photos of the Castles with family and friends.

"What can I do for you, Officer?" Ron asked, still typing. He wore a red cardigan, with a white shirt and dark blue slacks. Tim wondered if he'd dressed that way to match the room. He also wondered if any of Ron's loved ones had ever sat him down and told him how bad his toupee looked.

"I was hoping to talk with both you and Mrs. Castle," Tim said, standing in front of Ron's desk. "Is she home?"

"No. She's visiting her mother on the mainland."

"Really?"

Ron finally took his eyes off the computer screen and looked at Tim. "Yes, Mrs. Castle's mother is in a nursing home with Alzheimer's. We had a little emergency last night. I'm expecting Mrs. Castle back soon." He sat back in his big, black leather chair. "In the meantime, what can I do for you?"

"Um, do you mind if I sit down?" Tim asked, taking one of the twin cane-backed chairs in front of Ron's desk.

Ron made a little face. "I'd offer you something to drink, but I don't have a lot of time. I'm quite busy with some important e-mails here."

"This won't take long, Mr. Castle," Tim said. "And I really appreciate your hospitality," he added with a straight face. "I thought you and Mrs. Castle might help fill in some blanks. You see, Mrs. Shaw is starting to remember things. She remembers going to Silverwater Creek with your wife. I believe they went there together on the night Mrs. Shaw's son ran away."

His mouth slightly open, Ron stared at him.

"Can you tell me anything about that?" Tim asked.

Ron shook his head. "No, I think Mrs. Shaw must be mistaken," he said. "The last time either Mrs. Castle or myself were at the Silverwater Creek campsite was late August. I'm sorry I can't help you."

"So—you don't know anything about a meeting or an event at the campsite three Fridays ago? This would have been at night."

Ron shook his head again.

The telephone rang, and he quickly answered it. "Yes, hello?" He frowned a bit at Tim as he spoke into the phone. "Well, yes, but it's not a good time for me to talk right now . . ."

Tim got to his feet, then ambled over toward the array of framed photographs on the wall. There was Ron and Linda posed in front of the Lincoln Memorial; a photo at a party with Angela and Harlan Shaw; a shot of Linda with Harlan and Walt; and another one with Linda, Ron, and a woman Tim didn't recognize—at least he didn't recognize her at first. The three of them stood at a lookout point in Seattle. The Space Needle was behind the woman's shoulder. She was a brunette with a slightly flat nose.

Ronnie. The waitress's name choice made sense now. Ron had probably put her up to the little charade. Roseann had said Ron had been sitting at the counter when she'd gotten sick that morning. Then *Ronnie* had come in to take over for her.

". . . just don't do anything until I call you back," Ron was saying into the phone. "Okay . . . Bye."

Tim heard him hang up the phone. He pointed to the photo, and glanced back over his shoulder at Ron. "Who's this in the picture with you and Mrs. Castle?" he asked.

Ron looked annoyed at him and let out a wheezing sound as he pulled his large body out of the chair. "I really am busy here, Officer," he said, frowning. He waddled over to Tim's side and stared at the photo. "That's Zoya Wiseman, the widow of a very good friend of mine."

"Does she live in Seattle?" Tim asked.

"Yes, that's the Space Needle in back of us," he said, condescendingly.

"Is Zoya—by any chance—involved in the food service industry?" Tim asked.

"No, as I said, she's a widow, and a very old friend of Mrs. Castle's and mine." He sighed impatiently.

Studying the photo, Tim wondered if Zoya knew the severity of what she'd done. Had Ron and Linda told her she was poisoning someone with those berries? Or did she think she was merely playing a joke on a friend of theirs? Whatever the case, it was clear that Ron and Linda had recruited this woman to do their dirty work.

"Officer, I'm afraid I don't have any more time for you just now," Ron said. "Let me show you to the door . . ."

Tim felt Ron's hand creep up between his shoulder blades, and together they walked to the front entryway. Ron opened the door for him. "Sorry to rush you out," he said. "But give me a call, and I'm sure I can make some time for you. Then you'll have a chance to talk with Mrs. Castle too."

Tim paused in the doorway and nodded. "Oh, yes, we'll talk when Mrs. Castle comes home."

Claire paced around the ugly little hotel room.

She wondered if all the Guardians were involved in the Davalos murders, or had it been the job of only a select few? Had they killed Brian and Derek too? Certainly, Linda, Ron, and Harlan were all part of the cover-up. She wondered if that cover-up campaign included the various attempts on Tim Sullivan's life.

Claire went to the window and opened the drapes a bit. She looked out beyond the rain-beaded glass.

He was there.

She gasped.

The man in the stocking cap quickly ducked behind a camper parked in the lot. His army fatigue jacket almost blended with the bushes in back of him. He moved so fast, he was just a blur.

Trembling, Claire stared out the window. She watched him thread around several others cars—until he disappeared in back of the hotel.

She shut the drapes, then raced to the door, and made certain it was double-locked.

The telephone rang.

It gave her a start. For a moment, she couldn't move. She was afraid to pick it up. What if the caller was the man she'd just seen?

The phone kept ringing. Claire thought it might be Tim—with an emergency. She hesitated, then reached for the receiver. But the ringing stopped. She let out a sigh.

Suddenly, someone pounded on the door.

"Oh God," she whispered, backing toward the bed.

"Maintenance man!" the person called from the other side of the door. The doorknob rattled. It sounded as if he was inserting a key in the lock. But she had the door deadbolted. He continued to struggle with it.

"Hotel Maintenance!" he called again.

"Come back later, please!" Claire nervously called back.

She waited. No response. She didn't hear a thing, just the rain outside. Frozen, Claire stared at the door for a few more moments.

Finally, she reached for the phone and dialed the front desk.

"Operator. Can I help you?"

"Yes, hello," Claire said, trying to keep calm. "Um, I'm in room 19. Did you send maintenance person to this room?"

"Yes," the woman answered. "We're checking out the heating systems in all the units. I hope he didn't disturb you."

"Oh, no, no. It's okay," Claire managed to say. "Thank you."

She hung up the phone, then laughed. But she started to cry at the same time.

Someone knocked on the door again.

"Yes? Who's there?" she called, her voice cracking.

"Claire?" He paused. "It's Tim. Can you let me in?"

She hurried to the door, unlocked it, then flung it open. Claire threw herself into his arms, kissed his face, and started weeping.

Tim pulled her back inside, then closed the door. He held onto her, and stroked her hair. "What's wrong? What happened?"

Claire shook her head. For now, she didn't say anything. For now, she just took comfort in his arms.

Chapter 25

Tim gave Harlan's workroom door another forceful kick. There was a splintering sound. The door seemed to give a little.

"I think you almost have it," Claire said. She stood behind him.

Tim wanted to get at Harlan's computer. He wondered if all the Guardians were involved in these multiple murders.

Last night, Walt Binns seemed truly concerned about Fred Maybon's behavior. Was Harlan's friend on the level? How many people on this island were Guardians or connected to them? Harlan and Walt; their friend, Ron; Fred Maybon; the judge, Ward Fanning. Linda Castle was supposed to be the *Guardians' Angel.* And Judge Fanning had recommended all those "runaway" juvenile delinquents to his Guardian pal, Dr. Linus Moorehead.

Tim remembered Ron typing away on his computer. *A lot of important e-mails,* said the semiretired homebody and full-time Guardian.

Tim hoped Harlan had more than just work files on his computer in that private little room.

Leading with his shoulder, Tim slammed into the door again. It hurt like hell, but the door flew open, then banged against a cabinet. A chunk of wood broke off the door frame—along with part of the lock. Several items sailed off the cabinet shelf, including a bottle of Jim Beam that shattered on the floor. Tim's shoes were dowsed with bourbon.

"Oh my God," Claire murmured. She switched on the light.

Stepping over the shards of glass, Tim turned on Harlan's computer. "Him and his one-beer-for-the-night," Claire said, almost to herself. "I had a hunch he might be drinking down here."

"Let's see what else he's been lying about," Tim muttered, hunched over the computer. "Do you know his password?"

"Oh, God, I'm sorry, I don't," she whispered.

Tim typed CLAIRE in the password boxes, and six asterisk symbols came up. So did the response: *"Password Invalid."*

Glass crunching under her shoes, Claire stepped behind Tim and looked over his shoulder. "Try Tiffany," she suggested.

Tim typed it in, then pressed enter. The menu popped up. "Bingo," he said. He started typing furiously. "Okay, let's check out what we got here . . ."

Claire picked up a big piece of glass, and threw it in the wastebasket.

"What we got here is Harlan's alibi for Linda's death," Tim announced. He pulled the most recently viewed Web site addresses off the internet access box. "Your husband was down here looking at porn from one-forty until four this morning. *Siamese Sluts, Naughty Nymphs, Lesbian Action, Tahitian She-Devils*. Huh, and you were giving me shit for looking at one little *Playboy*."

Claire slapped him on the shoulder with the back of her hand. She sighed. "Well, at least we know he didn't murder Linda."

Tim kept bringing up the porn sites Harlan had been checking out recently.

"You can stop doing that now," Claire said

"I'm checking for bondage, S and M stuff, or anything

else that might run along Rembrandt's taste," he said, eyes on the screen. "Hmmm, I don't see anything here, but it still doesn't vindicate him as far as I'm concerned."

Tim went back to the main menu. He clicked on the mail icon. "Spam, spam, spam," he muttered, scrolling down the current mail list. "Who's this?"

He opened up a letter from *drlinus@glc.net* with the subject matter,

Update:

Harlan,
*   Claire has an appointment with me at 5:30 tonight. I'll e-mail you later. As we've discussed, she still doesn't trust you or Linda, and she's beginning to remember things. I'll see if I can get anything out of her about possible involvement with the policeman. Your concerns may be unwarranted. We'll see.*

—Linus.

"So much for doctor-client confidentiality," Tim murmured.

Claire was reading over his shoulder. "God, he's probably been giving Harlan updates on me all along."

Tim clicked in the "previous mail" box, but it was empty. "I think Harlan's been deleting his mail as he reads it. I'll double check the recycle bin before I finish." He scrolled over the other current mail. More ads, and then another message from *drlinus@glc.net*. There was no subject heading.

The e-mail had gone out to seven other addresses:

Fellow Guardians,
*   In light of the current police presence on the island, I won't be making any decisions concerning the Gutterman matter for another couple of weeks.*

—Linus.

"Do you know anyone named *Gutterman?*" Tim asked.

Sighing, Claire nodded. "Oh, he's sort of the town drunk. Vernon Gutterman. It's sad really. He's probably my age, and looks sixty. You might have seen him hitting people up for change on Main Street. He has a lot of problems. He was fired from the plant, and he's been arrested a few times."

"And Judge Fanning has probably recommended professional counseling," Tim concluded.

Staring at Moorehead's letter on the computer screen, Tim shook his head. "My God, they have it down to a system. Fanning recommends the criminals to his 'Guardian' buddy, Dr. Moorehead. Then Linus makes a decision that he shares with a select group of 'Fellow Guardians.' "

"What do you mean?" Claire asked. "What kind of decision would he pass along to the Guardians about a patient?"

"Whether or not the patient should be killed," Tim said. He glanced up at Claire. "All of those runaways and missing persons spent time on Moorehead's couch. Apparently, this Vernon Gutterman is seeing him now. How soon before he's missing or dead? See what's going on? Dr. Moorehead decides which 'problem cases' should die. Then the Guardians carry out his orders. It's for *'the good of the community.'* "

"Is that what happened to my son?" Claire whispered.

"There's a way to confirm it," he said soberly. "Moorehead doesn't throw away his old files. If we could track down his records on your son, and Derek, and these others, then we can check what he's written down about them—notes and recommendations."

"And death sentences," Claire said. She glanced at her wristwatch. "Tim, I—I have an appointment with Moorehead in twenty minutes. We need to see what's in those files."

"Things are better between Harlan and myself lately," Claire said. She sat in the club chair opposite Linus Moorehead.

He looked very relaxed and dapper in a black V-neck sweater. Nodding, he scratched his goatee, then scribbled on the notepad in his lap.

Rain tapped on his office windows, and the wind was howling outside. Claire's hair was still a bit damp from the downpour.

Tim had driven her to the office. Harlan had called as they'd been leaving the house. He'd said he wouldn't be home from work until seven-thirty. Claire wondered what he was up to.

"I trust him now," she lied to Dr. Moorehead. "Before, I didn't want to believe Harlan about Brian running away. But now I accept it. I'm also accepting the fact that I'll probably never see my son again."

"What brought this on?" Moorehead asked.

"I don't know." Claire shrugged. "I should have given up on him a long time ago. You saw Brian for a while. You must have come to some decision about him."

"What do you mean?"

"Did you think he was beyond help?"

Moorehead shifted in his chair. "I can't really answer that, Claire. I—"

A loud wailing from outside interrupted him.

"What's that?" Claire asked.

Moorehead got to his feet. "I think it's my car alarm," he said. He went to the window and peered down at the alley. Snatching his jacket off the coat hook, he hurried toward the door. "Sorry, Claire. I'll be right back."

"It's okay," she said. "Take your time."

As soon as Moorehead stepped out the door, Claire jumped up from the chair and ran over to the file cabinet. She tugged at the top drawer. Locked. "Damn," she muttered.

Claire checked his desk, and found some keys in the side drawer. All the while, Moorehead's car alarm continued to blare.

Back at the file cabinet, she tried two keys before the third one worked. Her hands were shaking. The top drawer was full of office supplies. Claire tried the next drawer down. She was in luck. The files were labeled with the patient's name—and in alphabetical order. There were even plastic yellow tags sectioning off each letter-group. She dug into the F's, but didn't find any record for *Ferguson, Brian*. Was the file somewhere else?

She sifted through the D's, and found the file for *Davalos, Hugh*.

The car alarm shut off. For a second, Claire froze.

Then she quickly closed the file drawer, and raced back to Moorehead's desk. Grabbing the phone, she dialed Tim's cell phone. He answered after half a ring-tone. "Yeah?"

"I need more time," she whispered. "Set it off again in five minutes."

From behind a Dumpster in the alley where Moorehead parked his BMW, Tim watched him shut off the car alarm for the second time.

The rain was coming down heavily now, and Tim was soaked.

Moorehead had brought his umbrella along for this trip. He stood by his car for a moment, glancing around.

Tim didn't move—even when Moorehead seemed to look right at him. He didn't see any change in the psychiatrist's expression. He just looked annoyed. Finally, he turned and wandered back toward the door to his building.

Tim had the phone on pulse. He felt it vibrate in his pocket, and quickly pulled it out. "Yes?" He stepped in a doorway to get out of the rain.

"I've seen the Davalos files," Claire whispered. "There's an attachment for the police, an evaluation. In each one he says '*This patient is a threat to the welfare of our community.*' Derek's file didn't have an attachment. But Moorehead's own personal evaluation was there. '*Belligerent and hopeless,*' he said. The thing that sets these files apart from all the others is a red dot by their name on the folder. I think that's how he marks the ones who are killed. I still haven't found Brian's file. Maybe it's under 'Shaw.' If you could set off the alarm again—"

"No," Tim interrupted. "I can tell, he's getting suspicious. Let's not take any more chances. He's on his way up. I'll pick you up at six-thirty. I'll be at Fork In The Road until then."

"Okay, bye." Claire said.

Tim heard a click on the other end. He shoved the phone back in his pocket, then ran half a block in the rain to the Fork In The Road Diner.

The restaurant wasn't very crowded, probably because of the storm. He took a table by the window, so he could sit and watch Moorehead's building down the block on the other side of the street.

Tim was hanging his wet jacket on the chair, and hoping they had chicken noodle soup, when the cell phone went off again. With the ringer off, it made a low, humming sound.

He dug the phone out of his jacket pocket, and switched it on. "Hello?"

"Tim, it's Troy Landers. I'm calling from my patrol car. Sorry about the reception. It's all this stinking rain. I've been checking the Logan cabin every couple of hours. I just saw a guy go in there. But I didn't get a good look at his face."

"Did he see you?" Tim asked.

"I don't think so. As far as I know, he's still there. He isn't wearing a stocking cap, but he has on the army fatigue jacket. I called the sheriff. He's over on the west side of the island, where they've lost some power. Do you want to come out here? I'm down the road from the cabin at the Evergreen Drive turnoff."

Tim hesitated. He glanced out at Moorehead's office window. Then he checked his watch. Claire still had forty minutes of her session left.

"You there?" Deputy Landers asked.

"Yes. I'll see you in ten minutes."

* * *

For the last ten minutes, while Claire talked with Dr. Moorehead, her eyes kept wandering over to the file cabinet behind him. She desperately wanted to look up Brian's records in there. She needed to see if Brian had a red dot by his name.

Moorehead got to his feet. "Claire, I talked with Dr. Beal at the hospital in Bellingham," he said, moving behind his desk. "We both agreed, considering what you've been through, we should get you on a mild antidepressant."

"Really?" Claire was surprised to see him pull the bottle of pills from his desk drawer.

"Yes. I'm very encouraged by some of the things you've told me in this session. You seem to be accepting the loss of your son, but that's not easy. You may have some difficult times ahead." He went to his little refrigerator, and pulled out a bottle of Evian water. "One pill twice a day," he said. "And I'd like to get you started right now."

He handed her the Evian bottle, then opened the bottle of pills. He shook one into her palm.

Claire stared at it. Something was very wrong. This medication wasn't coming from a pharmacist. It was something he'd hidden in his desk drawer.

"What's the matter?" Moorehead asked, standing over her.

"Um, I'm just wondering about side effects," she murmured.

"You might feel a little drowsiness at first. That's normal. Some people experience dry mouth, but there are no severe side effects. This is a very mild antidepressant."

She hesitated. He was still standing over her.

Claire put the pill in her mouth, then pushed it to one side with her tongue. She pretended to wash it down with Evian water.

As Moorehead walked back to his chair, Claire plucked the wet, filmy tablet from her mouth. She stuffed it under the cushion of the club chair.

"Good girl," Moorehead said. Then he sat down and smiled at her.

*   *   *

The wipers slashed back and forth on the windshield, and rain beat heavily on the car roof. Tim was at the wheel, headed up Evergreen Drive. He had Al's gun in the glove compartment, and the cell phone in his pocket.

He wasn't sure he could completely trust Troy Landers. Another deputy, probably Troy's predecessor, had spoken to Steven Griswald three years ago, and obviously he'd been with the Guardians. Was Troy with them?

Tim pulled out the cell phone and speed dialed Sheriff Klauser. There was a lot of static on the line.

"It's a goddamn mess here on the west side of the island," the sheriff reported. "We have a power line down and a couple of roads washed out. What's going on?"

Tim told him about the call from Troy Landers.

"Yeah, I know," the sheriff replied hurriedly. "He called me. Are you on your way to the Logan place?"

"Yes. I'm wondering if I should get back up help from some of the Guardians. Um, is Troy a Guardian?"

"No. I had a deputy who was also a Guardian about two years ago, but I fired him. His name was Parker. Guardians gave him the heave-ho too. He was a real pain in the ass. He moved off the island. Anyway, I wouldn't call any Guardians yet, Tim. Let's just see who's out there first. I gotta go."

Tim clicked off the cell phone as he approached the turnoff. He spotted Troy Landers in a police rain slicker at the edge of the street. Troy turned on a flashlight and waved it. Tim flashed his brights for a second.

Turning onto the little road, Tim switched off his headlights, then came to a stop. He noticed the patrol car, parked along the pathway.

Troy stepped up to his window. He had the hood up on his rain slicker. But his face was still wet. Tim killed the ignition, and rolled down his window. "Is our guy still there?" he asked.

Troy nodded. "I just checked a couple of minutes ago. I saw him in the kitchen. I don't recognize him at all. But he's a jumpy son of a bitch. He keeps looking out the windows, and twice he's stepped out on the porch. I think he knows we're out here. Do you have a gun? I have an extra rifle in my trunk you can use."

"Thanks, but I'm okay." He grabbed Al's automatic out of the glove compartment, then tucked it in his jacket pocket. He glanced at his wristwatch. Claire still had another thirty minutes with Moorehead.

Tim rolled up his window, then climbed out of the car. "Troy, we'll have to work real fast," he whispered. "I need be somewhere in about a half-hour. I'm looking after Mrs. Shaw, and it's important that I—"

He didn't finish. Without warning, Troy Landers hit Tim in the stomach. It was a sucker punch that knocked the wind out of him. Tim doubled over in pain. He couldn't breathe.

Troy didn't stop there. With his fist, he socked Tim in the jaw. Tim was stunned. He reeled back into the mud.

"That's for having me put on stakeout duty, you mother-fucker," he heard the deputy growl.

The rain beating down on his face, Tim lay on the wet ground, unable to move.

Troy hovered over him. He pulled the gun out of Tim's jacket pocket, and tucked it inside his rain slicker. Then he took the cell phone, ambled over to a tree, and smashed it against the trunk.

"You don't need that anymore," Troy Landers said. "You won't be talking to anybody—ever again."

"Claire, are you feeling all right?" Dr. Moorehead asked. He leaned forward in the club chair.

Sitting across from him, Claire slumped to one side and stared back at Moorehead with half-closed eyes. "I'm just so tired," she murmured. "I don't know what it is . . ."

He got to his feet, stepped over toward Claire and picked up her purse from the floor. He returned to his chair, plopped the purse in his lap, and started searching through it.

Claire gazed at him listlessly. She chided herself for not

kicking him in the groin a moment ago when she'd had the chance. She could have made her escape. Then again, that might have been totally unnecessary. She didn't know what he was up to. The business with the antidepressants was awfully suspicious. And as she pretended to grow more and more sluggish over the past several minutes, Moorehead didn't seem a bit surprised.

At the moment, feigning fatigue was her only defense. Moorehead's guard wasn't up. A kick or a punch in the right place, and then she could run like hell to the Fork In The Road, where Tim was waiting.

Dr. Moorehead took the bottle of pills from Claire's purse. "I bought these up in Vancouver. They're Rohypnol, the 'date-rape-drug.' Sorry, Claire, but I need to steal these back, and put them where the police will find them."

"What?" she mumbled vaguely. She pretended to be more interested in the storm raging outside his window.

Moorehead stood up again, and headed for his desk. "This bottle of Rohypnol will be in Tim Sullivan's room at The Whale Watcher Inn. They'll think he gave you this stuff."

She couldn't see what he was doing behind his desk. He reached for something in one of the lower drawers. "But before I do that, I'll need to make sure at least one of these little pills gets in your system."

She heard a strange snap. It had a thin, rubbery sound to it. She realized he'd just put on a surgeon's glove. He came around the desk with a handkerchief in his gloved hand.

"I know you didn't swallow that pill, Claire," he said.

She sprang to her feet.

All at once, Moorehead was on her. He grabbed her arm and twisted it behind her back. Claire shrieked, but he cut off her scream. Moorehead pressed the handkerchief over her mouth and nose. It was soaked with something that burned and made her eyes water. She tried not to breathe.

Claire struggled, but she felt herself slipping out of consciousness.

"Don't fight it," Moorehead whispered. "Just breathe in,

nice and quick. I don't want to rub this in your face. Chloroform can irritate your skin."

His lips brushed against her ear. "And I don't want any burn marks, Claire. I want you to look pretty when they find you."

Beep.
"Claire? Sweetheart? You there? C'mon, pick up. I'm still at the plant. Where are you? It's past seven. You should be back from your appointment with Moorehead by now. I can't believe you're not home. I tried your cop friend's cell phone, and I'm not getting an answer there either. What the hell's going on? I can't believe you're out in this weather. Well, I'll be home soon. I hope you'll be there when I get in. Bye."

Walt Binns and Ron Castle stood in their friend's pantry and listened while Harlan left the message.

"If we'd written a script and had him read it over that machine, it couldn't have suited our plans any better," Ron said glumly.

Ron had entered the house with a spare key Harlan had given Linda ages ago. He and Walt had already packed a small overnight bag for Claire: makeup, toiletries, perfume, her sexiest nightgown, slippers, and a robe.

Ron knew Harlan kept a semiautomatic in his workroom. He and Walt had been surprised to find the door broken in and a smashed bottle of bourbon on the floor. They couldn't figure out what had happened.

"You know how this will look?" Ron had said to his friend. "It'll look like he didn't even stop to get the key. He was so mad, he broke down the door to get his gun."

They'd fetched Harlan's gun for him, and made certain it had a full clip. It was all part of a plan, conceived at a secret meeting of the Guardians earlier today. They'd come together to discuss a solution to the "Claire Shaw problem."

The way they were setting it up left little room for doubt.

Harlan Shaw, his wife, and that rookie cop would be found in a remote cabin the Guardians had already chosen. It was the Miller place, about two miles down the road from Walt's cabin. Investigators would determine that all three victims were shot with bullets from the semiautomatic Ron had taken from Harlan's workroom. The gun would be in Harlan's lifeless hand. And the naked corpses of his wife and that rookie cop would be nearby—in the cabin's bedroom.

They hated to lose a good man like Harlan, but it was a necessary sacrifice. There was no other way.

They already had Harlan on tape, expressing concern and anger over his wife's attraction to the handsome cop. Dr. Moorehead had recorded a ten-thirty session with Harlan this morning. Ron would also recount for investigators an incident weeks ago at a Seattle police station when Harlan violently attacked Officer Tim Sullivan.

The message Harlan had just left Claire was like a bonus.

"I'm telling you," Ron said, as they took one last look around his friend's family room. "There won't be any loose ends here. This thing will be wrapped up even tighter than the Davalos matter."

"You don't have to sound so goddamn smug about it," Walt grumbled. "I'm losing my best friend."

"Hey, he's my buddy too." Ron patted Walt on the back, and they started toward the front door together. "I feel as bad as you do. But Harlan brought all this on himself, you know. He never should have taken Claire to that Guardian assembly. She just wasn't ready. We all told him so. But Harlan wouldn't listen."

Stepping outside, Walt paused in the doorway. He shifted Claire's overnight bag from one hand to another, then turned up the collar to his jacket. He looked out at the rain and sighed. "I keep thinking of poor little Tiffany, an orphan."

Ron opened up his umbrella. "I was just mulling over the same thing. She's a sweet little girl. Maybe Linda and I can adopt her."

* * *

"Slow down, and hang a right up ahead, sport," Troy Landers said. His back against the door, he rode in the front passenger seat of Tim's loaner car. He'd pulled down the hood of his slicker. A cocky smile on his face, Troy had Al's gun pointed at Tim. "Pull in front here," he said.

Wordlessly, Tim followed his directions. His jaw was still throbbing from where Troy had hit him. They'd been driving in the hard rain for the last fifteen minutes. Tim recognized the cabin at the end of the narrow, gravel path. It was the same cottage the Killabrews had rented three summers ago.

"Looks like we're the first ones here," Deputy Landers announced. "Kill the engine."

Tim switched off the ignition. "We're expecting company?"

"Yep, your girlfriend, Mrs. Shaw, will be here in about a half hour. Her husband's coming too—along with some others."

"Guardians?"

"Yep, it's gonna be a regular party."

"I didn't know you were a Guardian," Tim said.

"I'm not—yet." Troy smiled and hoisted his gun a bit. "We're a little early. So relax, sport. Keep your hands where I can see them. By the way, nice job driving."

"Thanks," Tim said, staring out the rain-beaded windshield.

Troy snickered. "Yeah, you're pretty good behind the wheel. After that number I did on your brakes the other day, I didn't think I'd be seeing your pretty puss again."

Tim unbuckled his seat belt and turned toward him. "That was you?"

Troy nodded.

"Is that the kind of work they require from a Guardian-wanna-be? Or did they ask you to shoot a couple of teen-agers too?"

"Smart guy," Troy muttered, his smile waning. He still had the gun pointed at him.

For a few moments, they didn't talk. Rain tapped on the car roof, and the wind was howling.

"Is the sheriff a Guardian?" Tim asked, finally breaking the silence inside the car.

Troy laughed. "Hell, no. The sheriff's clueless. So is Ramon. The Guardians and I are doing their jobs for them, and they have no idea."

"Did the Guardians kill Brian Ferguson?" Tim asked.

Suddenly, part of a tree branch fell across the windshield, then rolled off the car's hood. It didn't do any damage. It merely startled them—and distracted Troy.

All at once, Tim lunged for the gun. He grabbed Troy's hand and twisted it. A loud shot rang out. There was an explosion of glass as the bullet pierced through the windshield. "Fuck!" Troy bellowed. "My eyes!" It was like a cloud of glass-dust in the front seat of the car.

Though blinded, Troy wouldn't let go of the gun. He was relentless—until Tim slammed his elbow in the deputy's face. Troy reeled back and banged his head against the passenger window. Blood leaked from his nose, and the whites of his eyes had turned red. He looked dazed.

Tim realized he had the gun. He hurled back and struck the butt end of it across Troy Lander's temple.

The deputy went limp and flopped against the dashboard.

Tim caught his breath. The windows had fogged up inside the car, and he couldn't see outside. Troy's Guardian buddies were due any minute now—along with Claire and Harlan. Tim wondered what kind of plan they had in the works.

He grabbed Deputy Landers by the front of his rain slicker, and pulled him up to a sitting position. Blood still trickled from Troy's nose. Tim frisked him and found a gun. He was hoping the deputy had a cell phone on him, but he didn't. "Shit," Tim muttered.

He took the keys out of the ignition, opened the car door and stepped outside. Unlocking the trunk, he popped it open, then hurried around to the passenger door.

Deputy Landers stirred a bit as Tim pried him out of the

car. With the rain pelting them, Tim dragged the deputy's heavy, limp body toward the back of the car. He hoisted Troy up, then dumped him inside the trunk. His body hit the trunk floor with a thud.

Just as Tim shut the hood, he saw a pair of headlights in the distance, piercing the darkness.

He hurried back into the car and started it up.

The other day, when he'd been here with Walt, Tim had noticed a little alcove and a back road. He couldn't see it in the dark, not with a cracked windshield, and all the rain. But Tim crept along the narrow drive with the headlights off, and eventually he found the inlet behind some bushes.

He shut off the engine, and climbed out of the car again. He'd wanted to check that cabin for a phone so he could call the sheriff—and Lieutenant Elmore. He needed backup. But he was too late. The other car was pulling up in front of the house. Tim recognized Fred Maybon's Honda Accord.

But he didn't recognize the man climbing out of the car with Fred. Another Guardian, obviously. Fred had his assault rifle with him.

Tim stayed hidden behind some shrubs. Because of the rain, he couldn't hear much of what they were saying. Fred's friend carried an umbrella, and they huddled under it as they approached the front door. Fred pulled out a set of keys. ". . . *Should be here with that cop by now,*" Tim heard him remark.

Suddenly, there was a loud banging sound. Tim swiveled around. The noise was coming from the trunk of his own car.

He turned to look at Fred and his pal. Pausing at the front door, they squinted toward him. Fred seemed to have his rifle ready.

Tim didn't move. Could they see him from where they stood?

The banging noise stopped. Troy must have hurt his foot with all that kicking. After a few seemingly interminable moments, Fred shrugged his shoulders, then the two men stepped inside the cabin.

Tim ducked back into the car, and quietly closed the door. He could feel Troy rolling around in the trunk. The car wobbled.

Tim glanced at his wristwatch. Troy had said Claire was due to arrive in a half hour. He only had about fifteen minutes left. He didn't know how many of them were gathering at the cabin tonight. But he was pretty certain Fred Maybon wouldn't be the only one carrying a gun.

He was outnumbered. If only he could get to a phone. Claire's life depended on it.

"Get me out of here!" he heard Troy bellow. Troy began kicking at the trunk hood again.

Tim started the car. He had to take Troy someplace, then tie him up and gag him. He remembered Walt Binns's cabin was about two miles down this back road.

And he remembered that Walt's cabin had one of the only working phones in this part of the woods. He could call for back up.

With his headlights off, Tim headed down the muddy road toward Walt Binns's cottage. All the while, he listen to the rain on the car roof, and to Deputy Landers screaming and banging against the trunk hood.

Claire kept drifting in and out of the chloroform-induced stupor. She felt a burning sensation on her face from the chemical's residue.

She was in the passenger seat of Moorehead's BMW. Partially restricted by the safety belt, she slumped against the door. Her right foot felt cold. Had she lost her shoe? Claire didn't remember being carried to the car. Everything was kind of muddled.

She briefly glimpsed Moorehead at the wheel, then she closed her eyes again. They were moving. She listened to the rain. One of his windshield wipers squeaked.

She had a moment of déjà vu, of another long drive at night. But she hadn't been in Moorehead's car. No, she'd been lying across the backseat of Ron and Linda Castle's SUV. Her hands and feet had been tied, and they'd stuck a piece of duct tape over her mouth. Ron had knocked her over the head with something. They'd drugged her too.

Claire felt sick. She breathed through her nose, and listened to the SUV's engine. Occasionally, another car's headlights or a street sign illuminated the SUV's interior for a moment. Then it was dark again.

Ron was at the wheel, and Linda sat in front with him. *"We'll just have to use her own makeup,"* Linda was saying. *"It won't match with the others, but it'll have to do."*

Claire heard the squeaky windshield wiper again, and realized that she was in Linus Moorehead's car. There weren't any lights. They were driving into the woods. Where was he taking her?

Moorehead had tried to give her a pill earlier tonight. Yet she could almost hear Linda insisting that she take a tranquilizer: *"You need it, Claire. You've been through a lot tonight. This will calm you down."*

She took Linda's pill. It made her so drowsy, she thought she might pass out. She was sitting on the bed in her and Harlan's room. Listlessly, she watched Linda packing clothes and cosmetics in her overnight bag.

"You ought to sleep over at Ron's and my casa tonight." Linda's voice seemed to be coming through a fog. *"We'll have a girl's day in the city tomorrow. You need to get away . . ."*

The memories were coming to her in fragments. Suddenly, she was cold and shivering. The SUV's back door was open. The chilly air had an underlying stench.

"Well, how do you expect a garbage dump to smell, hon?" Linda was telling her husband. She leaned over Claire in the backseat of the SUV, and hurriedly patted rouge on Claire's cheeks. Linda was practically jabbing at her face with the brush.

"Looks like she's coming out of it," Ron said.

"She's been in and out of it for the last twenty-four hours," Linda replied, taking out a mascara wand. *"Just keep the*

flashlight on her, hon. I need to see what I'm doing. This isn't easy, y'know."

Claire remembered Ron holding her while Linda pulled a clear, plastic bag over her head. They were in standing in the middle of a junkyard. Claire tried to struggle, but her hands and feet were still tied.

Through the steam-fogged plastic, she saw Ron Castle take something out of his jacket. It looked like a gun.

She heard a shot go off. It seemed to echo in the quiet night. All at once, she felt a terrible blow to her chest. It burned. She couldn't breathe. Claire felt herself falling.

She gasped, and started to lurch forward. But the seat belt held her back.

Claire realized she was in the Dr. Moorehead's car. She heard the rain on the roof and that squeaky windshield wiper. She caught her breath and gaped at him.

Sitting behind the wheel, he smiled at her. "What is it, Claire? A bad dream?"

Tim stood in the downpour, staring at the house and shaking his head. The window shutters were all closed. Walt's cabin had been boarded up and battened down for the impending storm.

From over where he'd parked the car, Tim could still hear Troy's muted protests. *"Get me out of here, goddamn it!"* He kept pounding and kicking against the trunk hood.

Tim tried the cabin's front door. Locked. Having checked out so many of these shacks in the last couple of days, he'd become an expert at finding where some of the owners hid their keys. Tim felt along the top of the doorway frame, and checked under the mat. He tipped over two potted plants near the front stoop, but still couldn't find a key.

He tried kicking down the door. It didn't budge.

Wet and shivering, Tim went from one boarded-up window to the next, pulling at the shutters. It wasn't any use.

A couple of tree branches had fallen in the yard behind the

house. Tim glanced up at the power and phone lines. They were still intact. He looked back at the tool shed by the patio and barbecue. Maybe Walt had the house key hidden in there. At the very least, Tim figured he might find a crowbar or something to pry open a window shutter.

He ran to the shed, only to see the door had a padlock on it. "Jesus, God, give me a break!" Frustrated, he kicked at the door. The hinge holding the lock rattled.

Tim glanced around for a rock or something to break it off. He spotted a rusty spatula and a large fork hanging from the side of the barbecue. He grabbed the fork, and jiggled on the lock hinge until it snapped off.

It was dark, but very tidy inside the little, windowless shed. The rain echoed on the tin roof. Astroturf covered the floor. Tim found a flashlight on the shelf. He switched it on, and shined the light on an extension ladder, leaning against the wall, where rakes, shovels, and hoes were hanging.

He figured he could pry open one of the window shutters with a shovel. Tim grabbed a long-handled spade, and started to back out of the shed. But he accidently knocked a couple of things off the shelf. As they fell to the Astroturf floor, there was a strange, loud snap.

Tim shined the flashlight on a rat-trap, which must have been activated when it hit the floor. Next to it was a box. Keeping the light steady, Tim read the label: *U.S. ARMY K-RATION MEALS—3 PACK.*

"My God," he whispered.

In the autopsies, they'd found K-rations in the stomachs of three Rembrandt victims.

Tim turned the beam of light toward the shelf, where several more boxes of K-rations were stored, along with a case of bottled water.

He glanced back at the boarded up cabin. Was Tess Campbell locked away in there?

Heading out of the shed, Tim almost tripped over a patch of Astroturf that was askew. He kicked at the carpet, flipping it over to expose a section of the cement floor—and what looked like a piece of wood. Tim kicked at the Astroturf again, exposing more of the cement beneath it. He realized it wasn't a piece of wood in the middle of the cement foundation. It was a little door.

Tess's hands were raw and bloody, but she didn't stop digging. She chipped away and gauged out the soil with the make-shift pick. The aluminum bar from her bed-frame worked a hell of a lot better than the shoes. The earth seemed softer, more pliable.

Against the dirt wall, a large mound of earth had accrued under the tunnel opening. But it wasn't solid enough for Tess to stand on. She'd shoved the rickety little table beneath the crater, and precariously balanced herself on that. She could almost stand inside the tunnel now. But every time she took a breath, she'd get a mouthful of dirt and soot.

Still, Tess figured she was getting much closer to ground level—and fresh air. She kept hoping the next clump of soil she'd scoop out would have grass on it.

Suddenly, the tunnel caved in on her, and she was suffocating. For a moment, she was trapped. Tess struggled to back out of the crater, but the soil encased her head and arms. Flailing her legs, she dislodged herself and slid out of the hole. A pile of earth followed her.

Gagging, she spit dirt and pebbles out of her mouth. She had soot lodged in her ears, and up her nose. Blindly, Tess crawled around the cold floor until she found the bottled water. After rinsing out her mouth, she located the flashlight and switched it on. She was still having difficulty breathing, and it wasn't just the dirt in her nose and throat. There didn't seem to be much oxygen left in the little bunker. Not much left of the water supply either. Only one bottle remained.

Tess shook the dirt out of her hair and her ears. That was her third cave in; and so far, the worst. But she was breathing a little easier now.

She heard a noise from above.

Suddenly she couldn't breathe again.

He was back. How much time had passed since he'd last checked on her? Was it four or five hours—or just one? She wasn't sure anymore. He hadn't done anything the last time. She'd just heard him walking around up there.

Now Tess listened to his footsteps once more, and she wondered if he was just checking on her again. Or would he be coming down this time?

Grabbing the flashlight, she scurried back toward the dirt wall and searched for the aluminum bar. She'd dropped it during the cave in. She couldn't think of anything else she could use to defend herself.

He was still up there. She heard him. He'd just dropped something.

Tess pushed aside the plastic tarp, and frantically dug through the pile of clothes and dirt. She couldn't find the damn aluminum bar.

He was dragging something across the floor.

Tess stopped to look up toward the trap door. A light shined through cracks in the wood. He was coming to get her.

"Oh, God, please, please," she whispered, trying to find the aluminum bar. Tears streamed down her face.

She heard a hinge rattling. *"Tess Campbell?"*

She switched off her flashlight, then froze. The portal above her started to open. She saw his silhouette, hovering over the trap door. He shined a light down into the pit.

Tess heard rain on a tin roof. She could smell the damp, fresh air. She half-hid behind the plastic tarp. "Tess?" he said. "Tess Campbell, are you down here? I'm a police officer . . ."

She almost called back to him, but hesitated. She still couldn't see his face.

"Is anyone down here?" he asked. The flashlight beam wove around the confines of her bunker, then it stopped on her. "Tess? Are you okay?"

Trembling, she squinted up at him.

"I'm a cop. I'm a friend of Claire's . . ."

"Oh, thank God!" she cried.

"Are you okay?"

Tess let out a delirious laugh. "Christ, no . . ."

"Hold on," he said. "There's a ladder here. I'll come get you."

Stepping under the opening, Tess anxiously watched as he lowered an extension ladder into the pit. She couldn't believe it. She could breathe again. She was talking to another human being.

"I'm Tim Sullivan," he said, climbing down a couple of rungs. He paused and shined the flashlight on his own face so she could see him.

Tess smiled. He was a handsome guy. "It's pretty damn terrific to meet you," she managed to say. "I didn't think—"

A loud shot rang out.

Startled, Tess gazed up at the trap door. Someone else was there.

Tim Sullivan dropped his flashlight. It knocked against the bottom rung of the ladder, then rolled onto the bunker floor.

A moment later, Officer Tim Sullivan fell down on top of it.

Chapter 26

Claire listened to the squeaking windshield wiper. She still felt dizzy and tired. She wanted to roll down the window—just a tiny bit—for some fresh air, but Moorehead wouldn't let her.

Vacantly, she stared at one of her loafers on the floor. Until now, she hadn't noticed she wasn't wearing the shoe. It must have fallen off when Moorehead had been loading her inside the car. With her toe, she moved the loafer around.

Rain continued to tap on the roof of his BMW. They were driving on the wooded back routes, and even in her stupor, Claire could tell Moorehead wasn't having an easy time of it. The roads were slippery and littered with tree branches. They'd skidded twice already.

Strapped in the seat belt, Claire closed her eyes and hoped for another memory. Now that she was trying, nothing came. Even in her mind, she couldn't escape from Moorehead's car.

She tried to make sense of the memory fragments that had come to her earlier. The story Linda had told the police must have had some half-truths in it. Now she remembered Ron and Linda coming over on that Friday night. Linda had given her the tranquilizer. *"She's been in and out of it for the last twenty-four hours,"* Linda had said later at the garbage dump. It must have been the following night, Saturday, when they'd shot her. Obviously, they'd wanted it to look like a Rembrandt murder. But why did they want her dead? Did it have to do with an incident at Silverwater Creek? Or was it related to the sudden disappearances of Brian and Derek?

She closed her eyes again, and wished she could remember. "Was Brian a *'threat to the community,'* Dr, Moorehead?" she asked. She kept moving the shoe around the car floor. "Or was he like Derek, *'belligerent and hopeless'?"*

Claire opened her eyes. Moorehead glanced at her for a moment, then turned his attention back to his driving.

"I've seen your files," she said, taking a deep breath. "But I couldn't find Brian's. I need to know, does he have a red dot by his name?"

Moorehead gave her a little smirk. "So—you figured out my system. Smart girl."

"You make all the decisions, don't you?" she whispered. "You decide whether they live or die. Did you get to play God with my son, doctor?"

Claire stopped poking her toe in the loafer, and shoved it to the side, between the edge of her seat and the car door. She sat up. Suddenly, her heart was racing. It was as if she were waking up from an awful nightmare, only instead of fear, she felt a terrible rage.

"Did you give the order to have Brian killed?" she pressed.

He threw her a warily amused look. "I think you might need another whiff of nighty-night, Claire. Looks like that dose is wearing off." Eyes on the road, he started to pull over toward a turnaround area. "The truth is, this community— this island—is well rid of your precious son."

Dazed, Claire studied the smug profile of this man who had ordered her son's murder. An intense anger surged through her. She wanted to kill him.

Claire felt around for her loafer, and grabbed it. With all her might, she swung the shoe at his face—and the heel connected with his right eye. There was a bone-crunching pop, and Moorehead howled in pain.

Claire reeled back to hit him with the shoe again, but the BMW lurched forward. His foot had slipped onto the gas, and the car was out of control. Claire braced herself.

Moorehead brought a hand over his face. "You bitch!" he wailed. "Goddammit . . ." He couldn't have seen where the car was going. But Claire could. They were about to crash into the trunk of an evergreen tree.

Walt Binns hoisted the extension ladder out of the bunker. From the shed, he looked down at them through the open trap door.

Tim Sullivan was curled up on the floor. Crying, Claire's friend hovered over him. It was so dark down there, he couldn't quite see if Tim Sullivan was dead. Alive or dead, he wasn't going anywhere.

With his foot, Walt kicked the trap door shut. Then he bent over and readjusted the Astroturf carpet. While tidying up the shelf, he could still hear Tess Campbell's muted screams.

Walt stepped out of the tool shed, and frowned at the broken hinge on the door. He opened his umbrella, then started for the house.

He'd originally swung by the cabin for a bottle of wine. Among other duties, Walt was in charge of props for tonight. Harlan's gun was a necessity, of course. But Claire's overnight bag would help set the scene, and Walt figured a bottle of wine on the bedroom nightstand would be a nice touch. He had a respectable Merlot at his cabin. So he'd bypassed the rendezvous spot, and drove the extra couple of miles to his place.

He'd thought about adding a couple of wineglasses to the set as well, but figured that was a little too refined for the cop. Wine in jelly glasses was more his speed.

How ironic, he'd been thinking about Tim Sullivan just as

he'd pulled up to the cabin and spotted Tim's car. He hadn't planned on seeing his lady-in-waiting until much later tonight.

Well, now she had some company in her little waiting room—even if that company was a corpse.

Walt retrieved the bottle of Merlot from his cabin. On his way back to his Range Rover, he passed Tim Sullivan's car again. Earlier, he'd ignored Troy Landers—pounding and yelling inside the car's trunk. And Walt continued to ignore him now. He'd never cared much for Deputy Landers, ever since Nancy Killabrew had told him during one of their secret meetings that Troy had come on to her.

"Who's there?" Troy barked. He pounded against the trunk hood. "Let me out, goddamn it!"

Huddled beneath his umbrella, Walt tucked the wine bottle under his arm, and opened the back door. He grabbed the bag of magazines he'd given to Tim Sullivan last night, then he peeked inside. *Good.* The hotel coupons were still in there.

He needed to remove everything that connected him with the death scene. Walt wouldn't deny knowing Tim, if asked. But he saw no point in having a bag of magazines he'd purchased last night—along with his hotel coupons—found in Tim Sullivan's car.

Actually, those coupons with the date stamped on them didn't make for such an airtight alibi. Yes, he'd checked into the hotel in Victoria the weekend Terrianne Langley had disappeared. He'd checked into the same hotel several weekends when "Rembrandt" had been a bad boy. Those weekends, the hotel bed never got slept in. Those weekends, he didn't see his married friend, Suzanna.

"Who's there?" Troy bellowed. "Goddamn it, I can hear you! Lemme out!"

With his wine and his bag of magazines, Walt hurried back to the Range Rover. Before starting up the car, he took out his cell phone and dialed.

Ron Castle answered. "Yeah?"

"Missing anything?" Walt asked.

"Uh-huh, I'm here at the cabin, scratching my balls. The doc and Claire are MIA, and there's no sign of Troy and the cop—"

"Don't worry about Officer Sullivan. I have him tucked away. He's not going anywhere. In fact, I'm pretty sure he's dead already. I had to shoot him. But I used Harlan's gun—so let's not sweat it. I have all the other props with me."

"Where the hell is Troy Landers?"

"Oh, he'll be fine. I'll come by with him and Officer Sullivan after I pick up Harlan." He started up his Range Rover. "You said Moorehead and Claire still haven't shown up?"

"Yeah. I've called his cell several times. No answer."

"Well, some of those back roads are washed out. I'll bet he's stuck somewhere. You have the Jeep, Ron. Why don't you try Heritage Way, and see if he's out there?" One hand on the wheel, Walt navigated the muddy pathway by his cabin. "In the meantime, has Harlan left the plant yet?"

"Not yet. Ken's been keeping him busy. He'll call when Harlan takes off."

"I'll go wait for Harlan outside his house. See you at the cabin in about a half-hour."

"Huh, yeah, maybe by then we'll track down Claire and the doc," Ron said. "Christ, what a day. On top of everything else, I haven't heard from Linda at all. I'm really worried about her."

Eyes on the road, Walt smiled. "Oh, I'm sure she'll turn up."

With her last bottle of water and one of the towels, Tess washed out the wound in Tim's shoulder. She studied it with the flashlight. There was a lot of blood. From what she could tell, the bullet had entered his back and come out just above his chest.

She'd moved him to what was left of the dismantled cot. Half-draped with canvas, it looked like a broken-down beach chair. "You're not dying on me, pal," she said, catching her breath. "Not with a lousy little shoulder wound."

She took his hand, then set it over the towel draped on his shoulder. "Keep applying pressure. It'll slow down the bleeding." Tess rolled up one of her predecessor's sweaters, and set it behind his head. She covered him with the army blanket, and even tucked it under his chin. "How's your foot feel?"

"Like I broke something," Tim said. "Sorry I'm not much use to you."

"The hell you're not," Tess shot back. "I'm digging a tunnel. You can tell me what's up there. Are we under someone's basement or what?"

"No, we're beneath a tool shed in his backyard."

Tess shined the flashlight on one side of the trap door above them. "You came down the ladder from that angle," she said. Then she trained the light along the dirt wall to a huge tear in the plastic tarp, and the mouth of the tunnel. "I'm headed up that way. So far, I've hit everything but oil and gold. I must be near the surface. Tell me. Am I going to end up in his backyard or underneath a patio or something?"

Tim nodded. "You should be okay." He shifted a bit beneath the blanket, then pulled out a gun and handed it to her. "Take this in case he's still around. There's a phone in his cabin. You need to call the police, the Coast Guard, whoever you can. Tell them you're in the woods near the east shore of Deception Island. If you get the local sheriff here, we're at Walt Binns's cabin. Two miles down the road, there's another cabin, and these guys are planning to kill Claire there tonight. They probably have her there already."

"Oh, no," Tess murmured, clutching the gun.

"So just keep digging," Tim said, "Don't bother coming back for me. Just look out for yourself."

"I'll be back for you," Tess said.

She kissed his forehead, then turned away and hurried back to work on the tunnel.

* * *

Claire grabbed Moorehead by the scalp, and pulled him off the steering wheel. The BMW's horn stopped blaring.

But smoke continued to spew from under its mangled hood. The front of the car was wrapped around the evergreen's trunk.

Dr. Moorehead was unconscious, slumped back in the driver's seat. He had a gash in his forehead. He'd hit the steering wheel when they'd smashed into the tree.

Except for being shaken up, Claire had escaped injury.

In fact, her adrenaline must have been pumping, because she'd managed to pry Moorehead—with all his dead weight—out of the car. Then she dragged him off the roadside. The cold rain actually felt good for a few moments.

Claire climbed into the driver's seat. She prayed the car would restart. She held her breath and turned the key in the ignition. To her utter relief, the engine turned over. It was a sweet sound.

Claire backed the car away from the tree. She heard a grinding noise from the metal shifting. The smoke from under the hood seemed to get worse.

Still, she turned the wreck of a car around, and headed toward town. She wondered if—by any chance—Tim was still waiting for her at the Fork In The Road.

Standing beneath his umbrella, Walt waited for Harlan in the Shaws' driveway. The rain had quelled to a dull drizzle.

Harlan's Saab came up the cul de sac. Walt gave him a solemn wave. Then he stepped aside as Harlan pulled into the driveway. Harlan didn't shut off the ignition. But he rolled down the window. "What's going on?" he asked anxiously. "Is Claire all right?"

"I just know what the sheriff told me," Walt said. "They think Rembrandt has her in one of the summer cabins near Alliance."

"Oh, Jesus," Harlan murmured, stricken.

"They just found out," Walt continued. "I guess the detective—um, Tim, he's out there too. They've phoned the state police, but it might be a while before they can helicopter over in the storm. It's a lot worse on the mainland coast."

"Hop in," Harlan said. "We need to get over there."

Walt ran around to the passenger side, then jumped into the car. "How's the road to Alliance?" he asked.

"Half under water," Harlan said, backing out of the driveway. "I got here by the skin of my teeth. Stalled out twice."

"Half the island's without power too," Walt said. "Listen, it'll be rough going, but I think we're better off taking my boat around to the Alliance harbor. Then we can use one of the company cars."

Harlan nodded. He turned onto Evergreen Drive—and sped toward the center of town. "Walt, if anything happens to her, I don't want to live anymore."

Walt Binns just patted his friend's shoulder. He didn't say anything.

The BMW had both headlights broken, a cracked windshield, and smoke belching from under its dented hood. With all this going against her, Claire could barely navigate the dark, wooded road. She may as well have been driving through a sea of mud.

It was another three or four miles to town. Claire prayed the mangled car could make it there without breaking down, stalling, or catching on fire.

Up ahead, she saw a pair of headlights. She was instinctively wary. Whoever it was, they probably couldn't see her yet, because of her smashed front lights.

Spotting a little pathway that veered off the gravel road, Claire steered onto it. The trail was rough, with potholes, fallen branches, and puddles. The wounded BMW buckled over each obstacle. But Claire managed to turn the car around. Then she headed back toward Heritage Way. She wanted a better look at this other vehicle, and this person who was driving in the middle of a rainstorm, in the middle of the woods.

She recognized Ron and Linda's Jeep as it sped by. Ron was at the wheel. Claire figured it wouldn't be long before he discovered his fellow Guardian, Dr. Moorehead, along the roadside up ahead.

Claire waited until Ron's taillights looked like red pinpoints in the darkness, then she turned back onto Heritage Way. As the BMW picked up speed, the smoke only grew more dense.

She found it almost easier to navigate by looking at the treetops on either side of the road. Occasionally, the car went over a small branch in her path, and Claire felt her stomach tighten. She kept checking her rearview mirror. How much time did she have before Ron Castle's Jeep would reappear?

She noticed the town ahead, shrouded with darkness—except for a few tall harbor lights that must have been running on generators. The BMW began to cough and sputter as Claire turned onto Main Street. It seemed to be taking its last few gasps.

Claire finally coasted into an alley, then turned off the ignition.

Abandoning the car, she started on foot. The rain had died down. The Fork In The Road was only three blocks away, and Claire started running for it. She glanced over her shoulder, still no sign of Ron's Jeep.

She saw the restaurant up ahead. "Oh, no," she groaned, slowing down. There weren't any lights coming from the squat, white-brick building. The diner was closed.

Claire stopped and caught her breath in the restaurant doorway. A canopy above shielded her from the drizzle. The center of town looked deserted. It was as if the whole area had been shut down and evacuated.

Suddenly someone stepped out from the restaurant parking area. With the street lights off, she could only see his silhouette.

"Tim?" she said.

He came forward. His face was still swallowed up in shadow. But Claire recognized the stocking cap and army fatigue jacket.

Claire gasped, and bolted toward the street. She started running toward the hotel. She glanced back, and saw the man chasing after her. He darted in and out of the shadows along the store fronts.

Claire kept running. A block ahead, she noticed a car speeding down Harbor View Lane, toward the dock. She screamed and tried to flag it down. Then she recognized Harlan's Saab.

Claire just froze.

The car turned and headed toward her. Its brakes screeching, the Saab came to a halt only a few feet away from her. Harlan jumped out from the driver's side. "Claire, oh, thank God!" Opening his arms, he rushed to her.

She started to back away. But Harlan grabbed her, and covered her face with kisses. "Oh, baby, they told me you were . . ." He shook his head, then kissed her again. "Never mind. You're okay. Nothing else matters."

Claire numbly gazed at him, then she looked up and down the rain-soaked street. She didn't see the man with the stocking cap.

"What happened to you, sweetheart?" Harlan asked. "Where were you?"

She caught her breath. "You don't know? You're not in on it?"

"In on what?" he asked. "What are you talking about?"

A couple of short beeps came from the Saab's horn. Then Walt stepped out of the passenger side. He was waving his cell phone. "I just called the sheriff to tell him you're okay, Claire," he said. "He's in Alliance. They have Rembrandt cornered in one of the cabins. They could use some help—now."

"Well, you go," Harlan said. "I'm not leaving Claire alone. Besides, what the hell could I do?"

"No, they want Claire to help identity him," Walt said.

Dumbfounded, Claire shook her head. How could the police have Rembrandt cornered someplace on the other side of the island, when she'd just seen him a couple of minutes ago? She was about to tell Harlan and Walt that she never had any contact with Rembrandt, that Ron and Linda had tried to pull off a copycat killing.

"That policeman, Tim Sullivan," Walt continued. "They think he's hurt. Rembrandt has him hostage. And your friend, Tess, they're looking for her."

Claire felt tears stinging her eyes. "We—we really should go out there," she heard herself say. She squeezed Harlan's arm.

"No, it's too dangerous," Harlan argued. He pulled her toward the car.

"You heard what Walt said. They need me to identify Rembrandt."

She knew that was impossible, but she would use any argument she could to persuade Harlan. Her two friends were in trouble, and she had to go to them. "Please, honey, I need to go there. I want to help any way I can."

Harlan sighed. "All right, but you're not leaving my side."

"Let's get a move on," Walt urged them. He opened the back door for Claire. "They're waiting for you."

As they drove toward the dock, Claire kept glancing out the rain-beaded window for that man with the stocking cap. But she didn't see him.

In the front seat, Walt was already giving Harlan first-mate instructions for what promised to be a choppy voyage. Claire didn't tell them anything about her brush with Dr. Moorehead, or what Tim and she had discovered about some of the Guardians. She still didn't know if her husband and his friend were part of it.

When Harlan pressed her about why she was running

down Main Street in the storm, she put him off. "I'll tell you
on the boat, honey. I'm still kind of shaken up. Let me just
catch my breath here."

Once on the boat, the two men worked quickly to prep
Walt's Chris Craft for the short trip around the island. Claire
tried to stay out of their way. She sat near the edge of the
boat, and gazed out at the dock.

Suddenly, she noticed someone. He was running along
the pier—in and out of the shadows.

Claire stood up. He was still following her. She was about
to scream for Harlan. But the man in the stocking cap
stopped under one of the harbor lights, and she saw his face.
His sweet, handsome face.

"Brian?" she whispered.

He quickly darted behind a tall storage box near the end
of the pier.

"Brian!" she screamed. The boat's engine started up, drown-
ing out her voice.

Her son peeked out at her from behind the box.

Claire waved anxiously at him. "Brian! Oh, my God!"

The Chris Craft started moving. "No!" Claire screamed.
"No, stop!" She didn't realize it, but she started to climb
over the edge of the moving boat.

All at once, Harlan was grabbing her from behind. "What
are you doing?" he yelled. "You want to kill yourself?"

Claire fought and screamed as he pulled her back onto
the boat deck. Didn't he understand? Brian was alive. She
saw him on the pier. Harlan wouldn't let go of her. Claire got
more and more hysterical as they drew farther away from the
dock. Crying, she slapped and kicked her husband. She
couldn't see Brian any more.

"Get her down below!" Walt barked. "I need your help
here!"

The Chris Craft rocked and listed back and forth on the
choppy water. Claire couldn't keep her balance. She and
Harlan stumbled on the deck. She still fought him.

"Damn it, Harlan!" Walt yelled. "We're in trouble here! Put her in the second closet down there. Lock her in!"

Harlan picked her up again. Claire struggled as he dragged her down to the cabin. "What's gotten into you?" he asked. "Honey, please—"

"Let me go!" she cried. She bit his hand.

"Goddamn it!" he hissed, hauling her toward the closet door. The boat was still teetering.

All at once, Harlan was shoving her in a narrow closet. The door slammed shut in her face. Then she heard the lock click.

"Damn it, Claire," he said on the other side of the door. "Why did you make me do that?"

"Harlan, get your ass up here!" Walt yelled from the deck.

Claire pounded and kicked at the door.

"Just calm the hell down, and I'll be right back," she heard Harlan mutter.

The boat lurched again, and she stumbled against the closet wall. Claire broke down and cried. She would have collapsed, but there was no room to fall over in the tiny closet. Instead, she sank down and curled up on the floor. Engulfed in blackness, she couldn't see anything except her son's face. Brian was alive. They hadn't killed him.

But they'd murdered Derek.

"It's not murder," Linda had told her. "In many ways, it's like a mercy killing. He's a potential threat to this community and our children. Really, when you get down to it, we're saving him from himself. What's happening here is for the best."

Claire was in the passenger seat of the Castles' Jeep. Across from her, sitting behind the wheel, Linda sighed heavily, closed her eyes, and murmured something under her breath. Was she praying?

It was a beautiful, clear starry night. The Castles' Jeep was one of six vehicles parked at the Silverwater Creek campsite. The cars were lined up with their headlights on—illuminating the meadow in front of them. The small grove almost looked like the setting for a night baseball game. Different men were getting out of their cars, which they'd left idling. All of them carried rifles. All of them were Guardians.

Claire saw her husband among them, along with Ron Castle, Fred Maybon, and some others. She didn't see Walt. A few of the men had dressed in hunting gear.

Harlan had wanted her to come to this Guardian Assembly. She'd sided with him so many times against her son, Harlan must have thought he was infallible. He hadn't told her what this special meeting tonight was about.

Claire watched in horror as two Guardians led Derek Herrmann out of the back of a SUV.

"What the fuck is going on here?" Derek asked, laughing.

"He's sedated," Linda said solemnly. "Really, this is quite humane."

"Hey, what the hell do you think you're doing?" Derek yelled. But he didn't resist as his two captors started to undress him. Derek even stepped out of his jeans for them.

"They're not really going to do this," Claire murmured.

They led Derek toward the illuminated field. They'd stripped the tall, skinny teenager down to his white briefs.

Ron Castle came up to the Jeep with the gun in his hand. He leaned up to Linda. "I'll pop him one in the head for you, hon," he whispered.

Claire watched him walk away. He joined six other men, who lined up along the edge of the field.

Derek didn't seem to notice them. He didn't seem to notice the two men at his side were leaving him.

"We're not going to let this happen, are we?" Claire asked Linda, who had her eyes closed. "We can't just sit here! We have to do something . . ."

Linda opened her eyes and turned to her. "Pray, Claire."

Nearly naked, Derek seemed to bask in the spotlights directed at him. He laughed, and blew a kiss in the direction of the cars.

Claire jumped out of the Castles' Jeep. She started screaming. All at once, Derek's two Guardian "escorts" grabbed her.

"Derek! Get out of there!" she cried, struggling with the two men. "No, you can't do this!"

Derek froze for a moment. He squinted toward the lights with a goofy smile on his face. "Hey, Mrs. Shaw. Is that you?"

Suddenly, the shots rang out.

Claire's heart seemed to stop for a moment.

Then she broke free from the two men, and ran to Harlan's Saab. The engine was already idling.

She tore out of the lot. All she could think about was saving Brian from the same fate. If her son's best friend and partner-in-mischief was killed for *"posing a threat to the community,"* then Brian would be next.

Please, Brian, be home. Please, be home.

As soon as Claire came in the front door, she started calling his name. She could hear the music coming from his bedroom downstairs. She grabbed the local Yellow Pages, and tore through it until she found a charter speedboat company in Anacortes. They told her a boat would be at the Deception dock in forty minutes.

Claire hung up the phone, and started screaming down to Brian again.

"Yeah, Mom. What's up?" he replied, from the bottom of the basement stairs. He was wearing a sweatshirt, jeans, and white socks. He must have just gotten out of the shower a few minutes before, because his light brown hair was in damp ringlets.

Claire raced down the stairs, brushed past him and headed into his bedroom. "What the hell's going on?" he asked.

"I want you out of here," she replied. "You need to leave right now."

"What are you talking about?"

She pulled Brian's overnight bag from his closet, set it on his bed, then threw some clean underwear inside it. "Start packing," she said. "You have two minutes."

Brian kept asking what was the matter. She told him to put his shoes on, and he now had ninety seconds. "Isn't it clear enough?" she snapped. "I want you out of this house!"

Back upstairs, she took out her checkbook, and wrote her son a check for five hundred dollars. Her hands were trembling as she made out another check for the charter boat company.

Brian came up from the basement with his duffle bag. "I'm not going any place until you tell me what this all about, Mom."

"I'll tell you in the car," she said. "Get your coat."

She took the long way to the center of town—in case the Guardians were looking for her. All the while, Brian kept protesting. "What happened, Mom? C'mon, talk to me! Why are you kicking me out? What did I do?"

Her eyes fixed on the road ahead, Claire reached into her purse and took out the checks. "One of these is for you, and the other one is for the charter boat," she explained as calmly as she could. "You've run away before. You're good at this. You even stole a boat the last time, Mr. Gannon's boat."

"Mom, what the hell are you talking about?" He stared at the checks, and shook his head.

"You'll be all right," she said resolutely. "You know people in Anacortes—and Seattle. Maybe you can stay with someone there."

"You're really kicking me out?" he asked, his voice cracking a little.

Claire couldn't talk past the painful lump in her throat. She just nodded.

They parked down at the dock. Claire was terrified one of the Guardians would see them. She kept looking over her shoulder as she walked with Brian down to the pier. He was angry at her, and sulking. He'd stopped asking for her to explain his sudden eviction.

Claire folded her arms in front of her. She longed to hug Brian, but she couldn't. She needed to make it so he'd *want* to leave.

She saw a light from the charter boat on the dark, placid water. The sound of its motor grew louder.

"Listen," Brian said finally. "You'd tell me if you were in some kind of trouble, wouldn't you, Mom?"

"You're the trouble," she made herself say. "I want you gone."

His eyes—so much like his father's—started to tear up. "You can't mean that," he whispered. "Is Harlan making you do this?"

"No," she insisted. "But I'm doing it for him. I don't want to lose him. You—you're ruining it for me. Neither one of us want you in that house."

"Mom, please . . ."

Her heart was breaking. She had to shout over the sound of the approaching charter boat. "I don't want you calling. I don't want you trying to come back."

"Mom, I swear, I'll get along with him better, I mean it."

Brian reached out to her, but Claire brushed his arm away.

"I'm sick of your promises. I'm sick of you ruining my life. Now, get on the damn boat!"

Stunned, he stared at her for a moment. Then Brian obeyed his mother.

Claire knew he never would have left if he knew the truth—that his best friend had just been executed for being *a potential threat to the community*. Brian wouldn't have gone away if he'd known that his mother faced possible repercussions for interfering with the Guardians' work. If she'd gone with him, the Guardians would have tracked them down. Brian was better off alone. So Claire had to lie.

She didn't break down and cry until the charter boat sailed away with her son on it. Her arms ached from wanting to hold him.

She remembered now. In a daze, she drove back to the house, where Harlan, Ron, and Linda were waiting for her. To her utter astonishment, no one was upset at her. Harlan just kept apologizing for insisting she come to the Guardian Assembly.

"I told you she wasn't ready," Linda chimed in. "Poor thing. It was a terrible shock for her."

Harlan tried to hug her, but she wouldn't let him. She ran up to Tiffany's bathroom.

A few minutes later, Harlan was knocking on the door. "I'm really sorry, honey," he called to her.

She opened the door for him, then turned toward to the mirror and blew her nose. Her eyes were red from crying. "It's not just what happened at Silverwater Creek," she managed to say. "It's Brian. He's run away again. I don't know what I'm going to do . . ."

Once more, Harlan tried to hug her, but again, she recoiled.

Linda said she might feel better spending the night at their house. She started to pack Claire's overnight bag. She also insisted that Claire take a tranquilizer. *"You need it, Claire. You've been through a lot tonight. This will calm you down . . ."*

Claire remembered now.

She'd made Brian feel so unwanted that he was afraid to show his face on the island. Tim had told her that her "stalker" had found refuge in either one of the boats in the harbor or one of the summer cabins.

She'd never seen that army fatigue jacket or the stocking cap on her son before. She might not have recognized the clothes, but she should have recognized her son. She should have known he wouldn't have stayed away. All this time, he'd been watching over her.

The boat hit another rough patch, and Claire bumped against the closet door. She stood up, and felt along the wall for a light switch. She found one by the door. Except for a thin mat pushed against the wall, the tiny closet was empty. Claire had been on enough boats to know there wasn't such a thing as wasted space in a boat cabin. She wondered what Walt used the little room for.

Claire reached for the doorknob and twisted it. Why would he have a lock on the door to an empty closet?

There were scuff marks and indentations by the knob, like someone had kicked at it with their shoe. Earlier, she'd kicked at the door herself, but only a few times. The whole bottom half of the door panel was marred with dozens of those marks.

Claire suddenly realized what Walt used this little closet for. She wasn't the first woman to be locked inside it.

The boat was still moving at a brisk clip when Claire heard someone come down to the lower deck. She listened to the footsteps getting closer, and then a key rattled in the door.

"Sweetheart, are you okay?" Harlan gently called.

"Yes, Harlan," she answered.

He opened the door, and gave her a sheepish look. "Sorry to lock you in here, honey. But you were acting crazy. I didn't know what else to do."

Not budging, Claire just stared at him.

"Walt's sorry too," Harlan continued. "He said there's some brandy down here in the galley if you want some."

"Harlan, can I ask you a question?"

He nodded.

"Walt went out with Angela before you started dating her, didn't he?"

Harlan let out a bewildered laugh. "Well, yeah, but—"

"He was in love with her, wasn't he?"

Squinting at her, Harlan shook his head. "Claire, why are you asking me this stuff about my first wife?"

"Tracy and Angela were best friends, weren't they? Did they wear the same makeup? The same lipstick?"

He laughed. "Christ, I don't know."

Harlan reached for her, but she jerked away.

"C'mon, get out of there," he said, frowning. "You're starting to act crazy again."

Claire edged past him, and backed toward the galley. "It's important," she said. "Can you remember if Tracy and Angela wore the same lipstick?"

Harlan shrugged. "They might have. Angela mentioned something along those lines." He nodded. "In fact, yeah. Angela said that for her birthday, Walt went out and bought Tracy a bunch of lipsticks—all the same color as hers. *Scarlet* something. It was that birthday Walt gave her the car too, the Miata."

"The one they were killed in?" Claire whispered.

Harlan nodded. "Why are you asking about all this?"

"Because I don't think Walt ever really got over Angela."

"Hey, I need my first mate up here!" Walt called from the boat's deck—for the second time. *"C'mon, Harlan, help me out!"*

"I better get up there, sweetheart," Harlan said, patting her shoulder. They stood in the galley. "Maybe you should come up too," he suggested. "It's stopped raining. You could probably use some fresh air."

He turned toward the steps.

"Wait a minute," she whispered, grabbing his arm. "Does Walt keep a gun down here?"

Harlan squinted at her. "No." He patted her shoulder again. "Honey, don't worry about Walt. Everything will be fine. You just get some rest."

"My God, you haven't listened to one word I've said."

Frowning, he let out a long sigh. "I've been listening. One minute, you're telling me my best friend is the Rembrandt killer. But he didn't try to kill you. No, that was Ron and Linda. And the reason you were running down Main Street like a crazy woman tonight was because Linus Moorehead tried to kidnap you."

Claire shook her head. "I know it sounds crazy—"

"You've been under a lot of stress, that's all," Harlan said. "Why don't you rest down here? We can stay on the boat while Walt joins the posse. We'll just take it easy." He went to kiss her on the forehead.

Claire pulled away and glared at him. What was she thinking? What good did it do to confide in him? He was one of them. He was a murderer.

As Claire watched her husband climb up to the deck, she figured he was right about one thing: she was under a lot of stress. Why else would she think he would help her? Why did she even want his help?

Maybe because, despite everything, she had a feeling that Harlan really loved her, and he didn't have a clue what his Guardian friends were up to. Yes, he was a "soldier" in the Guardian firing squad for *the good of the community.* But he'd decided not to hide it from her. In fact, he was so honest—and so ignorant—he'd thought she would appreciate a front row seat to that lynching.

Was it possible Ron and Linda had tried to kill her on their own? Had they deceived Harlan? He probably trusted them as much as he trusted Walt—and Dr. Moorehead. There was nothing in Moorehead's e-mail to Harlan today about a plan in the works for drugging and abducting her.

She had no idea where Walt planned to take them. Was he working for the Guardians right now? Or did "Rembrandt" stand at the helm of this boat?

Maybe Harlan knew, or maybe he was being set up. Claire wasn't sure. Either way, she couldn't count on her husband to help her.

When she'd first met Harlan, she felt as if he'd come to her rescue. But that wouldn't happen tonight.

She was alone in this.

"Look who's come up for air," Walt shouted over the engine noise. He stood at the boat's controls with Harlan at his side.

Claire paused at the top of the cabin steps. She stared back at him. The wind whipped through her hair. She'd found a rain slicker in the supply closet. She'd also found a flare gun, and four cartridges. The gun was in her hand—inside the slicker pocket.

"Feeling better, honey?" Harlan asked.

"We'll be docking at Alliance in fifteen minutes," Walt announced. Then he smiled apologetically at her. "Sorry to make you a stowaway for a while, Claire. We were in trouble with the boat. It was an emergency situation. Desperate times, desperate measures. Forgive me?"

Claire didn't respond. She kept staring at him, and wondered if he'd killed Tess yet.

Harlan stepped toward her. But then he glanced over his shoulder, and stopped. "Hey, Walt. Who's that on our tail?" he asked.

In the distance behind them, Claire saw a speck of light in the choppy, black water.

"What the hell?" Walt said, obviously not expecting company. He had Harlan relieve him at the helm, then studied the other vessel through his binoculars. "I can't make this guy out," he said, grabbing the controls again. He handed the binoculars to Harlan. "Check him out with the cheaters. Maybe you recognize him." Walt reached for a switch, and the lights on the Chris Craft went out. "This might make it easier for you to see," he said.

Harlan spied the other boat. "Oh, yeah, it's Phil Gannon's sloop. Maybe he's come to help."

"What for?" Walt shot back. "He's not a Guardian. I mean—no one would have called him."

Claire gazed at the tiny light against the dark water. The last time Brian had run away—on his own—he'd "borrowed" Phil Gannon's boat.

He was following them.

The Chris Craft lurched forward, and she realized Walt was boosting the speed. He hadn't turned the boat lights back on yet. Claire had a feeling he didn't plan to either, not until he'd eluded the other boat.

He turned to Claire. "It'll get a little wet out here," he said. "You might want to go down below."

She glanced back at the light on the night sea. It seemed to be fading. Walt was losing him.

"Are you still mad at me for having you locked up?" Walt asked, yelling over the engine noise. "Hey, I should be ticked off at you, Claire. Your husband said you were telling him some pretty fantastic stories about me."

"You said down at the dock that they were looking for my 'friend,' Tess," she called. "How did you know that Tess is my friend? Did she tell you after you abducted her? Or did you see us together in the hospital when you were stalking me?"

Walt laughed. "Jesus, Claire, I don't know what you're talking about."

Holding onto the railing, Harlan frowned at her—and then at his friend.

"Why did Linda and Ron copy you when they tried to kill me?" she asked, over the motor's churning.

"You're talking crazy, Claire," he said, an uncomfortable smile plastered on his face. Then he turned to Harlan. "Hey, buddy, I'm sorry. But I think we took her out of the closet too early."

"You weren't in on their plan to kill me, were you, Walt?" she pressed. "You were busy that weekend with one of your victims. But you came to the hospital, because you were curious about 'Jane Doe,' and this copycat. You didn't know Linda and Ron were behind it. You didn't know it was me."

"Claire, you're not making any sense—"

"It was no accident Linda and Ron decided to imitate Rembrandt, was it? Did Linda know about you? Was it your little secret? How did she find out? I'll bet Ron didn't know. She must have used what she had on you to pull as many strings as she could. I'll bet she did that copycat job on me to watch you squirm. Is that why you killed her?"

Walt was shaking his head. "Harlan, you better take her down below—"

"Linda's dead?" Harlan asked numbly.

"I mean it," Walt said. "Get her out of here."

"Why? Am I slowing you down?" Claire glanced back at the dark seascape. She couldn't see the boat light any more. She pulled the flare gun out of her pocket, and raised it toward the sky.

"Hold it right there," she heard Walt say.

Hesitating, Claire glanced at him.

Walt stood at the helm, one hand on the wheel, and the other holding a gun. It was pointed at her.

"Jesus, what are you doing?" Harlan said. "Walt—"

"Put it down, Claire," Walt warned. "Just toss it on the deck."

"That's my gun," Harlan was saying. "Walt, what the hell—"

"For Christ's sake, tell her to drop it!" he yelled. The boat listed to one side, and water sprayed onto the deck.

Shaking his head, Harlan stepped toward his friend. "No, no, Walt, this isn't . . . you can't . . ." He trailed off as Walt turned the automatic on him.

"Stay there, Harlan!" he cried.

Claire raised the flare gun in the air, and fired.

"Goddamn it!" Walt bellowed. He swiveled toward her with the handgun.

The Chris Craft suddenly jolted to one side, and waves lashed onto the deck. All at once, Harlan lunged at his friend, and made a grab for the automatic. The boat was out of control, speeding and snaking through the choppy water.

Claire tried to keep her balance as she pulled out another flare. Her hands were shaking.

A shot rang out.

She looked up, and saw her husband stagger back from his friend. Walt still had the automatic. Harlan was clutching his throat. Blood oozed between his fingers. A look of shock and disbelief seemed frozen on his face. He reeled back toward the railing edge, and toppled over the side of the boat.

For a moment, Claire was paralyzed as she watched her

husband die. Then the boat took another jolt, and she almost dropped the flare. She clung onto the railing by the cabin entry to keep her balance.

Walt was coming at her. He shoved the gun in his jacket pocket.

Teetering, Claire loaded the cartridge into the flare chamber. Tears streamed down her face. She looked up again. Walt closed in on her.

He grabbed her by the front of her rain slicker. His other hand was pulled back in a fist.

Claire felt the flare gun slip out of her hands. She felt a hammer-like blow across her face.

Then blackness.

Chapter 27

For a while, he'd lost sight of them. It was as if the Chris Craft had disappeared. Brian only saw a dark horizon ahead. He couldn't even guess at the other boat's destination—maybe Victoria, or maybe one of the dozens of San Juan Islands. For several awful, interminable minutes, he thought his mother was lost to him.

Then the flare shot across the night sky. He could see them. They were headed for the plant dock on the Alliance side of the island.

He knew his mom had shot off that flare.

After she'd sent him away three weeks ago, he'd hitch-hiked to Seattle, and stayed with friends. Brian figured something was wrong when he phoned Derek's house, and got Mr. Herrmann, who sounded as if he had a snootful. "Derek's gone to Europe, backpacking," he said. "You can't reach him." Brian knew the Europe story was a lie.

Though his mom had said she didn't want to hear from him, Brian phoned the house anyway. He kept getting the machine—or Harlan—and he would always hang up.

Borrowing a friend's fatigue jacket and a stocking cap, he returned to Deception on the ferry. He saw "Missing" no-tices—with his mother's photo—posted around town. He should have known his mother had been in trouble when she'd sent him away.

For the next week, he followed Harlan around. He didn't want anyone seeing him—not even his friends on the island. His mother and best friend had mysteriously disappeared, and he wasn't taking any chances.

Even when his mom returned, he was reluctant to make his presence known. After all, she'd been pretty convincing when she'd told him she never wanted to see him again. And no one was posting any "Missing" notices for him. From the forest in the backyard, he kept watch of the house. As far as he could tell, his mother seemed to slip back into her normal routine. Still, he needed to make sure she was all right. So he kept an eye on her.

Maybe she'd given up on him, but Brian wasn't ready to give up on his mother.

For the last ten days he'd been sleeping in deserted summer cabins or stowing away in boats at the marina. He lived on junk food. The five hundred bucks his mother had given him was quickly running out.

Today, he'd slept late aboard Mr. Gannon's sloop. He made a trip to the forest behind the cul de sac, but didn't see his mom at home. It wasn't until he returned to the marina that he noticed her in the parking lot of The Whale Watcher Inn with that *dude*. Brian wasn't sure who he was, but he'd seen the guy come over to the house a couple of times when Harlan wasn't there. Watching them slip into a hotel room together, Brian figured the man was his mother's secret boyfriend. Was this good-looking guy the reason she'd sent him away?

Brian decided he'd seen enough. His mother seemed to have been doing just fine without him.

He took refuge from the storm in the cabin of Mr. Gannon's boat. Once the rain let up, he headed for Lyle's Stop and Sip. He needed food, and the clerk didn't know him there. Brian was in the alley behind some shops when he spotted his mother running down the deserted, rain-swept Main Street.

She looked half out of her mind.

Brian started to approach her, but she ran away. Defeated, he watched her drive off with Harlan and his friend, Walt Binns. The three of them boarded Walt's Chris Craft.

Then she spotted him from the deck. His mother cried out his name. In fact, she almost jumped off the back of that stinking boat to get to him.

But Harlan dragged her below, and they sped away. Brian had never trusted Harlan much. He used to think Walt was okay, but had never entirely forgotten that the easygoing, youthful-looking man was Harlan's best friend.

Brian followed them in Mr. Gannon's sloop. After a while, they must have caught on he was behind them, because they picked up speed and even shut off the Chris Craft's lights. They were trying to lose him.

They'd almost succeeded too.

But now he knew they were headed for Alliance. His mother had let him know.

Ten minutes after seeing the flare, Brian pulled into the plant harbor. Walt Binns's Chris Craft was already moored beside a couple of Chemtech company vessels.

The plant's main facility was a long, squat, brick and concrete monstrosity with smoke stacks belching out black fumes. There were at least a dozen other, smaller buildings on the site, along with a parking lot.

Brian, Derek, and some of their friends sometimes broke into the plant at night. The night watchman was a total slacker, who just watched his portable TV, ate, and slept while there. Brian and his pals would climb the tall chain link fence, and ride their skateboards in the vacant lot. He and Derek also figured out how to break into the company cars on the site. They'd drive around the lot like maniacs. They had six vehicles to choose from. The key to each one was kept in a magnet-box under the rear passenger door. Derek often talked about ripping off one of those cars, but Brian wasn't interested. Even if he was into stealing cars, he wouldn't have wanted one from that collection of beat-up old Cavaliers and Monte Carlos. Besides, the lot entry had a gate with a padlock.

But tonight, he was very interested in stealing one of the those beat-up old sedans.

As Brian tied Mr. Gannon's sloop to the dock, he glanced over at the company cars in the lot nearby. Instead of the usual six, there were only five of them.

He figured Harlan and Walt had driven off with his mother in one. Walt's cabin was only a couple of miles down the road. They were probably headed there.

Brian ran over to the row of vehicles. He found the key box under the rear passenger door of the last Monte Carlo at the end. He started up the car, and tore toward the lot exit.

Harlan was the plant manager, and had a key to the gate. Hell, Walt probably had one too. He'd worked at the plant for a while.

But Brian didn't have a key. What he did have was guts—and the recklessness of a seventeen-year-old boy.

Heading toward the gate, Brian pushed the accelerator to the floor. The tires let out a screech as the Monte Carlo charged the fence. The car crashed into the big gate, and after the initial jolting impact, Brian felt something give. Several broken metal links hit the windshield like bullets. He realized they were pieces from the chain padlock that had broken apart. The smashed gate flew open, then slammed against the other side of the fence.

At the same time, an alarm went off.

Brian hesitated just long enough to figure out the car was still working all right—except for the cracks in the windshield and a busted headlight.

He raced for the plant exit. The night watchman was obviously alerted. No doubt, he'd come out there, and try to stop him.

But Brian wasn't going to slow down.

His mom was in trouble, and she needed him.

* * *

Claire's head throbbed, and the side of her face hurt. She felt cold. She was naked—except for a thin, white sheet covering her.

She didn't know how long she'd been unconscious, but she was no longer on the boat. Lying on what felt like a massage table, she became aware of the binding around her wrists. The taut rope must have run under the table from one wrist to the other. Her ankles were tied in the same fashion—so her legs were spread across the width of the padded gurney.

Claire tried to open her eyes. But she could only get her left one open. The other eye was glued shut with a false eyelash.

"Now, that was clumsy of me, wasn't it?"

Walt Binns stepped into her view. He wore a surgical gown and gloves. There was a spotlight behind him, over his shoulder. He reached toward her face and carefully readjusted the false eyelash. "There now, better?"

She blinked a few times, then glanced from side to side. He'd cut her hair. Shorn chestnut-colored clumps rested around her neck and bare shoulders.

To her right, she saw a narrow cabinet on wheels. An array of cosmetics, brushes, combs, and astringents were laid out on top of it. A tortoise shell lipstick container was among them.

"Is that Lady deMilo Scarlet Passion lipstick?" Claire asked.

"Yes," Walt said. "Leftovers from my late wife's supply. Guess I'm just sentimental." He was applying liquid foundation to her jaw, apparently trying to cover up a mark he'd left there after slugging her. "Harlan said you were asking about the lipstick when he let you out of the storage locker. How did you know about the brand? Did your policeman friend tell you?"

"Yes," Claire answered, wincing as he continued to dab at her sore jaw. "Where is he? At the dock, you said 'Rembrandt' was holding him hostage."

Walt smirked. "Rembrandt is." He dabbed some foundation under her eyes. "Tim Sullivan is in a holding room with your friend, Tess. By the way, you were right. I first saw Tess at the hospital. I think she might have even had a little crush on me."

Claire watched him reach for the rouge. She noticed a pair of hair-cutting sheers on the table. If only she could get at them. She tried loosening the rope around her wrist by rubbing it against the edge of the gurney.

"Clever, the way you caught me on that slipup about Tess," he continued. "But what really amazed me was the way you nailed the Linda situation. You pretty much had it down pat, Claire."

He let out a bitter laugh. "Linda was such a meddling, control-freak bitch. I had no idea she did that number on you. I didn't put it together until a couple of days ago."

"How did she find out about you?" Claire asked.

He gently applied the rouge to Claire's cheeks. "Linda knew I was interested in this girl, Nancy, who was vacationing with her family out here a couple of years ago. Nancy was engaged to some fellow in Wenatchee, a high school sweetheart. I didn't want her to, but she married him anyway. When Nancy ended up dead a year later, Linda put it together that . . ." He shrugged. "Well, Linda knew I don't get over losing a girl very easily."

"Like Harlan's first wife, Angela," Claire said. "Is that why they're all made up to resemble her? Is that how you're making me up now—like her?"

She kept trying to wiggle loose the rope around her wrist. Walt was so focused on her face, he didn't seem to notice her hand moving under the sheet.

"I liked her looks," he replied.

"Tim said you enjoyed the challenge of transforming your victims into Angela's likeness."

Sighing, Walt picked up the hairbrush. "Well, Tim isn't talking much any more. I shot him about an hour and a half ago, and left him locked up with your pal. Unless Tess picked up some nursing skills while she was in the hospital, I'm pretty sure he's dead by now."

Claire jerked at the rope. She couldn't hold back. She started to tremble. Tears slid down from her eyes.

"Now, don't do that," Walt said, reaching for a tissue. "You're ruining it. God, I hate when I get criers. I didn't think you'd be one of them, Claire."

"What about Tess?" she asked, her voice cracking.

"You're warming up the table for her," he said. "Maybe Tim was right. I'm looking forward to the challenge with Tess. I want to do something to cover that birthmark of hers."

"You'll never get away with this," she said.

He sighed. "Yes, I know. I'm not sure how much I'll like life as a fugitive. Then again, maybe I'll enjoy the challenge."

He carefully brushed her hair over her forehead and to the side. "You know, there was a little party earlier tonight down the road about two miles," he said. "It was a kind of 'surprise party' for you, Harlan, and Tim Sullivan. Something clever Moorehead and the Guardians had hatched out. I just called and busted it up a half hour ago. I said the three of you had just died in what would conveniently look like a boating accident."

Walt chuckled. "So they've all gone home. They're waiting to hear the sad news from the Coast Guard. They'll be in for a surprise in the morning. I'll be long gone by then."

While he hovered over her, Claire kept trying to wiggle her hand free from the rope. "You should listen to yourself, Walt," she said. "Harlan considered you his best friend, and tonight you shot him in the throat. Don't you have any remorse at all?"

He stopped brushing her hair for a moment, and gazed down at her. "To tell you the truth, Claire, part of me kind of enjoyed it."

*   *   *

From the end of the muddy pathway where he'd parked the Monte Carlo, Brian couldn't see any lights coming from Walt Binns's cabin. As he came closer to the house, Brian noticed all the window shutters were closed. There didn't seem to be anyone home.

Still, he crept along the trail, hoping to find the Chemtech car parked on the other side of Walt's front porch. If they hadn't taken his mother here, where had they gone with her?

Approaching the chalet, Brian darted behind one tree and then another. The army fatigue jacket made him nearly invisible—at least from a distance.

He spotted a car in the alcove beside the porch. But it wasn't a Chemtech vehicle. It belonged to that guy his mother was seeing. Brian skulked toward the car, then suddenly stopped. "Holy crap," he murmured.

The trunk was popped open. Three bullet holes perforated the hood. Brian felt his stomach turn.

He was staring at a dead man, curled up inside the trunk. Blood leaked from holes in his yellow slicker. His eyes and mouth were half-open. The face was frozen in a rigor-mortis grimace. It was Deputy Landers.

Brian staggered back from the car. He thought he might be sick.

He bent forward and took a few deep breaths. As he straightened up again, he saw a beat-up white Taurus parked in front of the other car—closer to the backyard. It was unmistakably a Chemtech company vehicle.

They had his mom here, somewhere inside this cabin.

Brain reached up and tugged at one of the window shutters, but it didn't budge. He crept around back and tried another window shutter. No luck. He was about to move onto the next window, but a noise stopped him. He froze, and glanced over his shoulder.

A large raccoon lazily crawled up the trunk of an evergreen tree beside the cabin.

"Jesus, you scared the shit out of me," Brian muttered to the animal. He took another couple of deep breaths, then tried to jiggle open the shutter. Like the others, it was firmly fixed in place.

Brian hurried toward the back of the house. "Please, God . . ."

He started crying. He was thinking about his mom. They'd already murdered a cop. God only knew what they were doing to his mother right now.

"Excuse me a moment," Walt said. He turned and switched off the spotlight.

Claire raised her head from the table, and watched him walk over to the window.

He didn't say anything about the scraping noise along the side of the cabin just seconds ago. But obviously, he'd heard it. She'd heard it as well, and her heart leapt a bit.

Was it too much to hope that someone was out there? Maybe Tim, or Brian, or the police?

Walt pulled up the shade, opened the window, and then the shutter. Meanwhile, Claire tried to loosen her hand from the rope. It burned against her wrists. She stole a glance at the scissors on the side table.

"Claire, someone has come here to rescue you," Walt said. Grinning, he stepped back from the window.

She could see a raccoon scurrying up the trunk of an evergreen tree. The light from inside the cabin reflected in the creature's eyes.

Walt secured the shutter back in place, then he closed the window and lowered the shade. He turned toward her again. "Now, where was I?"

From behind a tree in the backyard, Brain watched Walt close the window shutter. Why the hell was he wearing a surgeon's gown?

He turned and glanced at the tool shed by the patio and

barbecue. Maybe he could use something in there to break inside the cabin, something that could double as a weapon.

He stopped in front of the tool shed's door. The lock had been broken off the hinge. He hesitated before stepping inside.

Suddenly, something brushed against his ankle.

Brian reeled back. Stunned, he gazed down at the ground. It was moving.

Something poked out of the earth. It scratched and clawed at the soil.

"Oh, my God," Brian whispered. He was staring down at a human hand. It seemed reach out to him.

The lights flickered.

Leaning over her with an eyebrow pencil in his hand, Walt hesitated. "They must still be having problems with the power," he remarked. "I hope I won't have to work in the dark."

But Claire had a feeling he was almost finished with her. He'd already fixed her hair and eyes, and liberally applied the Scarlet Passion lipstick. Now, with the pencil he drew a beauty mark on her cheek. It was probably his finishing touch. Tim had said the beauty mark was like Rembrandt's second signature.

She kept twisting at the rope around her wrists—to no avail. "You know, Tim told me something about the 'Rembrandt profile,' " she said. "He said Rembrandt likes to terrorize his victims and watch them suffer. It turns him on." She sighed, then suddenly continued in a calm, soothing tone. "But you know, Walt, you don't have to resort to that. You're better than you think. There's such a thin line between giving pain and pleasure. Why don't you untie me? Cross the line, Walt. You have me looking like Angela now. So why not make love to me? I've always imagined you'd be better than Harlan. Angela was a fool to let you go."

Walt hesitated. With a curious smile, he stared down at her. Then he let out a little laugh, and turned away.

Claire watched him retrieve something from the dresser against the wall. She frantically struggled to free her hands from the rope. But Walt turned around again, and she stopped.

He stepped up to the table with a see-through plastic bag and a roll of duct tape. He took the scissors from the side table and snipped off a long piece of tape. He stuck it to the edge of the side table, leaving the strip of tape to dangle there like fly paper.

"Touch me, Walt," Claire urged him. "Don't put the bag over my head. Make me squirm with your touch—not by putting some silly bag over my head. That's cheating. C'mon, Walt. I want you to pleasure me—the way Harlan never could. Please, Walt . . ."

He cocked his head to one side, then looked her up and down. He seemed tempted. But then a cold smile came to his face. "You'd say anything at this point, wouldn't you?" he asked. "Don't you know, at least half of the others before you have tried the same thing, Claire?"

He started to pull the plastic bag over her hair.

Claire jerked her head from side to side until she thought her neck might snap.

"You're not the first to try that trick either," he grunted. Suddenly his hand was on her throat, choking her. With the other hand, he tugged the plastic bag farther down over her face.

Claire tried to move her head, but she couldn't. She could barely breathe.

He let go, but just long enough to grab the strip of duct tape. He quickly sealed the rim of the bag around her neck. The tape pinched at her soft flesh there. She gasped, and the clear bag began to steam up.

Through the fog, she saw Walt hovered over her. He was smiling. "I won't let you suffocate, Claire," he said. "This is just round one."

As she twitched and shook on the table, Walt started to run his hand over the white sheet covering her body.

The lights flickered again. He stopped for a moment.

Suddenly, Claire heard a gunshot outside. She flinched.

Walt stepped away from her, then moved toward the door. While his back was to her, Claire inhaled deeply, sucking part of the plastic bag in her mouth. She chomped down on it with her teeth, then ground them together. It was tough plastic, but she managed to puncture it. She poked her tongue at the perforation to make the hole bigger. At last, she could breathe a little.

Another gunshot went off, startling her.

"What the hell?" Walt muttered.

Through the fogged plastic, Claire watched him reach for something in the dresser. It was Harlan's gun. Walt glanced over his shoulder at her, then he stepped out of the room.

He unlocked the front door and walked out on his porch. Walt had the gun readied as he looked out at the forest. It had stopped raining, but the drops were still falling from trees. Branches swayed in the light breeze.

"Who's out there?" Walt called.

"Drop the gun!" he heard someone say.

But Walt only raised the gun higher. He tried to figure out where that man's voice was coming from.

Suddenly, something banged against the back of his cabin. Startled, Walt began to retreat inside.

"Walt!" the man called.

He swiveled around. A man came out from behind a tree, yet he was still slumped against it.

Walt recognized Tim Sullivan—and the woman in back of him, covered with mud, Tess Campbell. Tim Sullivan had a semiautomatic in his hand. "Put it down, Walt!" he yelled.

Defiantly, Walt Binns pointed Harlan's gun at him.

A shot rang out.

* * *

The banging and pounding wouldn't stop.

Through the hot, steamy, suffocating bag, Claire heard wood splintering. Then glass shattered. Someone was breaking the window in Walt's little operating room.

She lifted her head up and watched a hoe smash through what was left of that window.

A moment later, Brian boosted himself up on the sill, and crawled inside. He was wearing the army fatigue jacket. But he didn't have the stocking cap hiding his wavy brown hair.

"Oh, Jesus!" he said, gaping at his mother. He rushed to her side. "Hold on, Mom. Hold on . . ." His hands shaking, he pried apart the plastic bag.

Claire gasped for air.

He reached for the scissors on the side table, then carefully cut the bag away. He kissed her forehead.

"You came back," Claire whispered. "My sweet boy, I can't believe you came back . . ."

He started to cut at the rope around her wrist. Suddenly, Claire panicked. "Oh, Brian. He's still here. He's got a gun. You—"

The gunshot silenced her.

Brian touched her hand, then moved away from the table. With the scissors poised, Brian crept toward the door. He stepped out of the room. She listened to his footsteps. A moment later, he came back.

Wide-eyed, Claire stared at him.

Brian went back to cutting the rope binding her wrists. "He doesn't have the gun anymore, Mom."

She didn't quite know what he meant. Claire shook her head. She was still trying to get her breath. "My friend, Tess . . . she's in trouble. She's trapped here someplace . . ."

"Everything's cool, Mom," Brian whispered. "Your friends are outside. They're okay."

At last, he cut through the taut rope.

Claire pulled the sheet up to her neck. She sat up and threw her other arm around Brian. She held onto him, and began to cry. She thought back to that moment on the dock, when she'd sent him away. How her arms had ached from not holding him.

She'd been waiting over three weeks for this. She held onto her son, and felt the pain wash away.

Epilogue

From the only working telephone among the cabins in the northwest forest of Deception Island, Brian Ferguson called the local and state police. Claire overheard her son talking to Sheriff Klauser: *"Yes, I know, Sheriff, I don't think I've ever called you before. Usually it's somebody calling about me . . ."*

Within hours, the tiny island was swarmed with hoards of police, Coast Guard, FBI agents, and reporters. The capture of "Rembrandt" was big news. But that bombshell of a story almost became eclipsed by the startling revelation involving Deception Island's men's club, the Guardians.

Fred Maybon was one of the first islanders questioned by the police. Hoping to strike a deal with authorities, Fred immediately blew the whistle on his Guardian buddies. He said the Guardians had orchestrated nineteen disappearances and seventeen accidental deaths of undesirable locals over the past eight years. Most of the accidents were forced drownings. In a few cases, certain individuals found the brakes had gone out on their cars. And in another situation, a family of four was killed in a fire. The majority of those subjects who disappeared or ran away were troublesome teenagers. They'd been executed at Silverwater Creek. Some were buried out there. Other bodies were taken by boat to the Strait of Juan de Fuca, weighed down, and dumped overboard. The boat engaged in these secret sea burials was the *Lovely Linda*, with Ron Castle at the helm.

Ron didn't wait for the state police and FBI to question him. News of Linda's apparent suicide reached him only hours before the island came under siege by police and federal authorities. They found him in his study, lying in front of his desk—on a woven rug with an American Eagle emblem on it. A gun was in his hand. Ron Castle had put a bullet through his brain.

Dr. Linus Moorehead managed to elude the police for two days—until they found him hiding out in one of the weekend cabins. His unshaven face was still cut, swollen, and bruised from running his BMW into a tree. With her shoe, Claire Shaw had also done some serious damage to his right eye, which was puffy and blood-red. Discovered cowering under a bed in his pajamas, Dr. Moorehead didn't go quietly. The police had to drag him out of the cabin. He shrieked and wept shamelessly. *"You can't do this to me!"* he kept insisting. *"I'm a doctor! You can't fucking do this to me!"*

Moorehead was the last of the group rounded up. Nine of Deception's more prominent citizens had already been arrested. Another eight were under investigation.

The day after Moorehead's arrest, Claire Shaw returned to Deception to attend a memorial service for Harlan at St. Mark's Church. Not even a week had passed since she'd made the congregation ill at ease by offering Special Intentions for her missing son and for Derek Herrmann. Many of those same people attended the service for their friend, Harlan Shaw. Several of them had husbands or fathers who had recently been arrested. Several others were currently under investigation themselves. Despite their loyalty to Harlan Shaw, they only had contempt for his widow.

Sitting in the front pew, Claire defiantly ignored their scornful stares. She dressed in a simple black dress and the string of pearls Charlie had given her so many years ago.

She held onto Tiffany's hand. She'd come for her step-daughter—and for Harlan too. Claire couldn't condone the heinous acts he'd committed with the Guardians. But Harlan had been her husband, and he'd saved her life.

Brian, however, didn't feel any such obligation to his stepfather. He didn't attend the memorial. They had tempo-rary lodgings on the mainland, and he'd already cleaned out his room in the house on Holm Drive. He'd told his mother he was never going back to the island.

After the service, in the vestibule at the front of church, Claire stopped to speak with the handful of islanders who were still talking to her—including Kira Sherman and Molly Cartwright. Others just passed her by with icy looks and dis-approving frowns.

One of the coldest scowls came from a lanky, tall, some-what homely man who stood in the corner of the vestibule. He was in his forties and dressed in a dark blue suit. Claire didn't recognize him. She hadn't seen him inside the church. But as she talked with her friends, she kept glancing over at him. He wouldn't stop glaring at her.

Claire finally asked Kira Sherman if she recognized the gaunt man.

"No, I've never seen him before," Kira whispered. "He sure is creepy looking."

Claire began to worry about Tiffany, who was talking to some of her classmates. She'd been out of school for the last three days. That Monday when she'd said good-bye to Claire and boarded the school bus, Tiffany had been worried that she would come back from her sleepover the next day and find her stepmother gone again. Instead, Tiffany lost her fa-ther.

She had no other family—aside from Angela's father, a sixty-seven-year-old widower. Harlan's estate was divided evenly between his wife and daughter. The will specified that Claire would take on guardianship of Tiffany. Claire had instructed the lawyers to accelerate the adoption process.

Tiffany said good-bye to her friends. Claire took her by

the hand, and started for the church door. That was when the tall, homely man stepped toward her. "Mrs. Shaw?" he whispered.

Claire's grip on Tiffany's hand automatically tightened. She pulled Tiffany behind her—so she was standing between the gaunt stranger and her stepdaughter. "Yes?" she said.

A little smile came to his homely face. "I'm Steve Griswald," he said. "I'm sorry, but I couldn't bring myself to go in there. I didn't come for him. I came for you. I wanted to thank you for helping bring my sister's killers to justice." He shook her hand. "I can lay it to rest now. Thank you for Violet and her family, Mrs. Shaw."

When Claire and Tiffany stepped out of the church, Brian was standing by the car, waiting for them. He wore khaki pants and an Irish knit sweater that used to be his father's. Brian smiled at them. In the sunlight, with his golden brown hair blowing in the wind, he looked so much like Charlie.

Tiffany ran up to him and hugged him. "Hey, pumpkinhead," he said, picking up his stepsister and giving her cheek a kiss.

"I thought you weren't ever coming back to this island," Claire said, managing a smile. But she had tears in her eyes.

Brain shrugged. "Well, I figured the natives weren't very friendly. I didn't want you to go it all alone, Mom."

Claire embraced him. "Coming to my rescue again," she said, patting his back. "How did you get here anyway?"

"I stole a car."

Claire pulled back and stared at him.

Brian rolled his eyes. "Relax, Mom. I'm kidding." He opened the back door for Tiffany. "Tess let me borrow her car. I parked it at the Anacortes terminal and came across on the ferry. Then I walked here. It's a good day for it."

Touching his cheek, Claire smiled at her son. "Yes, it's a good day," she said.

* * *

No one blamed Tess. She'd tried to clean the bullet wound in Tim's shoulder as best as she could. But she'd been working in the darkness of Rembrandt's make-shift "waiting room" with a bottle of water and an unsterilized towel. Tim had carried around that bullet in his shoulder for over four hours until the doctors removed it. The infection had already started.

There was only so much the doctors could do.

The day after Tim had been admitted to the hospital, the infection from the bullet wound had spread, and his fever had climbed to 104 degrees.

Claire had stayed at his bedside that evening. It reminded her of all those nights she'd spent, curled up in a chair in Charlie's hospital room, listening to her husband's rattled breathing. As the patient's wife, she'd been given some latitude with visiting hours.

But this time around, since Claire wasn't even related to Tim, she had to use her limited connections at the hospital to get past visiting-hour regulations. It helped that she'd become friends with Tim's nurse.

It also gave her some peace of mind knowing she hadn't left her son or stepdaughter all alone that night. Tess was with them. Her place was only a fifteen-minute drive from the hospital. In fact, Tess's house had become their temporary lodgings.

Claire and Tiffany stayed in her guest room, while Brian set up a cozy, make-shift bedroom—with a rented bed—in the basement. Tess said they weren't an imposition. "I got the place for a family, and now I have one," she told Claire.

Everywhere they went, the press followed them around. Dozens of reporters kept a vigil outside the hospital, and Claire always had to sneak in a side door to visit Tim.

Both she and Tess had become reluctant media darlings. They'd been approached by a score of agents, hoping to acquire the film and literary rights to their stories. But neither of them were interested in cashing in on what had happened.

When reporters asked her how it felt to be the woman who helped apprehend Rembrandt, Tess always replied, "Well, I missed out on a free make-over, but otherwise I feel pretty good about it."

Tim was in no condition to speak to the press. But his boss, Lt. Roger Elmore, wasn't at a loss for words. "Everyone on the task force is saying a prayer for our friend, Tim Sullivan," he was quoted in the newspapers. "Tim has always been one of our best and most respected officers, a real team player and a friend to all."

A few hours after Harlan's memorial service, Claire went to the hospital to visit Tim again.

The door to his room was closed, and his nurse stopped her from going inside. "I'm sorry, Claire," she said. "You can't go in there."

Claire numbly stared at her. "Why? What happened? Is he all right?"

"Oh, he's more than all right, honey," Sherita said, patting her shoulder. "He is one fine-looking man. He's just getting a sponge bath right now—his second today."

Claire squinted at her. "Wait a minute. When I was staying here, I got a sponge bath—something like, once every three days."

Sherita wrinkled her nose. "Don't say anything to him about that. You'll ruin things for half the nurses on this floor. They all want a turn. He's an absolute doll."

The door opened, and a heavy-set, baby-faced Latino man in a pale blue uniform stepped out of the room. He carried a folded up towel.

"Thanks again, Raul," Tim called.

The nurse peeked back into the room and nodded. Then he gave Sherita a sheepish smile and moved down the hallway.

Sherita nudged her. "I always knew you'd find your dream man eventually, honey."

Claire stepped into the room, which smelled of jasmine and eucalyptus. Raul must have used some fancy soap for

Tim's bath. And he'd combed his hair too. Tim was dressed in the burgundy pajamas Claire had bought for him yesterday.

He looked very handsome, but still a bit tired and frail. Sitting up in his hospital bed, he smiled at her. "Well, hey, how are you?" he asked in a sleepy voice.

"I'm good," Claire said. "How was your sponge bath?"

"Oh, really nice. He even gave me a foot massage."

"Yeah, they used to do that for me too," Claire lied. She pulled the chair over to his bedside.

"They're springing me out of here the day after tomorrow," he announced.

"That's wonderful," Claire said.

He would be staying with his brother's family in Seattle while convalescing. Claire felt a little pang in her heart, knowing she wouldn't see him for a few days.

She clutched the railing on the side of his bed. "Are you still coming to Tess's house for Thanksgiving?" she asked. "I'm cooking—turkey, stuffing, the works. We're eating around eight, because Tess promised to serve dinner at a homeless shelter until seven. I know Brian is anxious for you to be there. He's thrilled that his mom is friends with *Tim Timster*, the creator of *The Adventures of Private Eye Guy*."

Tim brought his hand up to bed railing and rested it top of hers. "I wouldn't miss it," he said with a strained smile. "But is that all we are, Claire? Friends?"

She shrugged. "For the time being, I think that's all we can be."

"It's all right. I'm a patient guy." Tim glanced over at their hands joined together. He gave hers a little squeeze. "Is this okay?" he asked.

Claire smiled, and her fingers interlaced with his. "This is more than okay," she whispered. "This is a very good start."

Two floors above them, a room in the north wing was under heavy police guard. The scores of reporters outside the hospital waited there mostly for any updates on the patient in room 416.

Tim Sullivan had shot Walter Binns in the knee. And like the officer who had struck him down, "Rembrandt" had developed an infection from his bullet wound. Before his condition developed to pneumonia, an impassive Walter Binns confessed to the murders of Harlan Shaw, Linda Castle, Deputy Troy Landers, eight women from Western Washington, and another two from Vancouver, British Columbia.

With his leg suspended in a traction harness, Walter Binns was strapped in his hospital bed. His fever ranging from 100 to 103, he drifted in and out of consciousness for two days.

A police guard was in the hospital room at all times, and two more armed guards were posted outside the door. Still, several nurses on the fourth floor specifically asked not to be assigned to the patient in room 416.

But there were some women who wanted to meet him. The photo of Walter Binns that ran in most newspapers captured his deceptively youthful guy-next-door good looks. Maybe it was the wavy dark hair or his crooked smile, or perhaps some people just wanted to know someone infamous. Whatever the reasons, over two dozen women had already written to Rembrandt, care of the hospital. They sent notes and Get Well cards to the ailing serial killer, saying they wanted to meet him.

But Staci didn't want to meet him. She wasn't crazy. She just wanted a look at him. She worked the desk at the Intensive Care Unit, and it had been a dull day. She was going out for margaritas later with her friend, Heather, and she wanted to tell her what Rembrandt looked like in person.

During her break at six o'clock, she walked over to the north wing. There was a window in the door to Room 416. She flirted with the guard a little, and he said it was okay if she wanted to peek inside.

Staci thought of all those poor reporters outside the hospital, just itching to be in her nurse's shoes right now. She stepped up to the window—which had criss-crossed, thin wire running through it.

A lamp was on in the corner of the hospital room, where a stocky police guard sat, reading a paperback.

The man in the bed appeared to be sleeping. The harness holding up his wounded leg hovered a few inches off the bed. He had kicked off his sheets. Straps from underneath the bed were tied to his wrists. The pale blue hospital gown he wore was blotchy with sweat stains. His dark wavy hair looked greasy, and his complexion was sallow. He'd looked a lot more handsome in his newspaper photo.

He turned toward her and opened his eyes.

Staci let out a little gasp. Those eyes were dark and puffy, yet mesmerizing. He was staring at her, and she couldn't move.

"That's him," she heard the guard say. "That's Rembrandt."

Walter Binns gazed at the nurse looking back at him through the little window in the door. She seemed frightened. He felt a tiny, delicious rush. He shivered, but it had nothing to do with his fever.

He locked eyes with the girl. She had pretty eyes.

Walter Binns thought about how he could make them even prettier.

When a Serial Killer Gets a Taste for Blood . . .
Years ago, the Seattle police were baffled by the Schoolgirl
Murders. The killer staged the scenes, dressing his female
victims in schoolgirl uniforms and saddle shoes. No woman
in Seattle felt safe, until they caught the man responsible,
and the case was forgotten. . . .

He Only Wants to Do One Thing . . .
Across the country, a killing spree is taking place. The first
victim is attacked in a taxi by a mysterious stranger. The next
is found strangled in a changing room. A hitchhiker is left by
the side of the road, his identity brutally stolen. The murders
are so bizarre, so random, no one would think to connect
them. . . .

Kill and Kill Again . . .
Only Seattle writer Gillian McBride sees the disturbing co-
incidences between all the murders—and it's hitting too
close to home. Somehow, she is the link between past and
present—and to a twisted serial killer who shows no signs
of stopping. With each terrible piece of a sinister puzzle, a
psychopath is carrying out a master plan, a killing spree
that needs a final trophy to be fully complete. . . .

Please turn the page for an exciting sneak peek at

**Kevin O'Brien's
KILLING SPREE**

coming January 2007!

Chapter 1

All the crazies were out tonight.

What did he expect? It was Halloween, and the streets of Greenwich Village overflowed with people—drunk, laughing, screaming people, all in their stupid costumes. Tonight he'd seen a husky, bearded man in a nurse's dress and cap; an attractive couple (and boy, didn't they know it) as Adam and Eve, wearing strategically placed fig leaves and nothing else; and innumerable gay guys dressed up as characters out of *The Wizard of Oz.*

Amid the partyers, one person stood out to him. Wearing thick glasses and a rather nerdish cardigan sweater, the young man walked down the street alone, his hands shoved in his pants pockets. He seemed timid and detached. Strapped around his stomach was what looked like six sticks of dynamite and an alarm clock. Only a few people seemed to notice him, and when they did, they laughed. But it was nervous laughter.

Greg felt a bit like that lonely nerd, like a human time bomb about to go off. If he didn't get out of the Village soon, he was going to explode.

Driving a cab in New York on Halloween night was pure torture.

Greg prayed that his next fare would take him to another part of town, far away from this crazy place. He planned to put one more hour on the meter before going home to his dumpy studio apartment so he could memorize an audition piece for tomorrow. It was a commercial for allergy medication, and he desperately wanted the job. Greg was living a cliché: the struggling thirtysomething actor by day and cabdriver by night. He'd convinced himself two years ago that driving a taxi would give him a chance to really study people and better develop his craft. Huh, what a crock. After a few months, the only thing he learned was that there were some real jerks in this world.

And a lot of them had come out tonight.

Greg spotted the couple, waving at him from the corner of Hudson and Charles. The guy was dressed up as Zorro—with the cape, hat, mask, and the sword. The girl had gotten dolled up in a Spanish dancer outfit—a yellow dress with black lace, an elaborate headdress and castanets. Approaching them, he heard her clicking those castanets and giggling. He saw her pretty face light up as he pulled toward the curb. She smiled.

Greg let out a grateful sigh. She looked like an angel.

She had long, light brown hair and a creamy complexion. The sexy-slutty señorita outfit looked so absurd on such a fresh-faced, sweet woman. He guessed she was in her late twenties. The way she weaved a bit, he could tell she was slightly drunk.

"Oh, thanks so much for stopping!" she gushed, climbing into the backseat with her masked boyfriend. "The last two taxis just sailed by—"

"Ten-seventeen West Thirty-seventh," barked Zorro, interrupting her.

Greg set the meter, then glanced at them in the rearview mirror.

The girl's eyes met his as she settled back in the seat and buckled her seat belt. She grinned and clicked her castanets once more. "Hola! And Happy Halloween. How come you're not wearing a costume?" She worked the castanets again.

"Cut that shit out," Zorro grumbled.

"Huh, grouch," she muttered, slipping the castanets in her little black purse. She gave Zorro a playful pout, then cleared her throat and called to Greg. "I'm having the best time! This is my third night in New York, and I love it! I don't ever want to go back to Portland." She raised her voice as if making a declaration: "I want to live in New York City and write bestsellers!" She laughed, then tapped Greg on the shoulder. "I'm getting a book published next month—my first. I'm an author."

"Congratulations," Greg said. "What kind of book is it? Will it—"

"You don't need to make friends with the driver, dopey," the man interrupted. He pulled her toward him. "Come here." He kissed her neck and cupped a black-gloved hand over her breast.

She squirmed a bit. Greg noticed her looking at him in the mirror. She seemed embarrassed at the way her boyfriend was pawing her. "Quit," she whispered.

"You fucking love it," the masked man replied, pulling away from her for only a moment. He shut the Plexiglas divider between the front and back seat. Then he started fondling her again.

From what Greg could see, she didn't seem to *fucking love it*. She tried to laugh and push the man away, but his hands and mouth were all over her. Greg saw her wincing. Her eyes connected with his. She seemed to plead for some kind of intervention. The man started to climb on top of her.

Greg had put up with couples fornicating in the back of his taxi before. But in all those cases, the women had seemed pretty damn willing. He could tell this woman wasn't the type. No, not at all. This guy was humiliating her.

Greg thought about stopping the cab, opening the back door, and throwing Zorro out on his ass.

A car horn blared, and Greg suddenly realized he'd drifted into oncoming traffic. He swerved the taxi back into his lane.

He felt someone kick the back of his seat, and heard a muffled cry. Greg checked the mirror again. "Shit," he muttered under his breath.

She wasn't resisting at all anymore. Zorro was on top of her, and one of her legs had wrapped around him. She clutched at the back of his cape. She had her eyes closed, but her mouth was open and her lips slid along his neck.

Greg was so disappointed in her. For a crazy moment, he'd felt a connection with this sweet, fresh-faced young woman from Portland. He'd even thought he could *rescue* her. But now, she was letting this asshole screw her in the back of his taxi. And she seemed to be having a swell time of it.

Frowning, Greg stared at the road ahead. Through the Plexiglas divider, he could hear muffled moaning back there. But thank God, the traffic and street noise mostly drowned her out. He didn't want to listen to her in the throes of ecstasy. He just wanted to get them the hell out of his cab. Jerks.

Greg turned onto 37th Street, and a section full of little specialty stores with apartments above them. He pulled up in front of the address the guy had given him. It was a travel agency, closed for the night. Was this the right address?

He heard the Plexiglas divider whoosh open behind him. Greg glanced over his shoulder. The pretty brunette numbly stared at him, catching her breath. Zorro had finished with her. "I'm in a hurry," the guy said. "She's paying."

Before Greg could respond, Zorro ducked out of the cab. His black cape billowed as he ran down an alley beside the travel agency. He disappeared into the darkness.

Greg shifted forward in his seat. "That's eleven fifty, ma'am," he grunted. He checked the rearview mirror.

He couldn't quite read the look in her eyes. She still seemed to be catching her breath. She muttered something back to him, but it was like a whimper. He couldn't hear her past the rumbling motor.

Then he saw the dark red smudges on the handle to the Plexiglas divider. Zorro had opened it with his gloved hand.

Greg saw that she had tears in her eyes, and she was trembling.

"I'm stabbed," she whispered. "Dear God . . ."

He swiveled around. Her hands clutched at the front of

her yellow dress with the fancy black lace. The material was slashed across her belly—and drenched with blood.

"Police in Manhattan are searching for a man dressed as Zorro," the pretty, Asian anchorwoman announced. She wore a tailored black suit, and behind her was a red, bloody *Z*, a grisly take on the "mark of Zorro." "He's wanted in connection with the stabbing of a twenty-eight-year-old Portland woman. The victim, whose identity is being withheld pending—"

"Her name was Jennifer Gilderhoff," the man said to the TV. "And she 'wanted to live in New York City and write bestsellers!' Huh, poor, sorry bitch."

"The victim was stabbed in the backseat of a taxicab, during the Halloween celebration in Greenwich Village," the news anchor continued. "She was rushed to Roosevelt Hospital, where her condition is listed as critical."

The man stared at the TV screen. "She's not dead?"

The TV anchor paused for a somber beat. "In Queens tonight, a Halloween prank turned into a four-alarm fire when a group of teenagers—"

He grabbed the remote and switched off the TV. He couldn't believe Jennifer was still alive. Of course, she wouldn't be for long. He'd studied surgical procedures recently, and knew those stab wounds he'd made were fatal. She was probably in a coma.

Half-dressed and with his hair still wet from a shower, he wandered over to the honor bar and poured himself a Scotch.

On the bed, with its hunter-green and maroon paisley spread, his suitcase was open and almost completely packed.

He chilled his drink with a few cubes from the ice bucket. Beside the plastic bucket on the desk was a paperback thriller, *The Mark of Death* by Gillian McBride. He'd been reading a passage from it earlier, and used a postcard to keep his place. He'd received the postcard in the mail several weeks ago. It announced the publication of a book by another author, Jennifer Gilderhoff, *Burning Old Bridesmaids' Dresses and Other Survival Stories*. The postcard showed the predomiantly pink book cover, with a winking cartoon woman brandishing a cigarette lighter wand.

Considering what he'd done to Jennifer tonight, he figured her lighthearted collection of "chick-lit" stories wouldn't fare so well commercially. It certainly had to put a damper on a reader's enjoyment when the author of such cutesy fluff got stabbed to death—or *almost* to death. He didn't think she'd last out the night.

He sipped his Scotch and flipped to the page he'd marked with Jennifer's postcard. He tossed the card aside. Moving toward the bathroom, he read the passage in Gillian McBride's *The Mark of Death*. He was very, very familiar with it:

> Her blood was still warm and wet on his hands as he raced toward the alley beside the beautiful estate. His Zorro cape billowed behind him. He listened to the material flapping in the wind. The Masked Man felt such a rush of adrenaline. He felt like a superhero. . . .

He stopped in the bathroom doorway, and closed Gillian McBride's book. He gazed at the bathtub. The water in it had turned pink. His Zorro costume was soaking. After another rinse or two, all the blood would be gone.

He glanced at the book in his hand. "I did it better," he whispered. "I did it better than you, Gillian."

Chapter 2

MEET THE AUTHOR! read the sign by the desk at the front of the Barnes & Noble store in Woodinville, Washington. *GILLIAN McBRIDE signs copies of her new thriller, BLACK RIBBONS: A MAGGIE DARE MYSTERY!*

The author photo on the sign showed a beautiful, haughty-looking woman who could have passed for twenty-five. Gillian hated the photo, but her agent and editor were crazy about it. "The picture says, 'I'm savvy, I'm smart, and I have best-seller-in-the-making here,' " her agent, Eve, had told her.

"I think it says, 'I'm smug, I'm arrogant, and I have absolutely no interests beyond myself, my hair, and what I'm wearing,' " Gillian had countered.

To the photographer's credit, he had taken about ten year's off Gillian's age (actually thirty-seven), and he'd erased scores of freckles from her face (they came with being a redhead). But he'd failed to capture Gillian's warmth and vulnerability. The woman seated at the desk, behind a stack of books, looked like the nice, down-to-earth, slightly older sister to that smug ice princess in the author photo.

Gillian wore a lavender silk blouse and black pants. Her shoulder-length, tawny hair was pulled back in a ponytail, and she kept a smile fixed on her face.

Some authors had throngs of rabid fans at their signings, roped-off lines of people around the store impatiently waiting for a brief moment with their favorite scribe. Gillian wasn't one of those authors. She'd been sitting at the desk for over ninety minutes and sold eight books so far. She had one fan show up—a very nice middle-aged woman named Stella who had read all five of Gillian's previous thrillers and e-mailed her once in a while. Stella had chatted with her for about ten minutes but had to rush off to meet a friend. Then Gillian was by herself again. "I'm sorry I've never heard of you" was what people usually said when they stopped by her table to check out one of her books. But most people didn't stop at all. They passed by her table and avoided eye contact—as if she were some panhandler on the street.

So Gillian sat there, forcing a smile, and wondering if people saw the desperation on her face. It was like eating alone at a fancy restaurant. She felt onstage—and very pathetic. She'd done these author signings dozens of times before and knew the score. *Just keep smiling.*

That was what Gillian told herself as she dealt with this new potential customer, a woman in her early twenties with a ratty brown pullover sweater, stringy blond hair, and heavy eye makeup. She was on her cell phone as she approached Gillian's desk. She glanced at *Black Ribbons,* then quickly put it down again. "No way, not if you're gonna get fucking drunk again tonight," she said into the phone. She picked up another one of Gillian's books, and scowled at the back cover. "You do so," the young woman continued on her cell phone, ignoring Gillian. "Why the fuck should I even plan on doing anything, if you're gonna be drunk most of the time? I mean it, you have a problem. I'm fucking serious . . ."

The blonde went through all six of Gillian's books, barely looking at each one before rejecting it. And Gillian wondered how many times this woman said *fuck* during a given day. Gillian felt invisible. Finally, she started drumming her fingers on the desktop and stared up at the young woman.

"Well, maybe I need to rethink our relationship," the

blonde was saying into her phone. Her gaze suddenly locked on Gillian. "Would you mind your own fucking business?" she growled. "Jesus!" She threw GIllian a sneer, then wandered away from the table. "No, I wasn't talking to you," she said into her cell phone. "There's this stupid woman in the bookstore . . ."

If I was in a relationship with you, sister, I'd be getting drunk every night too! Gillian wanted to yell at the woman. But she said nothing and kept smiling.

She saw someone else approaching.

"Are you the author?" asked a middle-aged woman with a stiff-looking helmet of black hair. She adjusted her glasses and picked up a copy of *Black Ribbons*. "I read three books a week. I haven't heard of you."

"Well, I'm Gillian, and—readers like you are my favorite kind of people." She held out her hand, but the woman was studying the back of Gillian's book. Gillian slipped her hand back under the table.

"Black Ribbons: A Maggie Dare Mystery," the woman muttered. "What's this about anyway?"

"Well, Maggie Dare is a seventy-year-old retired police detective," Gillian explained. "She's a very 'tough old broad.' This is my second mystery-thriller with Maggie. This time, Maggie's investigating a series of murders in western Washington." The woman said nothing, so Gillian continued. "Um, each time this particular killer abducts a new victim, he ties a black ribbon around a nearby tree, post, or landmark. And the body is always found twenty-four hours later—with a ribbon around the neck, in a pretty bow. It's not quite as grisly as it sounds. It's more suspenseful than gory."

The woman frowned. She put the book down on the table as if it were someone else's used Kleenex. "I don't think I care for that at all."

Gillian kept smiling.

"What about this one?" the woman asked, picking up another book.

"That's *Killing Legend,* my first. It came out two years ago."

"What's the plot?" she asked, scrutinizing the back cover. "Because I don't understand the title."

"Well, instead of a living legend, this man is a *Killing Legend.* I was inspired by the rumors after James Dean's death. People claimed he was still alive but so horribly disfigured by the auto accident that he'd faked his demise. Anyway, in my book, this *legend* is a sexy leading man, an overnight sensation in movies. And everyone thinks he's dead after a car accident. So now he's preying on all the people who made his life hell on his way to the top of the Hollywood heap. There's show business mixed with murder, plus a little—"

Gillian stopped as she noticed the woman shaking her head again. She had that same sour look on her face as she plopped the book down. "I hate stories set in Hollywood."

Gillian nodded. "Yes, well, it's not everyone's taste," she said lamely.

"What about this one?" the woman asked, picking up another book.

Are you for real? Did you come here to torture me?

Gillian kept smiling and explained the plot of her second thriller, *Highway Hypnosis.* It was a very creepy tale of a former surgeon who turned killing hitchhikers into big business. He sold the victims' identities on the black market—as well as their internal organs.

That wasn't Old Sourpuss's cup of tea either, Gillian could tell. The woman shook her head and clicked her tongue against her teeth. But before Gillian could thank her for stopping by, the lady sighed and picked up another one of her books. "What's *this* about?" she pressed, waving a copy of *The Mark of Death.*

Now it was Gillian making a face and shaking her head. "Oh, I don't think you'd like it. My books aren't for everyone. But thanks for stopping by." She felt as if she were trying to *break up* with her and let her down gently: *This isn't working out. It's not you, it's me and my books. We're not a good fit. Move on—please* . . .

The woman scowled at the back cover of *The Mark of Death* for another moment, then she set the book back down on the desk. "You're right," she said. "This one doesn't look very interesting either. So—where's the travel section?"

Fifteen minutes later, Gillian was walking across the mini-mall's parking lot. She'd signed a dozen unsold copies of her new thriller and all her backlist books combined. The events coordinator and a couple of clerks had bought copies of *Black Ribbons,* and she'd personally signed them. Pity purchases, most likely. But she was grateful just the same. They'd asked her to come back when the book was released, God bless them.

She'd signed at this particular store twice before—and both times had been Saturday afternoons. This was her first night signing here, and she hadn't realized until now that the rest of the mini-mall shut down early. All the other storefronts were dark.

Gillian hiked up the collar of her trench coat as she made her way toward an opening in a row of trees at the far end of the lot. The bus stop was on the other side of those trees.

She still had a few minutes to catch the 8:40 bus to Seattle. At one time, Gillian had a car, but not anymore. She'd been forced to sell her Saturn two year ago. Immediately afterward, the man who had made her sell it beat her so severely she'd had bruises on her face, back, and arms for over two weeks.

But Gilliam didn't want to think about that right now. Even though the problem hadn't quite gone away, she didn't want to dwell on it. Not tonight.

She had a bus to catch—then a transfer and another forty-minute ride back to Seattle. It was a hell of a long trip merely to sell eleven books, but that was part of the business of being a "medium-selling" author. She glanced back at the bookstore. Maybe for the next book signing she would drive herself here and find a line of people actually waiting for her. *Oh, dream on, Gillian.*

The wind howled. Leaves and debris scattered across the parking lot pavement. It was a cold, damp November night, and Gillian could see her breath. There were fewer cars around the farther she moved away from the bookstore. It was also darker at this end of the lot. The opening in the line of trees was just ahead.

Gillian thought she heard something behind her—a clicking noise or footsteps. She glanced over her shoulder and didn't see anyone. One of the floodlights above was sputtering. Maybe that was what made the strange noise.

As she turned around again, Gilliam saw a minivan slowly pull into the lot. Its headlights swept across her, blinding her for a moment. The vehicle headed toward the bookstore, but then it pulled a U-turn. Once again, those headlights were in her eyes.

Then they went off.

The minivan pulled up alongside her. Gillian veered away from it, and picked up her pace. But she didn't break into a run. She didn't want them to think she was scared. There was no else around. She couldn't see the driver—or anyone inside the car. But the way the minivan inched alongside her, she could tell the driver was looking at her.

Gillian carried a little canister of pepper spray in her purse, but it always took forever to find *anything* in that satchel. With a shaky hand, she frantically dug into the bag and groped around for the pepper spray. She kept walking toward that opening in the trees, and pretended to ignore the minivan just a few feet away from her. She could hear traffic noise on the other side of the trees up ahead. But would anyone hear her if she screamed?

The minivan picked up speed, then stopped between her and the trees at the edge of the lot.

Gillian stopped too. Suddenly, she couldn't move. Her feet froze up and became rooted to the pavement. She stared at the driver's door as it opened.

A tall, gangly man climbed out of the front. The baseball cap he wore cast a shadow over most of his face, so all she could see was his unshaven jaw and a crooked smile. His denim jacket was slightly askew; he had his right arm in the sleeve and the other in a cast. The left side of the jacket was draped over his shoulder, half covering the bandaged arm.

Gillian thought about Ted Bundy. That was one of his ploys. He sometimes approached his victims with one arm in a cast—and a friendly smile.

Gillian kept searching for the pepper spray in her purse. It was too dark to see anything in the bag, and when she looked up, he was coming toward her. She backed away.

"Pardon me," the man called. "Mind if I talk to you for a minute?"

Staring at the man, Gillian took another step back. She thought she felt the pepper spray canister at the bottom of her bag.

"Aren't you Gillian McBride, the author?"

She said nothing.

"I recognized you. Is it too late for an autograph?" He hoisted his bandaged arm. "Think you might sign my cast?"

Gillian hesitated. She heard another door click open, and she glanced over at the minivan. A young girl—about twelve, with a ski jacket and her hair in pigtails—jumped out of the passenger side. "Is it her, Dad?"

Gillian let out a little sigh. As the girl came up to her father's side, Gillian noticed a well-worn copy of *Black Ribbons* in her hand.

"The wife is a big fan of yours," the man explained. "She's home with the flu, otherwise she'd be here. You really scared her with this new book."

A hand over her heart, Gillian cracked a smile. "Well, tell your wife you got even with me tonight."

Gillian autographed the book for the man's wife, and signed his cast too. Rolling up her coat sleeve, the daughter asked Gillian to autograph her arm. Gillian complied. She talked with them for a few minutes. The man asked if she needed a ride someplace. Gillian lied and said she was fine. As the man and his daughter pulled away in the minivan, Gillian waved. And when she was sure they could no longer see her, she started to cry.

Those few moments with that man and his daughter had made her feel important. Maybe the long bus trip here was worth it after all. So why was she crying?

She'd been doing that a lot lately—when she was sure no one was around to see her.

Gillian found the pepper spray in her purse while fishing out some Kleenex. She dried her eyes at the bus stop.

There was something else in Gillian's purse—her mail. They'd been late delivering it today, and she'd grabbed it out of her mailbox on her way to catch the bus to Woodinville. Now, on the near-empty 409 back to Seattle, Gillian glanced through it—and tried to ignore the unabashed gaze from a creepy, bearded man with a bad toupee, seated in one of the Handicapped Only spots.

Most of the letters were bills, some past due. But she'd also received a postcard from her best friend, Dianne Garrity, vacationing in Palm Springs. She and Dianne had grown up together. As a kid, Dianne had been considered a weirdo because she had scoliosis and wore a back brace through tenth grade. But that didn't bother Gillian, who was never very athletic or popular anyway. They read each other's diaries, and Dianne was the first person to tell Gillian that she should be a writer. "I mean it," Dianne had said back in high school. "You're going to be a famous author someday." She was saying the same thing when Gillian was trying to sell her first thriller to scores of uninterested agents and publishers.

Saw "Black Ribbons" in a Walgreen's here in Palm Springs, Dianne reported in the postcard. *You were at eye-level, right next to Stephen King—well, okay, NOW you're there. I moved it . . .*

There was also a letter from her agent. It was a xerox of

the first few paragraphs of a New York *Daily News* article. Her agent had attached a Post-it. *Doesn't this seem familiar?* it said.

The bus went over a few potholes, but Gillian barely noticed. She was studying the headline: POLICE HUNT FOR "ZORRO KILLLER." The article told of a stabbing on Halloween night in New York. A man dressed as Zorro had sliced up a woman in the back of a taxi. The clipping was only a portion of the story, and the victim's last name had been cut off: ... *visiting from Portland, 28-year-old Jennifer—*

Biting her lip, Gillian set down the news clipping.

The story was familiar, all right.

Author Photo by Marc Von Borstel

KEVIN O'BRIEN grew up in
Chicago's North Shore, but now
lives in Seattle, Washington.
He is currently working on his next
thriller and can be reached at
authorkev@aol.com.

SOMETHING SHE CAN'T REMEMBER

When Claire Shaw wakes in a Seattle hospital, she remembers nothing of what has happened to her. She doesn't recognize the concerned faces of her husband and friends. She knows only that she is lucky to be alive, the single surviving victim of a vicious serial killer.

SOMEONE WHO WON'T FORGET

She was a mistake—not like the others. She didn't understand. That was obvious now. But she would come to understand. Next time, there would be no escape—and her eyes would fill with that perfect, beautiful terror...

SOME THINGS YOU CAN'T IMAGINE

On an island isolated from the mainland, Claire has returned to a life she barely knows anymore. A town that feels as if it, too, is hiding something in its dark woods, remote cabins, and chilly smiles. Bit by bit, Claire's memory is taking terrifying shape in a place where fear is very much at home...

PRAISE FOR THE NOVELS OF KEVIN O'BRIEN

"Another taut page-turner."
—*Seattle Post-Intelligencer*

"O'Brien does what he does best: keeping the suspense at unbelievably high levels."
—*The Midwest Book Review*

Visit us at www.kensingtonbooks.com

ISBN 0-7860-1847-X

PINNACLE
U.S.$4.99
CAN $6.99
PRINTED IN U.S.A.